Carrie Brown

THE ROPE WALK

Carrie Brown is the author of five novels
and a collection of short stories. She has
won many awards for her work, including
a National Endowment for the Arts fellowship, the Barnes and Noble Discover Award,
and the Janet Heidinger Kafka Prize. She
lives in Virginia with her husband, the
novelist John Gregory Brown, and their
three children. She teaches at Sweet Briar
College.

THE ROPE WALK

THE
ROPE
WALK

A Novel

Carrie Brown

Anchor Books
A Division of Random House, Inc.
New York

FIRST ANCHOR BOOKS EDITION, MAY 2008

Copyright © 2007 by Carrie Brown

All rights reserved. Published in the United States by Anchor Books, a division of
Random House, Inc., New York, and in Canada by Random House of Canada Limited,
Toronto. Originally published in hardcover in the United States by Pantheon Books,
a division of Random House, Inc., in 2007.

Anchor Books and colophon are registered trademarks of Random House, Inc.

Grateful acknowledgment is made to Houghton Mifflin Company for permission to
reprint excerpts from *The Journals of Lewis and Clark*, edited by Bernard DeVoto. Copyright
© 1953 by Bernard DeVoto. Copyright renewed 1981 by Avis DeVoto. All rights reserved.
Reprinted by permission of Houghton Mifflin Company.

The Library of Congress has cataloged the Pantheon edition as follows:
Brown, Carrie, [date]
The rope walk / Carrie Brown.
p. cm.
1. Girls—Fiction. 2. African American boys—Fiction. 3. Friendship in children—Fiction.
4. Intergenerational relations—Fiction. 5. AIDS (Disease)—Patients—Fiction. I. Title.
PS3552.R68529R68 2007
813'.54—dc22
2006024869

Anchor ISBN: 978-0-307-27809-8

Book design by Wesley Gott

www.anchorbooks.com

Printed in the United States of America
10 9 8 7 6 5 4 3

To all the children
but especially
Harry Walker Brown and Margot Alexander Pleasants

To my mother
for giving me time and a place

and

to John,
as always

THE ROPE WALK

The Rapex War

ONE

IT WAS GOING TO BE a beautiful day.

Alice climbed onto her bedroom windowsill and sat down, wrapping her arms around her legs. Early morning mist hovered in mysterious levels over the lawn below. In the tree branches that inclined near her window, the low sun ignited little white signal fires that flashed at Alice from the velvety spaces between the leaves. It was dark still beneath the ragged hems of the firs at the side of the house, and a cool, musty smell rose from under the old rhododendron bushes, but across the front lawn, downy stripes of sunlight began to unfurl between the long shadows of the trees. Beyond the lawn, and then farther out beyond the low border of the stone wall, fields revealed in the growing light raced away to the wooded horizon.

On her windowsill, Alice waited, watching. The full energy of the day, like a parade assembling its drums and cymbals and marching players, lay just out of sight, gathering strength at the edge of the world. Any moment now, the day's brimming cup would spill over the far treetops and flood the hour with light.

Today, the twenty-ninth day of May, was Alice's tenth birthday. When she was younger, her brothers had told her that the

3

annual Memorial Day parade in Grange, the creeping procession of fire engines and floats and flag bearers that Alice watched with shining eyes from atop her father's shoulders, was held in celebration of her birthday, as if she were a princess whose subjects collected for her pleasure. Now she could not remember what it had felt like to believe this fiction, though she was assured she had believed it. She could only remember the uncomfortable dawning of her doubt: the gravity of the white-haired soldiers formed into a trembling V whose size diminished each year; her correct linking of the word *memorial* with the word *memory*—this, she puzzled, was not language for a birthday celebration; and her adding up of the other signs, too. No one saluted her as they went past. No one came to one knee before her. No one said happy birthday.

She could not remember what it had felt like to believe in Santa Claus, either. That faith, too, had slipped away from her with casually troubling ease. Like discovering a hole in her pocket through which a precious trinket had dropped and been lost, she could not pinpoint when the miracle had left her.

Out of loyalty, each spring the family still attended the Memorial Day parade, shabbily reinforced over the years by opportunistic floats from other jurisdictions: a pickup full of people in *Star Trek* costumes, a van from the television station in Brattleboro, a Frito-Lay truck from which employees in matching black polo shirts tossed bags of chips, a woman in her pink Mary Kay car trailing ribbons like a honeymoon vehicle.

But now there was a birthday party, too.

Already someone—one of the boys, probably—had carried the rush-seated dining room chairs outside for the party and arranged them haphazardly on the front lawn beneath Alice's windowsill; one had toppled over onto its side into the wet grass.

Alice made a box like a camera lens with her fingers and looked down through the aperture at the fallen chair. The trees' monumental shadows, cumbrous as ocean liners as the sun climbed higher in the sky, lay across the lawn. Alice followed them with her camera over the dewy grass and back to the house. A red, white, and blue bunting had been hung over the front door, and a rippling candy stripe of crepe birthday streamers wound along the porch railing . . . and there were the black-handled kitchen scissors, too, their tiny jaws agape, forgotten on the porch floor. Alice pretended to take a picture of them. How strange things looked when they were not where they were supposed to be.

She hitched around on the narrow sill and raised her camera a degree to fix on the cloud bank of white balloons tied to the flag-pole and holding sway over the daffodils. Past the yellow heads of the flowers and over the stone wall, the tall grass in the fields, still heavy-headed with dew, lay down in silver waves all the way to the horizon, a rough pinking-shears strip of dark green woods against a blue sky. Alice swung her imaginary camera back and forth experimentally, like an eyeball rolling wildly in its socket, and the world whistled and winked and nodded its shining head at her, beckoning and calling. The fields, the orchard, the lawn and flower borders near the house, all of it rolled beneath her, twinkling and flashing in the spring sun as if mirrors were turning in the grass and among the leaves of the trees.

Alice's heart strained against the cradle of her ribs. She had lived in this place all her life, in this house in a small town in the rocky southern hills of Vermont, with her five older brothers and her father, who was a Shakespeare scholar and a dean at the nearby college. She could not imagine ever leaving. Indeed, she thought she would fight like a lion, roaring and biting and tearing limb from limb, if anyone tried to separate her from this place, these people. It was interesting, horribly and yet irresistibly interesting, to imagine being inspired to such heroic lengths, though sometimes she frightened herself with the possibility of danger and loss, forces that might surround her and try to drag her away.

This was a recent development, the idea that something could happen to threaten the world and her place in it.

Valiant in play, armed with a painted cardboard sword and wearing a blue velvet cape sewn for such games by her late mother, Alice liked to leap from tabletop or tree branch or the back of the couch, brandishing her weapon at the empty air. Usually victory was effortless and inevitable, a ballet of acrobatic thrusts and parries and swirls of the cape, after which her invisible enemies fell left and right or scuttled away howling into the trees. She was prince, captain, and knight, poised on a rock, sword point aimed triumphantly skyward.

Recently, though, her games had begun to unsettle her. Now her imagination supplied not just the juvenile idea of adversaries—witches with long greasy hair, slit-eyed goblins worrying something inside their bulging cheeks, monsters squatting on warty green haunches, ready to spring; it also whispered the truth, which was that suffering was real. She did not know how she knew this, or when the change had taken place. But she would not play now in sight of her brothers, whose teasing she had once failed to notice, or, if she had noticed, to mind. Suddenly this year she did not want to be watched as she struck out on all sides, for now there were things against which she felt truly helpless—the actual misery of the world, things that were unfair, *wrong*—and she came home quietly at the end of an afternoon of play in the woods, her long sword stuck in her belt, her face a mask.

The world of her childhood, with its endless days and deep,

certain sleep and quicksilver possibilities, had been abraded, roughened, its perimeter made vulnerable by the apprehension of dangers—death and poverty and terror and war and sickness—arriving from the real world, things that rose up against the clumsy, makeshift enemies, the dear enemies of her youth, and opened their hideous red mouths to swallow whole the fragile companions of her play. Now when she looked out into the world from her windowsill, it was with the knowledge that she could lose it. She did not know how or when. But she knew it was possible, and that made all the difference.

The night before, Alice had dreamed again that she could fly. Usually these dreams were deeply pleasurable. She swam through warm air, her body undulant as an otter's. Up from the earth came the familiar scents of pine and hay and river and blackberry. When she ran through the long grass in the meadows, reservoirs of granite, marble, slate, and talc lay beneath her feet. Beneath those, from a time long ago when the northern hemisphere's arctic sea covered what are now Vermont's grassy slopes, and when the places Alice knew and loved did not yet exist, rested the bones of ancient beluga whales. This year in school, her class had studied the geology of the Champlain Basin, and they had been taken on a trip to see the bones of a prehistoric white whale found underground one hundred and fifty miles from the nearest ocean. The whale had been named Charlotte, for the town in which she had been unearthed, said their young, ponytailed museum guide, and she had been twelve feet long. The shortest child in her class, Alice had been urged to stand up front at the exhibit, grave and watchful, her face inches from Charlotte's long, blunt, grizzled skull. Charlotte had died peacefully, the young man informed the children. No violence here. Her teeth were intact; her bones had drifted gently into the sediments of an offshore estuary.

Since then, whenever Alice flew in her dreams she saw below her the familiar acres of her house in its surrounding fields and also the swells of topography and what lay buried beneath the woods and tumbled rocks. The sleeping bones of whales and dinosaurs, prehistoric birds whose notched wings spread like the carbon shadows of kites over roads and meadows, barn roofs and the twisting curves of the river lay exposed as if in an X-ray. In her flying dreams she saw far and wide: a little vole scrambling over acorns in the oak woods; the crashing falls of the river where it tumbled into a green basin of bubbles and foam; the arrangement of bones sleeping under the hills.

Alice never fell in these dreams. But last night, for the first time, there had been a shocking vertiginous drop, as if the fabric of the dream were thin in places, her own weight too heavy for it. She had awoken with her hair damp and sticking to her face, her breath coming fast.

Now Alice blinked into the sunshine, the soft, gauzy morning air growing in brilliance as the day advanced. Down on the grass, a crow flapped heavily over the lawn and landed on the overturned chair. Already the light had crested the treetops, careening over the fields.

Soon, the guests for the birthday party would arrive.

Alice had been told repeatedly that the windowsill was a dangerous place to sit, but it did not feel precarious to her. She had never been afraid she would fall. She pressed the knobs of her spine against the window's frame and flexed her bare feet in the groove of the sill. Once, Alice had tried to draw from memory everything that was in the bedroom behind her. It had been surprisingly easy, one recalled detail leading quickly to another, like a bird alighting from branch to branch and leading the way through an unfamiliar wood. Inside the glass-fronted bookcase, the spines of books gleamed. The slipper chair striped in worn barbershop red and white that had been in her father's childhood bedroom was nearly buried under a messy heap of discarded clothes. Alice's old stuffed monkey Sinbad, with his bashed-in Egyptian fez and tattered red jacket, sat on the dresser. Everything in this room was known and familiar; she could recall it down to the smallest detail, even with her eyes closed.

A white tiger moth had died in the casement overnight. Alice reached down to touch it carefully with a fingertip. It fell over stiffly like a boat capsizing, submitting to her its yellow, furred underside. Three black dots stared up at her from its belly. When she was younger, Alice had held solemn funerals for butterflies and beetles and the tiny gray voles eviscerated by the cats, using a spoon to bury them under the azaleas and gagging over the headless voles. She could not decide which she hated more: headless bodies or bodiless heads? But the reality was that too many creatures died every day; even at seven and eight years old she'd seen the impracticality of arranging last rites for all of them, and she had lost interest in the events' theatrics. Today she turned ten, and she could no longer worry about innocent ants crushed under people's shoes or helpless mosquitoes slapped unfeelingly against someone's arm, not when history, let alone the present, offered up such moving tales of human endeavor and peril. She loved a painting that hung in the lobby of the library in Grange, a vivid and lifelike rendering of the First Thanksgiving celebrated by the Pilgrims and the Indians, the canvas so large and full of life that it seemed one could step into the painting, perfectly to scale, and join the figures gathered there at that feast of gratitude and hope. This year suddenly, after being taught the song about the lone wandering pilgrim, she found that she could not get through it, so moved was she by what she now understood as the Pilgrims' great bravery and equally great tragedy. Would she have been brave enough to step aboard one of those first vessels setting sail for the new world? She admitted that she would have been afraid.

The dead moth was a shadow cast over the morning. She liked moths, their modest, dusty colors and twilight journeys, the comical way they marched around in circles on the tabletop as if they'd been wound with a key. This one had the shaggy head of a statesman, laid out in death like a plenipotentiary in ermine robes, or a judge, eyes closed beneath his powdered wig. Her brothers hunted butterflies and pinned the specimens of monarchs and painted ladies and viceroys behind glass in a case in their bedroom, but Alice held back from these pursuits, averting her gaze from the needle and her brothers' hands and the butterflies' slender bodies, their little waists pinched between thorax and abdomen.

A breeze reached her now from over the fields, touching her shoulder and cheek. The white curtains shifted and bulged beside her, and at her feet the moth's wings stirred, too, a deceptive, tantalizing flutter. There had been a time, even just a year ago, when that little movement would have beguiled her, the laws governing the universe so much less appealing than the powers of her imagination, the possibility of a moth's resurrection. But today, with the inevitable capitulation from nine years old to ten, from the era of single digits to double, she had arrived at the age of scientific empiricism: she knew that there were no other possibilities for this moth. All summer long there would be more of them, anyway, legions of gentle pilgrims who would blunder into her bedroom at night to bump their noses against the yellowing shade of her bedside lamp. And every night another one would expire in the windowsill, fallen onto one wing like a soldier upon its shield. Alice thought the windowsill was a terrible place to die, almost as bad as the gutter. In the stories she had read, the gutter was always where the poor orphan nearly expired.

Carefully she lifted the tiger moth and held it out on her palm to the breeze. In an instant the wind picked it up. It blew away off her hand like a fighter jet veering suddenly out of formation. She raised her hands quickly, tried to find the tumbling moth inside the frame of her imaginary camera. At first the lawn tilted and held, a wedge of the blossoming lilacs obtruding into her view like an enormous purple mountain. But the moth was gone. It had disappeared, a speck crossing the frame of the picture like a shooting star and falling out of it into the void, into the world where sky and grass, flagpole and balloons, overturned chair and blur of yellow daffodils jostled and collided against the blue sky, the arrangement of everything that belonged to her tenth birthday holding still for just a moment. In heaven, in what Alice thought of as the parallel universe where everything that died could be set gently on its feet again and given a push with the tip of giant finger, the moth would be restored. But for now, as far as Alice could see, it was lost.

The day was innocently beautiful, the air milky and calm and full of the scents of pollen and flowers and the new grass of May. The morning was intoxicating, irresistible; Alice wanted to turn handsprings over the lawn or run through the orchard with her arms outstretched like an airplane's wings. All her life, she thought, she would want to remember the feeling of spring inside her this morning, the birds going mad with joy and purpose in the trees, the silky warmth, the glamorous light. She wanted never to forget this day: not the moth, not the daffodils, not the heat on the back of her neck. It was all in the details, she sensed, the paint chips from the windowsill stuck to her bare feet; the feel of the silver bangle, her birthday present from her father, sliding coolly up and down her arm; the sunlight laying a bright path over the grass like a jingling of bells.

She leaned over and like a kitten quickly touched her kneecap with the tip of her tongue, tasting the rough, salty surface of her own skin, its strange heat; the taste was irrefutable evidence of herself, satisfying and private and known. This was who she was, Alice MacCauley, ten years old today in the town of Grange, state of Vermont, United States of America, continent of North America, the planet Earth, the World, the Universe.

She raised her hands again and tented her fingers into the box of her camera. She looked at the morning, the wobbling lawn, the careening tableau of the chairs and lilacs and balloons, the pink and white bunting shuddering along the porch rail in the breeze like a snake trying to shed its skin. It was impossible to believe that one day it would all disappear like poor Charlotte the whale, the whole of Alice's world and everything she loved sinking under a glacier or lost like Pompeii under the ash of the volcano.

Ba-boom, ba-boom, ba-boom; a bumblebee thudded close by Alice's ear, startling her.

The wind advanced, an invisible army bending the tops of the pine trees. The tiny mirrors hidden in the grass, faceted like the compound eyes of insects, flashed and flew. Something powerful stirred in the air, rippled over her shoulders, and caught the wild beating of her heart.

A little protest rose in her, competing with an instinct for valor. She wasn't ready, she wanted to say.

But she would have to be.

Any moment now, the guests would arrive.

TWO

ALICE ATTENDED to the sounds of the household as they floated up the stairs. From the kitchen came the bouncing tempo of polka music. Elizabeth Tranh, the MacCauleys' Vietnamese housekeeper, played the radio at a volume uncomfortable for most other people. She had poor hearing, the result of an infection acquired during the six weeks in 1979 she had spent in an open boat on the South China Sea with her son and daughter-in-law, two grandchildren, one of them an infant, and a dozen other Vietnamese fleeing their country. After many months in a camp in Hong Kong, the family had been taken in by the United States under the Episcopal archbishop's fund for refugee relief. Alice's mother, Beryl MacCauley, who had belonged to St. Barnabas Episcopal Church in Grange, had become Elizabeth's American sponsor when the family was resettled in nearby Brattleboro. The year Alice's twin brothers were born, Beryl offered Elizabeth a job helping with the house and the children, and Elizabeth had stayed with the family ever since. Alice knew her to be devoted to the MacCauley family and tireless in an impatient, sometimes militant way. Once Alice had asked Elizabeth about being adrift in the boat for so many weeks, but Elizabeth had waved away her questions. "Hot," she said. "Thirsty. Boring. What do you think?"

From her place on the windowsill, Alice heard the rumble of her father's voice calling something to Elizabeth and Elizabeth's shouted reply. Alice could tell by the sound of his voice that he was facing the mirror in the downstairs bathroom, jutting out his chin and fumbling with the knot of his bow tie.

Already that morning, Alice's brothers had brought her breakfast in bed, a family tradition on birthdays. The five boys, teeth unbrushed, hair stiff with sleep, in sour-smelling T-shirts and boxer shorts, had banged open her bedroom door, James bearing the old bamboo tray laden with French toast and vanilla ice cream. They had jumped on her, shocking her out of sleep, tickling her and blowing into her ear and making farting noises with their mouths against the back of her neck when she buried her face in the pillow, squealing. Happy birthday, they'd shouted. Happy birthday, Alice!

She had rolled over, shrieking and struggling inside the vice of her pajamas and the twisted sheets, and they had swamped her. Where's Alice, they had asked each other, sitting on her while she screamed and hiccupped with laughter and tried to fight them off. Who's seen Alice? It's her birthday today!

When the screen door to the front porch below Alice's window opened, offering up its familiar rusty squeak, Alice leaned over from the windowsill to see who was coming. Tad and Harry could imitate anything: countless lines of dialogue from movies, various birds, the ascending whistle of the teakettle, the sound of Elizabeth's rubber-soled shoes on the kitchen floor. The squeaky screen door below Alice's bedroom window was a character the twins referred to as the Bishop, its voice a whine of hysterical, nasal complaint that Archie forbade the boys to perform at the dinner table. Once they had made Alice laugh so hard milk came out her nose.

In a game begun by Alice's mother, a piece of furniture in nearly every room of the house had been named and its character established. Alice understood that her mother had been silly, playful in a sentimental, old-fashioned way, an instigator of traditions still observed years after her death: charades on New Year's Eve, candlelight for birthday dinners, pajamas worn inside out in hopes of snow, the bestowal upon the troubled or faint of heart of a certain stone from the Cornwall shore reported to bring good luck and cheer. Beryl had been a kisser of dogs and horses, children and women and men, creative in a slapdash, comic vein, such as the trail of black footprints she'd once painted across the pine floor of the kitchen, its outline still just barely visible. Since her death, the children had continued to refer to the selected pieces of furniture by their assigned names, as if to give up the game would have been to acknowledge that they had, gradually, forgotten her. As a result, they all referred to the uncomfortable black rocker by the fireplace in the living room as Vulgar, their mother's name for it, and whenever someone unsuspecting sat in it, the twins went into a contorted performance Alice loved known as Violated Vulgar, clawing the air as if they were drowning and sputtering absurd, made-up epithets, usually inspired by Shakespeare, thanks to their father's influence: *Thou deboshed fish, thou.*

The pair of high twin beds with the pineapple posts in Alice's bedroom were known as the idiotic Molly and Polly, who squealed and giggled when Alice lay down at night and shrieked like virgins, as Tad and Harry said, when one of the boys stretched out on the spare bed to read to Alice at night. The telephone bench in the front hall, with its voluptuous lines and worn velveteen cushions, was the lascivious Brigitte, a cameo at which Harry excelled, swaying down the hall like a giant, six-foot-three drag queen past whoever sat on Brigitte to make a phone call. Tad and Harry were the most protective of these old traditions; they had been nine when their mother died, Alice knew, old enough to remember something, but only details so shadowy and elusive that later they were not sure whether they might have made them up.

Eli and Alice had no memory of their mother at all.

In Beryl's old dressing room, though no one ever went in there, the chaise longue upholstered in slippery polished cotton was known to all of the children as Auntie Lola. There had been no reason to speak of Auntie Lola for years, all ten years of Alice's life, in fact, nor to enter the darkened room under the eaves with its faded Chinese wallpaper and dressing table with its still skirt of blue silk concealing the desolate space beneath. Yet Alice knew all about Lola and her Pekinese, the collection of little pillows with their bunched pansy faces and button noses gathered against the seatback.

On Alice's dresser was a picture of her mother as a child astride a rakish black and white pony. Alice knew in detail the story of her parents' marriage: in 1978, the red-cheeked daughter of an Oxford don—nineteen years old, pretty, and thought by her parents to be a bit wild—fell in love with Archibald MacCauley, a pipe-smoking young American scholar visiting England on a Rhodes fellowship. He and Beryl married at her parents' house in Oxford, and their first son, James, was born in a London hospital five years later, Wallace a year and a half after that. Then, after nearly a decade away from the United States and in the face of an offer of a tenure-track position from the American college near the house in which he had been born and raised, Archie flew home with his English wife and two small sons to live in the old

Vermont farmhouse in which Archie himself had come into the world. The twins were born two years later in 1987, Eli sixteen months after that. Then, in 1995, seven years after the arrival of their last son and a month after giving birth to her only daughter, Alice, Beryl MacCauley died in a fall from her horse.

She had written one cookbook and edited another; given birth to six children; raised two litters of Labrador puppies; bought, trained, and sold two horses; planted a hundred feet of gardens; and cooked countless meals, including—Alice had been told— some especially memorable Moroccan-inspired tagines for her family and friends.

Too young to be aware of her loss, Alice was spared the first grief of her mother's death. Over the years, though, she had grown jealous of other girls who had their own mothers to fight with and complain about and love. She was jealous of her brothers, too, especially James and Wallace, who were old enough to reliably remember their mother. Alice had nothing but stories about her mother's affection for other people, and photographs, including just one of her and her mother together, in which Beryl, a patterned scarf tied around her head, leaned back in a canvas chair on the lawn in front of the Vermont house, cradling the newborn Alice in her arms and smiling. At Beryl's feet, in a detail Alice had studied, one of the family's Maine coon cats had rolled onto its back, four paws batting the air as it begged for attention.

Yet Alice would not have said she was lonely. The presence of her five brothers meant that for most of Alice's life, her house had been full of people, not only her father and Elizabeth and the boys but also the boys' friends. It was a house that more and more over the years, despite what Alice witnessed as Elizabeth's increasingly shrill efforts, had fallen sway to the corruption of children, their chaos and theatrics, their games and hysterics and crimes and hidden kindnesses and cruelties; this was how Alice knew it, as a series of stages on which play was enacted, Alice bringing up the rear in helmet or horned Viking headdress or feathered mask, bearing light saber or wand or pennant on a pole, whatever was left over, whatever she was handed. In James and Wallace's bedroom, a span of real ship's rigging, excellent for climbing, was fixed to one of the beams on the ceiling. Alice had been netted and caught here and hung upside down; she'd been a hostage, a stowaway in a crow's nest, Peter Pan. At six she'd broken an arm swinging onto one of the beds; at nine—a fly being drained of its blood by a spider—she had required five stitches in the top of her head after being cut loose while her hands were still tied behind her back. She never played a girl in any of these games; it never occurred to any of them, including Alice herself, that Alice should play a girl's role, Wendy instead of Peter Pan, for instance. Who would want to be Wendy?

In the long gallery that ran the length of the back of the house, a summer porch that had been closed in long ago and lined with cupboards for the boys' boots and skis and tennis rackets, a rope swing had been suspended from two sturdy eye hooks in the ceiling. Here, when the boys deserted her for their more grown-up activities, Alice swung through the rainy afternoons, sailing over mops and rusty buckets, heaps of dead wasps in the dusty casement windows, her toes grazing a battered ball that traveled slowly, inevitably, to the corner where the floor sloped.

Children loved the MacCauleys' house. There was a fireman's pole that ran through a hole from the upstairs porch to the downstairs porch, and, in the branches of a maple tree, a tree house with a drawbridge on a pulley that let down into Tad and Harry's bedroom window. Explorers in the house, Alice silent and unnoticed in their wake, found soon enough the telescope in the attic window, the liquor bottles in the closet with its tiny hidden sink in Archie's study, the false bottom in the drawer of the desk in the living room, the secret opening beneath full of old copies of *Playboy* which the boys, when Alice first discovered them, snatched away from her.

This year, with all her brothers gone off to college, Alice sometimes walked aimlessly through the rooms in the quiet that came over the house, and over herself and her father, when the boys were away. She had the notion that along with all the silly voices—those of the Bishop, Vulgar the rocking chair, Brigitte the love seat—that fell silent when her brothers were not at home, her mother's voice was murmuring somewhere at an undetectable frequency in conversation with the possessions among which, as a living, breathing presence, she had once moved. Alice let her hands brush these objects and thought about how her mother's hands had once touched the same places.

All the family's fun, Alice understood, had begun with her mother.

Squeak went the Bishop again, and there was Archie. Alice leaned over and watched her father from the windowsill. He was fifty-six, but already his hair had gone completely white. It shone in the sun, flawless as the wings of the moth prince who had perished in Alice's window casement. Archie, his progress grave as a butler's, came down the steps of the porch bearing a tray of glasses, proceeding one step at a time in a careful sideways attitude like an old man, and made his way through the dining room chairs arranged haphazardly across the front lawn. High above him in her windowsill, Alice detected the tinkling of the glasses trembling on the tray.

A terrace had been built on the foundation of the old summer kitchen that had burned down before Alice was born, and here a table with a snowy cloth had been laid. The lilacs had dropped a snowfall of tiny purple blossoms over the dishes. Elizabeth had set out platters of sandwiches under a drape of cheesecloth, glass bowls of berries, and an enormous sagging gelatin mold jeweled with pineapple and mandarin oranges. The ice cream—peach and strawberry in brown cardboard five-gallon buckets—would be brought out later.

In the apple orchard beyond the stone wall that bordered the lawn, Alice could make out from her window her brothers moving under the trees and hear snatches of their distant voices, mostly Tad's and Harry's. They were making a rope walk for her.

The night before, at dinner, James had leaned over the dining room table, his hair falling over his forehead, and had drawn scribbled curlicues with his finger on the table's mahogany surface, explaining it to her. Many girls had fallen in love with James over Alice's lifetime. Archie said James's romantic lock of black hair worked on them like a hypnotist's watch on a chain.

"It's like a big spiderweb," James had said. "The idea is that everyone has a string, and you have to untangle it to get your surprise. There's a surprise at the end of every one, a present," he said. "How do you like the sound of that?"

The rope walk sounded fine. But then Alice liked almost everything the boys did, except when they excluded her from their adventures. Eli had turned seventeen that year. Tad and Harry, April fools, had recently celebrated their eighteenth birthdays. Wallace was twenty; James, the elder statesman, twenty-two. This year, they had all left for college on the same day, including for the first time, Eli. Alice, embarrassed to cry in front of Elizabeth and Archie, had gone upstairs to lie on her bed with her face in the pillow. At least Tad and Harry stayed in Vermont to attend Frost, where Archie was a dean. Alice knew that it had to do with their bad grades and their general failure to take anything seriously that the twins had not, like their father and grandfather, and like James and Wallace and now even Eli, gone to Yale. They didn't seem to be sorry about it, though. They had come home to attend her piano recital in November, where they stamped their feet and whistled appreciatively as she made her embarrassed curtsey. In March they had showed up for public speaking night at school, where they made faces at her from the audience in the auditorium and succeeded in making her laugh, and then, her face aflame with mortification, fall silent, unable to remember another word in her recitation of "Hiawatha."

Usually Elizabeth went home on Friday evenings—she had kept her own house as long as she'd been with the MacCauleys; various grandchildren had moved in and out over the years—but she had stayed last night to bake Alice's cake, a three-tiered coconut one with curls of real coconut on it. Alice had been given the hammer the night before and had aimed several ineffectual blows at the coconut, but it had been Eli who'd cracked it finally, the milk splashing onto the floor.

Pushing open the door with her hip, an avalanche of the boys' ironed shirts over her arm, Elizabeth had been upstairs once already this morning to check on Alice after her bath.

Alice was on the forbidden windowsill, still in her undershirt, when Elizabeth surprised her, looking around the door.

"Alice! Get *down* from there! You going to fall off! Get down, get down!" Elizabeth glared at her. "You find your shoes? Eli polished them last night. He said he put them on the stairs."

Alice swung her legs around hastily so that her feet grazed the floor. Yes, she'd found the shoes, the black patent leather smelling of polish. Yes, she'd hung up her towel. And yes, her dress had been where Elizabeth had said it would be, hanging up in the airing cupboard off the upstairs back hall where the ironing board was kept, a fancy white dress with a blue sash and bunches of cherries appliquéd on the collar. She hated the dress. It was a baby's dress, chosen by Elizabeth.

"Fix your hair," Elizabeth said on her way out.

Archie called the sweaty tumble of red curls on Alice's head her glory; he liked to brush his hand over the coils. Alice hated her hair. It was painful, having Elizabeth brush it, and she herself only tore ineffectually at her head with her mother's old ivory-handled hairbrush. She would have to brush it today, even though it was her birthday.

Squeak went the Bishop.

Alice leaned over again to look. Archie had gone back indoors, and the lawn below was empty now except for the dining room chairs. Already the morning shadows had contracted, drawing in on themselves to become soft shapes disappearing against the brightening grass. Soon the guests would arrive and Alice would come downstairs in her dress. There would be lunch, and running among the children, and the singing of happy birthday and the cutting of the cake, the first slice to go to the youngest guest and the next to the eldest and the very last to Alice herself.

People did not look at the MacCauley boys and necessarily think of the boys' mother, but Alice knew they remembered her when they looked at Alice, perhaps for the likeness between them, both of them red-haired and red-cheeked and mottled on the neck when upset or anxious, or perhaps just because Alice was a girl. Alice sensed that she was regarded as unfortunate by some of the MacCauleys' friends and neighbors, a girl in a house full of boys, a girl in a house that lacked a mother's touch, a girl in a house that contained neither hair dryer nor drawers of makeup in the bathroom, nor even, thanks to Alice's own perverse preference for pants rather than dresses, more than one summer dress and one winter one, an old-fashioned blue velvet with a white bib of a collar picked out by Elizabeth that made Alice feel like an orphan dressed up to impress prospective parents. People had relegated Alice, she believed, to the shadowy underground of the woebegone and misbegotten, the world of those who had suffered bad luck; those who had attached themselves, even unwittingly, to something sad; those who always reminded people of someone no longer living. In that dark place, misfortune, ugly as a stepsister, would always follow at your heels. You would have to be very brave, Alice thought, to escape. You would have to be heroic.

Still, despite their mother's early death, they had a talent for happiness, the MacCauley children. That was what people said, admiring them at parties—all of them (except Alice) so tall and boldly colored, the twins like Alice and Beryl with Nordic strawberry-colored hair, the others dark-haired and blue-eyed like Archie, with Archie's handsome features. Surely Alice, too, feeling as she did on this morning of her tenth birthday with the world sparkling beneath her, could hold on to a share of that happiness?

Downstairs, Wally began banging on the piano: *ta-ra-ra-boom-de-ay, ta-ra-ra-BOOM-de-ay,* faster and faster. The door in the face of the cuckoo clock in the upstairs hall sprang open, and the little bird sang out the hour. Alice flung her legs outside the window frame, dangling her feet and thumping her heels rhythmically against the clapboard. Beside her, the window curtains inflated with the wind, rising and falling against her. Alice took deep breaths, puffing out her cheeks and exhaling gustily, her breath filling her up, and up, and up until she was light-headed. She felt as if she might float off the windowsill; the only thing keeping her tied down were her feet, which had grown pleasantly heavy.

And then she heard the first car crunching down the long gravel drive between the pine trees, approaching the house.

The party was about to begin.

THREE

THE FIRST IN A PROCESSION of cars turned slowly onto the grass of the field. Alice yanked her legs inside and dropped off the windowsill onto the floor. Her ironed party dress was ridiculous; she did not want to be seen in it. Girls her age wore blue jeans, even to parties, but Elizabeth did not think this was suitable party attire, and Archie helplessly deferred all such decisions to Elizabeth.

After a minute, Alice peeked up over the edge of the windowsill. The first arrivals were picking their way over the rough ground of the field toward the house, calling greetings to Archie, who descended the porch steps and strode out across the lawn to meet them. As Alice watched, nose above the windowsill, Mr. Casey, who owned the Grange Inn in town, sailed down the driveway on his bicycle, his dachshund standing up in the wicker bicycle basket and barking hysterically at Lorenzo, the MacCauleys' affable black Labrador, who wound joyfully among the guests.

A balloon slipped free of the porch railing and rose silently into the leafy shadows of the maple tree near Alice's window.

When Alice heard Archie call her name, she sank back hurriedly to the floor again. She could imagine him taking a step backward on the lawn to search her window, shielding his eyes with his hand. But she did not want to go downstairs in her foolish dress with its starched pleats and silly cherries, in her shiny shoes and babyish white socks. Everyone they knew in Grange had been invited, and people would feel obligated to make a fuss over her, which would be embarrassing. Few of the families in Grange had children exactly Alice's age. There were a couple of teenage boys who would have complained about having to come to the party, Alice thought, and who had probably stayed home, and then there was a group of children much younger than Alice. But this event and an annual Christmas party fulfilled Archie's sense of his social obligation for the year, and though Alice suspected that, like her, he did not really look forward to either occasion, he pretended bonhomie. In any case, no one ever asked Alice whether she wanted a birthday party or not.

Alice's door opened with a soft click. She looked up, stricken—was Elizabeth coming to get her?—but it was only Wally, who smiled down at her on the floor.

"Not a very good hiding place," he said.

Alice looked at her feet. "I'm not hiding."

Wally came in, closed the door behind him, and sat down on the bed. "You have to go down there sometime," he said.

Alice watched him take a small glass ashtray out of one pocket and a cigarette and a book of matches out of another. He tapped the cigarette against his wristwatch and then lit it. Alice had spent a whole weekend leaving handwritten warnings about the dangers of smoking in Wallace's bedroom, filling the pockets of his coats and stuffing them inside the tight rolls of his socks. "You stink," some of them said. "Cigarettes kill," said others. Archie occasionally smoked a pipe, and Alice had papered his belongings, too, dozens of little skull-and-crossbones notes. This had been Alice's year for furious letter-writing campaigns: against the war in Iraq (Archie was opposed). Against relaxed state laws controlling snowmobiles (Archie was opposed to this, as well). In support of increased fines for littering, this having been the collective cause of the fourth grade at her elementary school. One day, pedaling her bicycle along a mile-and-a-half stretch of West Road, Alice had affixed fifty hand-lettered signs to the trees, warning violators about tossing trash out their car windows. Tad and Harry, who discovered the signs on one of their trips home that fall, had arrived in time for dinner asking who'd put all that garbage on the trees on the road and causing Alice to flee from the table in mortification.

Wally was the tallest of the five boys, the most serious, and the one she could usually depend on for respectful consideration of her questions. His nose was big and beaked, and his jaw had a ferocious edge like an ax blade, but his eyes were dark and tender. He was the musician among them, sensitive and brooding. Alice knew that Archie expected Wally to be famous someday, and he'd already played a lot of concerts and won some important competitions. Alice thought Wally was mournfully heroic looking, like Abraham Lincoln. She knew James was considered the more conventionally handsome of the two, but she thought she preferred Wally's romantic look.

"What do you feel when you have a birthday?" she asked him now.

"Nothing," he said. "It's just another day, isn't it?" He blew a cloud of smoke toward the ceiling. "Once I might have felt something," he said. "I can't really remember."

Alice looked down at her white socks and her party shoes. "Archie doesn't want you to smoke in the house," she said primly.

"I know," Wally said. He sighed. "It's just stress making me do it. Sorry." He stood up. "Come on. Let's go."

When Alice didn't move, he said, "It's just the first moment that's bad. After that, nobody will notice you." He stubbed out his cigarette, stood up from the bed, and came across the room to reach down and take her hand. She let him pull her to her feet and then leaned into him for a moment. He smelled like cigarette smoke and something sour: grass clippings, she thought.

"Courage," he said, and pushed her toward the door.

"Here you are!" Archie looked relieved. He met them on the porch and put his arm around Alice's shoulders, bearing her with him down the steps and over the grass toward Helen O'Brien, who stood waiting on the brick path, leaning on her cane and smiling.

"Happy birthday, dear Alice," Helen said. She kissed Alice's cheek. "You look perfectly beautiful."

The O'Briens were the MacCauleys' nearest neighbors. Helen's husband, Tom, known to most people simply as O'Brien, was Archie's oldest friend, an engineer who built bridges for the state of Vermont. Like Archie, he had grown up in Grange. Helen had been stricken by polio when she was young, and she wore a brace on one leg, a complicated affair of Velcro straps and buckles and metal splints. Alice had seen a picture of Helen from when she was a child in the hospital in Boston, flanked by smiling nuns in wimples who surrounded the frail little girl like a merry fleet of sails. She was gentle and kindhearted, beloved by the MacCauley children.

Helen seemed distracted. "Now, where has that boy gone?" She took Alice's hand between her own and held it, gazing around. "I wanted to introduce you. We have Ann's boy visiting with us, you know, he's—"

Ann's boy? Alice had never met Helen's grandson, but she knew the interesting fact that Helen and O'Brien's daughter, Ann, who was several years older than James, had run off to New York City when she was still in college and married a black man with whom she'd had a son, and that they did not come to Grange to visit. Helen spoke wistfully about Ann sometimes, and about the grandson, who was close to Alice's age.

"He's all right, Helen," Archie said. "I saw him tearing around like a fire engine. Come and sit down." He put a hand under Helen's elbow and led her along the path toward the terrace. Alice trailed behind them.

"Aren't you glad to have them all home?" Helen said to Alice, taking a seat in the chair Archie held for her.

"Tad and Harry brought a new dog with them," Alice said. "They're keeping it in their room."

"Another dog! What does Lorenzo say?"

Alice knew she was being teased, but she didn't mind. "He's a three-legged dog, with blue eyes," she continued, ignoring Helen's tone. "They're training him to count. A professor at Frost is doing an experiment."

"Well!" Helen's eyes were smiling. "I hope it doesn't distress him when he figures out that all the other dogs have *four* legs."

The lawn in front of the house had filled with people. They came by and shook hands with Archie, chatted with Helen, and smiled down at Alice, remarking inevitably on how tall she had become. Alice could see across the driveway into the barn, where Eli had opened the doors and where a few little children inside waited for turns on the swing suspended from the rafters. Tad and Harry, each bearing a tray of glasses of lemonade, stopped to kiss Helen in greeting and moved on.

"What have you done with O'Brien?" Archie asked Helen, taking the chair beside her finally and pulling Alice close to him with one arm. Alice leaned against him, safe from the barrage of well-wishers.

"Oh, he's coming," Helen said. "He's a little out of sorts."

Alice watched Helen look significantly at Archie over the top of her lemonade glass. She was about to ask why O'Brien was out of sorts, but Archie pushed himself out of his chair.

"There are the Fitzgeralds," he said. "I'll go give them a hand."

Alice watched the Fitzgeralds' old car turn slowly onto the field. Miss Fitzgerald had been Wally's first piano teacher, though the arrangement had not lasted long. After less than a year, when it was clear that Wally was significantly talented, Archie had offended Miss Fitzgerald by finding someone at Frost with whom Wally could study instead. Alice did not like Miss Fitzgerald; none of the MacCauley children did. Alice felt distrustful of Miss Fitzgerald's apparent interest in children, which seemed to Alice to be fabricated at great effort. She never bent over to shake hands or rest a palm on your head; in fact she seemed to put her hands deliberately out of reach or to busy them with something—change in her purse, an umbrella, a sheaf of papers— so as to avoid having to shake your hand, as if she feared that invisible germs were leaping off you like fleas. Yet Alice felt the tug of an unpleasant tide when she was around Miss Fitzgerald. Something happened between them, something neither of them liked or wanted to happen, but against which both of them were helpless: they had a peculiar awareness of each other that made Alice feel exposed, like when someone opened the door of her cubicle while she was changing into her bathing suit at the

YWCA in Brattleboro, where Alice went for swimming lessons. It was not just that Alice felt a strange sympathy for Miss Fitzgerald, though she was certainly aware of the desperate degree of Miss Fitzgerald's discomfort. It was that Miss Fitzgerald made Alice remember all the bad things she'd ever done in her life, and though there hadn't been so many, and most of them were trivial enough—petty thefts from her brothers, once a math test at school when she had looked at the answers of the boy beside her in class, various lies to Archie about whether she had done her piano practice or helped Elizabeth with the ironing or the dusting—the resurgence of guilt she felt in Miss Fitzgerald's presence was powerful enough that she had never confessed this to anyone, not even Wally, who, Alice thought, might have understood.

The boys' imitations of Miss Fitzgerald singing "For Those in Peril on the Sea" in a shivering vibrato were familiar stock in the MacCauley household. It had caused hurt and bitterness when Archie, sympathetic to Wally's complaints, had severed the piano arrangement. Even now, if Alice and Archie happened to run into Miss Fitzgerald while doing errands in town, Alice was aware of Archie's careful effort to appease her whenever she asked after Wally with an injured, studied politeness.

"You were the beginning of it all, Hope. Thank goodness you were there and saw what he had," Archie always said diplomatically.

Helen turned around in her chair now to watch Archie cross the lawn toward Miss Fitzgerald's car.

"So the great Kenneth has arrived," she murmured. "Poor man." After a moment she added, "Poor Hope."

"Who's Kenneth?" Alice said.

"That's Miss Fitzgerald's brother."

This was interesting news, that Miss Fitzgerald had a brother.

Alice, who considered herself an expert at brothers, did not like to acknowledge any further similarities between herself and Miss Fitzgerald, however. She watched with dismay as Miss Fitzgerald got out of the car and stood fussing at Archie's shoulder while he struggled to unload an old-fashioned cane wheelchair from the trunk. It was the strangest-looking chair Alice had ever seen.

Helen made an exasperated noise. "Where on *earth* did she find that old relic?" she said. "I bet it was in her attic."

They watched Archie wrestle with the seat.

Helen glanced at Alice. "Do you want to know a secret about Kenneth? It's not really a secret anymore. Plenty of people know it."

Alice nodded.

Helen lowered her voice. "He's Anonymous."

Alice gazed back at her, mystified.

"The library!" Helen said. "*Your* library. Kenneth Fitzgerald's the anonymous donor!"

Despite its dreary aspect, Alice had been a frequent patron at the dark old library building in Grange. It had smelled of mice and mold, and the heavy yellowed shades pulled down over the windows had submerged the rooms in a permanent dusk. On the walls had hung a collection of faded botanical prints, spotted with age, and the children's book collection had been so old that sometimes bits of the books' pages had come away in Alice's fingers like flakes of dry leaves. When Alice was seven, the old building had closed for a year while, thanks to an anonymous donor, it was restored and expanded by two new wings, one of which was devoted to children's books. This had quickly become Alice's favorite place in Grange. The high-ceilinged reading room was filled with heaps of brightly colored beanbag chairs and so many books that Alice knew she would never be able to read them all. Presiding over the children's wing was Carmel Murphy, a young woman whose name always made Alice think of creamy caramels and whose shining auburn hair and wide-open blue eyes and soft sweaters inflated by the gentle rounds of Miss Murphy's bosoms held Alice's attention with rapturous power; Alice, bearing her customary armload of books to the counter to have them checked out, knew she stared at Miss Murphy and knew it was impolite, but she could not take her eyes away from her, the pulse fluttering in her pretty white throat and the hypnotic action of her fingers deftly rifling the pages of Alice's books.

Tall windows in the children's wing let in the bracing winter light or rippling summer shade. The tables, made of smooth, pale wood finished to a silvery shine, were cool to the touch and satiny. Alice spent hours in the library, nestled in a beanbag chair dragged into a shaft of sunlight, or on rainy days curled up in a corner in one of the adult's leather armchairs, a delicious persimmon color. Besides the books, her favorite thing in the library was the pair of mobiles that hung from the high ceiling in the children's reading room. Alice liked to lie on her back on a beanbag, staring up at the mobiles moving gently in the air far above her head, the shapes suspended from a branching series of long curved arms. She could not decide if the shapes were like leaves and coral and flowers, or whether they were more like creatures: a seahorse, a diving otter, a Klipspringer, the dainty little antelope that ran over Africa and which she had seen a drawing of in Archie's encyclopedia.

Alice nursed a secret fantasy that Wally and Carmel Murphy would fall in love one day and get married. Whenever Wally came along to the library to keep Alice company and help her carry home her books, she tried to catch him secretly following Miss Murphy with his eyes, but he did not seem as impressed by her as Alice did. Wally was not as successful with girls as James, a fact that made Alice feel protective of him. Yet he was not foolishly theatrical around them either, like Tad or Harry. He unself-consciously stretched out his long frame on the floor of the reading room alongside Alice, lacing his fingers behind his head and watching the mobiles, the shadows of the shapes flickering over them like the shadows thrown by the quicksilver minnows across the sand in the riverbed. Alice hoped that, one day, Miss Murphy would look up and notice Wally. Yet this charitable feeling was complicated, for there was her own ardent admiration of Miss Murphy (and Miss Murphy's failure to notice anything special about Alice), as well as Alice's possessive feelings for Wally; none of her brothers paid as much attention to her as Wally. If Wally didn't seem interested in having a girlfriend, she had decided, she wasn't going to hurry him into finding one.

In Alice's estimation, the person responsible for the beautiful new library would be someone truly important. She and Helen watched Archie get the seat of the wheelchair in place and start around to the far side of the car.

"Hope always wanted Kenneth to come back to Grange," Helen said now. "She's been alone for so long, since her mother and father died. You know, O'Brien and Kenneth were friends as boys, long ago, and your father, too, I think, though he would have been a good bit younger, of course. But now . . ." She paused. "Well, I don't suppose Hope expected it would be like this."

Alice had never thought of Miss Fitzgerald as someone who might be lonely. She seemed instead like a very busy person, a person burdened by busyness, in fact, often showing up at the house with petitions she wished Archie to sign.

"It's Miss Fitz," the boys would say, giddy with excitement, tearing into Archie's study to warn him. "Hide! Hide!"

And Archie would hush them and get to his feet and go to meet her at the door.

She had a habit of wearing scarves over her hair, tied under her chin in a way that forced you to concentrate unhappily on her face, bulging from the scarf's constricting hold. In a rare moment of irritation, Archie had once said aloud that he wished she would keep her snout out of things she didn't know anything about, and since then Alice had never been able to look at Miss Fitzgerald without thinking of a rat. Long-nosed, cheeks working nervously as if she were chewing something, eyes watering, she had the look of a bad rat in a picture book Alice had once read. Also, she seemed to Alice to be more of a male rat than a female one, a confusion that added to Alice's distress around her.

Alice watched Archie come around from the far side of the car. He was pushing the wheelchair and leaning forward as if he were listening to something the man seated in the chair was saying to him.

Kenneth Fitzgerald looked as if he was made of birch bark. He was frail and pale-skinned, and Alice could see that, even sitting down, he was elegantly tall, with a long neck and endless legs. But his expression, his posture, didn't look like that of a sick man's. He loafed in the wheelchair in an old-fashioned seersucker suit, knees apart, elbows sticking out; Alice was always told, when she sat like that, to sit up properly. Alice looked away; there was something wrong with him, or else he wouldn't be in the wheelchair, and you did not look at people who had something wrong with them, she knew, sick people or dwarfs or retarded people like Barrett and Rita's son, Eric, who helped at the general store in Grange and who could sometimes be heard wailing in a back room while Rita hit the keys of the cash register with a stony face, ringing up Alice's shameful candy purchases.

Yet she did not think she felt sorry for Kenneth Fitzgerald the way she felt sorry for Eric, with his blubbery face and untidy clothes. Kenneth Fitzgerald had a pointed widow's peak of snowy hair and hooded eyes and a knowing expression, and despite his slouching he loomed in the wheelchair like a king or a sorcerer. He made Alice remember a story she had read about a magician, a complicated figure who'd thrown a long shadow of wickedness over a kingdom that under his tyranny had turned to an eternal winter, bleak miles of snowy plain before a final darkness. In the story, the magician himself had been under an enchantment, and another enemy, a magician even more knowing and powerful, had to be defeated before the good magician could be released from his spell and return to save the kingdom.

Kenneth Fitzgerald was speaking to Archie. He threw out his arm in a grand gesture, as if tossing a swarm of bees to the wind. Alice heard her father laugh, bent over the handlebars of the wheelchair. It was a surprising sound, and Alice took note. Archie rarely laughed aloud.

Alice wanted to ask about the library—had Kenneth Fitzgerald been responsible for the mobiles, too? Something about that gesture of his, his long fingers fluttering, had made her think of them—but at that moment a boy came running up to them, panting.

Alice stared at him. He had wiry sandy-colored hair and skin the color of the cloudy honey Barrett sold at the general store. An assembly of objects hung from his belt: a loop of thick rubber bands, an empty sheath for a knife with something bulging at its center, a hank of fraying rope.

"*Here* you are!" Helen looked up, smiling, and put out her arm to draw him to her side. "Oh, Theo. You're soaked. What have you been doing?" She handed him her glass of lemonade. "Alice, this is our grandson, Theo Swann. Theo, this is Alice. She's the birthday girl."

"Someone was chasing me!" the boy said breathlessly. He

gulped the lemonade, his chest heaving. He didn't acknowledge Alice.

"Chasing you?" Helen took the glass from him.

"A dog!" Theo said.

"Well, that's not some*one*. That's some*thing*," Helen said. "Not that silly dachshund of the Caseys? I know it wasn't Lorenzo. I don't believe I've ever seen Lorenzo run."

Alice had met Ann O'Brien only once, on a trip to New York last year with Archie and O'Brien and Helen. They had taken her to see *The Nutcracker* and the shop windows and the tree and skaters at Rockefeller Center. O'Brien had wanted to go see the place where the airplanes had crashed into the World Trade Center buildings, but Helen had said he would have to go alone; she didn't want Alice to see such a sad and gloomy place. On their last afternoon in the city, before the ballet, Alice and Archie had picked up Helen and O'Brien at a restaurant where they'd had lunch with their daughter. Alice couldn't remember whether anyone had said anything about this boy then, though she had known he existed. She had wanted to ask about him; she knew he was around her age. But something, some anxious unhappiness in Helen's expression that afternoon, had stopped her. Ann had been a small woman like her mother, with exquisite, almost hypnotically perfect skin; she had gazed sleepily at Alice when they were introduced, and Alice had thought that Ann looked as if she were sick or recovering from being sick. The husband, the black man, had not been there.

Suddenly, Alice remembered Tad and Harry's dog. She turned to Theo. "Did the dog have three legs?"

He looked at her as if seeing her for the first time. "Yes!"

"Did it have blue eyes?"

Theo's jaw dropped. "Whoa!" he said. "*Yeah* it did."

"He must have escaped," Alice said to Helen. "I've got to go catch him."

When Tad and Harry had brought the dog into the kitchen a few days before, cringing and shaking on its leash, Alice had felt an unhappy confusion over the fact that the dog had only three legs. What had happened to the other one? It was terrible to think about. She had followed them when they had taken the dog outside, where it sniffed around urgently in the tall grass behind the barn.

"Want to hold the leash?" Tad had said, offering it to Alice, but she had put her hands behind her back. The dog had made her feel pity and also a shameful squeamishness; she had wanted to be brave enough to take its leash while it squatted pathetically on its three legs to pee into the grass, but she had not been able to make her hands come out from behind her back. Now the thought of it on its own, bewildered and limping along, its haunch above the stump of its missing leg moving horribly, aroused in her a confidence she had not felt the night before.

"I'll come, too," Theo said suddenly.

"Where was he?" Alice said.

"Over there." Theo pointed toward the apple orchard.

Alice began to run, and Theo ran after her. They sprinted away together, veering around a group seated in the dining room chairs pulled into a circle on the grass. "Happy birthday, Alice," somebody called as they ran by, and Alice waved, a giddy lightness in her heart.

Oh, *this* was what she had wanted to do all morning, she thought. She had only wanted to run, flying out of her windowsill and over the grass. Some of the other children started up behind them, caught by the contagion of the runners.

Now here was the stone wall to be leaped, rearing up in front of her. And here, as she teetered atop the stones, was the strange surprise of the rope walk in the apple orchard, a mysterious tangle of colored strings wound trunk to trunk like an enormous enchanted spiderweb, just as James had said. She balanced on the top of the wall, breathing hard.

"Follow me," Theo called, for suddenly he was beside her and then past her, leaping to crest the wall and sail over it, his legs flying. His striped T-shirt blazed in the sunlight.

She hesitated for a moment, glancing behind her. She saw Archie, still with his hands on Kenneth Fitzgerald's wheelchair, look up at Theo's shout. He said something, and Kenneth Fitzgerald moved his head to look in her direction. He didn't look at her, exactly; his head moved like a periscope, as if an invisible eye were guiding him in her direction. Perhaps his nose was sniffing her out as she stood on the wall in her starched party dress, her feet in their patent leather shoes slipping on the stones.

Archie began to raise his hand; he meant to call her back, Alice thought.

And so before he could issue the command, before she could be accused of disobedience, Alice jumped.

FOUR

A **SPRING THUNDERSTORM ENDED** the party prematurely. The last guests ran for their cars or were supplied with umbrellas from the hall closet and drove away up the lane to the West Road. Alice sat at the kitchen table and watched Elizabeth bustle around, putting away the last few dishes, wrapping the leftover sandwiches in plastic and setting them in the fridge. Finally, Elizabeth was finished. She went to the bathroom to change her shirt and came back, tying a plastic rain bonnet under her chin. "*Birth*day present, under your *pi*llow," she said in a teasing, singsong voice. "From me. Don't forget to look." She bent to kiss Alice. Elizabeth always gave Alice money for her birthday, crisp one-dollar bills in amounts equal to whatever age she had reached.

"I won't forget," Alice said. "Thank you, Elizabeth." She put her arms around Elizabeth's neck. Sometimes she wished Elizabeth didn't go home on the weekends, but Archie had said that they must never ask more of Elizabeth than she wanted to give them; she did so much for them all as it was.

Alice went to the window and watched the taillights of Elizabeth's station wagon disappear up the driveway in the darkness of the rain. Then she sat back down at the kitchen table. In the hall, the grandfather clock struck four p.m., the exact hour when Alice had been delivered into the world. Alice held her breath; now she was truly ten. The moment slid past slowly, chime after chime. The clock's voice rasped, its old gears struggling free for each stroke. When the clock fell silent, Alice stayed in her seat, but she did not feel any different than she had a moment before.

After the noise of the party, the house was quiet and lonely feeling; the rain fell with a sighing hush that was like the ocean Alice heard inside the goliath conch kept on the top shelf of the cabinet in the dining room. When Alice was younger, Archie would bring down the shell collection for her to play with under the dining room table. Alice had loved the shells, each like a miniature world with its glistening interior and elaborately carved and crenellated surfaces, its mysterious, sad smell of salt, the faint reminder of its old life in the sea. Lying with her elbows propped open before the *Golden Guide to Seashells of the World,* Alice had learned the names of all the shells: Miracle shells, Babylon Turrids, the Noble cones, tiny Rose murex, cowries with their grinning mouths, Venus clams and cockles and whelks. Words in any arrangement—lists, names, snatches of verse— came easily to Alice, first pronunciation, for which she had an instinctive gift, and then sense; when she was only five or six Archie had enjoyed getting her to memorize, which she appeared to do effortlessly, and then recite lengthy bits of doggerel or silly Ezra Pound or Shakespeare's sonnets: *Let me not to the marriage of true minds admit impediments. Love's not love which alters when it alteration finds.* She had not been allowed to lift down the shells herself, and now she didn't ask for them anymore, but when she was younger she had spent hours under the table playing with them.

Now someone put on music in the living room. It was probably Wally. He was the only one of the boys who liked classical music. Alice got up to go find him.

Wally hadn't turned on any lights, despite the darkness outside. He sat sprawled on the rug, leaning against a pillow propped up against the couch, smoking a cigar and blowing ostentatious smoke rings that sank slowly in the heavy air.

Alice poked her finger through one as she came across the room.

"You ruined it," he said. "I'm trying to get a bull's eye."

"One to go through the other?" Alice stopped to watch as he exhaled, executing two ghostly, wobbly rings that collided in midair.

She climbed onto the couch behind him and lay down, gazing across the premature dusk of the room at the armchairs with their frayed armrests, the long table covered with the darkly patterned Kashmiri throw and stacks of books, the faceted glass lamp whose beaded shade winked in the half-light. Between the two high windows at the far end of the room, through which quivering flashes of lightning could be seen, stood her mother's tall secretary desk. Behind its glass doors, the pale moon faces of two porcelain Chinamen stared forth from between the books. Alice made her imaginary camera again and looked through the knothole made by her fingers: two jade temple dogs on the desk's surface, their teeth bared, held a messy row of telephone and address books and papers. On the stained blotter, a silver cup shone dully in the light. The cup had been won by her mother long ago in an archery tournament and was filled now with stubs of pencils and odd pens and a hawk's boldly striped feather.

Alice dropped her camera. In a deepening drowse that seemed to be taking hold of her limbs one at a time, she watched the mirror over the fireplace where lightning pulsed distantly like something in another world. The morning of just a few hours before, when she had sat in her room and waited for the party to begin, seemed far away. Now her dress was rumpled and stained, the patent leathers lost in the tall grass of the orchard where the rain would ruin them. Elizabeth would complain, Alice knew, about the condition of the dress and the missing shoes. But that didn't seem to matter right now; she felt so sleepy. Alice gazed at the mirror in a somnolent stare. The light in the room dimmed another degree. Wally's cigar smoke hovered like a mist. Alice loved twilight for the appearance of fireflies, for the day's last giant shadows, comically oversize, for the way the color blue seeped into everything. Today would end without twilight, though, swallowed up by the rain and gloom; day would slouch into night like a hearse with drawn curtains.

Alice stretched and crossed her arm over her eyes. Her skin smelled of grass and dog. The three-legged dog, which had been captured eventually earlier that afternoon with the aid of a quarter-pound of hamburger meat supplied reluctantly by Elizabeth, had been braver than Lorenzo about the approaching thunderstorm. Usually at the first sound of thunder Lorenzo made straight for Archie's bed at a scrabbling run, crawling into the space beneath it, shaking and whimpering. The three-legged dog, on the other hand, confined again to the twins' bedroom, had put his front paws on Harry's pillow, his body quivering, and stared out the window at the branches whipping back and forth in the high wind that preceded the rain.

"What happened to his leg?" Theo had asked Harry, and Harry had regaled Theo and Alice with a long, upsetting tale about how the dog had been caught in a trap and had chewed off his own leg, a story to which Theo and Alice had listened, horrified. Cruelty to animals was an unbearable idea to Alice, and Theo had seemed as moved as she was by the idea of the dog's suffering. "Those traps," he had said fiercely after the twins had left the room, bored by Alice and Theo and the dog. "A hunter should get *his* leg caught in one."

Watching him as he knelt on Harry's bed and patted the dog's trembling back, Alice had realized that Theo had completely conquered his initial fear of the dog. When they had first discovered the dog racing about wildly in the field behind the vegetable garden, Theo had drawn up behind her, a restraining hand on her arm. "Don't scare him," he'd whispered, and she had shivered at his breath in her ear. But she had known it was Theo himself who was frightened. They had stood there, Alice herself suddenly unsure about how to proceed, while the three-legged dog snuffled frantically in the grass. When Tad and Harry arrived, armed with the hamburger, Alice had been disappointed. She wanted to have been the one to return the dog to safety. But Theo had gone darting out to help, firing questions at the twins: What was the dog's name? How old was he? What kind of dog was he? Where did they get him?

Once the dog had been restored to the bedroom, Theo had disappeared briefly, returning minutes later with a toolbox, a battered red tin case that held a messy collection of odds and ends and broken parts of things: a sprinkler nozzle, a hammer missing a claw, various screwdrivers, a bent section of radio antennae, coils of copper wire, a penknife with a floppy blade, miscellaneous screws and nails and washers and unidentifiable mechanical parts, a cell phone with a smashed face, a television remote missing its back. He had opened the toolbox on the floor of Tad and Harry's bedroom, rifling busily through its contents.

Harry, a plate of sandwiches on his knee, had leaned over to look inside. "Nice junk," he said.

"We can maybe rig him up a fake leg," Theo said to Alice, ignoring Harry. "A wheel or something . . ."

Alice had seen Harry roll his eyes at Tad. She had felt embarrassed for Theo; it was obvious even to her that the toolbox didn't contain anything that could make the dog a new leg. But after

Tad and Harry had left, Theo had rifled through the drawers of the desk until he found paper and a pencil. He had not asked for permission to do this; he'd just done it, a trespass Alice herself would not have committed in a stranger's bedroom. Lying on his stomach on the floor and smoothing out the paper with his palms, he had drawn, tongue between his teeth, what Alice recognized immediately as an extremely good likeness of a dog, his hindquarters suspended in a rolling cart strapped to the dog's shoulders with a device like the stays of an old-fashioned buggy. From this beginning they had imagined all sorts of tasks the dog could perform thus equipped: trundling objects from place to place, fetching the newspaper, delivering mail, hauling rocks, conveying messages. He could even be recruited as a moveable lemonade stand. Even while she had known that these things would never happen, that the dog would be taken back to Frost with the twins, it had been easy to forget that truth, to pretend otherwise. It had been fun, planning the dog's future with Theo. He had a good imagination.

Now, as Alice lay on the couch, the sounds of the thunder and the rain and the cello seemed to fill up the room and overflow, as if the walls were dissolving. Wally's cigar smoke rings made ghostly wreaths in the air. She blinked against their wavering shapes, and her eyes closed. When she heard someone come to the door of the living room, her eyes felt too heavy to bother opening.

It was James's voice. "Success?" he said.

Alice heard Wally shift on the floor in front of her, felt his eyes on her. "She's asleep," he said after a minute, turning around again. "Worn out with partying."

Alice felt too sleepy to correct Wally. She had occasionally deliberately pretended sleep in order to overhear something that might not have been said aloud in her presence, though she had never heard anything interesting this way; people usually just tip-toed away. Once, though, she had been discovered hiding inside the kneehole of Archie's desk when Archie was confronting James about a girl whose upset parents had called Archie on the telephone; James and the girl had driven to Key West for a week during high school, leaving behind cheerful notes of explanation that seemed to assume that no one would mind. Alice, fascinated by the drama, had been listening intently, but when Archie noticed her at last, he had hauled her out from under the desk, her elbow hurting inside his grip. This past Christmas, shooed away repeatedly from her brothers' conversations, she had lain waiting under Tad's bed for what had seemed like hours, aware of the dusty coils of horsehair inside the box spring above her like something alive enlarged to terrifying proportions under a microscope. When the boys had finally congregated in the bed-room, Harry tossing a tennis ball against the wall with madden-ing regularity, the only thing she had heard that was at all interesting was Tad and Harry's report that Archie was in fact quite a popular professor at Frost. His worst offense, Harry said, was that he was thought to be "unknowable."

"Which means he doesn't drink with them," Tad had said.

"Or sleep with any of them," Harry added. "Thank god."

Alice had not understood why Archie should want to go to sleep beside any of his students, but she had sensed dangerous, uncomfortable territory. Afterward she was a little sorry she'd eavesdropped.

Another set of footsteps approached the living room. With an effort, Alice opened her eyes enough to see Archie appear beside James in the doorway. Through her eyelashes he looked as if he were crosshatched by the enormous shadow of palm fronds. The layer of bitter cigar smoke shivered in the air.

"Radio says they're having hail in Newfane," Archie said, speaking above the rain. "Poor Alice."

"Oh, she'd had enough," Alice heard James say. "Look at her."

There was silence for a moment. Alice felt their eyes resting on her and she stayed very still, trying to take only the shallowest breaths, a pantomime of deep sleep.

"All parties should end early anyway," James said. "Then people go away saying it was the best party they'd ever been to."

Alice heard Wally laughing quietly.

Finally Archie spoke again. "The rope walk was a good idea. You boys were good to do that for her."

They'd had to hurry through the game at the end of the party, the sky already threatening, scattered raindrops striking high in the trees. Some adults had played, too, helping the younger children through the maze. When Alice had found herself face-to-face with Theo, he had seemed electrified with excitement in the strange light, his strange bushy hair standing up on end. But they had easily untangled their lines from each other's, Alice slipping under Theo's arm, Theo twirling around her, both of them seeing instantly how it should be done. She had watched him as he vaulted through the maze, his line eventually leading him back to her. The other children had shrieked with excitement, but Alice had been quiet, watching the lines gradually unwind from one another, waiting until she was brought back face-to-face with Theo.

Once, when she had stopped near the stone wall, she had heard Miss Fitzgerald's voice, speaking from behind her where the adults had gathered to watch.

"Who's *that* little boy?" Miss Fitzgerald asked someone. "That's not Helen and O'Brien's little black grandson, is it?"

Alice knew that Theo's father was black, but Theo himself was tawny like a lion, his burr of blond hair like the head of a thistle. She liked his color; it made her think of the desert in Kipling's *Just So* stories, the rhinoceros with his skin stuffed full of itchy yellow cake crumbs, the crazy Parsee dancing on the sand in glee.

The prizes at the rope walk had been good; nothing disgusting. There were yo-yo's, boxes of colored pencils, Hershey's bars, and harmonicas, all fished out of the old bins at Barrett and Rita's store in town. In the end, Theo had traded a box of crayons for Alice's Slinky, packing it away inside his toolbox.

"We should have played music," Wally said now. "It would have been more fun. Horns, maybe, or Fats Waller. Might have sped things up, too."

Alice looked through slits; she watched James and Archie's shoes and their pants cuffs cross the floor toward the couch, heard the sound of them sitting down. Perhaps she could stretch now, she thought, and pretend to wake up.

But then James spoke again, freezing her into stillness. "How *is* Alice?" he said. She could not understand his tone; he sounded as though she had been diagnosed with a fatal disease and everybody knew it but Alice. Coldness crept over her. It was one thing to pretend sleep and listen to people talk about inconsequential things. It was another thing when they began to talk about you. Either way, she thought, it was miserable in the end. "Come out from under there," Archie had said to her the day he'd found her hiding in the kneehole of his desk, gripping her by the elbow; his roughness, the sense of Archie's barely contained anger, had shocked her. Archie never lost his temper, never shouted as she knew some parents did. She had stood in front of him, cheeks burning. "Go to your room," he'd said. "No supper." This was the only punishment Archie ever meted out, but it was terrible, far worse, she thought, than the groundings and the long lectures—and the whacks on the bottom—she had heard about from her schoolmates. The sound of dishes clattering and conversation at the table reached you alone in your room, along with the smells of meat loaf or baked beans or macaroni and cheese cooked in the red casserole dish. You would be left alone for hours, waiting and growing more and more hungry, and at last, after dark, Archie would come upstairs to say good night, and he would kiss you sadly as you lay in your bed. Then he would reach into his pocket for the saltines, which he always brought with him, and he would stack them neatly on your beside table. It was those saltines, and the sight of his blunt, squared-off fingers shuffling them into a neat little stack that always broke you, and you would weep then, turning your face away in shame.

The two worst sins in the MacCauley house were lying and deliberate cruelty. Pretending you were asleep when you were not was like telling a lie.

Archie didn't answer James right away. Alice felt sure her face was bright red with shame.

Finally Archie said, "Alice is lonely. But Elizabeth is here." He reached up and took off his eyeglasses. Alice heard them click shut as he put them away in his pocket. "Did I ever tell you—" he began.

"About the live frog found in a hailstone." Wallace and James said it in unison.

"Ah," Archie said. "I repeat myself."

There would be no answer to this, Alice thought. Archie *did* repeat himself, more and more often now. But she was being distracted by their conversation. Wait, she wanted to say. Am I *lonely*? Is *that* what this is?

In front of Alice, Wallace's shoulder, sculpted like a mountain in his white shirt, stood out in the melancholy light.

"Were we lonely?" she heard James ask.

"Well," Archie said. "You had each other, didn't you?"

Lying on the couch, Alice felt herself growing small, like a stone dropped from a great height. She wanted to stretch, to sit up suddenly, blinking and yawning: the birthday girl awakes! Everyone say Happy Birthday! Yet she knew she was not equal to the performance this would require. They would suspect her of listening, and they would be right.

The rain seemed to be intensifying, hammering on the porch awning outside. James had told Alice once that thunder was the sound of rocks being rolled away from a giant's cave in the sky, a notion that for years had terrified Alice. Only repeated comic performances by Tad and Harry, who were forced to enact on Alice's twin beds the bumbling, slapstick boxing match of two crybaby giants, could restore Alice's equanimity. She was not afraid of thunder anymore, but still a storm left her with a feeling of disquiet, of doom and gloom, like being sick with a fever. She wished she had not heard Archie, but there was no undoing it now.

She *was* lonely. *She* alone, of all the MacCauleys, was a lonely child. Her brothers had had each other.

And then sleep took her, like a hood pulled down over her face. She slept deeply, though perhaps it was only for a few minutes, a refusal to stay awake and consider her sorry plight. When she opened her eyes, she saw that her father and James had fallen asleep, too, side by side on the couch, Archie's finger still trapped inside his book, James's head resting near Archie's shoulder.

Suddenly, Wally turned around.

She jumped.

"You've been awake this whole time, haven't you?" he said. "I felt your eyes."

Alice turned her face away. "I have not," she said. She felt disconsolate, disoriented. She had dreamed vaguely of banishment, a dream of wetness and coldness, damp stones on a shore, her voice an echo in the fog.

She rolled back over and looked at Wally. The room had grown very dark. Archie, with his mouth open, looked like he was dead.

"When are you leaving?" she said. She knew Wally would be gone for the whole summer, but she wanted to accuse him now, accuse him of leaving her, just as he had accused her of pretending sleep. Wally had won a coveted apprenticeship with a conductor at a summer music festival in Michigan, where he would lead a youth orchestra. It was a challenging program for young musicians, not to mention a young conductor, Wally had told the family at dinner a couple of nights before: Beethoven's *Coriolan Overture;* Weber's *Invitation to the Dance; Songs of a Wayfarer* by Mahler, with a baritone soloist; Schubert's "Unfinished" Symphony. James, too, would be gone soon; he was going to law school in the fall, but he would spend the summer at the governor's office in Montpelier on an internship. Sitting beside Wally on the floor the day before while he'd gone through Archie's ancient record collection in the living room, Alice had asked Wally what it would be like at the governor's house.

"Grand," Wally had said. "Perfect for James." He had slipped an old record out of its cardboard jacket, regarded the label.

James was full of charm and confidence. He liked to ruffle Archie's hair, sling an arm around his brothers, catch up Alice in a theatrical way and swing her around. He was full of plans and ideas, keeping Archie in his seat at the dinner table for hours after the dishes had been cleared while he talked and asked questions. He usually had a girl with him, too, someone pretty who clung to his arm. Wally never brought home a girl.

Soon the house would be empty again. Tad and Harry, after a week or so of carousing with their old friends at home in Grange, would return to Frost, where they were living over the summer in the basement of the college infirmary, working with the grounds crew to mow the lawns and surrounding fields and in the evenings acquainting themselves, as Archie had put it, with the girls in town. Only Eli would stay at home with Archie and Alice, and Eli was the quietest brother, slender like his mother, tall like Archie, who had staked out for himself, perhaps particularly in the wake of the twins' boisterousness and Wallace and James's separate and pronounced interests of music and politics, the peaceful world of the garden. It was Eli who, as a young teenager, had revived his mother's perennial borders, who had built the path down to the river, stones quarried with a single-minded patience from the riverbed, and who hired himself out every summer to their neighbors in Grange for general yard work and improvements. Alice tagged along after him on these errands while he moved stolidly from one project to another, but he never talked much. Eli was inscrutable, Wally said.

Alice watched Wally take a long pull on his cigar. He grimaced and then leaned over to flick it into the fireplace where it glowed for a minute in the darkness. He didn't answer her question about when he was leaving. He'd already invited her to come along when Archie drove him to the airport, and she knew he understood that she was baiting him now out of meanness and sadness. She felt a sudden flare of longing like homesickness. She liked it when Wally took her with him on his nighttime walks, the two of them crossing the fields into the woods, walking along the old logging road near the river in the dark and then circling back to approach the house again through the orchard. She liked the feeling of coming upon her beloved house as a stranger would. Long and low, with black shutters under a green roof, the original white-painted farmhouse had been extended by ad hoc additions supplied over the years to meet the needs of the growing generations of family. The ground floor of the original building, built in the early 1800s, had been converted long ago into Archie's study, where a tiger skin rug lay on the floor. The tiger's mouth was open in a silent roar and all its yellow teeth were bared at the French doors through which a raccoon had crept once while Archie sat up late one evening, working. At the sight of the tiger, the raccoon had arched its back and let out a scream so bloodcurdling that Archie had fallen out of his chair in shock. "Thank God it wasn't a skunk," he'd said later. There was a tale about the tiger having been shot by one of their mother's forbearers in India, but Wally said it was apocryphal.

Suddenly Alice sat up. "Look!" she said, pointing to the window.

Outside, a strange glow had filled the air. Alice scrambled off the couch and ran to the window. "There's ice in the birdbath," she said from across the room.

Wally got to his feet and joined Alice at the window. The sound of the rain had changed again. Little tacks fell against the porch awning now with a hushed noise, like sand filling a bucket. The birdbath was heaped with a mound of crystals; patterns of snaky trails of ice beribboned the lawn.

"Did I ever tell you," Wally began in his Archie voice.

"About the live frog," Alice said, in the same tone.

Together they stared out the window. Behind them, the arm on the record player lifted, reversed itself with a click. The music ceased and the sound of the hail pattering on the awning and on the tin roof filled the room.

Archie awoke with a snort. "Alice?" he said. His voice sounded worried, querulous, an old man's voice.

"We're here," Wally said, turning around. "It's hailing, Arch. The world is raining frogs."

"I've been asleep," Archie said, unnecessarily.

Alice stared out the window. The spring day had been arrested by a false winter as transparently unreal and strange and magical as the fake snow that had tumbled through the footlights on the stage at school for the Christmas pageant, where Alice had been a candy cane, dressed in tap shoes and a red bathrobe onto which one of the other children's mothers had sewn a winding white stripe. Now everything had turned silver and gray. Steam rose from the ground. The new green leaves hung down from the branches, defeated and dark as soot.

"You'll remember this day forever, won't you?" Kenneth Fitzgerald had said to her at the party after Archie had introduced her finally. He had looked at her gravely. A little clump of white spittle had gathered at the corner of his mouth, and Alice had wanted to look away, but his eyes had been brimming and shining. "For my tenth birthday I was given a boat," he'd said to her, and perhaps because he was at her height, sitting in the wheelchair, it was as if Archie and all the party melted away; it was only the two of them left there on the lawn. "It was called the *Alice Fitzgerald*," he said, holding her eyes with his own, "named for my mother."

Alice had stared back at him, struck of course by the coincidence of the names—her name being Alice, his mother's name being Alice; plus, it was hard to think of this old man as a boy, let alone a boy with a boat of his own. But she had been surprised mostly by the way in which he seemed to have read her mind, or at least her feelings, so inchoate but powerful that morning when she had sat in her windowsill and felt the exultant light of the spring day enter her body. Now his words seemed to her like a prophecy, for here in the silvered world outside the window, in the cups of the daffodils filling with ice, in the spikes of grass frosted white, was an ending to the day so strange she knew she really would never forget it, the day it hailed in May on her tenth birthday.

As she stood there in her party dress facing Kenneth Fitzgerald, Theo's voice had piped up behind her.

"*I* have a boat," he said.

Alice saw Kenneth Fitzgerald's eyes slide from her face to take in Theo in his dirty T-shirt. Somehow she knew Theo didn't have a boat; Kenneth Fitzgerald knew it, too, she thought, and suddenly there was between them a complicity that made her uncomfortable.

"Come on, Alice," Theo said rudely then, and Alice caught Archie's frown as she struggled.

But Kenneth Fitzgerald's eyes had come back to her face. "Happy birthday, Alice," he said. "Go with your brave friend."

And so she had run off with Theo, relieved and embarrassed, and yet somehow strangely thrilled.

"Look, Archie," she said now, and she raised her hand to the cold glass, the world outside the window, the memorable, memorable world. "Look at the poor lilacs, all covered with snow."

FIVE

ALICE HESITATED on the porch—the air was full of hissing and a hushed tinkling of ice—and then she ran down the steps and out onto the cold grass. She cringed as the hailstones bounced off her arms and the back of her neck, but she was mostly just surprised; they didn't really hurt. The air smelled bitter, like the inside of the rusted old freezer case in Barrett and Rita's general store in Grange, with its tempting, meringuelike crust of ice to which Alice had once unwisely touched her tongue. She had been shocked at the taste, cold and somehow burnt, and the roof of her mouth had stung for hours afterward. She'd been afraid to tell anyone what she'd done, though. She was always being told not to put things in her mouth.

It was exhilarating to be outside, the spring day majestically transformed into a winter theatrical in its effects. A group of adults staged a play in Grange every summer; Archie had been recruited to help with some of the Shakespeare productions. Alice had once played a fairy in *A Midsummer Night's Dream,* but she'd preferred being backstage and conscripted for sound effects, rattling lengths of sheet metal and banging pot lids and ringing bells and firing an air horn in *The Tempest,* hunched down in the wings with some other children, a flashlight taped to a broom handle and suspended over a music stand so they could follow the script. Tad and Harry, on ladders, had let loose a bed sheet full of tissue paper confetti for hail and fired a volley of painted cardboard lightning bolts that jerked across the stage on a pulley and rope.

One of Alice's favorite illustrations came from a book, *The Wind Boy,* in which the North Wind, cheeks puffed out and lips pursed, blew swirling gusts across the page. She could feel the face of that colossus above her now, eyes streaming, curled locks of gray hair disarranged. The mild, perfumed May afternoon had been replaced by a reckless cold. Alice ran in circles, slipping on the grass, and when she stopped running the hail collected like fallen stars in her hair and in the lap of her dress, which she held out like an apron. High above, the hailstones tore noisily through the leaves of the trees and piled up in curving tracks over the grass. It wasn't true, was it, Archie's story about finding a live frog in a hailstone? She examined one: they were like marbles, gray and knobbed and dirty looking, as though they brought with them on their screaming ride toward the earth particles of outer space, a gritty planetary grime like fireplace ash. She scooped up another handful; they were strangely dry.

Then she felt the pace of the hail pick up. The sound intensified overhead, a moaning in the wind. The hail began to clatter like a train wreck on the roof high up and invisible in the crazily blurred sky.

"Ouch!" she cried, as a hailstone struck her face. She ducked and held her hands over her head as she ran.

"Alice!" She heard Archie's voice; he was calling to her from the porch, leaning over the rail. "Alice, come inside!"

But this was too wonderful, too strange and wonderful, not to be out in it. She slipped on the grass and fell. From the porch she could hear Wally laughing as she scrambled to her feet, the whoosh of the hail filling her ears.

"Ouch!" she cried again, and then in surprise, "Ow!" for it really hurt now and she skidded back toward the house, bent double under the storm of ice. Safe on the porch, panting, she shook her head like a dog. Crystals of ice flew off her.

Wally jumped back. "Hey!" he said.

Archie hustled her inside past James, who held open the door, smiling.

"Mad girl," Archie said, pushing her in front of him. In the hall he stood, breathing hard, looking down at her. "Go have a bath," he said. "Go and have a bath, mad birthday girl."

In an hour it had all melted away. The air grew cool and heavy, the twilight full of drowsy, stunned mosquitoes and a haze that drifted in layers over the lawn. Alice wandered downstairs from her bath in bare feet and jeans and an old sweater.

James and Eli were in the kitchen, the windows fogged with steam from a pot of water boiling on the stove. Just as Alice stepped into the room, Tad and Harry came in the back door, the three-legged dog scrabbling at the end of a leash behind them.

"Here. Hold him, okay?" Harry handed Alice the leash and crossed the room to open the refrigerator.

Alice took the leash and sat down in a kitchen chair. When the dog pushed past her knees to go under the table, the leash wrapped around the leg of the chair and Alice followed him to untangle the line. The dog sat down with the top of its speckled head grazing the underside of the table. The stump of the dog's leg held Alice's gaze; she found she could look at it for longer now, though she still wasn't ready to touch it. Suddenly the dog darted its head toward her. Alice froze in alarm; was he going to bite her? But he only licked her hand swiftly and then looked away. She stole her arm around him, her fingers in his rough coat. He began to pant.

They sat to eat finally with a clatter of knives and forks, a scraping of chairs. Alice came up from under the table and took her seat between Archie and Tad, who reached over to give her a horse bite on the thigh; Archie frowned at them as he uncorked a bottle of wine fetched up from the basement, his glasses pushed back on the top of his head. Then he gave Alice a second look and leaned toward her, the corkscrew still in his hand. "Did the hail do that to you?" he said, staring at her forehead.

Alice put her hand up to her face, the little cut just above her left eyebrow she had noticed when she cleared a circle on the steamed-over mirror in the bathroom. It had stung in the bath, just for a moment, when she'd soaped her face and slipped under the hot water. "Maybe," she said. "I don't know."

Archie's eyes were fixed on her forehead.

"What?" Alice said.

"It's very strange." Archie's eyes roved over her face.

Alice stared at him.

"Your mother," he began, his eyes returning to her forehead, "your mother had a little scar." He raised a finger and touched his own eyebrow. "Just here, where that hail got you."

"I remember that," James said suddenly from the other end of the table.

The other boys had fallen silent.

"I do, too," Wally said after a minute. "How'd she get it?"

Archie put down the corkscrew and picked up his wineglass. He glanced down the table at the boys and then back at Alice, and his look, when Alice met it, was full of loneliness.

She reached to put her hand up to the place above her eyebrow where the hailstone had struck her. No one said anything.

"She got it from a hailstone," Archie said finally. "When she was ten."

"You're kidding?" Harry stared at Archie.

"That's so weird," Tad said. "Really?"

Alice did not say anything. The little cut above her eyebrow burned for a moment and then buzzed, and then the sensation died away. She felt excited. Coincidences such as this were part of her understanding of the world, the same part that contemplated stories without questioning, whether their events were believable or not, but this instance of concurrence drew her close to her mother in a way that felt especially strange and important. Archie had read enough Shakespeare to Alice for her to see that even stories for adults sought conclusions, couples marching off together paired like swans, or the apparently dead returned to life, or twins parted by shipwreck finding each other at last. The pattern of revelation, resolution, restoration was familiar to her. Alice had a pop-up book—supplied to her by Elizabeth—that displayed various anatomical parts with a startling three-dimensionality; erect penises leapt up out of the book's pages, a woman's abdomen was peeled back like layers of an onion to reveal a uterus, a pair of ovaries nestled like pears in her belly. On one page, an umbilical cord was strung from margin to margin like a watch chain. But though Alice knew she had been linked physically to her mother, this bridge between them—mother and daughter struck at the same age and in identical places by a hailstone—carried with it an extraordinary, even Shakespearean dispensation. Her brothers did not have scars caused by hailstones.

Alice looked back at Archie. He seemed so sad to her sometimes. He rarely laughed, he often seemed tired, his shoulders sloped and hunched. This incident likewise seemed to have failed to charm or even amaze him. On the contrary, he looked more serious than usual, though Alice, with the communication of this revelation, felt blessed, singled out for special attention. Yet such moments in stories, she remembered suddenly, usually preceded something significant, a test of some kind. An ordinary boy discovers that he is actually a member of an ancient, magical race, destined to save it from destruction. A girl to whom heavenly creatures are revealed discovers that she must rescue her father from a terrifying enchantment. Alice had always admired the children in these stories, the ones who found themselves in the midst of bewildering adventures, charged with something terribly important. Was this one of those moments, she wondered? A little shiver ran over her.

At that involuntary movement, Archie seemed to wake up from the trance of his inspection of her. His eyes widened a fraction, and then, after a moment, he gave her a rare smile. *"There are more things in heaven and earth, Horatio, Than are dreamt of in your philosophy,"* he said. He looked back at his wineglass and took a long swallow. Then he raised his eyebrows and surveyed the table. "Well? Anyone?"

"Uh, Lear?" James said.

"No," Eli said quietly. "It's Hamlet."

Archie pointed his fork at him. "Horatio's your clue. Exactly," he said. "Ten points to Eli."

After dinner, Tad and Harry went out to the barn to play Ping-Pong. From the back door of the kitchen, Alice looked across the grass at the parallelogram of light that fell from the open barn door and illuminated the daffodils, most of them flattened by the hail, that ran along the stone wall. Only a few of the pale heads floated above the mist. Faintly Alice could hear the

Ping-Pong game, the dull plocking sound. This was the hour when the pair of doves that roosted in the birch tree near the back door made their good-night noises; and there they were, with their fussy, throaty warbling sounds. Where had the doves gone during the hail, she wondered? The leaves of the trees rustled in the darkness, as if something were settling itself there, staring out at her.

Alice helped carry plates to the sink and stood waiting with a towel while James washed the dishes. She could see their reflections wavering in the dark glass of the window, James's tall shape in his white shirt, Archie far off behind them where he sat reading at the table, the lenses of his glasses glinting. Her own face, when she stared at her reflection in the windowpane, was soft and smudged as a thumbprint. In a photograph from her parents' wedding, her mother wore a bright red dress with a gold pin shaped like a whorled feather that Archie had given her; Alice had studied the photograph in minute detail. She had had to ask what the pin was, because it was too small in the photograph to make out clearly. She had been unable to see the scar on her mother's forehead, for instance, though of course she had not known to look for it. Wally crossed the room behind her. His shirt bloomed blurrily against the mirror of the windowpane for a moment, and Alice startled and nearly dropped the glass in her hand.

James glanced over at her and grinned. "See a ghost?"

Archie pushed back his chair from the table, folding the newspaper and slapping it against the table's edge. Eli, who had been sitting at the table beside him looking through an old gardening book of their mother's, didn't look up. *"What fools these mortals be,"* he said; this was what Archie usually said when he read the newspaper.

"Quite right," Archie said. He stretched. "Let's go," he said to Alice.

Alice had been waiting for this, the moment when she and Archie would leave the house together and walk down to the river. This was their tradition on her birthday, a tradition begun by Archie for Alice alone. It did not have the gaiety of the rituals developed by Alice's mother; it was instead a grave occasion. But Alice loved it. Now Archie helped Alice root in the drawers of the pantry until they found a candle stub; it was too tall, and Archie sliced off the end with his knife. Then he sat down at the table again to fold the tinfoil boat into which they would affix the candle stub and set it to sail in the big, calm pool of the river. The ceremony, the embarkation of the little boat with its flickering candle, had filled Alice all her life with a serious pleasure.

The little cut on her forehead gave a sudden twinge, reminding her; the wonder of it, the strangeness of the coincidence, filled her again for the second time that evening. She felt very small suddenly, like something floating in the river and approaching the gnashing, tumbling confluence of the many branching streams that met just above the falls.

Outside, when they stepped into the darkness, the sky overhead was streaked with clouds like ghostly ponies' tails, the moon's face blazing down at them.

"Time is like a fashionable host . . ." Archie began when they were seated on stones at the river's edge, listening to the water.

All the MacCauley children were handy with Shakespeare. Tad and Harry, especially, had an endless store of lines taught to them by Archie which they used as ripostes or insults or excuses or purely irrelevantly. *"Now, infidel, I have thee on the hip!"*

Where was Harry? Someone might ask Tad, and he would be unable to prevent himself from striking a pose and replying: *"I saw young Harry with his beaver on."*

"Potations pottle-deep," they warned Archie, who liked his wine with dinner.

Chided, they hung their heads and confessed: *"I have a kind of alacrity in sinking."*

Archie looked down at Alice now. "Well, somehow you've gotten very old," he said.

Above their heads, bats crossed the river in the black sky in pursuit of the night's insects. The stones were black; the little rills and rapids in the river frothed white in the darkness.

"You know, I'm always grateful to Eli, whenever I come down his path," Archie said into the silence that was filled with the musical rippling of the water, the childish sound of bubbles and splashing. "The older I get, the more grateful I am. It's a wonder none of you ever sprained an ankle coming down here at night to swim."

Alice sat on crossed legs beside her father. The stones did not hurt her. She was able to fit the sharp bones of her backside into comfortable little hollows, shifting the stones around beneath her. She loved to be outdoors at night. Everything smelled different, as though during the day the sun bleached away the scent of things; only at night did the cool darkness release them, a mysterious intoxication. She lifted her nose to the breeze, like a fox.

She felt Archie reach for her, his arm fall around her shoulders. She turned to look up at him, and he touched the little wound above her eyebrow with a fingertip.

"What are we to make of that," he said quietly, but it wasn't a question.

She leaned against her father's shoulder. He reached into the pocket of his coat and found the candle and matches. From the breast pocket of his shirt he unfolded the tinfoil boat and tweaked it clumsily until it held its shape. He offered it to Alice and opened the box of matches, striking one, and holding the flame to the bottom of the candle, letting it drip a pool of wax into the saucer of the boat. When he was done he affixed the candle and returned the matchbox to his coat pocket. Alice, looking up into his face, saw him glance upward as if suddenly aware of something that had passed swiftly over them, a rush of wings. His eyes were wide-open and startled, and Alice felt the hair rise on her arms.

He looked down at her after a minute. "Owl," he said. "They're so quiet."

Alice watched him raise himself painfully from the stones of the beach. She took the boat from him when he held it out to her. Together they crouched by the water, and Archie fished in his pocket for the matchbox and lit the candle. Then Alice released the craft with her fingertips into the water. They watched it wobble out and catch in the current, a little light that brought the darkness in close around them.

Alice lifted her imaginary camera, made a silent click against her teeth with her tongue.

Then suddenly the light sped away, borne off in the flow, and in the next moment it had gone out altogether, the fragile boat toppled and the candle extinguished.

"Ah, well," Archie said into the darkness beside her. "Another year come and gone."

They came up from the river and walked toward the house through the shadows in the orchard, between the old stone posts that had marked where the gate had once stood, and into the field. A length of white ribbon from the rope walk was still tangled in the branches of one of the trees, an end trailing over the grass in the darkness, shiny and out of place. They stopped for Archie to shake it free from the branch. He gathered it up and stuck it in his pocket. As they crossed the lawn toward the back door, Alice looked up toward the house and saw James at the screen, silhouetted there as if he'd been watching for them. When he saw them, he stepped forward and held open the door.

"O'Brien called," he said as Archie and Alice drew near. "He's on his way over here."

They stepped inside. "What is it?" Archie said.

James glanced down at Alice for a second. "It's Helen," he said to Archie.

At that moment they heard the car in the lane. Archie went out the door again, letting it bang shut behind him. The headlights of O'Brien's car blazed in the dark, illuminating a stretch of the lawn and the crabapple tree with its twisted Oriental posture, the one Alice had pretended, when she was younger, was the enchanted figure of a princess trapped inside like Daphne, the girl who had been turned into a windswept laurel tree to protect her from Apollo. From the back door, Alice saw Archie lean in the driver's window, his hand on the top of the car. After a moment, he stood upright again and opened the back door. Theo climbed out. Archie shut the car door and put a hand on Theo to draw him onto the grass away from the driveway. The tires squealed once as O'Brien backed up, reversed, and then headed up the driveway. Alice watched Archie look down at Theo standing beside him in the darkness. Theo had cinched his belt very tightly; even more objects seemed to be hanging from it. His waist looked as tiny as a grasshopper's.

Alice glanced questioningly at James standing quietly beside her.

Wally came up behind them, his hands in his pockets. "He got here fast," he said.

"What's happened?" Alice asked.

Nobody answered her. James was watching Archie and Theo standing in the dark, Archie saying something softly to Theo. Wally took his hands out of his pockets and crossed his arms over his chest, his fists tucked under his armpits.

"What *happened*?" Alice asked again. She had begun to feel frightened. "What's wrong with Helen?"

But then Archie and Theo were coming toward the door. James leaned out and opened it for them.

Theo was carrying a suitcase and his toolbox. He didn't look at Alice or say hello.

Archie reached down and took the suitcase from Theo and set it on the floor. He made an expression of mock surprise. "Good Lord. What do you have in here?" he said. "Rocks?"

Theo looked up at him. "A couple."

Archie looked surprised. "Well, you can never find a rock when you need one. Good to keep a few on hand," he said after a moment. He glanced at James. "How about some cocoa?"

"Sure thing." James moved away.

Alice wanted to ask again what had happened, but Theo's silence stopped her. Whatever it was, it must have been very bad; Helen must have been hurt in some way. When Alice's grandfather, Archie's father, had died a few years before, the news had arrived in the same way, people speaking in low voices, their heads close together. No one had told Alice immediately; no one had ever actually said the word *dead*. That evening when she had gone to find Archie and say good night, he had been sitting in the armchair in his study, a glass of whiskey in his hand. Alice had climbed into his lap, and he had closed his eyes and put his arms around her. There had been wetness on his face, and Alice had felt that she could not bear it. It was like the feeling that came over her whenever she heard "Puff the Magic Dragon," the sorrow of the song too powerful, too overwhelming, little Jackie Paper gone away forever and leaving Puff alone. Sometimes the boys played the song just to torment her and sang along with it in lugubrious voices, trailing after her through the house, even under the dining room table where she went to escape; then she flew at them with her fists. Once Archie had punished Tad and Harry for this.

As she had sat there that sad night on Archie's lap in his study, her face against his chest, part of her had wanted to jump up and run away. That night, after she had gone to bed, she had gotten up again and found her wooden sword; thus armed she had leapt back and forth from bed to bed in her room, plunging the sword into the darkness, whirling savagely on her enemies until she was sweating and trembling.

Archie bent to pick up Theo's suitcase. "Why don't I take these rocks upstairs?" he said. He rested a hand briefly on Theo's head. "I'm sure your grandmother will be all right," he said. "Not to worry."

Theo did not move from his place by the door. His demeanor of that afternoon had changed entirely. He stared at the floor.

Confused, Alice leaned back instinctively to find Wally. Where was he? When she felt him there behind her, she reached up to hook her arms in his. He lifted her off the floor for a moment before setting her back down, and she realized that she had stopped breathing for a minute. The air filled up her lungs again, a relief.

"Want to unload that box?" Wally said to Theo, gesturing at it.

Theo shook his head and looked at the floor.

"Well, come on and sit down," Wally said. "The cocoa chef will fix us up in a minute."

Wally frog-marched Alice over to the table and heaped her into a chair. Alice hooked her legs around the chair legs and reached out to toy with the salt-and-pepper shakers. After a minute, Theo crossed the room and sat down across from her, his toolbox on his lap.

Alice looked at Theo. "Did you see the hail?" she asked.

Theo looked down at his toolbox. He didn't say anything.

Alice hesitated, confused. "Once Archie found a live frog in a hailstone," she offered at last.

Wally returned to the table with mugs. "That's what we like to call a tall tale, otherwise known as bullshit," he said. He looked down at Theo's bent head. Alice glanced up at Wally, but he was still watching Theo.

James came over to the table with the steaming saucepan and a ladle and began filling the mugs. "You know what?" he said. "I remember your mom, Theo. We thought she was the most beautiful girl in Grange."

"Really?" Alice thought this was interesting information. She reached out and pulled her mug closer.

"Definitely," James said. "I mean, she's older than me—how old is your mom?"

Theo's face turned red. "I don't know," he mumbled.

James and Wally exchanged a look. "Well, she must be, maybe, thirty," James said. "Something like that."

"I think she's thirty-three," Theo said.

"That'd be about right," James said easily. Alice felt a sudden rush of warmth for James. He was so good at making conversation.

"She looks a lot like your grandmother," James said. "Watch it, it's hot."

Theo had lifted his mug to his mouth, but he set it down quickly.

"So, she took a fall, huh?" James went on. "The rescue squad came?"

Theo nodded.

"They'll fix her up," James said. "Don't worry about it, okay?"

"I don't even know her," Theo said. He didn't look at any of them. "I've never been here before. I only came because my mom is sick."

James and Wally exchanged another look. "Well, we're glad you're here now," James said easily.

Archie came back into the room, pulling on a jacket. "I'm going down to the hospital," he said.

James turned around in his seat. "Anything we can do?"

Archie stopped at the table. "I'll call," he said. He looked down at Alice. "You see that Theo has everything he needs, Alice."

Alice nodded.

Archie went out the back door, and they listened in silence to the sound of the car heading up the lane. Theo bowed his head over his mug.

A moment later, Tad and Harry banged in through the back door. "Where's Archie going?" Harry said.

Wally looked up at them. "Later," he said, and gestured with his head toward Theo.

Tad and Harry stopped, staring. Theo's shoulders had begun to shake. He bent his head miserably over his mug.

Alice stood up. After a moment's hesitation, she went around the table and stood by Theo's chair. "Hey," she said. "Let's go find the dog."

Theo brushed his arm over his face, but he got to his feet, hoisting his toolbox.

Alice turned to Tad and Harry. "You never told us his name," she said. "The dog's name. What's he called?"

"Lucille," said Tad. At the same moment, Harry said, "Sweetums."

"Sweetums Lucille," Tad said.

Alice looked at them in astonishment. "He's a *boy* dog," she said.

"Yeah, we know." Harry shrugged. "What can you do? That's what it said on his tag."

"I have a dog at home," Theo said suddenly. They all turned to look at him. Alice felt a little freezing inside her; there wasn't any dog at Theo's house, she thought. He'd been too afraid of this one; he'd even been afraid of Lorenzo.

"His name's Ray," Theo said. "He's named for a boxer my dad knows."

"Yeah? Your dad knows a boxer?" Tad sat down at the table.

"My dad boxes. He's a really good boxer."

Wally stood up suddenly. "Let's go find that dog," he said.

Alice woke up sometime in the middle of the night. She came fully awake instantly, so awake that she wondered for a moment if she were dreaming. She sat up in bed. Outside, the moon framed in her window spilled bright light over the lawn. Theo had been put to bed in the guest bedroom over Archie's study. The furnace had been turned off already, but the night had grown steadily cooler; Alice had helped Tad set and light a fire in the old fireplace in Theo's room. The window seat under the dormer window was heaped with needlepoint pillows made by Alice's mother, a collection of wildflowers native to New England.

Theo didn't seem to have brought any pajamas with him. He had opened his suitcase on the floor by the bed—a huge powder blue case with tape on one corner—bent over it secretively, and extracted a T-shirt, striped like the one he had worn at her party. Then he had followed Wally, who took him off to show him where the bathroom was so he could brush his teeth. Alice had sat cross-legged on the foot of the bed in the guest room, waiting, and watching the fire. Archie still wasn't back from the hospital. She hadn't wanted to ask Theo what had happened to Helen; she had sensed not to. She'd been to the hospital in Brattleboro a few times, once to have her arm set when she'd broken it, once to have her head stitched up. The gray floor of the halls there had been highly polished, treacherous like water or ice. Her shoes had squeaked as she'd walked across them.

When Theo came back into the room, he climbed immediately into bed and lay down, facing the fire.

"Ten minutes," Wally said, sticking his head around the door frame. "Then you guys have to go to sleep."

"I have a fireplace in my room at home," Theo said after Wally left the room.

Alice kept her eyes on the fire. She didn't believe this; it was the same as the boat and the dog, she thought, and she began to feel hopeless. How could you believe anything this boy said? Then he surprised her by saying, "It's boarded up. A fireplace is dangerous. If there was a fire in our building we'd have to go down the fire escape to get out." He sat up in bed. "You don't have a fire escape here."

Alice glanced at the window. You could climb out of it into the fir tree and get down if you needed to. "There's the tree," she said. She pointed at the window. "You could get out that way. It's okay."

Theo lay back down and turned his face into the pillow. After a moment he spoke again in a muffled voice. "These smell like their house," he said.

"Who? Helen and O'Brien's?"

Theo didn't answer right away. "It was scary," he said then, and Alice realized he meant whatever had happened to Helen. She felt that freezing, breathless sensation come over her again.

"She fell off her chair," Theo said.

This description gave too exact a picture of Helen's suffering. Alice stared at the dancing flames. Helen always came to parents' night at school with Archie in the fall, even though she wasn't any blood relation to Alice. Alice would write letters to both her father and to Helen, welcoming them to her desk and telling them what she'd been doing at school, leaving them in a folder with a picture she had drawn. She was happy to be able to write two letters, when her classmates only wrote one. Helen would leave her a little bouquet of flowers in a jar and some chocolate kisses and a note that said she was proud of Alice. The note was always signed with lots of Xs and Os.

"He came in and yelled at me and got down on the floor with her," Theo said, speaking from the depths of the pillow. "Then he called the ambulance."

Alice didn't want to hear any more. She put her chin in her hands. Her head felt heavy, and her stomach had begun to hurt. She had never heard O'Brien yell. She had only heard Archie raise his voice a couple of times, both times at Tad and Harry, once for crashing the car, once for not coming home one night.

"I want to go home," Theo said.

Alice looked over at him. When Eli had left with the other boys last fall to go off to college, Alice had gone around gathering talismans from each boy—a scrap of paper on which one of them had scribbled a telephone number, a comb left behind in the glass in the bathroom, the statute of a frog playing a violin made out of cork that had sat on Wally's bureau, James's edition of Stephen Spender's poems—and laid them under her pillow along with an old compact of her mother's, the powder caked and hard, its little mirror silvered. Elizabeth had taken them out from under the pillow, but she had put them on Alice's bedside table, setting up the frog statue on top of the book.

"Archie will take you," Alice said. She was sure of this; Archie would not want a child to suffer. And Theo was obviously worried about his mother being sick; she must have been very sick to send Theo here. But why couldn't his father have taken care of him? This was a question to which Alice could not provide an answer, but she was sorry anyway about the prospect of Theo leaving, and about Helen, and even about Theo's mother being sick.

Alice wanted to sweep it all away, to go back to the afternoon, when she and Theo had made plans for the dog—she couldn't call the dog Sweetums Lucille; that was just Tad and Harry, teasing them. Theo had talked about the dog delivering mail in a wagon, about building a house for it. He had seemed to ignore the fact that Tad and Harry would be taking the dog back with them to Frost. Theo had wanted to know about swimming in the river, about going down the river in a raft and making a camp, about staying out all night. He had so many ideas, things she hadn't even thought about doing. A wave of helplessness came over her. Helen and O'Brien were too old to entertain a boy all summer; he would have come down to the MacCauleys' house every day. They could have played in the attic, in the barn, in the woods. He was the kind of boy she didn't think she would get tired of.

"I miss my mom," Theo said.

Alice did not miss her own mother; she longed for her, a distinction she understood was significant. She thought it would be terrible to miss your mother and not be able to see her. And she had never been parted from Archie, so she did not know what it would feel like to miss him. But she could imagine it. That was a new and terrible thing; now she could imagine it.

Theo had turned his face into the pillow again. He pulled the blanket over his head. Under the quilt, he drew his legs up and away from her.

Alice had never been away from home by herself except occasionally to a friend's house to play for the afternoon. There was always somebody at home, Elizabeth or Archie or one of the boys. There was always someone there to take care of her. Helen did a wonderful thing with her fingertips on Alice's forehead when Alice's head hurt. Archie ran a fist up and down her spine in an absent way when she went to stand beside him and lean against his shoulder. Even Tad had picked her up once when they had found a possum, probably rabid, its sickening tail dragging in the dust, lurching down the driveway. Sometimes Elizabeth read to her from *Reader's Digest,* even though Alice could read perfectly well herself; they would sit in the armchair in the kitchen by the fireplace, Alice perched on the arm of the chair and leaning against Elizabeth, while Elizabeth read the jokes to her, her finger following the words, or the articles about dogs rescuing people from burning buildings, or about mirages, how someone had found water in the desert. Elizabeth loved *Reader's Digest.*

Alice glanced over at the bundle of Theo buried in the blankets. The fire hissed in the fireplace, making a quarreling, squeaking sound; the little faces in the flames grimaced and drew their lips back over their teeth. She heard Wally coming back upstairs. "I can go get the dog," she whispered. "He could sleep in here with you."

But Theo didn't answer her.

When Wally came to the door of the guest room, Alice slid down off the bed. At the doorway she paused and Wally took her hand. She turned around. "Good night," she said.

At first Theo didn't say anything. Then he surprised her again by sitting up in bed. "It's the end of your birthday," he said. "Your birthday's almost over."

The day had held so many strange events, the strangest of them all, she thought, this boy who was sitting up in bed now looking at her. For a moment she remembered the feel of the hail on her arms, the way it had filled up the birdbath. "You'll always remember this day," Kenneth Fitzgerald had said to her, and she thought that it was, truly, as if he had known something about all the events to come, the hailstorm, and Helen, and now Theo, here in her house, the wind moving the leaves of the trees outside like a restless, unquiet, unhappy spirit. What kind of man was Kenneth Fitzgerald to know such things?

Suddenly Theo scrambled out of bed and opened his suitcase again, his back to them. "Wait a minute," he said. Then he turned around, his fist concealing something. "Here." He put the object into her hand.

It was a rock, a smooth white stone crossed with a helix of winding blue veins.

"It's a good luck stone," Theo said. "I have a rabbit's foot, so I don't need this."

"Thank you," Alice said. As Wally turned her to lead her away, she looked back at Theo. Standing by the bed in his striped T-shirt and underpants, he raised a hand to her in salute.

Later that night, Alice swung her feet over the edge of her bed and listened. Something had woken her. After a minute she heard voices from downstairs. She crept across the floor to her door and pulled it open a little wider with her fingertips. A cool draft swept over her shoulders, making her shiver. Archie was in the hall downstairs. It must have been the car that had woken her.

She heard a second set of footsteps, then a third and a fourth. She saw Tad and Harry's red heads pass though the hall below. Wally came out from the living room and sat down on the stairs, his black hair ruffled up in the back as if he'd been sleeping on the couch.

"He's going to stay there," Archie was saying to James. "I'll go back in the morning."

James said something she couldn't make out. She pushed the door open a little wider.

"I don't know," Archie was saying. And then he said something else she couldn't make out. He moved out of the hall toward the living room, the boys following. Alice could hear their voices in the living room, louder now, but too muffled for her to distinguish their words.

Alice stood up and peeked around her door. The upstairs hall was empty; someone had left the light on in the bathroom at the head of the stairs, and a light was on in James and Wally's room, though the door was closed. Lorenzo, looking like a sea lion in the dark, huge and obdurate and whiskered, was stretched across the doorsill to Archie's room. He lifted his head when Alice stepped into the hall. She was halfway to the stairs when she heard Archie in the hall below; she darted back to her room, but she heard his heavy tread on the staircase.

She was in bed in a second, but Archie came to the doorway a moment later. "Why aren't you asleep?" he said.

She sat up in bed. "Did you see Helen?"

Archie came in and sat down on the bed. "I saw her."

She wanted him to say something else, something reassuring, but he didn't. "Can I see her?" she asked.

Archie didn't say anything for a minute. "Not tomorrow," he said. "Maybe later."

Alice lay back down. Archie put a hand on her forehead, as if she were sick and complaining of a fever.

"Is she going to be okay?"

"I hope so."

Alice closed her eyes. That was what grown-ups said so they didn't have to give you the bad news right away, she thought. It wasn't a lie to hope that things would turn out in a particular way, even if you knew they wouldn't. Maybe this was what had been lying ahead at the end of this day, she thought. Helen dying. She felt for a moment as if she were falling, as if she had been pushed over a building's edge.

She thought of all the people who would be sad about Helen dying. O'Brien, of course. And he wasn't the sort of person who could take very good care of himself, Alice sensed. And Ann, their daughter . . . losing her mother, as Alice had lost hers. And Theo, even though he didn't know Helen very well. Then the image of Helen as a little girl on her canes, her brave bright face looking up from between the nuns at the camera, came to Alice, and she thought she would start to cry, so she opened her eyes instead and spoke. "Is Theo going to stay here?"

Archie pushed his glasses up onto his forehead and rubbed his eyes. "For a while," he said. "Yes. We'll see."

• • •

When she woke again, the room was utterly dark. The moon had disappeared from her window, and Archie was pushing through her doorway, opening the door quietly with his shoulder, something in his arms. She thought she was dreaming now; the darkness felt close and warm, and there were no lights on in the hall. She heard someone crying, very close by, and she wondered for a moment if it were herself, crying in a dream, because she felt so sad, so forlorn, as if she had been left behind in the oak wood with its silent cathedral corridors between the trees, a place Alice had never visited without feeling that something magical and important had happened there, was happening still perhaps, a resonant throbbing under her feet as though the soldiers of an invisible army were gathering around her, their swords and shields clashing silently. She was afraid of being lost, stolen like the boy Wild Robin who had been taken by the fairy queen to her palace, where his teeth grew long and pointed and he rotted on candy and selfishness and threw hysterical, dangerous tantrums.

Archie came between the beds, his back to her, and leaned over to put down whatever he'd been carrying.

Alice turned her head slowly—it felt as though she were swimming in heavy dark water—and saw the stripes of Theo's T-shirt, the blond burr of his hair. Archie leaned over him, murmuring something, his hand patting Theo's back, pulling up the blankets.

SIX

WHEN ALICE WOKE UP the next morning, the bed beside her was empty. She knew it had not been a dream, though—Theo's arrival there in Archie's arms the night before—because someone, at least, had slept in the bed. Now the sheets had been flung back, and the bedspread pooled on the floor. Across the room, the window glass was white with sunlight. She couldn't see anything through it, as though the world outside had been replaced by an infinite brightness, a brilliant nothingness. Her door stood wide open, and downstairs Wally was playing the cello.

Usually Alice was the first person awake in her house. Archie was a night owl and slow to rise in the morning, but Alice was often up and reading in the kitchen, a mug of hot chocolate at her elbow, when Elizabeth arrived to fix breakfast. Now, hearing the music downstairs and voices in the kitchen, Alice sat up in bed, disoriented. On the occasions when she was sick and slept through an afternoon fever to wake at dusk, the day having been replaced by a dismal, lackluster twilight, Alice could not defend herself against sorrow; it was as if she had fallen through a hole in the air into a place eerily familiar to the world she knew and yet somehow not the same at all, full of strange shadows and objects freighted with menace and loss. Soup spilled on a tray in her bedroom, a glass of flat ginger ale with its bent straw, the tired dishevelment of her blankets—all these things conspired to make her both weary and ill at ease, as if she needed to keep exhausted watch against whatever surprises this place, this silent night that had descended on her after no day at all with the sudden, final weight of a coffin lid, might throw up into her path.

Now, a little of that same menace, the sense that things were not as they should be, that they had been altered insidiously in nearly imperceptible ways, crept into the room, despite the brightness of the morning. She got out of bed and stood on the floorboards. They were already warm under her feet from the sun, a comforting corrective against everything that felt so strange and chilling. But what had happened to Theo?

She found him on the porch downstairs. He was sitting on the floor in the shade with his back against the clapboard wall of the house. He glanced up when she opened the porch door, but he didn't say anything. He only raised one slow hand in greeting, and then his dreamy gaze returned to the lawn, his chin resting on his arms crossed over his knees. He wore the same striped T-shirt he had worn to bed the night before.

Alice sat down near him. The night before, with its confused comings and goings, the infectious misery and fear of the crying boy carried into her bedroom at some late, disturbed hour, Alice's awareness of Helen's peril, whatever it was—these events reached through the warmth of the morning sunlight with the disconcerting tread of a bad dream remembered. Yet, as she sat quietly beside Theo listening to Wally play, Alice thought that the music, like the morning itself, was brimming with light and warmth and playfulness. Wally had taught her to listen to music with her eyes closed, to see the pictures it made in her mind: water tumbling over rocks in the river, bumblebees going up and down like sentries in the orchard, armies massing on the horizon, a ship turning slowly in the wind. Sometimes it seemed to her that music didn't so much make pictures as it expressed what it was possible to feel, things you had felt but had not known how to shape into the idea of what they were. And music could explain not only what you *yourself* might feel; Alice sensed that it could also make you feel what other people felt, people you didn't even know, or people who had lived a long time ago, like the women who stood on the white stoops of the windmills in Holland in the gold-framed painting that hung in Archie's study. Music, Alice thought, could make her feel what those women had felt, standing there holding on to their white hats, with fleecy clouds in the pure blue sky above them and the watery green axis of the fields stretching away into the endless distance. Music could even show you what *things* felt, trees or the wind or the ocean as it touched the shore.

Usually Alice thought the cello sounded sad. The instrument itself suited Wally, she felt, whose face looked like the mask of tragedy, with deep dark eyes and a sober, downturned mouth. But this morning the cello had a happy, almost teasing sound. Alice watched a pair of robins, their breasts high and inflated, hop over the lawn in front of Theo. They almost seemed to be moving in time to the music . . . in waltz time, Alice realized. How funny. She sighed and stretched out her legs and flexed her toes in the sunlight.

When Wally stopped playing, Theo straightened his back as if he'd been sitting still in one position for a long time. The night before, when he'd stood in front of Alice extending to her his lucky stone, his face had been creased and worried, like something folded up in a pocket for a long time. Sleep—or maybe it was Wally's music, Alice thought—had transformed him. He looked rested, puckish, and playful, his hair standing up in tufts like the golden grass in the field.

The sun felt hot across Alice's legs. It was hard to believe that the world had been covered in ice the afternoon before.

"That's a violin, right?" Theo said to Alice.

"Cello," she answered.

Theo nodded as if she'd confirmed his guess. "I really like it," he said. "That's the instrument I'm going to play." This morning he was wearing his belt crossed bravely over his chest like a military sash. Alice saw that he'd brought his toolbox outside with him.

"I'm named for a musician, you know," Theo said. "So it's in my blood."

"What musician?"

"Thelonious Monk. He's my dad's favorite."

Alice had never heard of him. She thought Thelonious was a strange but impressive-sounding word.

"Hey, Alice. Do you have a raft?" Theo said abruptly.

"Tad and Harry have a rubber one," she said. His questions had a way of catching her off guard, and she had to think for a minute. "Maybe it's got a hole in it, though. I'm not sure."

"We could fix that," Theo said. "It's easy to fix punctures. All you need is a patch kit. Do you have a patch kit? One should have come with the raft from the manufacturer." He went on, "Or we could *make* a raft. You just lash logs together. It's easy. Where does that river go?"

Alice realized that she'd never thought about it; she didn't know where the river went. Why hadn't she ever asked? Now that Theo had posed it, it seemed like a reasonable question. "We could look on a map," she said. "Archie has lots of maps."

"Well, all rivers run to the sea eventually," Theo said. "It would be good to have a map, though. We should get one."

It sounded as though he'd made plans already to float down

the river in a raft. But it also sounded as though he meant to have Alice beside him. He expected her to come along.

Just then, the porch door opened and Archie stepped outside. "There you are," he said. "Your beds were empty. I thought you'd run away or been carried off by spirits."

Theo looked up at him blandly, but Alice got up and went to Archie and put her arms around his waist.

He rested a hand on her head. "Eli's making eggs," he said. "And Elizabeth left us blueberry muffins." He addressed Theo. "Are you hungry?"

Theo looked up at Archie; then a surprised expression came over his face. "I didn't have any dinner last night," he said.

"Ah." For a moment, Archie's hand stopped moving on Alice's head. "Well. Extra rations for you this morning then."

Alice looked up at Archie. "Where's Helen?"

"She's at the hospital. O'Brien's there with her." Archie looked away from her to take in Theo. "You'll be staying here with us for a little while, if that's all right, Theo," he said. "I promise that we'll feed you."

Alice turned inside Archie's embrace to look at Theo. So he *could* stay, if he wanted. There would be no need to escape, setting off down the river in search of his mother. She wanted Theo to want to stay now, but she understood that he missed his mother, that such a feeling would need to be respected. If he wanted to go home, Archie would take him, Alice knew.

But Theo did not make her wait for his answer. He jumped to his feet and assumed a kind of Oriental fighting position, knees and elbows cocked; then he began vigorously boxing the air toward Alice, leaping from foot to foot. He danced near Archie and Alice and boxed the air temptingly in Alice's direction. "C'mon," he said. "C'mon, Alice. Come and get me."

"I think I am to take this display as an expression of your approval and enthusiasm," Archie said.

Alice whirled around and put up her fists, mimicking Theo's bouncing dance. They sidestepped down the length of the porch facing each other, feinting blows. When they came together, grappling, Alice inhaled, taking in Theo's particular smell: this was *who he was*. But what did he smell like? Who *was* he? It was a completely unfamiliar smell, like looking down a long hallway in a strange building. Then a drape at the far end was swept aside, and an idea of Theo's life appeared to her: a history of different beds, and unfamiliar food served on plates with patterns she did not recognize, and music playing that she had never heard before. There was his lifetime of being steeped in the details of his own world, so different from hers, and all of these details had flowed into him, into his skin and his hair and his breath. Her nose and forehead were mashed against his chest as they struggled; she held his arm pinned behind his back. And then Alice was seized by homesickness like a tide swirling around her knees, threatening to take her down. How she loved the old familiars of her own life: the oval shape of the mirror above her dresser with its bunch of chipped plaster grapes at the bottom of the gold frame; the ship model sailing on its dusty green felt sea in the glass box on Eli's desk; the dining room rug, whose pattern of black lines and cream-colored diamonds and rust-colored hills and green rivers was like a topographical map over which she had moved her armies; the pin-headed pieces from the Sorry game; the lollipop-colored tiddlywinks, their perfectly smooth wafers so satisfying when she tested them between her teeth.

With a grunt, Theo released her, and she staggered back.

Archie held open the door. "Dance this way, please," he called to them, beckoning them in. "Eli's eggs will be cold."

Theo stopped bouncing then and took a deep breath, fists

cocked at Alice. Alice stopped, too, fists held before her face. They locked eyes, breathing hard.

Then Theo grinned at her, faked a jab at her belly, and took off toward Archie.

"This way, this way," Archie said, waving him past. He raised his eyebrows at Alice. *"He capers, he dances, he has eyes of youth, he writes verses, he speaks holiday, he smells April and May."*

She stopped, looking up at him. How did Archie know she had been trying to figure out what Theo smelled like? But that was it. He smelled like spring, like the month of May.

Archie bent to kiss her head as she went past. *"Now, our joy,"* he said. *"Although the last, not least."*

During breakfast, the telephone rang. Archie pushed his chair away from the table and went into the front hall to answer it. All the boys had cell phones, but Archie had steadfastly refused to get even a cordless telephone for the house, claiming that he wanted to keep his conversations short and to the point and that wandering around while talking loudly to someone on the telephone was a sign of boorishness and not having enough to do.

Theo had eaten two platefuls of eggs and had said that he was still hungry; now he was standing beside Eli at the stove, watching as Eli cracked more eggs into the frying pan and scrambled them with the back of a fork. "Don't you guys have a television set? I have PlayStation," he said. "Don't you have any video games? Do you even know what a video game is?" By the time Alice heard the rumble of Archie's voice saying goodbye in the hall, she had almost forgotten that he had been on the phone; whoever had called had talked for a long time before allowing Archie to say anything in reply.

When Archie came back into the kitchen, his hand lingered on Alice's head. "That was Miss Fitzgerald," he said.

"Oh, no." Harry hunched over his coffee cup, a pantomime of misery.

Archie sat down at the table again and began gathering up the newspaper. He ignored Harry. "Your help has been requested," he said. "All of you. I've said you'll be over after breakfast."

James came into the kitchen, a towel around his neck, his hair wet. "Where are we going?"

Archie pushed his glasses onto his head. "I gather there's some furniture—" he began.

A chorus of groans came from the boys. Archie held up his hand. "And some weeding."

James poured himself a cup of coffee from the stove. "At the Fitzgeralds'? When do we have to do this? *Now?*"

Archie stood up. "Fortify yourselves appropriately," he said. "But don't keep Miss Fitzgerald waiting." He picked up the newspaper. "I'm going over to the hospital, and I trust you to behave like gentlemen. Mr. Fitzgerald would like some things rearranged in the house to accommodate his possessions. I don't suppose it will take you very long, big strapping boys like yourselves." Then he looked down at Alice. "And you have been especially requested, Alice," he said.

Alice looked up at him in surprise. What would Kenneth Fitzgerald want with her? And yet, as she looked up at Archie, she felt herself blushing.

"I gather that Mr. Fitzgerald requires your services in particular," Archie said. He was looking at her oddly. Then he glanced over at Theo, waiting at the stove for his eggs. "And you, too," he said.

Theo's jaw dropped.

"You're to choose something to read aloud to him," Archie said, returning his attention to Alice. "It can be anything you like, apparently. His eyesight has deteriorated, and he . . ." Archie hesitated. "It will be a kindness, Alice." He hesitated again, as if there was something else he wanted to say. But after a moment it seemed he had thought better of it, for he only took his glasses off his head and put them in his shirt pocket.

After Archie had left the room, Wally lit a cigarette.

Tad stood up, his plate in hand. "Someone said he's got AIDS," he announced.

Wally looked up at him sharply. "Shut up, you asshole," he said. "Can't you see there are children in the room?"

"Fuck you, Wally," Tad said, surprised. But he looked embarrassed.

"I know what AIDS is," Theo said.

"Yeah, me too," Alice said, defensively.

Wally took a drag of his cigarette and exhaled. Then he smashed it out on his plate. He didn't look at Alice and Theo, but his words were clearly directed at them. "You can't get it from him. You can't get AIDS from him. You know that, right?" he said, finally looking up at Alice. "It's not contagious like that."

She nodded.

"You can't get it just from reading to someone, or even from shaking their hand."

"We can only get it if we shoot drugs with them or have sex," Theo said.

James began to laugh.

Wally stood up. "I just didn't want there to be any confusion," he said loudly over James's hooting, but only Eli and Alice and Theo were watching him. Tad had taken his plate to the sink and stalked out of the room. Harry was bent over the newspaper, ignoring them all. For a moment Wally stood beside the table.

Alice, stricken silent, was appalled at his expression, at the way his voice had shaken, with anger or with something else, she couldn't tell. "They just shouldn't be afraid of him," he said finally, and he looked around the room at his brothers, and at Alice and Theo, as if in challenge. Finally he pushed back his chair violently and walked out.

James was still laughing as Wally left the room.

James decided that Alice and Theo could walk over to the Fitzgeralds'. "Don't dawdle," he said to Alice. She gave him a resentful look. She was usually on time; it was the rest of them who were dawdlers, slowpokes who never seemed ready to go anywhere when the time came, causing Archie to stand outside by the idling car and bellow for them in impatience.

Upstairs, Theo had to look for his shoes. "Do you have a haversack?" he asked Alice. "We need a haversack."

"What for?" Alice got down on her knees to retrieve one of his sneakers from under the bed.

"Provisions," Theo said. "Maps."

"We're only going to the Fitzgeralds'," Alice said, handing him his shoe and looking around the room for the other one. For a boy with only one suitcase, he seemed to have brought a lot of possessions; clothes were strewn everywhere, all over the floor. She had peeked into his suitcase. There weren't many clothes in it, but he had brought a lot of Legos.

Theo looked at her pityingly. "Never go anywhere without a map, Alice," he said. "You might get lost. Do you have a compass?"

They decided to bring the rest of the blueberry muffins from breakfast, a map of the state of Vermont, two screwdrivers from Theo's toolbox, a coil of rope from the barn, a box of matches, and some Christmas tree ornament hooks Theo discovered while rifling through a drawer in the pantry.

Alice was uncertain about what books to bring. What did you bring to a man who had AIDS? She didn't know quite as much about AIDS as her comment at the breakfast table had suggested. She did not understand fully about the issue of sex that Theo had raised, though she did understand that one should not poke a needle that had been used by an infected drug user into one's arm, an admonition that seemed so far from Alice's frame of reference that she had not really even bothered to think about it. She knew that a lot of people were dying from AIDS, and she knew that many of them were black people in Africa, or people called "gays." But she was not sure exactly what "gay" meant, though she knew it had something to do with sex—boys liking boys instead of girls—and she was not sure exactly what *that* entailed, either. Nicholas Papaver, who lived in Grange and was a few years older than her, a fawning, greasy-haired acolyte to Harry and Tad, who did not really like him, had once pulled down his pants behind the MacCauleys' barn and invited her to look at his willy. Alice, who had seen a few of these before, living with five brothers, had stared at it dispassionately. But when it started to twitch like a rusty garden hose and then rise, her eyes had flown up, shocked, to meet Nicholas's gaze, and he had blushed bright red and turned away hurriedly to zip himself up. She knew that willies had something to do with sex, but not exactly what their role might be.

Regardless, it did not seem that someone like Kenneth Fitzgerald, AIDS or not, would appreciate the books most beloved by her—the Harry Potter books, C. S. Lewis's Narnia chronicles, *A Story Like the Wind* by Laurens van der Post, Kipling's *Just So Stories, The Once and Future King, The Wind in the Willows*—and she felt in any case that these stories, her pleasure in them, was private. She did not want to read aloud from them to Kenneth Fitzgerald, even if he was sick and suffering and deserved her attention. He seemed, in a way, to know too much about her already, and these stories that she loved, she felt irrationally, would give him a strange access to her and her feelings. The way he had looked at her and spoken to her, the things he had seemed to know about her . . . he was not like other adults, and Alice was uncomfortably aware of being flattered by his attention, almost as much as she was disconcerted by it. Most grown-ups barely seemed to notice her.

Alice and Theo stood in front of the bookshelves in Archie's study. Finally, thinking of Archie, Alice took a volume of Shakespeare's sonnets, a collection of short stories by a writer named Chekhov that Archie always said were an inspiration to him, and, at Theo's urging, a book about Meriwether Lewis and his expedition with William Clark across the American territories. Theo had taken the book down from the shelf and opened it at random. " 'Every man on his Guard and ready for any thing,' " he read aloud. "I know about them. They walked across the whole country or something. This sounds good."

They set out into the bright morning, following a track down from the MacCauleys' driveway into the lower field. At the margins of the meadow, the white bark of the birch trees stood out against the shadowy darkness of the woods beyond. Both the MacCauleys' property and the Fitzgeralds' bordered the river, and Alice knew she and Theo would be able to walk the whole way through the woods near the water until they came to the falls, where they would have to climb up to the road.

The stretch of river below the falls and through the MacCauleys' land was broad and shallow, easily flooded during storms and heavy snowfalls. Over time, the river had branched across the low ground into winding streams, bowered invitingly by branches and full of musical tinkling, that looped through the woods, creating chains of tiny, private islands easily reached across the rocks. The boys had played their wildest games here, defending the islands from enemies, setting up camp, and building forts. Even though she was conscripted in these games for boring duties such as wood gathering or cooking, when she would be given a battered pot and a stick for stirring and left at "camp" to prepare a soup of berries and moss and river water, Alice had not minded the domestic nature of these roles. She had squatted alone over a campfire—sometimes a real one, though Archie had expressly forbidden them—shivering with happiness as the boys' war whoops or floating whistles sounded through the trees. Through the smoke she caught flashes of them running fast through the greenery and heard their feet splashing through water, the sound of their hard breathing.

The boys gradually grew too old for these games and Alice was left to play by herself, but she had never been afraid to go down into the woods alone, out of sight or even earshot of the house. Sometimes she was gone for hours. She could not have accounted for her time there, nor was she ever asked to. She would have been speechless if she had been called on to describe what she did when she went out to play. She was aware of a change that came over her, though, when she left the bright sunlight of the fields and made her way into the shade of the trees: a boundary between her own body and the world seemed to vanish then. She was attentive to the way things felt and smelled; she could identify her brothers by smell alone. It was a game they played sometimes, Alice blindfolded on the telephone bench in the front hall, the brothers coming silently one by one to stand before her and let her sniff the air; she could even name some of their friends this way, and she was rarely wrong. Over the years she had come to associate the smell of the woods with her own smell, and she felt at home there. For a long time, she had played that she was a fairy flying through the trees or a gnome child hunched on a moss-covered log. She sprang from stone to stone along the edge of the river, or hid in the grass and watched the insects darting over the water, the birds in the undergrowth. She did not feel alone during these games, or lonely; she sensed the hidden gaze of the world, unseen companions who watched her, their eyes blinking among the grasses.

Though the MacCauleys' land was friendly territory, perfectly proportioned for children's play, the Fitzgeralds' property bordered a more dangerous mile of water, where the river narrowed toward the falls and its high chasm. Sheared-off straggly junipers and cedars dug roots into the rocks and leaned out over the water, and the steep hillsides were covered with aspens and ash and maple and red oaks. Canoeists and kayakers had to portage here, carrying their boats through the woods and down the perilously rocky paths. The deep pool below the falls was known as Indian Love Call, for the melancholy way the air, full of mist and spray, held an echo and for the rumors of the ghostly voice of a young Indian squaw who could be heard weeping for her lover. Occasionally swimmers made their way through the woods from the road to swim in the pool below the falls; for many years, a rope had been tied to the branch of a tree that clung to the edge, and Alice knew from her brothers that boys dared one another to swing out over the water and drop. You had to know just where to let go, they said, when to drop the rope and let your body plunge straight as a needle into the black water, your arms at your sides, or you could be dashed to bits on the rocks. Alice knew that Archie had forbidden the boys to swim there, even in the pool where the river widened out past the falls and where the water was deep and wide and smooth, full of a mysterious cold blackness. There were too many temptations there, Archie had said, too many risks; the whole place wore what he called *"the cunning livery of hell."* But Alice knew that all the boys had disobeyed him; Tad and Harry had even swung out over the water on the rope, probably more than once.

She herself was wary of that stretch of the river. The stories about the ghost, who was said to have lost her life going over the falls, were troubling, even if Alice didn't exactly believe them. And the strength and power of the water felt hypnotic to her, tempting in a way she found frightening. When you drew close to the falls, the air had a deep, concussive ringing, and you felt compelled to try to creep closer to the tumult of water, inching along on the tumbled wreckage of rocks. One winter afternoon, walking with Wally in the woods, they had come across a deer, its neck caught in the fork of a tree that had fallen over the river a hundred yards below the falls. The poor creature, slipping on the rocks, had fallen in and been swept downstream until it was trapped by the forked branch, held there in the water while it froze to death. The deer's body had been encased in a cataract of ice like a gruesome sculpture, tiny hooves protruding helplessly through the frozen waterfall. Alice had never forgotten the sight of it; it stayed there in her mind like a talisman against the place, and sometimes she thought of it at odd moments. That day, Wally had taken her hand and helped her back over the rocks away from the water, into the woods silent in their winter white and gray, silent in a way that made Alice think of their cold, speechless witness to the deer's terrible death. She had wanted to cry at the thought of the creature's suffering, its slow dying in the freezing water, its desperate velvet mouth turned upward through the icy spray to catch at the air. Sometimes when she lay in bed at night, especially when she was aware of the pleasure of her own sleepy warmth and cleanliness after a bath, and of the cheerful sound of the radio being played quietly downstairs, the comforting glow of the yellow lamp on the Chinese chest in the upstairs hallway . . . then she thought of the deer, and she froze inside at the proximity of such suffering alongside her own comfort. It was guilt that she felt, and pity, but also something more complicated; she would turn then and look for a long time at the photograph of her mother holding the infant Alice, and when sleep slowly took her away in its black-sleeved arms, she went as an orphan, a wide-eyed survivor, all alone on the deck of a boat sailing into the darkness.

The garden in front of the Fitzgeralds' house was badly over-grown. Weedy saplings with leaves like big flapping hands waved over the picket fence. Alice and Theo stopped on the sidewalk and looked over into the yard, where the browning heads of peonies and the heavy canes of old rosebushes had fallen over into the tall grass. The MacCauleys' car was parked on the street, and from the direction of the garage, Alice heard the sound of a motor—a lawn mower, or maybe it was a chain saw—catching and then dying. Eli must have decided there was more serious work to be done than weeding.

The house was high and square, painted white with black shutters, although both house and shutters needed painting, Alice noticed. The Fitzgeralds' was among the more formal of Grange's residences; most of the houses on the street, with their narrow front gardens and sheer curtains at the front windows, were what Alice thought of as town houses, with additions that led back away from the street toward the woods and the river, not country houses like her own. The piano lessons, Alice remem-bered, had been held in a room at the back of the house, reached through a separate entrance by a slate path that ran downhill along the side of the house between overgrown boxwood bushes.

Archie had not sent Alice to Miss Fitzgerald when it had been her turn to begin music lessons, and Alice didn't think Miss Fitzgerald knew that Alice played. She hoped that Miss Fitzgerald would not find out somehow, because Alice felt sure that Miss Fitzgerald would see it as another disloyalty on Archie's part. She didn't know if anyone took piano from Miss Fitzgerald anymore.

Alice knew that she and Theo had lingered too long in the woods—most of the morning, in fact—despite James's injunction not to be late. They had longed to stay there and play, and it had not been easy to leave. On their way up to the road, Theo had consoled himself with grand plans for the afternoon. He wanted to build a shelter on the island highest in the stream, the one with the best vantage upriver. All the way to the Fitzgeralds' he had described how they would set out fishing lines and string a hammock in the trees (making a hammock was easy, he'd said; all things seemed easy to Theo). He wanted to plant a flag, like the explorers of Everest. He wanted to tame a deer and went on at length about how they might accomplish this; he seemed to know all about it. He wanted to raise a baby raccoon, too—he said he'd seen a nature show on television about this, and to Alice he made it sound inevitable that they would stumble across an orphaned baby raccoon in need of nursing. He wanted to fix up the twins' raft and moor it near the island, too.

Beneath his eyes he had painted dirty pairs of black stripes like Indian paint, and he had taken off his shirt to tie it around his head. After he'd finished painting his own stripes, he had turned Alice to him, both hands on her shoulders, and looked critically at her face. Then he knelt down and mixed a little spit with the dirt at his feet and with his thumb planted a muddy print on each of her cheekbones, leaning back to examine the effect. Blinking back at him, Alice had noticed that his eyes were golden, like a lion's, and that his eyelashes curled up tightly. For a moment, she thought of Helen, and her happiness was crossed by a shadow. It seemed wrong that Helen's accident, or illness, or whatever it was, was the cause of Alice's happiness at this moment.

As she and Theo stood on the step at the Fitzgeralds' front door, Alice realized that her hands had gone clammy. She could feel the telltale prickle of heat on her neck, where she flushed when she was shy or worried. She wasn't sure how long they'd stayed in the woods, but she knew it had been too long. She wiped her hands on her T-shirt and then saw that she had left rusty streaks down her front. She glanced at Theo; he was no cleaner. His hands and knees were filthy and his face still bore the streaks of his war paint. He'd put his shirt back on, though.

Alice reached up and lifted the knocker.

Suddenly, beside her, Theo said, "I've got to pee." He began to hop up and down in agitation.

Alice glanced around. "Go back there, over by the garage," she said, trying to keep her voice low. "Hurry up."

Just as he raced away around the corner, the front door opened.

Miss Fitzgerald stood inside behind the screen, her outline dark and indistinct, like a giant puff of black smoke. Alice stared up at her. Miss Fitzgerald seemed to be about to take a step back and close the door again; it was as if she didn't see Alice standing there on the doormat, though there she was, plain as day. The hallway behind her was dark.

"It's Alice," Alice said, for suddenly it occurred to her that maybe Miss Fitzgerald might not know who she was, might not remember her. Miss Fitzgerald had never actually spoken to Alice directly. When she came by to see Archie, her eyes would graze over you, even if Archie politely introduced you to her. And yet

Alice felt sure somehow, as she stood there separated from Miss Fitzgerald by the insubstantial and distorting surface of the screen door, that Miss Fitzgerald *did* know who Alice was; that she knew her, and she knew Alice knew her in turn, despite the fact that they never spoke, and that she could not bear something about that mutually reluctant acknowledgment that passed between them.

Miss Fitzgerald's form approached the screen from inside the hallway, as if she were trying to get a better look at whatever had addressed her from the doormat. Behind the mesh of the screen, her face looked like a terrorist's with a stocking pulled over it, featureless and flat and vaguely frightening. Alice felt her heart begin to pound inside her chest.

"Go around to the side. Your feet are terribly dirty," Miss Fitzgerald said and closed the door.

Alice's cheeks burned, but she backed off the front step obediently. She was not used to being spoken to like this. Elizabeth was dictatorial about baths and clothes and manners at the table, but Alice understood that this was Elizabeth's job; she was supposed to be severe about such things, and she was not mean, anyway, just no-nonsense: *give me none of that yakking,* Elizabeth said, or *hurry up, time's up.* She was never rude.

Alice glanced around for Theo. She called his name in a loud whisper but he didn't answer.

She jumped when the front door was abruptly opened again. From inside, Wally pushed open the screen door. He had a small, rolled-up carpet over his shoulder.

"Where have you been?" he said. He resettled the rug on his shoulder. "Where's Theo?"

"He had to pee," Alice said. "He went by the garage."

Wally craned out the front door to look in that direction, but there was no sign of Theo. "Well, you'd better come in," Wally said. "I'll leave the door open for him."

Alice hesitated. "She told me to go around to the side. She said my feet were dirty."

Wally's eyes widened. "She's worried about your dirty feet?" He gave a snort. "Come on," he said. "It doesn't matter. You'll see."

Inside, there was hardly enough room for Alice and Wally to stand side by side. The dark hallway was lined with stacks of boxes and paper, some as tall as Alice herself. Alice followed Wally down a little path between them. A carpeted staircase rose up to their left. It, too, was crowded with piles of things. Alice could see cobwebs like garlands looping from place to place across the flocked wallpaper.

"See what I mean?" Wally said quietly over his shoulder.

At first Alice thought that all the boxes and bags and piles of loose papers were Kenneth Fitzgerald's belongings, that he had moved in and been too sick or weak to arrange anything. But soon she saw that the teetering stacks were made up mostly of old newspapers and broken-down boxes, crates heaped with clothing and dishes and bits and pieces of things: she saw doorknobs, drawer pulls, casters, lampshades, hangers. She followed Wally carefully along the narrow passageway, her mouth hanging open.

"Pretty much the whole house is like this," Wally said from in front of her, his voice still low. "He's got the addition at the back of the house, where she used to do the piano lessons. It wasn't as bad back there, and we got it pretty much cleared out already. Tad and Harry took a load of stuff to the dump in the truck. He said not to even look at any of it. Just to get rid of it." Wally hoisted the rug higher on his shoulder. "She says she's collecting for the poor."

Alice was speechless. She clutched the books close to her chest, her elbows held in tightly along her sides, so as not to brush against anything. The air smelled terrible—like maybe something had died somewhere in the heaps of stuff. She tried to breathe through her mouth.

Ahead of her, Wally turned a corner in the hall and descended a half flight of stairs. The walls on either side were hung thickly with framed photographs. Alice tried to see the faces in the portraits, but the images were obscured behind a layer of dust. Wally shifted the rug on his shoulder again and opened a set of double glass doors. The sharp scent of lemon furniture oil cut through the stale air. Though more of the same stacks lined the walls, a long mahogany dining table was completely clear, glowing with fresh polish; it looked as if the occupants of a recent feast had vanished, along with their dishes, into thin air. Wally dropped the rug from his shoulder and pushed it out of the way with his foot against the far wall, near a window seat piled with what looked like folded blankets and coats. The heavy drapes at the window were gray, nearly colorless, though once they'd had some sort of pattern on them, Alice saw. Wally turned around to face Alice. She could hear, from somewhere distant in the house, her brothers' voices, the thud of their footsteps. Miss Fitzgerald was nowhere in sight.

"It didn't used to be like this," Wally said after a minute, staring around the room. "It was always kind of cluttered, but . . ." He looked back at Alice. He regarded her for a minute and then gave her a rueful smile. "You'll catch a fly in there," he said.

Alice closed her mouth.

"Come on," he said. "He's back here. There are a couple of rooms that are pretty much just his stuff now. They're okay."

The first room into which Kenneth Fitzgerald had been installed was at the end of the house. It was long and lined with bookshelves under a low ceiling. A small fireplace beneath a thick mantelpiece that appeared to have been made out of a single, massive timber stood at one end of the room. Alice knew enough about old houses to guess that this might have been a summer kitchen once. A set of French doors in the middle of the room opened out onto a flagstone terrace, and beyond the terrace, an overgrown expanse of lawn, the long, silvery grass stirring in the breeze, stretched to the edge of the woods. The floorboards inside had been recently mopped and polished; Alice could smell the lemon polish again. A large round pedestal table stacked with books had been pushed into the center of the room, and several armchairs, their red leather seats shiny with age, arranged around it. Near the table was a heavy settee with a faded green velvet slipcover and a fur throw. Several tall boxes that, because of their shape, Alice thought must contain paintings leaned against the bookshelves. On the floor by the French doors, where bees buzzed in from the garden, stood a tall glass vase of enormous white and purple irises, their heads heavy and their scent overripe and sweet. Near the flowers, a white rag lay on the floor as if it had been thrown down in surrender.

Alice looked up and saw herself and Wally reflected in an oval gold-framed mirror at the end of the room over the fireplace; their figures were tiny, like two people hesitating at the mouth of a cave.

At that moment, Miss Fitzgerald bustled into the room from the terrace outside, carrying a mop and an empty bucket. Instinctively, Alice drew near to Wally. Miss Fitzgerald's apron was the sort Elizabeth would have laughed at, all French frills and a big bow behind. She moved busily past them.

"I've just mopped," she said briskly, as if she cleaned and mopped all the time. "Don't track anything on the floor in here." She did not meet their eyes as she hurried past them.

Alice did not know where to look. When Miss Fitzgerald had left the room, Alice glanced up at Wally.

He puffed out his cheeks. "Has Archie ever said anything

about this, Alice?" he asked quietly. "About the house being like this?"

Alice shook her head. But how would someone have described it, anyway?

Wally rubbed his forehead. "Either she's completely crazy and can't see what a mess this place is, or she's so mortified she can't let on that she sees it . . . because that would mean that we're seeing it, too. I don't know what Kenneth must have said to her to get her to call this morning and ask for help." He looked down at Alice, who was still clutching her books. "Alice," he said quietly. "This is really strange."

Alice looked away from him and gazed around the room. The sense of cleanliness and order here, the glimpse through the French doors of the overgrown stretch of lawn beyond the terrace, the feeling of fresh air in the room, the sounds of the birds, the vase of flowers—even if they were, oddly, on the floor— all these were a relief after the horrible clutter of the rooms they had just passed through. It was as though this room had been enchanted, or perhaps spared the terrible enchantment that had fallen over the rest of the house.

"What good will it do to read to him?" Wally appeared to have posed the question rhetorically. He gazed around the room. "But maybe Archie is right, that it will be a kindness." He stopped once more, and then, seeming to remember that Alice stood there beside him, he squatted down in front of her. "Are you afraid?"

Alice shook her head, but Wally's question had unnerved her.

"There's nothing to be afraid of," Wally said. "He's just like anybody else. Only now he's sick. And that's not his fault. Do you understand that?"

Again, Alice nodded, though she wasn't sure what Wally meant.

"He's out on the terrace, in the sun," Wally said. "Come on."

THE ROPE WALK

Kenneth Fitzgerald was sitting with his back to them at the edge of the terrace on a black metalwork chaise longue heavy with fancy scrolling. He wore a battered straw hat on his head and in his lap he held what looked to Alice like an open sketchbook. When Alice and Wally stepped outside onto the terrace, he closed the book and turned around in the chaise longue.

Alice could not prevent her sharp intake of breath, an audible gasp, at the sight of his face. Her heart seemed to have leapt up into her throat.

One of Mr. Fitzgerald's eyelids had been hitched open and pinned to the jutting brow bone with a narrow X of white bandage tape. The eyeball, unmasked, stared out at her, horrifying and malevolent. And yet the other eye was sad and blue, small and rather lost-looking in his face; it was as if one side of his face wanted to terrify her, while the other side asked for her forgiveness and her pity.

"Word of the day," he said. "*Rara avis*. As in, Alice. Thank you for coming."

Wally put a hand on Alice's shoulder.

"A rare or unique person or thing. *Rara avis*." Mr. Fitzgerald began to try to raise himself from the chair.

Wally moved forward to offer his arm, but Mr. Fitzgerald waved him off. "I have something—" he said breathlessly, struggling to his feet, his hands on a cane. "Something inside, for Alice."

Alice could smell him from where she stood, a bitter smell, like burnt leaves. She wondered if it was the medicine he had to take. It wasn't his clothes; his white shirt had been starched and pressed, and his trousers were creased and clean. But his feet were bare, and they were horrible, Alice noticed suddenly, recoiling: they were purple, bulging, with thick dark nails that snaked over the end of his toes. He stood shakily. Alice looked away from him and swallowed hard. And then she saw, just beyond the terrace, Theo's head emerge at the top of the tall grass. His face was still streaked with dirt. He caught sight of her and beckoned madly with one hand. He must have crawled across the lawn through the grass on his hands and knees.

Wally stepped backward, drawing Alice against him, to allow Mr. Fitzgerald through the doors and back into the shade of the big room. Alice glanced quickly over her shoulder at the grass again, but Theo had ducked down out of sight. She allowed Wally to steer her back inside.

Mr. Fitzgerald was leaning over a box on the floor, one hand gripping the bookcase; with his cane he poked around inside the box. "Goddamn it," he said. "I can't find anything. I'm afraid it will have to wait." He straightened up and glanced at them, his face a lopsided mask of horror and appeal. He reached into his pocket, withdrew a handkerchief, and touched it to his mouth. "You've seen the house, Alice," he said. "This is what happens to the sick. We lose all our dignity when we can longer protect our secrets. I should have done something about it long ago. I knew it was like this, didn't I?"

Alice didn't know what to say. She felt embarrassed for all of them—Mr. Fitzgerald for looking so terrible, his sister for having her house like this, herself and Wally for having to see it.

"Your great big enormous brothers have been an enormous help," Mr. Fitzgerald said. "I'm very grateful to them."

Wally murmured something indistinct, a protest, Alice thought. She wanted to turn around and see if Theo was still hiding in the grass, but she didn't dare look. Mr. Fitzgerald came toward the table in the center of the room, leaning on his cane, and took a seat. He beckoned Alice to join him. "You've brought books." He held out a hand. "Your father said you read very well."

Alice approached the table.

"Will you call me Kenneth?" he said. His voice had a pleading quality. "My mother called my father Mr. Fitzgerald. That was how they addressed each other—Mr. and Mrs. Fitzgerald, even in their nightclothes, I suspect." He stopped abruptly, as if he'd said something in front of Alice that he shouldn't have. "And I shall call you, Alice—not Miss MacCauley. That's all right?"

Alice nodded.

He reached up and touched the X of white tape at his brow. He looked at Wally. "Can I trouble you, Wallace, to make the trip to the kitchen and ask Sidonnie—she's my cook, and pray, don't offend her; I've had to lure her here from New York at an exorbitant rate—if she'd be kind enough to bring us something to drink? Lemonade? Or would you rather an iced coffee?" He turned to Alice.

Alice had never had coffee in her life. "Iced coffee," she said, and saw Wally raise his eyebrows at her.

Why had she done that? She didn't even like the smell of coffee. She looked away, down at the books she still held, her cheeks burning.

"And for yourself and the others," Mr. Fitzgerald called after Wally. "Anything you'd like."

When Wally had gone, a silence fell in the room. Alice felt the heat of the flush on her neck and face. She was afraid to look at Mr. Fitzgerald—at Kenneth; could she call him that?—and his terrifying eye. She stared down at her own hands.

After a moment, he spoke. "My mother—*my* Alice," he began, and when he said her name, Alice glanced up. His bad eye was watering fiercely. He reached with a handkerchief to mop clumsily, almost brutally, at his face. "My mother read aloud to me when I was a child, everything from the Bible to Dickens to Kipling to Shakespeare. It changed my life, I'm sure of it. And I find it a comfort now. Thank you for coming to oblige me in this way."

Alice did not know what to say. She was aware of the quiet in the room, the swooning perfume of the irises, the buzzing drone of the bees drifting in and out of the French doors. It was strange to think of this man, this ruined old man, as a little boy, being read to by his mother.

"I've brought some Shakespeare," she said at last. She put the books on the table and pushed them toward him.

He lifted the books one at a time and inspected them. "And you can read Shakespeare aloud, can you? Well, you are your father's daughter . . . and here's Chekhov, one of my favorites. Excellent. I knew you'd choose well. And what's this?" He smiled, tapping the journal of William Clark and Meriwether Lewis, the book Theo had selected.

"Do you know?" Mr. Fitzgerald said. "This contains one of my favorite accounts, that of the bear who takes ten bullets, five to the lungs and one to the heart, one to the shoulder, one to the leg, and two to his lights, and who yet manages to swim across a river, bellowing with fury, and chase off his attackers. That was in the Thwaites edition, but I suppose it's in here. I would like to hear it again. Courage, eh?" He clapped his hand to his chest and smiled, but it was such a terrible smile—so angry, Alice realized after a moment—that she looked down at her hands again. He stacked the volumes on the table, his hands trembling.

"Is your friend," he said then carefully, not looking at her, "afraid of snakes, by any chance?"

Alice felt her jaw drop, and the blush flame over her neck and face again, as if someone had touched a match to her skin. He'd seen Theo out there in the grass.

"Perhaps he'd like to come in and join us before he's frightened to death by one of those garter snakes that so loves a neglected lawn." Mr. Fitzgerald tapped his fingers on the book and then glanced over at her. "It's all right, Alice," he said after a moment. "You can call him in. He was the very picture of stealth and it was only an accident that I happened to see him. Hope nearly doused him with her mop water."

Alice stood up.

Quickly, Mr. Fitzgerald reached out and caught her arm. His fingers felt dry as paper. "Alice," he said, "he's appointed himself your guardian, your hero. I envy him." He dropped her arm. "I wouldn't have you—either of you—afraid of me, you know."

Alice looked down at him in consternation. "Okay," she said. She couldn't think what else to say. She meant to apologize for Theo lurking in the grass, for Mr. Fitzgerald's sickness, and his horrible eye, taped open like that. For his awful sister and the state of the house. And also, she realized, for something else, something that felt like both an admission of her innocence, her ignorance—she did not understand everything that she had seen this morning—and a plea; she did not want to know as much as he seemed her to want to know of his life, the sad, adult errors of his life, everything that had gone wrong, or been neglected, or pushed aside.

He smiled up at her, the eye watering freely, as if a river of tears ran down his face. "Go. Call him in," he said.

Alice ran out to the terrace. The sun was directly overhead, and the day had grown hot; a breeze ran over the grass, ruffling it like the surface of the sea. Theo was nowhere in sight.

"Theo." She called him in a stage whisper. "Theo!"

Fifteen feet away, his head popped up out of the grass. He looked like a tawny little lion cub, stripes on his nose.

"He's seen you," she said, from the edge of the terrace. "He wants you to come inside."

Theo's surprise, she thought, mirrored her own. His jaw hung open.

Slowly, Theo stood up all the way and then began struggling toward her through the grass as if he were plying deep water, his arms doing the crawl. "How'd he see me? His sister almost dumped a bucket of water on my head. Is he *mad*?"

"He's not mad at us," Alice said. "He just wants—he just wants us to read to him. His eyes—there's something wrong with his eyes." She thought about how to prepare Theo for the sight of Mr. Fitzgerald's face, but then she realized that Theo had already seen him.

"*Yeah*," Theo said, as if she'd said the most obvious thing in the world. "It's disgusting. What's wrong with them?" With one finger he lifted up his eyelid in a grotesque way and then let it drop. "You know what? I know a boy who can turn his eyelids inside out."

He climbed up onto the terrace. He was barefoot; she wondered where his shoes had gone. She was aware of Mr. Fitzgerald waiting in the room behind them. She was aware of everything she had seen that morning: Miss Fitzgerald's desperation, the cluttered, filthy house, even Mr. Fitzgerald's own effort with her and with Wally, his watering eye, his horrible feet—in the face of Theo, standing there panting and dirty in front of her, all of it seemed to shiver a little and break up, like an image reflected in a pool of water. Suddenly Alice wanted to hug him.

"I'm really, really hungry," Theo said. "Do you think they have anything to eat?"

Wally returned with a tray of glasses of iced coffee and a plate of buttered raisin bread. The other boys trailed in, sweating and dirty. Hesitantly, Alice took a sip of her coffee and immediately added milk and two heaping teaspoons of sugar to the glass. She thought she could manage to drink it down if it were sweet enough. Theo took three pieces of raisin bread, unashamedly stacking them on his palm, but he refused the coffee, pulling a face. With his mouth full, he motioned to Alice to take another piece of bread and pass it to him. She helped herself quietly to another piece and passed it to him under the table.

In the silence, Alice watched James and Wally exchange a glance. No one seemed to know what to say.

It was Eli who finally broke the silence, speaking in his quiet, matter-of-fact way.

"The lawn mower needs to be repaired, Mr. Fitzgerald," he said, setting his empty glass back on the tray. "I took it down to Wilson's and left it there, if that's all right. It probably just needs to be cleaned. I'll pick it up tomorrow and come back to do the lawn." He cleared his throat. "I cleared out the side yard some, but there's more that can be done there. The irises need to be thinned when they're done. The lilacs are beautiful; they're old ones."

Mr. Fitzgerald, nodding vigorously, seemed eager to agree to anything. "My mother planted those lilacs," he said. "I'm grateful for anything you can do. I'm afraid my sister . . . I'm afraid it's all been—neglected. Shocking. You must just tell me . . ."

It was Tad and Harry who asked the question none of the rest of them had been willing or able to ask.

"Your sister seems to maybe want to go through some of this stuff before we take it out," Tad said.

"She seems kind of upset with us," Harry said.

For a moment Mr. Fitzgerald didn't reply. Alice wondered if he hadn't heard somehow; his attention seemed to be drifting. Then he said, "I told her I wouldn't disturb her bedroom. She's safe in there. But the rest . . ." He waved a hand. "All of it . . .

Well, it must go, mustn't it?" But he didn't mean it as a question. He put one hand up over his bad eye, as if the light were hurting it; the other eye gazed out the French doors. With the staring eye invisible behind his hand, he seemed diminished somehow, Alice thought, ordinary, just a sick old man. A sick old man who'd come home to a crazy house.

James said then that they would come back that afternoon and again the next day, as there was still more to be done. Wally would be leaving in a couple of days, and James himself, soon after that, but Tad and Harry—James shot them a meaningful look—could stay on and work for a while, if Mr. Fitzgerald needed them. Eli volunteered that he'd continue to come and work in the garden as long as Mr. Fitzgerald wanted him.

"Not to presume, sir," James volunteered, "but you might want to have someone come in and . . . clean. Or paint, even. We can ask Archie or Elizabeth if there's someone in Grange who might be able to . . ."

Alice wondered about the cook Mr. Fitzgerald had brought with him, the one with the strange name who'd made the coffee—he'd pronounced it Sih-doe-nee. What did she think of this house? Alice wondered.

"Yes, yes," Mr. Fitzgerald agreed. "Of course. Yes, I must do that."

After the boys had gone, Mr. Fitzgerald crossed the room leaning on his stick and went to the settee, lifting his legs painfully one at a time to the fur throw and then leaning back against the cushions with a small, almost inaudible groan. He put his arm over his eyes.

Theo and Alice, sitting at the table, watched him for a minute or two and then looked at each other.

Is he asleep? Theo mouthed at Alice.

She looked at Mr. Fitzgerald for a moment and then back at Theo. She shrugged.

"I'm not asleep," Mr. Fitzgerald said.

Theo and Alice jumped.

"I snore," he said. "That's how you'll know."

Another silence followed. Theo made aggrieved faces at Alice, gesturing to the French doors, walking his fingers through the air. She shook her head at him; Mr. Fitzgerald might be watching them. *No,* she mouthed back. *Wait.*

"I told your father that I wanted someone who could read to me, Alice," Mr. Fitzgerald said suddenly into the quiet. Theo startled again, but Alice had been ready this time, as if she were growing used to the long pauses between his sentences. She waited.

Alice leaned forward in her chair. Theo did the same.

"Theo," Mr. Fitzgerald said. "Would you recognize a box cutter?"

Theo looked surprised and then thrilled. "A box cutter? Yeah."

"I thought so." Another long pause followed this.

Theo made an aggrieved face of impatience at Alice.

"I think it's on the floor, near the lamp," Mr. Fitzgerald said finally. "Can you find it? Now, leaning up against the bookshelves," he continued. "One of the boxes . . . it's marked 'Bridge.' "

Theo, box cutter in hand, began inspecting the crates. "Here it is," he said.

"Careful," Mr. Fitzgerald said. "Don't drive it deep. Just go gently down the seam on the front."

Theo and Alice got the crate open and plied back the lid to reveal a lightweight wooden frame and the back of what looked like a canvas.

"Careful," Mr. Fitzgerald said again. "Lift it out gently and turn it over." He laid still on the settee, his arm over his face. He didn't look at what they were doing, as if he trusted them completely, Alice thought.

Together Alice and Theo lifted out the frame—it was surprisingly light, though taller than either Alice or Theo. Taped down to the other side was a complex mass of copper shapes and fragile-looking metal arms.

Alice recognized it instantly. "It's a mobile," she said. "Like in the library." She looked back at Mr. Fitzgerald on the settee. "You *did* make them."

Below his sleeve, Mr. Fitzgerald's mouth curved into a smile, but he didn't respond to her comment. "Next," he said, and then he went on to describe how they should screw an eye hook into the ceiling beam—they could stand on the table for that; Theo would find the tools over there on the bookshelf—and then release the mobile from its board and suspend it with a length of monofilament.

These maneuvers were accomplished. Once hung, the sculpture fell away like a shower of snowflakes through Alice's hands, springing into shape, floating gently in the air above their heads. Its circumference, over five feet across, was wider than Alice's reach when she stretched out her arms beneath it in both directions. Several of the pieces were hinged together like the treads of an arched Chinese footbridge; Alice was reminded for a moment of Charlotte the whale, her long, curved backbone. Above the bridge floated a long shape like a wisp of cloud, and below it a mass of silvery whorled shapes like the concentric rings made by stones thrown into water. It was complicated, ephemeral; it made Alice feel aware of the air around her, as though she were submerged in lazy currents of water. She twirled slowly beneath it, looking upward. Theo blew a gust of breath up toward it and it moved faster. Beside Alice he stared up at the mobile, too, watching it drift.

"Do you like it?" Mr. Fitzgerald spoke from the settee.

"It's *great*," Theo said. "It's *so* cool."

Mr. Fitzgerald didn't say anything else for a few moments. Alice and Theo stood under the mobile, watching it.

"Alice?" Mr. Fitzgerald's voice, when he finally spoke again, was faint, as if he spoke from a great distance.

Alice turned to him. The light in the room had changed, she noticed, the sun having passed around the corner of the house. The room was dim and warm, with just one band of golden light running low around the base of the bookshelves. She was aware of the irises again, their heavy perfume.

"Alice?" he said again.

"Yes," she said. "I'm here."

He seemed to sigh a little. "The Lewis and Clark," he said. "From the beginning."

Alice went to the table and found the volume.

"Time to lie down, Theo," Mr. Fitzgerald said, as if he were speaking to an unruly dog; he sounded suddenly very tired and short of breath. "Under the bridge. Listen. No interruptions. No questions."

Theo, perhaps too surprised to object, perhaps in a kind of trance worked by the mobile and the fatigue of their long morning, the growing heat of the afternoon, the shadows in the room, lay down promptly as ordered, his arms crossed under his head.

Alice picked up the book and opened it. She looked at the page. It felt as if it were she, and not just Lewis and Clark, who was beginning an expedition. Just days ago, her summer had seemed to promise such ordinary sorts of pleasures; she had even worried that she'd be bored, with all the boys except Eli gone. Many of the children in Grange went away to camp or to a grandparent's or to the beach in the summer, but Archie didn't like to be away from home and they rarely went anywhere.

And yet now she had Theo—she took a deep breath—and she had *this*. They could come every day to read to Kenneth, she thought. She wanted to see all the mobiles in the boxes, for she felt sure that's what they contained. Was he an artist? She thought her father had said he did something with the theater.

He had not frightened her. Wally had told her not to be frightened, and she hadn't been, not really. Kenneth seemed really and truly glad of her company, and Theo's.

For a moment she hesitated—her eyes felt heavy, and she needed to shake her head a little, clear it—and then she put her finger on the page and began reading.

"It is full summer on the Missouri," she read aloud, *"which means ferocious heat broken by sudden, violent storms. Storms endanger the boats; so do the many snags past some of which they have to be towed by handline, an operation made risky by the swiftness of the current."*

Alice stopped and flipped ahead through the first few pages, her eyes skimming the text. Many of the real dated journal entries had been included in the book, and she could see that they had been left just as Lewis and Clark must have written them, with weird spellings and random capitalizations. These were going to be hard to read, she thought, just like Shakespeare was sometimes puzzling. But there was something about the authenticity of those misspelled diary entries that she liked, the real thoughts of these two men, composed at the time without desk or lamp, sitting beside a river and writing in a journal balanced on a knee or a convenient rock or a fallen branch. It made the hair rise on her arms. She glanced down at Theo—his eyes were wide and unblinking, fixed on the mobile above his head—and then she bent to the page again. *"June 29,"* she continued. *"Hall given 50 lashes for stealing whiskey and Collins 100 lashes for being drunk on post and for permitting the theft. July 3 first sign of beaver. July 4 celebrated by the discharge of a swivel gun and an extra issue of whiskey, and Joseph Fields bitten by a snake, apparently a rattler . . ."*

She was not sure for how long she read. She would have said it was a half hour, maybe much less. Lewis and Clark made their way along the river, fighting mosquitoes and shooting deer, facing standoffs with the Indians.

No one came to the door to check on them. The house was quiet. The mysterious cook Sidonnie did not appear, nor Miss Fitzgerald. Nor did Alice's brothers return, though every now and then she heard their voices in a distant room or the sound of the truck's engine. Alice could hear the buzz of the bees in the irises and every now and then the rough cry of a bird outside. Otherwise, it seemed to her that she and Theo and Kenneth might have been the last people on earth, forgotten by the world. She sat, aware of her own pulse. Her throat was dry. Not a sound came from Kenneth or Theo.

After a minute, she closed the book and leaned over to look down at Theo. His eyes were closed, his face relaxed, his cheeks flushed from the heat. His mouth had fallen open. How could he be a black boy? she thought again. He was so like the color of a lion, all butter and syrup and honey. Suddenly, his eyelids fluttered open, and he was staring up into her face; he looked confused for a moment, as if he didn't know who she was or where they were. Then his face cleared and he smiled up at her; quickly he turned his head to look at the settee on the far side of the room. As if on cue, a snore came from the figure reclined there—it sounded almost like a groan, finishing on a shuddering note of discomfort.

Theo swiveled his head back toward Alice and then sat up on his elbows. "Come on," he whispered. He rolled over and began to crawl toward the French doors and the terrace outside on his elbows and knees, a guerrilla fighter moving through the underbrush.

Alice glanced at Kenneth on the settee and then, after a minute, dropped to her knees and crawled after Theo.

Out on the flagstones, Theo scrabbled up to his hands and feet and did a scuttling crab walk toward the grass, dropping off the edge of the terrace in a low roll like a soldier ducking from enemy fire.

Alice followed and rolled right on top of him. The two of them burst into hysterical giggles.

"*Shhhhh.*" Theo reached up and clamped his hand over her mouth. "*Shhhhh!*"

Before she had thought about it, Alice's tongue darted out into the sweet saltiness of his hand. She licked him, the marshmallow white color of his palm.

For a moment he held his hand to her lips, his eyes wide and looking into hers, and then like a wrestler he flipped her over; she felt him against her, beginning to laugh again. And then he sprang off her and crawled away into the grass.

Alice lay on her back for a moment, breathless, and then she rolled over, too, and followed him. When they got to the edge of the woods they scooted behind a tree and then peered back at the open French doors. They had left a little trough in the grass, but otherwise nothing had changed. No one appeared on the terrace, shielding his eyes against the sun and looking for them. The black metal chaise longue on the terrace seemed to float along the waving tops of the golden grasses like a strange Egyptian vessel, a pharaoh's empty boat headed for the open sea.

Alice raised her hands and made her imaginary camera, her fingers forming the box in front of her eye. With one finger, she depressed the pretend shutter. She clicked her tongue once against the roof of her mouth.

Theo looked over at her when he heard the click. "What are you doing?"

"Nothing," she said. "Just taking a picture."

SEVEN

THE NEXT MORNING, Alice and Theo stretched out on their stomachs on the sun-warmed floor of the porch. Lorenzo lay beside Alice, steaming in the sun like a black seal. Discarded on the porch floor were the remains of the panniers Theo had spent some minutes after breakfast trying to fashion for the dogs, paper grocery bags threaded by coat hangers and roped onto a saddle made out of an old bath towel. It had been his thinking that Kenneth could use the dogs, or perhaps a dog of his own that might be trained accordingly, for fetching and carrying things. "Saint Bernards and Newfoundlands are excellent at that kind of work," he had told Alice. "I saw a show about them on TV."

When a battered panel truck rumbled down the driveway, scattering stones into the grass, the dog lifted his head sleepily.

Theo sat up. "Who's that?"

"It's Mr. Moon," Alice said. It seemed a shame to Alice that Mr. Moon, who did odd jobs for people in Grange, looked nothing like his name. He was as red-haired as Alice, with long, old-fashioned coppery sideburns and bulging muscles in his forearms. His hands were knotted with arthritis—they looked to Alice like dragon claws—but the condition did not seem to interfere with his ability to work. He raised bees and had told Archie that he took bee pollen for the inflammation in his hands and made sure to get himself stung every day as some sort of treatment, a prescription that struck Alice as terrible. He stuck one arm out the window as he drove past the children, his cudgel of a fist raised in greeting.

Alice and Theo ran down to the garage, where Mr. Moon had stopped the truck, to investigate.

"Something for *you*," Mr. Moon said to Alice from the driver's seat. He opened the door of the truck and climbed down. "From Mr. Fitzgerald."

Alice gaped at him.

"There's one for him, too." Mr. Moon gestured at Theo, and then went round to the back of the truck and began rolling up the rear gate. "If his name is Theo."

Alice and Theo exchanged a mystified look.

The crates in the back of the truck were the size of freezer chests. Theo craned around Mr. Moon. "They're mobiles," Theo said in excitement. "They're in the same kind of box as the other ones. But these are *big*!"

A thrill fountained up inside Alice's stomach. Kenneth had sent them two of his mobiles. Were they a gift?

"Someone home could give me a hand?" Mr. Moon asked Alice. He climbed up into the truck and began winding a leather strap around the first crate.

At that moment James stepped out onto the porch, followed by Archie, blinking into the sunlight and tucking a book under his arm.

"They're for us," Theo called to them in excitement. "They're mobiles." He raced up and down alongside James and Archie as they walked down to Mr. Moon's truck. "I know how to open them," he said. "I can do it. I opened one before."

"Kenneth sent them," Alice said, in response to Archie's questioning look.

He looked at her blankly.

"Mr. Fitzgerald," Alice said quickly.

Archie's eyebrows lifted in surprise. "Ah," he said finally, regarding her. He kept his gaze on Alice for a moment before turning away to climb up into the truck and examine the crates.

"Here's the letter," Mr. Moon said. He held it out as if he wasn't sure who to give it to.

Archie took it and looked at the envelope. "It's addressed to you, Alice," he said.

Under his gaze, Alice felt the heat blossom over her neck. She hadn't *asked* for the mobiles, she thought. She would never have done that. She looked up into the truck at the two enormous boxes. No one except Helen, who one winter had ordered Alice a glamorous white fur muff and mittens from a department store in New York, had ever sent her anything. Harry and Tad, holding their hands cupped piteously like little paws against their chests and putting on pathetic, buck-toothed expressions, had told Alice that the muff and mittens were probably made of baby rabbits. Alice had been so horrified that she couldn't even look at the gifts after that, let alone wear them. Archie had made Tad and Harry write letters of apology to her for spoiling her present— Archie believed that writing about something was the surest way of learning it, and all the MacCauley children had been forced to pen letters of contrition over the years—and he had promised her that the fur wasn't real. Not a single hair on a rabbit's head had been harmed for her lovely muff, he told her. But it was too late. She couldn't bring herself even to open the box.

Mr. Moon and James carried the crates onto the lawn.

"I know how to open them," Theo said, dancing around the men. "All I need is a box cutter."

When James headed for the porch to go inside and find a knife to open the crates, Theo scampered along behind him. "All we need is a box cutter," he said again. "I know how to do it."

James leaned over and clamped a hand over his mouth. "I'm going to cut a box," he said. "A *voice* box." He threw Archie an exasperated look.

Alice sat down on the steps of the porch. Suddenly she felt deflated, as though the lovely pleasure of Kenneth's gift to them was being ruined, exactly as Tad and Harry had ruined the muff.

"Go ahead." Archie gestured toward the letter. "Open it."

Alice looked down at the envelope in her hand. Carefully she took out the heavy paper and unfolded it. Kenneth's handwriting was large and heavily slanted, veering unevenly across the page as if he might have written it with his eyes closed, feeling for the margins with his fingers.

Dear Alice, he had written. *I would be honored if you and Theo would accept* Monkey Man *and* Old Soldier's Beautiful Daughter. *They are too large to hang inside an ordinary house, but a tree branch is fine. It won't hurt them to be outside. I hope you will come see me today. There is no one to talk to except my loony sister (!) and Sidonnie, who I fear does not like Vermont and will be leaving me soon.* There was a little break on the page before the writing began again, like a postscript. *Word of the day: I think you and Theo will become my* camarilla. He had underlined the word *camarilla. Do you remember yesterday's word? You're it.* Rara avis. *Your friend, K.F.*

Alice looked up. Archie had turned away from her, squinting at the lawn and the field beyond, the sun shining on his face. His hair floated up around his head in the breeze, white and feathery.

"What's a camarilla?" Alice asked.

Archie turned around. "What?" He frowned. "Oh, it's a king's inner circle, I think, sort of a cabal. Clever schemers who advise the king. Why?"

"He's giving us two of his mobiles," Alice said. She imagined herself and Theo dressed in heraldic mail like Knights of the Round Table, with lions on their breasts. She was surprised that Kenneth had called Miss Fitzgerald "loony" in the letter. But then Alice had seen the house; he wasn't telling her anything she didn't already know. Also, he'd put that exclamation point there; Alice had mistakenly called them "excitement" points when she was younger. The mark of punctuation seemed to suggest he had a lighthearted view of his sister's housekeeping failures. Last night, when Archie was back at the hospital, she had asked Wally if the boys had told Archie about the house. "The twins did," he had told her. "I'm sure he thinks they're exaggerating. I told him it was beyond even the twins' imagination."

Archie came to sit beside her on the steps of the porch. "Well. That's something," he said. He hesitated for a moment before going on. "You know, Mr. Fitzgerald is an important artist, Alice," he said finally. "I suspect these are worth a good bit of money. He's made us a very valuable gift."

Not *us,* Alice thought. *Me.* Me and Theo. She looked down at the letter in her hands.

"Ken's had an extraordinary life," Archie went on, leaning his elbows on his thighs. "One adventure after another. Climbed all sorts of mountains in India and Pakistan, designed sets for ballets and operas in theaters all over the world. As I say—he's quite famous." He paused for a moment. "I read something once about him. It was in an interview, I think. He said he got the idea of the mobiles from mountain climbing, looking down on the world and seeing the shadows of the clouds . . ." He trailed off.

Alice looked up at him.

"It's just that it's probably a lot of money, Alice," he said. He straightened his back and rubbed a hand over his head, disarranging his hair.

Did Archie mean they would have to give them back? "They're a *present*," Alice said.

Archie was silent for a moment. "Not your ordinary sort, though," he said. "I want to think about it."

"Think about *what*?"

"Whether we ought to accept them."

Alice felt alarmed. He *did* mean to send them back. "He gave them to *us*," she said. "To me and Theo."

Archie sighed. "Let me think about it, Alice."

Alice stood up and looked down at Archie. "I want to open the boxes," she said. She rarely argued with her father; it startled her to hear her voice now, the note of anger in it. But why was he being so . . . careful, she thought in resentment, so careful and old and *slow*. Archie always wanted to think about things. He always wanted to *consider* matters before venturing an opinion or making a judgment, as if everything were equally important, what to have for breakfast and—she cast about for a parallel construction—whether to go to war. And of course they *weren't*, she thought now in frustration. Some things just didn't matter all that much. For a second she felt a shocking blaze of hatred for her father, a sensation utterly unfamiliar and powerful. It was as if all her blood had suddenly been exchanged for fire and then just as quickly extinguished, leaving only a smoldering gunpowder trail.

Archie looked up at her. "He must like you very much, Alice." He reached to take her hand. "What did you do to besot him so already?"

But Alice took her hand away. Sometimes when Alice went in search of Archie in his study, she found him in his tufted leather chair, the one their mother had called Sleepy Hollow for the deep well of its cracked seat. He would be staring vacantly past the book open on his lap, the room dark except for a single light shining onto the page, the lamp's occult ceramic finial, an Egyptian eye, watching the shadows in the corners of the room. Archie would look up at her knock, startled, and when he saw her, peeping around the edge of the door, he would close the book and smile. But it was a sad smile he offered her at those moments, and she understood that she had seen a side of her father he ordinarily took more trouble to conceal. Behind the mild expression Archie presented to the world—his calm manner, his quiet voice, his wry, economical utterances—lay this sadness, Alice knew, all the years of missing Alice's mother and struggling alone to raise their children. Yet even more troubling than the sadness was the indifference Alice sometimes detected behind her father's melancholy, as if he simply could not rouse himself to care sufficiently about either the questions posed to him in this world or the answers he would supply. On those evenings when she came to say good night to him in his study, when she found him so inert and helpless and far away, Alice would run for his lap and put her arms around his neck and bury her face in his shoulder, unwilling and unable to look at him.

Archie's face, turned to her now as he gazed up at her on the porch steps, looked old and tired and defeated.

Suddenly, surprising herself, she jumped to her feet and leaped down the steps to the grass two at a time. She did not want Archie to look at her that way. On the lawn, in the heat of her confusion, she turned a violent handspring, and then another.

Theo banged through the screen door onto the porch. "No box cutter," he announced.

Archie had no practical skills; the boys joked that he couldn't even change a lightbulb. He had never maintained the kind of respectable tool bench O'Brien had set up in his garage, for instance.

James appeared a moment later, a steak knife from the kitchen in his hand.

They slit open the boxes and the mobiles appeared, fixed to the boards with huge staples, like creatures caught in mid-flight and pinned to the wood. At first Archie wanted to leave them attached to the boards and not hang them, but Theo and Alice set up such a complaint that he relented. The children stood under the maple tree on the front lawn, and James brought around the ladder and set it against the tree to climb up and hang the mobiles from the branches. Theo threw open his arms as the jointed black shapes of *Monkey Man,* with the distended belly of a starving child, arms and legs akimbo, mouth open in a howling O, jumped down and bounced on the mobile's metal arms, doing a Saint Vitus's dance in the air. The figure was nearly the same size as Theo, recognizable as a monkey but also human and vital, like a shaman caught up in a secret ritual.

When James affixed *Old Soldier's Beautiful Daughter* and let the pieces fall into place, a shimmering waterfall of tiny gold leaves dropped and spun like golden bees in the dappled shade under the tree. Elizabeth, who had come to work even though it was Sunday because she was finishing up the laundry for James and Wally's departures, came out onto the porch in her apron to watch. "*Wha!* So beautiful!" she said in surprise. "And what's that one? That one's you, Theo, jumping around like a monkey!"

Inside, Wally began playing the piano, a complicated passage of notes that ran up and down the scale. When Alice had gone by his bedroom door on her way down to breakfast that morning, she had seen his suitcase open on the bed, a stack of ironed shirts folded on the bedspread, and his tuxedo, magisterial and black, draped like a mourner over the footboard, his black shoes side by side on the floor. Tomorrow he would leave for Michigan, but inside the living room now Wally played the exercise faster and faster; his hands must be a blur over the keys. Alice listened and imagined the notes running around and around the walls like birds trapped in a room. Since their trip to the Fitzgeralds' yesterday—since breakfast, really, when Wally had gotten angry—Wally had held himself apart from the boys. Even his playing now had a remote, concentrated energy to it, as if he were having an argument with himself.

Alice stood beneath the shower of *Old Soldier's Beautiful Daughter.* Beads of reflected light danced over her skin, and she tried to catch them in her fingers. Theo bumped into her as he spun around beneath *Monkey Man,* and they clasped hands, swinging each other in furious circles and then collapsing onto the grass.

Theo rolled her over and sat on her, victorious. He smelled like grass and dirt—*April and May*—and the bacon they'd had for breakfast and something else, something she was learning to identify as his own particular smell. She bucked violently and toppled him, but he had her pinned again in a minute, her cheek against the grass, his chest pressed against the wings of her shoulder blades.

"Surrender," he said from on top of her, panting onto the back of her neck. The sensation of his hot breath on her skin tickled her, a strange, hysterical tickle. She began to squirm beneath him, wrenching her shoulders and trying to throw him off, but she was laughing too hard to be successful.

"Got you," Theo crowed. "I've got you, Alice."

After lunch it began to rain, a steady spring drizzle, and Archie dropped Alice and Theo off at the Fitzgeralds' in the car. When they pulled up in front of the house, Alice hesitated. She wondered exactly what Tad and Harry had told Archie about the condition of the Fitzgeralds', what Wally had said, whether Archie himself had ever been inside. She wanted him to see it, the strange walled city of junk Miss Fitzgerald had built inside her own house. Archie would be able to fix things somehow, Alice thought. He would understand about Miss Fitzgerald's trouble and put it right.

She turned in the front seat beside him. "Can you come in with us?" she said. She wanted to put her arms around Archie now, to apologize for her anger of earlier in the day when he had been reluctant about the mobiles. She was suddenly sorry for having pulled away her hand. She did not *want* to hurt him, she thought in a painful spasm of loyalty, as if it were someone else who had thought all those mean things about him, that he was boring and old-fashioned and . . . old.

Archie glanced at his watch. "Not today. I have to run up to Frost to pick something up, and I want to go back to the hospital tonight. Tell Kenneth I'll come see him soon. Tell him—well, tell him thank you, of course."

Alice looked away from Archie out the window. The world beyond the wet glass appeared bent somehow, like a scene's disturbed reflection in a circus mirror.

"Call Elizabeth if it's still raining when you're ready to come home," Archie said into the silence.

Alice opened the car door. "Can we come to the hospital with you tonight?" she said, turning back to look at him once more. "To see Helen?"

"We'll see," Archie said. "Maybe." He waved at them as he drove away, the car's taillights reflected in the dark shine of the wet pavement.

Theo and Alice opened the gate to the Fitzgeralds' garden. The twins and Eli had been at work since earlier that morning. The grass had been mowed before the rain had started and one section of the fence had been cleared of weeds. The fence itself, denuded, was falling apart. It looked as though it would have to be replaced entirely. There was no sign of the twins or Eli now, though. They'd probably gone home for lunch.

"I'm not going to go," Theo said suddenly. He stopped walking.

Alice turned to him in surprise.

"I'm not going to the hospital to see her," he said.

Alice stared at him, bewildered. "Why not?"

"They don't like me," he said. "They don't like my dad."

Alice couldn't imagine Helen not liking anyone. She couldn't imagine O'Brien and Helen not liking their own grandson.

"They're racists," Theo said. "Especially *him*. He doesn't like us because we're black."

The rain was falling harder now; it dripped off the hood of Alice's raincoat and ran down her face. Theo had been given an old yellow slicker of Eli's. It was too large for him and it hung down over his hands and nearly to his knees. He had not put up the hood, and the rain fell on his bare head, his golden hair darkening, sticking up in wet tufts.

"You don't *look* black," Alice said.

"Well, I am. If you have even one little drop of black blood in you, you're black."

Alice thought about this for a minute. "*Why* don't people like people who are black?"

Theo shrugged. "They just don't."

Alice was troubled by these assertions, these revelations of dislike between Theo and Helen and O'Brien, though she wasn't sure she believed Theo's statement about Helen and O'Brien being racists and not liking their own grandson. It seemed baffling to her that people might not like each other because they were one color or another; they might just as easily decide not to like red-haired people, she thought uneasily. Having a lot of colors was much preferable to having only one, anyway. No child would ever be foolish enough to want a box of crayons with only one color in it, she thought. A girl in her class at school every year had a new box of seventy-two crayons, blissfully sharp and pristine. Alice, who was always told to rummage through drawers at home for stubs and broken crayons to fill her pencil box, any other practice being thought wasteful by Archie, was envious. She did not have time to consider any of this at length, though, because at that moment the front door of the Fitzgeralds' house banged open and slammed inward, the door meeting the wall inside with a loud report. Alice heard herself give a little shriek of surprise, and she and Theo grabbed on to each other. They stood on the path, clinging together. But no one came out the door. It just hung open, a dark hole. Theo and Alice stared at it, horrified.

"Let's *go,*" Theo said. He took off around the side of the house in the rain. Alice followed him.

They scrambled up the steps to the terrace and approached the French doors. They were shut, and Alice approached the house cautiously and leaned close to the glass to cup her hand. Theo stood next to her, panting. Rain splashed onto the bricks at their feet.

"Maybe somebody got him," Theo said breathlessly. "Maybe someone mugged him!"

Alice had never heard of anyone getting mugged in Grange, but she'd played games of cops and robbers with the boys, sometimes armed with a club or more often dragged around in handcuffs or tied up and gagged in the tree house. She peered through the glass. The room appeared to be empty, but a chair had toppled over onto the floor—that was strange, Alice thought—and a pool of blankets lay on the carpet beside the settee. Several cardboard boxes, their tops gaping open, stood in the middle of the room. The glass felt cool and wet on Alice's forehead as she leaned against it. The room was quite dark. There was only one light on near the settee, a lamp with its gooseneck twisted at a violent angle.

Theo leaned in beside her. Alice peered into the dim room. And then she heard Theo gasp.

"What's *that*?" he said in a tiny voice, as if the breath had been sucked out of him. He pressed up close beside Alice and pointed through the glass.

At his sharp intake of breath, Alice had reared away from the door as if something were about to come hurtling toward them out of the depths of the room, but now she leaned in cautiously, following the path of his pointing finger. And then she saw it. On the floor, a man's dark trouser leg, bent at the knee, extended from behind the settee. She couldn't see beyond that.

Her fingers found the latch and she pushed open the door and ran across the room.

Kenneth was lying on the floor behind the settee, his head cradled on a toppled stack of books. The wind, gusting across the floor through the French doors behind her, rifled the open pages in a way that made Alice's heart stop for a minute; she was reminded of the blur of calendar pages signifying the passage of time in old movies. How long had he been lying here?

She dropped to her knees beside him. What should she do? She didn't know what to do. She put her hand on his chest. Water ran down her sleeve and dripped onto his shirtfront. Under her palm she could feel the bony case of his chest barely rising and falling, as though something were happening a long, long way beneath his skin, a long way from the surface of the earth. His hair still bore the marks of the teeth of a comb. He wasn't wearing the cross of tape over his eye today, but she could see where it had left a mark against the white skin of his forehead. His lips were badly chapped.

Theo spoke from behind her, appalled. "He's *dead*."

She shook her head. "No, he's not," she said. "We have to get help." She turned around and looked up at him. He looked terrified, but she realized that she felt very calm inside, as if she was thinking in slow motion. When she spoke, she heard her own voice in her ears. She could feel every part of her hand where it lay across Kenneth's chest; she could feel his heart, very far away, offering up its exhausted beating through his shirt and against her palm. Wally had a heart murmur, and when Alice was younger and he had held her on his lap, she had put her ear against his chest to listen for it, the musical, murmuring voice she imagined, like the voices of the children in the auditorium at school, waiting for the principal to stand up and lead them in the Pledge of Allegiance. Wally's heart, she discovered, beat faster than other people's. Archie's heart, on the other hand, was slow. It sounded like muffled footfalls across an empty museum gallery, each beat a solemn echo of the last.

She got to her feet. "We have to get help," she repeated.

Across the room, the door was ajar. Alice hurried across the floor between the boxes; at the door she hesitated, but only for a second. Pushing it open, she leaned into the hall.

"Hello?" she called into the gloom. There was a window in the hall, but it was heavily curtained, the red panels finished with greasy silk fringes. "Miss Fitzgerald? Tad? Harry?"

"Try again," Theo whispered from behind her, making her jump.

But Alice heard the sound of a door opening overhead and footsteps, a woman's clicking heels, coming down the back stairs. A moment later, Miss Fitzgerald appeared.

She looked as if she had been asleep, bewildered and lost. She stopped ten paces from the children, almost as if she were afraid of them, Alice thought.

"How did you get in?" Miss Fitzgerald said. "I didn't let you in."

"We came in through the terrace," Alice said. And then she felt angry. It was irrelevant how they'd come in! Were they being accused of something? They had *found* Kenneth. "It's Kenneth," she said, and as she spoke she understood, as if an electrical cable had connected them suddenly, that Miss Fitzgerald loved her brother and that the sight of him motionless and silent on the floor would terrify her. An intimacy would be exchanged now between Alice and Miss Fitzgerald, bearers and receivers of bad news alike, against which Alice protested. Suddenly she did not want to be there, seeing what she was seeing. The powerful sense of indignation she had felt a moment before deflated inside her, like a balloon releasing trapped air. "I think he fell down," she said in a small voice.

Miss Fitzgerald brushed past them. In the doorway she gave a little cry when she saw Kenneth on the floor. She knelt beside him, exactly as Alice had done.

Alice and Theo watched from the door; Alice felt Theo reach over and take a bit of her raincoat sleeve in his fist, hanging on. She realized how hard her heart was beating. The deep, almost restful quiet that had dropped over her seemed to be breaking up, like fog burned away by the glare of sunlight. She was aware of the musty odor of their raincoats; they smelled like the closet under the stairs, like old leather and tennis balls and rubber boots. She was aware of her blood prickling in her fingertips and across her cheekbones and under her arms.

Miss Fitzgerald stood up and hurried to the telephone on the table. Alice felt instantly hot with shame, with the foolishness of her error. She should have remembered the telephone. She knew all about calling 911 in case of an emergency. She knew about how you were supposed to get down on the floor—stop, drop, and roll—if you caught on fire, not go running away. She knew that if you got caught in an undertow you were supposed to allow yourself to be carried out to sea where eventually the current would release you, even though your most powerful instinct would be to fight to return to shore. She knew that if you got caught in quicksand, the same logic applied: stay utterly still, don't struggle, hardly even breathe. She knew not to drink salt water, even if you were perishing from thirst. She knew that if you had been lost for days in the woods, you shouldn't suddenly eat a huge meal when you were rescued, because it would be too much for your body. It seemed that in order to save oneself, again and again, one had to fight one's own instincts, one had to gain mastery over all the urgent imperatives of flesh and blood. One had to be less of oneself, in order to try and preserve that self.

Miss Fitzgerald dialed with trembling hands and held the receiver to her ear. Her eyes slid to Alice and Theo in the doorway, and she deliberately turned her back to them, her green cardigan hanging crookedly over her shoulders like a small, lopsided cape. Her voice sounded breathless, but she gave her name, her address. She started to list the medications Kenneth took, but someone on the other end of the phone must have stopped her, because she fell silent then, answering in worried-sounding monosyllables. When she hung up finally, she put her hands to her cheeks for a moment, staring at Kenneth on the floor. Then she knelt beside him again, stroking the hair from his forehead.

A terrible sympathy rose in Alice; her throat tightened painfully. Miss Fitzgerald looked so old and pathetic, her ugly worried face bent over her brother. But Alice took an involuntary step backward when Miss Fitzgerald, as if sensing Alice's scrutiny, looked over her shoulder at Alice and Theo still riveted in the doorway. Alice was reminded of the feral cat that lived in the MacCauleys' barn, the calico that could be seen carrying its newborn kittens like dead mice between its teeth, moving them from location to location. She saw the cat sometimes, going out hunting at dusk; it always seemed to be looking over its shoulder. Alice left milk for it in a saucer, when Elizabeth wasn't looking.

"What mischief were you up to?" Miss Fitzgerald said. "What happened?"

Alice stared back at her, speechless.

But Theo suddenly came to life beside her. "We just found him like that!" he said. "We didn't do anything! Alice saved his life!"

On the floor, Kenneth gave a little moan.

Theo tugged hard at Alice's sleeve. *Let's go,* he mouthed, his expression furious.

Alice's feet felt wooden, but she allowed Theo to pull her along the edge of the room toward the French doors and the terrace beyond. Outside, she registered the rain on her face again, the wet grass sticking unpleasantly to her legs as she ran across the lawn. Theo wanted to keep running, but at the street Alice heard the siren and grabbed his sleeve to pull him back. They huddled down in the tall weeds under the eaves of the garage, watching while the fire truck and the town ambulance pulled up to the curb. Three men and a young woman—Alice recognized her from the YMCA in Brattleboro where she handed out towels and checked people's membership cards—ran up into the house. The front door was still wide open. Rain fell inside on the carpet, leaving a dark, spreading spot.

"Let's *go,*" Theo said again. "C'mon. *C'mon,* Alice!"

But Alice shook her head. It seemed wrong to leave, as if they would be abandoning Kenneth. They squatted under the eaves, the rain dripping miserably on them.

"You think somebody got him?" Theo said at last.

Alice glanced at him from under her hood.

"I mean, maybe he's a spy," Theo said. "He kind of seems like a spy. Maybe terrorists got him." Theo stood up and peered on tiptoes through the cobwebby window into the garage. "There's a car in there," he said. "Maybe it's got a car bomb in it." He looked down at Alice, his face miserable with indecision and fear.

Alice tugged him down beside her. "He's an artist," she said. "He just fell down because he's sick and he's got AIDS or something. He's not a spy. There aren't terrorists here, anyway."

Theo crouched beside her on his heels. "They're everywhere," he said.

Alice glanced at him again. His skin looked yellow under his hood.

"You just don't know that, because you don't live in New York," he said. "Terrorists are everywhere. Don't you watch TV?"

Alice didn't want to tell him that Archie didn't really ever let her watch TV. If there was something important happening in the world, Archie watched the news in his study; sometimes, caught up in front of the screen with a drink in his hand in the evening, he didn't notice when Alice came in quietly and stood there watching, too. She'd seen the footage of the planes flying into the World Trade Centers. She had been struck by the scary silence that had accompanied the images, especially the silence during which the minute black shapes of people's bodies—at first she had been puzzled, and then disbelieving; what *were* those things?—fell through the air, descending toward an invisible ground. There was hardly ever silence on TV, she'd noticed, and the strangeness of it during those moments had frightened her almost more than what she could see with her eyes. She'd seen the men pull down the statue of Saddam Hussein in Baghdad, too. That was supposed to have been an important moment, she knew, but the scale of the event had seemed too small to be truly impressive; Alice had been to football games at Frost where there were more people. And once she'd watched part of a show about how the Americans were trying to find Osama Bin Laden, who was hiding in a cave. The description of the cave—with bedrooms and pantries and roads and tunnels and computers and storerooms and garages—had been fascinating. Yet often it seemed to her that she was hearing the same news over and over again in a vaguely boring kind of loop: there were car bombs being set off in one city or another, a dozen people, or a hundred people, killed. Bad storms, kicked up by global warming, circled the globe like evil dervishes. The summer ice in Antarctica was melting. The air was dangerous to breathe. Usually, when Archie finally noticed her standing there staring at the screen, he would stand up and turn off the TV. "Enough of that," he'd say. "Let's go watch fireflies."

Still, she couldn't really claim to watch television regularly at home. "We see a news show at school in the morning," she said to Theo now instead.

"That's watered-down news for kids," Theo said. "You didn't see the real thing. You didn't see the planes going into the World Trade Center." He shook his head, like a jaded adult. "Unbelievable."

"Yes, I did," Alice said quickly. "I saw the pictures." Had Theo actually witnessed this sight? She felt the need to defend herself suddenly against what seemed like accusations of a criminal innocence. She looked at the pictures in the newspaper, and she even read some of the articles, or parts of them. It embarrassed her that Archie didn't allow her to watch television and that she had to amuse herself with reading, or colored pencils and paper, or holding a fishing pole baited with a marshmallow over the river, or practicing the piano, or just playing outside. At school, when kids asked her if she'd seen a particular show, she just shook her head mutely, smart enough not to lie and say she had. She'd seen TV at other people's houses, of course, and lots of movies—the wonderful one about the pig, Babe; she'd liked *Toy Story* and *Hook* and *The Princess Bride* and *Beauty and the Beast*. So it wasn't like she had never even seen TV. She'd been mesmerized in what had felt like a helpless way by the bright succession of images on the screen. But now it seemed that she had to apologize for having been denied regular access to this medium, this important conduit for information. She didn't think terrorists were everywhere; why would they be everywhere? *How* could they be everywhere? But even the YMCA in Brattleboro had a terrorist attack alert level sign in the lobby, though the paper it was printed on was kind of old now and torn at one edge; the warning level had been on yellow for as long as Alice could remember.

Maybe Theo understood something significant about the world that she did not, she thought now. Maybe everyone, everywhere, was at risk all the time. Maybe just over the mountains, or around the sharp corner of the road that hid what was ahead, there were people coming who wanted to do harm to her, not because she was Alice, but just because she was the enemy. It could be completely impersonal, being a victim. You might not have any opinions at all, you might not care one way or another about something, but still you would be struck down where you stood just *because,* just because you were accidentally allied with something that someone else hated. This was a new version of harm, she realized, a new and helpless version. In her nightmares she always knew her enemy—the monster who reappeared in her dreams from time to time, crunching down the street and uprooting telephone poles; the musketeer with a sickening rapier; even the ghoul rising from the icy marble of the morgue—and she understood that her enemy knew her, too, had been aiming specifically for her. It was a contest among declared foes, and her honor and bravery were at stake. But with terrorists? Well, it was so . . . random. And you never knew *when* to expect them, so you would have no opportunity for heroism before you were blown to bits, like all those people waiting in line in bakeries, or at a bus stop, or crossing the street. It didn't matter if you were ready for something, because how could you know what to be ready for, and when? At school they'd sent each child home with instructions for how to put together an emergency preparedness kit, and she'd had to beg Archie to make even a token gesture of compliance. Finally she had gone ahead herself and packed an old briefcase of Archie's with bottles of water and some dog food, granola bars, and batteries; she'd spent her own allowance money on garbage bags and duct tape, because the instructions had said you could tape up your windows with them against a chemical attack.

"No one is going to hurt you, Alice," Archie had said, putting on his glasses and reading over the instructions. "We live in the middle of nowhere. No harm will come to you here!" But he'd sounded exasperated rather than comforting.

Suddenly Alice and Theo heard voices. Two of the men appeared in the doorway carrying Kenneth on a stretcher. Miss Fitzgerald, holding a coat over her head, came out after the stretcher and was helped into a car. Alice saw Miss Fitzgerald's cardigan sweater fall from her shoulders into a puddle on the sidewalk. Nobody stopped to pick it up.

In a moment, the street was empty. The rain fell quietly on the grass and the black shiny surface of the road and into the fragile, heavy leaves of the trees that lined the street, their branches meeting in the middle to form an arch of watery green, submerging the street in a soft light. Water slid from the eaves of the garage in a curtain beside Alice and Theo, dripping into a groove like a long grave that rain from previous storms had worn in the earth. Where was the cook, Sidonnie? Alice wondered vaguely. Had she already left, gone back to New York?

She hiccupped unexpectedly. There was a wrenching in her chest, and with it the tears began, surprising her, bubbling up out of nowhere. She had thought Kenneth was dead. . . and perhaps he would die. And yet she hadn't been afraid to touch him. Through her crying she wondered at that; she hadn't been afraid then, only now. She had always thought she would be afraid of a dead body. Her teeth began to chatter.

Theo watched her for a minute and then scooted closer to her and put his hands on her shoulders. He lowered his face to rest his forehead against her own, a strangely grown-up gesture, like an adult comforting a child. Suddenly he was the one reassuring her.

"We'll get to the bottom of it," he said. "Don't worry."

For a moment Alice wavered. She knew—or, one part of her knew—the truth of the situation, which was that Kenneth Fitzgerald had fallen because he was sick. No one had crept out of the shadows to do him harm. But Theo's conspiracy theory, in which he and Alice were cast as detectives or spies, in any case as something larger and more potent and mysterious than they were, had the tempting quality of illusion to it; it wasn't real, and that, at least for right now, was its charm. She could believe it, if she wanted to, she thought; indeed, she could feel it happening, as though she were on a sled teetering at the crest of a long, steep hill, and the relief of this filled her with nostalgic longing, though for what exactly she could not say.

"Don't cry, Alice," Theo said, and his voice was sympathetic. "Don't cry."

They stayed like that for a while, hunched down side by side in the weeds, Alice snuffling. The rain fell off the eaves in beautiful silver chains.

When they got home they were soaking wet and Theo's teeth were chattering. Elizabeth drew them separate baths upstairs and sat on the side of Alice's tub in Archie's bathroom to pour water from a cup over Alice's head. Alice told her what had happened at the Fitzgeralds'.

"Tip back your head," Elizabeth said. "Eyes closed."

"She doesn't like me," Alice said.

Elizabeth didn't say anything for a minute. "She was upset," she said at last. "You know how she is." Elizabeth smoothed a hand over Alice's head, pushing away the soap. Alice heard the sound of tires on the driveway, and Elizabeth glanced out the window. "Okay. There's your father," she said. She straightened up and put a hand to the small of her back. Downstairs, the telephone began to ring. "I'm going to fix supper," Elizabeth said. "You stay in here. Soak."

When Alice came downstairs at last, Theo was already in the kitchen. She could hear him regaling someone with the afternoon's events. When Alice entered the room, Archie was standing at the kitchen table. He had the day's mail in his hand, but he had stopped in his perusal of it, apparently to listen to Theo. Wally was sitting at the table, his chin in his hand. Eli stood just outside the open kitchen door on the stone step, supervising the dog Lucille as he nosed around in the wet grass. Through the doorway, Alice could see his feathery tail waving as he loped back and forth, some scent under his nose.

The boys looked up when Alice stepped into the room.

Theo stopped talking. He looked around a little guiltily. No one said anything at first, and Alice wondered what Theo had told them.

"Well. Let's have supper," Archie said after a minute. "Someone go call Tad and Harry, please. And where is James?" He tossed the mail into the copper bowl on the fireplace mantel and pushed his glasses up onto his head. "Mr. Fitzgerald is all right, Alice. He just had a dizzy spell and fell and gave his head a knock. He's already been sent home from the hospital."

"What did you tell them?" Alice said to Theo when they were sent off to wash their hands for dinner.

"Nothing." Theo soaped his hands vigorously under the tap.

"You told them something," Alice said.

For a moment, Theo resisted. Then he said, "I just told them how you almost gave him mouth to mouth."

Alice, standing next to him at the sink, stared at him, appalled.

"Well, you almost did," Theo said. "You would have." He looked over at her. "I couldn't have touched him," he said. "But you weren't afraid."

"I *was* afraid," Alice said quietly. She looked away from him to hold her hands under the water, and she watched the soap drain off her fingers.

Theo reached across her for a towel. "That's the hero part," he said. "Being afraid, but doing it anyway. That's what my dad says."

Alice thought about the mysterious black man who was Theo's father. She hadn't seen all that many black people in her life. The custodian at her school was black. There were a few black kids at the elementary school, though none in her grade. She'd seen more pictures of black people than real black people themselves, photographs in *National Geographic,* for instance.

Standing beside her at the sink, Theo pushed her playfully with his shoulder.

Alice looked up and regarded their two faces reflected in the mirror.

Theo grinned at her.

After a minute, Alice pushed him back.

The hospital in Brattleboro was a gloomy brick Victorian building with capped turrets and gingerbread trim painted a dark brown. It had been used as a TB sanatorium for a time; many of the rooms, even those on the second and third floors, had private porches where the patients had sat out in the winter air, wrapped in blankets. Behind the building, jutting up out of a grove of spruce trees, a smokestack stood out grimly against the blue twilit air. Tad and Harry had told Alice when she was younger that the smoke coming out of it was from the dead bodies being burned in the basement morgue. She'd asked Archie about it one day as he was driving her home past the hospital after her swimming lesson at the YMCA.

"For heaven's sake," he'd said. "That's for the laundry, Alice. The bed sheets, the towels, the—" He had shaken his head. "Don't believe anything the twins tell you, all right?"

In the main hall of the hospital, Archie stopped to hand to Alice the bouquet of flowers Eli had picked for Helen. "I don't know that we'll actually be able to see Helen tonight, Alice. She's in a deep sort of sleep. But she'll know you've brought these for her when she wakes up."

Theo stood a few paces behind Alice. He had not said to Archie that he wouldn't go to the hospital—Alice thought he'd probably been afraid to refuse to go—but he had not said a word in the car on the way to Brattleboro. Alice, sitting in the front seat beside Archie, had noticed her father glance into the rearview mirror several times, watching Theo.

"She's in a coma?" Theo perked up now at Archie's description. "Uh-oh. That's bad."

Archie looked over Alice's head at him. He looked surprised, but he didn't say anything.

O'Brien met them in a poorly lit little lounge upstairs, where a lamp with a yellow sticky-looking shade listed on a rickety table. He looked exhausted, with deep, rubbery pouches beneath his eyes. His shirt and trousers were badly wrinkled. He accepted Archie's brief embrace, but he didn't speak to Alice or to Theo. He didn't even seem to notice that Theo was there, hanging behind Alice.

Alice saw Archie register this lapse. He moved to put his arm around Theo as if to bring him forward to O'Brien's attention. But Theo refused to move any nearer, shrugging away from Archie's arm. O'Brien didn't seem to notice this either, but Archie looked at Theo, his back turned resolutely to the two men.

"Why don't you let me stay here tonight?" Archie said to O'Brien.

O'Brien shook his head. "I wouldn't sleep anyway," he said. "It doesn't matter." He noticed Alice finally and smiled wearily at the bouquet of peonies and hydrangeas in her hand.

"Well, at least let me take you across the street for something to eat," Archie said. "We'll only be gone a half hour, just long enough to get a steak and a baked potato or something into you. Alice and Theo can stay here. They can come right across the street and get us if—"

O'Brien was shaking his head again, but at the mention of Theo's name he seemed to see him for the first time. He stared at him for a moment, but he didn't speak to him. He turned to Archie again instead. "I talked to Ann this morning," he said. "She's grateful to you for keeping him. She wants to make sure it's all right if he stays—"

"Of course, it's all right," Archie said. "Of course, it is."

"She wants to come, but she can't do anything for her mother.

She might just make it worse, and she's in no state right now . . .
Sorry about this. About the timing of everything." O'Brien
paused abruptly, as if aware of needing to take care with his
words in front of Alice and Theo. "She said *he* would come
and get the boy, if it's inconvenient, but I think right now they
need to—"

"It's no trouble," Archie said quickly. "You tell her just to take
care of herself, not to—"

"My dad could come get me." Theo had turned around to
stare at O'Brien. His chest was heaving with emotion. "Or they
could come together. He could drive her. He always drives,
because she doesn't like to drive, she hates to drive, it makes her
nervous, so he—"

O'Brien looked down at him. "That's enough, son," he said
after a minute and turned back to Archie.

Theo's face turned red. Suddenly he made an indistinct noise
and tore away, running down the hall. He was carrying his toolbox, which he'd insisted on bringing, and he ran awkwardly, the
box banging against his thigh.

O'Brien passed his hand over his forehead. "Jesus Christ," he
said, and then, more vehemently, "Oh, for *Christ's* sake."

Archie reached down and took the flowers from Alice. "Go
and find him," he said to her. "He doesn't know where he is. I
don't want him getting lost."

O'Brien had turned away to look out the darkening window,
one arm folded across his middle, a hand over his mouth.

Archie put a hand on Alice's shoulder. "It's all right," he said
quietly. "I'll see you downstairs."

Alice looked at O'Brien's back. She didn't love O'Brien the
way she loved Helen, but she thought she had been fond of him;
he was usually funny and jokey, and she felt that they doted
equally on Helen, a fact that united them. But he had been

unkind to Theo just now; he had not even said hello to him. Alice knew she did not understand why O'Brien was angry with Theo, for it seemed to her that's what he was, but she had to acknowledge that Theo might have been truthful when he said that O'Brien didn't like even his own flesh and blood if it had been spoiled, as Theo said, by that drop of black blood. She turned away, without saying goodbye and without saying she was sorry, which she had planned to say. Right now, her sympathies were with Helen, not with O'Brien—with Helen in her deep and dangerous sleep, and with Theo.

On the way home from the hospital that night, rain began to fall and lightning crackled across the sky, illuminating the curving road ahead and the steep hillside of trees on their left in flashes of unearthly white light. They drove along beside the river, and Alice watched the water appear out of the darkness, turbulent and black, in the flickering bursts of lightning. Thunder crashed overhead; Alice felt the force of the concussion in her teeth. Archie drove at a crawling pace, the windshield wipers sluicing buckets of water from the glass, and at last he turned the car down the driveway. The house was in darkness. The power must have gone out.

Archie swore quietly inside as they felt their way through the kitchen in the dark. He knocked over a chair. "Boys?" he called. "James? Wallace?"

"In here, Arch," someone called. It sounded like Wally.

The boys were sitting in the living room playing cards. There were beer bottles and a couple of candles on the table. Wally had another cigar going and the air was heavy with smoke.

Archie stopped in the doorway, Alice beside him. He waved

his hand against the smoke. "It smells like a goddamn tavern in here. Anybody think to close the windows upstairs?" he asked.

"Got 'em." Alice saw James look up from his hand at the tone of Archie's voice, the rare anger there.

"How's Helen?" Harry asked.

"The same." Archie ran a hand over his forehead. "No one located a flashlight, I suppose."

Wally stood up and brought Archie a flashlight. "You're late getting back," he said. "I've already lost ten dollars to James."

Archie didn't say that they'd spent over an hour looking for Theo, who had been discovered finally up in a tree near where they'd parked the car. Alice knew Theo was in trouble for having sat up there on a branch, watching Alice and Archie looking for him up and down the street, calling his name. Finally, returning alone to the car because she didn't know where else to go, she had heard, coming from above her, a strange, birdlike warble, three treble notes repeated and then repeated again. When she looked up, she'd seen Theo's face, staring down at her, and she had felt a wave of relief. She had wondered irrelevantly how he'd managed to haul his toolbox up there beside him, because she could see it, too, wedged into a fork of a branch. She felt a surge of gratitude to Archie for not telling tales on Theo now.

"Have you got another flashlight?" he said to Wally instead. "Alice and Theo can take one upstairs with them, and I'll go look for the lantern. They need to get to bed."

"I'll go up with them." Wally flicked on his flashlight. Theo, caught in the beam, averted his face, cringing.

Upstairs, Wally made a game of traipsing around, escorting Alice and Theo back and forth to the bathroom to brush their teeth, helping Theo find a T-shirt and a change of underwear. When he left Theo alone in the bathroom with the flashlight propped up on the edge of the sink, Alice tugged on Wally's arm in the dark hallway. "He should sleep in with me again." She shivered a little. "He's kind of afraid of the dark."

"Okay. I don't see why not," Wally said.

In her dark bedroom, Alice turned on her side in bed and looked across to the other bed where Wally sat, legs crossed, waiting for Theo.

"You're leaving tomorrow, right?" she said.

"Yup."

When a flash of lightning illuminated the window for a moment, Wally emerged in the strange light in black and white like an old photograph, the beaked bridge of his nose a dark gash down the middle of his face, his eyes wide. Alice lifted her hands quickly and made her camera. She pretended to take a picture; she knew she had just missed the burst of blue light, but the effect of the afterimage hung there in the air a moment, like fireworks blazing against the sky and then going out.

"What are you doing?" Wally sounded amused. "Taking a pretend picture?"

"Nothing." She rolled over onto her back, putting her hands at her sides. She felt sticky and damp. "What's the matter with Theo's mom?"

She heard Wally shift on the bed, the protest of the old bedsprings. "I think," he said slowly, "that she's what they call depressed. Sad. Blue."

Alice thought about this. "What's she sad about?" she said finally.

"I'm not sure," Wally said. "That would be a complex question. There's a little marital difficulty, I think. It's like—" he paused, apparently thinking. "It's like being dead, when you're alive. There's medicine for it, but sometimes people have to go into the hospital."

"Is she in the hospital?"

"I think it's being discussed."

At that moment Alice saw the beam of Theo's flashlight bouncing over the walls in the hall.

Wally got up from the other bed. "Scoot over," he said and lay down next to Alice.

From downstairs she could hear the boys arguing over the card game, Tad's wild laugh, a babble of voices raised in complaint.

"You're glad to be leaving, aren't you," Alice whispered. Suddenly their world—with Helen so sick, and Theo's mother so sad, and O'Brien so sad and angry and mean—seemed bleak, a place one would long to escape.

"No. Not really. I'll miss you," Wally said. "I get sick of the twins, though. They get on my nerves. I get sick of James, too, because he's such a pompous asshole sometimes. Excuse me."

"I don't care," she said. She sighed.

Wally put out a hand and stroked her hair. "I get sick of everyone except you . . . you and Eli; you kind of can't get sick of Eli, you know?"

Theo's light came ricocheting into the room.

"Okay, pal?" Wally said.

Beside her, Alice felt Wally's voice, rumbling and deep. It seemed to reach inside her, more a sensation than a sound. He smelled like cigar smoke and under that something that was both sweet and sour, like molasses.

Theo climbed into bed, the light from his flashlight careening madly over the walls and ceiling.

"When will the lights come back on?" he said.

"You two are full of unanswerable questions," Wally said.

In the dark, Alice snuggled up against Wally. Theo being there with them had distracted her from the looming fact of the boys' departure, especially Wally's, but she felt it ahead of her now, like a tree fallen across the road. She wondered how Theo could stand being separated from his mother and father for so long. He hadn't even asked to call them on the telephone, which Archie surely would have let him do. Maybe, she thought, he was scared to call home, afraid of what he would find out if he called. Was his mother sad about being married to Theo's father, sad that white people, maybe even her own father, didn't like him because he was black?

"I can't get down," Theo had said from up in the tree at the hospital, and she had had to call Archie.

He had come over and stood beside her, looking up into the leafy darkness at Theo motionless on his branch. Archie had stepped under the tree and held up his arms. "Let one leg down," he had said to Theo. "You can step right into my hand here. No, wait a minute. Give me that box of yours first. There you go. Now come on, I've got you. I won't let you fall."

Alice had seen Archie's hand go around Theo's ankle and grip it firmly, his other hand going up to steady the boy at his waist as he came down. For a moment Archie had held Theo in his arms before letting his feet touch the ground, and Alice had felt a fierce gladness at seeing them together.

She brought her knees up to her chest under her nightgown and ducked her head into Wally's shoulder, burrowing against him. It had been a long day, she thought. Then she remembered *Monkey Man* and *Old Soldier's Beautiful Daughter* outside in the storm, the black disjointed pieces of *Monkey Man* hanging heavy and sorrowful, stiff as a soldier, his face shut up against the rain, and the flickering body of *Old Soldier's Beautiful Daughter,* leaning on the wind and reaching her insubstantial arms toward her silent companion.

EIGHT

WHEN SHE OPENED HER EYES, the room was full of hot, dusty sunlight. From outside she heard the boys' and Archie's voices, the sound of car doors opening and closing. She lay still for a moment, registering these sounds, and then, when she realized what they could mean, she bolted out of bed and to the window.

James and Wally stood talking with Archie beside the station wagon in the driveway, Archie's hand on the roof of the car. On the lawn, Tad and Harry pitched a tennis ball back and forth at each other. She could see only Eli's back where he was bent over the car's open hood, adjusting something inside. She ran from the room and downstairs.

Wally was wearing an ironed white shirt and blue jeans. His hair was slicked back from his forehead in an old-fashioned style that made him seem suddenly years older to Alice. He looked up as she came tearing out the kitchen door. She ran across the wet grass in her bare feet and jumped into his arms, wrapping both legs around his waist.

"That's my clean shirt you're getting grass all over," he said, holding her.

She put her cheek on his shoulder and squeezed her eyes shut.

The plans had been rearranged last night after she'd gone to sleep, Wally explained apologetically. Archie had decided that James would be allowed to keep the car for the summer after all, so James would take Wally to catch his flight this morning, continue on to spend two days visiting a girl at her family's lake house, and then go on to his internship in Montpelier. Alice would not make the trip to see Wally off at the airport, after all. In fact, she had almost missed their departure altogether.

"I'm sorry," Wally said into her ear. "Sorry, Alice."

"Here. Give her to me," James said, and Alice felt herself handed over. She did not open her eyes for the transfer. She pressed her face to James's neck, smelled the aftershave he liked and, underneath it, the kittenish smell she always associated with his skin.

"How would you like a tour of the governor's mansion this summer?" James said, squeezing her. "Arch says he'll come for a weekend and bring you with him."

She nodded mutely. The shock of having nearly missed them—would they really have left without saying goodbye to her? It appeared that they would have—made her speechless with grief and bewilderment. Did they think she would make a scene, she wondered, and so they'd been too cowardly to wake her up? She had never in her life made a scene; had they not noticed her dignity at their departure last fall, when she had been proud of herself for not weeping? For a moment she was ablaze with anger, and when she squeezed James around the neck she knew it was too hard, a mean, furious squeeze designed to hurt. Then she felt Wally lean in close to her in James's arms. He lifted her hair and kissed the back of her neck, laying his cheek against her skin for a moment; she slumped in James's arms, defeated, the heat of tears under her eyelids. Then James tightened his arms around her, one more hug preparatory to letting her go, and for a moment she resisted being released, clenching her legs around his waist.

But her feet never touched the ground. Tad and Harry swept in, plucking her shrieking with surprise from James and bearing her high over their heads, marching off over the grass with her held aloft as if she were a catch bagged on safari.

"Roll her," Harry said to Tad, and she screamed. They spun her once around, bounced her gently, spun her again. She flopped helplessly, her breath trapped in her chest, her nightgown billowing around her. The white shape of the house seemed to topple; the lawn and trees slid up into the sky.

"There are cats that weigh more than this," Tad said, jostling his end of her.

"She's nothing but a bug," Harry said.

She screamed as they rolled her again, and while she screamed and laughed hysterically, she heard the sound of the car's engine starting up, the tires on the gravel. When they set her down, dizzy and breathless, the car was gone and the driveway was empty. She staggered a little into Tad, who put his hand on her shoulder. Harry crouched down beside her, his hands steadying her. It had been a conspiracy, she knew, all of them moving together, moving so fast that she hadn't even seen it happen. It was like when she was younger and stood in the middle of the lawn, her hands over her eyes, counting to one hundred while the boys and their friends scattered to hide. When she took her hands away, the world would be empty. The leviathan of the woods had swallowed them all.

She sat obediently at the kitchen table while Elizabeth brought her oatmeal and sliced bananas in a blue bowl, toast cut nicely into triangles, a glass of orange juice. It was a thoughtful breakfast, Alice knew, the whole household, including Elizabeth, aware of how Wally and James's departure would affect her. She looked mutely at the toast, feeling suddenly, inexplicably, suffocated by its evidence of solicitude. Behind her at the sink Elizabeth busied herself with the dishes. Archie had kissed her goodbye outside and driven off to Frost. Tad and Harry had disappeared. Eli, too, had vanished. Alice had been left behind, she thought, to be fragile and touchy and unhappy.

She was not hungry, but she picked up her spoon and began to eat automatically. Elizabeth did not tolerate wasted food. Whatever you didn't finish at one meal would be taken away without comment but then invariably served to you at the next. Sometimes it was far worse the second time around, and Alice had learned to clear her plate. The table was still cluttered with the dishes from the boys' breakfast, the Blue Willow butter dish, a honey pot with the twisted silver spoon, the sugar bowl with the lid on which a small blushing shepherdess held her chipped skirts coyly in one hand, her crook in the other. Wally had stubbed out a cigarette in a little glass ashtray beside his plate.

She was halfway through the oatmeal when she remembered Theo. She hadn't even looked to see if he was still in bed when she'd gotten up. Alice pushed back her chair and took the stairs two at a time.

His bed was empty, his toolbox gone. The morning had been full of vanishings; she imagined the worst.

She came back downstairs and stood stricken in the doorway of the kitchen.

"He's *gone,*" she said to Elizabeth.

He had run away, she thought, or O'Brien had arranged for him to be taken home. Everything today had happened while she had been asleep, as if she had been under the influence of a potion that weighted her limbs and her mind, pinning her to the sheets like a stone. Ever since her birthday, she realized, she had overslept in the mornings, as if her own internal clock had stopped functioning. She felt betrayed by herself, disgusted by this new person who missed the early morning hours she had always loved, who slept through conversations when significant decisions were made. For a moment she remembered her vertiginous flying dream, when she had pitched through rents in the cloud toward the ground. She was afraid she would cry.

Elizabeth turned around from the sink in surprise. "Who? Your friend Mr. Crazy Theo?"

Alice nodded.

"No, he's not gone." Elizabeth turned back to her dishes. "He was just up early. He's down at the river, playing."

Alice sagged with relief against the door frame. How strange that she felt like crying again. She seemed to be crying all the time now, she thought.

"Go on, hurry up. Finish your breakfast," Elizabeth said. "Then you can go find him. Also, Archie talked to Mr. Fitzgerald this morning on the telephone. You two are supposed to go over there after lunch today."

Alice took the path into the woods that she had taken with Theo two days before when they had walked to the Fitzgeralds', reasoning that he knew that route and would have taken it again. Also, he'd been particularly pleased with one of the little islands, wanting to build a camp there. Alice ran through the trees toward the sound of the river, jumping over fallen branches. She saw Theo—or saw the red stripes of his T-shirt—as she came out of the woods onto the bank of the river. He was upstream perhaps a hundred yards away, down by the water's edge.

When she drew near he looked up at the sound of her clattering over the stones and stood up, waving excitedly. At his happy greeting, Alice felt the morning's grief slide away from her. The river ran along beside her, the air cool and clean. The sluggishness that had kept her in bed these last two mornings seemed to float free; she felt as if she were coming back to herself, flowing eagerly into her fingers and toes, pushing up like rising sap against the bones of her shoulders and the brace of her collarbone, all the way to the top of her head and then down against the soles of her feet with a boundless, glad energy. She ran toward Theo, leaping from rock to jagged rock and over the crevasses between boulders, her arms held out for balance.

They spent all morning by the river, laboriously carrying stones from the water's edge up to the grassy shelf of the island for the foundation of a fort. Theo had made astonishing progress on his own, industriously dragging fallen branches that would form the roof into a heap by the low beginning of the stone walls. Alice had never imagined such an ambitious fort. The island jutted into the river, siphoning off a narrow stream that ran down a curving rocky channel under the trees and divided the island from the shore. Theo had positioned the fort at the tip of the island, its bowed front facing the oncoming water with a good view upstream. He had left room for a door, an opening in the rocks spacious enough for the two of them to sit side by side, that looked upstream. Already the walls were eight inches high, the stones fitted neatly against one another.

While they hauled rocks up to the site, Theo explained how the fort would look when it was finished, with a central beam, and branches laid like an airplane's dramatic wing across the top to create a broad overhang, providing shelter from the rain for the wood supply he envisioned. "We'll need some kind of a skin for the door," he told her, panting, as they struggled up the bank with their rocks. "Do you know if there's a bear skin anywhere around here?"

Alice staggered behind him under the weight of a long flat rock. "A *what*?" she said. She was learning that, to Theo, the world was irrational, even absurd, a place both perilously flawed—where your own grandfather could fail to love you— and at the same time rich with possibility: rivers to be followed to the sea, strange bear skins just lying around for the taking, for instance. Whatever caution other children possessed, whatever caution she herself possessed, seemed shrinking and cowardly beside Theo's conviction, the tireless work of his imagination. Here he was, separated from his mother and father, abandoned by his grandparents to whom he had been entrusted, staying with strangers, without any of the familiars of home on which Alice knew she herself depended for comfort and strength. And yet he was awake early, launched out into the daylight, into work, into purpose and pleasure, busy and untroubled. She thought she knew enough to say that there weren't any bearskins around, but that certainty gave her a sorry feeling, not a superior one.

"If there's bear hunting here, a hunter might shoot a bear and skin it and just take the meat," Theo said. "If you don't take the meat, it's immoral to kill the bear just for fun. Bear skins smell terrible, though, and it's almost impossible to get the smell out, so sometimes people just leave them."

How did he know these things? Alice wondered. She reached the top of the bank and dropped the rock near the others. Her arms, from straining at their sockets while she was holding the rock, now wanted to float upward of their own accord, light and airy as feathers. It was true that there were bears sighted from time to time in Grange, she thought, mostly upending the garbage cans behind Rita and Barrett's store. She'd heard it speculated that the same bear came down from the mountain every now and then, remembering the rich leavings of the store's garbage.

"What do they smell like?" she asked. "Bear skins."

"I forget," Theo said, bending over to move her rock into place. "Really bad cat pee or something. I saw a show about it on TV." He stood back and appraised the fort. "This is going to be great," he said, and glanced over at her, expecting confirmation.

It was great, she thought, taking a deep breath and looking around. It was the best fort she had ever seen.

After lunch, they decided to walk to the Fitzgeralds' by way of the river and have another look at their fort. It was hard to leave it, but they were both eager to visit Kenneth, to see how he was after his fall and to thank him for the mobiles. They began walking upstream, hopping from rock to rock, talking about improvements to their camp.

At one point, Theo stopped, listening. Behind him, Alice almost collided with him and nearly lost her balance; she put her hands on his shoulders, steadying herself.

"Is that a waterfall?" he said. "That sounds just like a waterfall."

Alice teetered behind him on the rock. She clutched at Theo's shirt for a moment and righted herself. She felt a flicker of unease. "We're not allowed to go there," she said.

Theo turned around to regard her with interest. "How big is it?"

Alice knew she didn't know exactly how high the falls into Indian Love Call were. "As high as the roof maybe," she guessed, reluctant.

"Of your *house*?" Theo sounded impressed.

"They're dangerous. Archie says so," Alice said. She began to march off the rocks and scramble for a handhold up the bank. The river had already started to narrow here. The banks were higher, pitted with holes and twisted with tree roots. The water, with its happy conversational rills and ripples further downstream, sounded more urgent, deeper and faster.

"Why can't we go? We won't go *in* them," Theo said patiently, as if such an idea were idiotic anyway. "Let's just go *see* them."

Alice reached the top of the bank and turned around. The falls weren't far, she judged, though in the summer, with the trees in leaf, the sound was muffled. It was easier in winter to hear the water pouring down into the dark pool, easier to feel chilled by the powerful sound of it.

"C'mon," he said. "It won't hurt just to see them. Do you know how big Niagara Falls are? A woman went over them in a barrel. She was a teacher, and she went in a *dress*. She didn't even take her shoes off. I saw it on TV. She was perfectly fine."

Alice looked down at him. He teetered on a rock below her, holding out his arms for balance. "Oops!" he said. And then he clowned around a little, pretending he was falling in.

Alice turned away resolutely. "I'm leaving," she said.

After a minute, she heard him behind her, scrambling up the bank.

"Behold the conquering heroes." Kenneth greeted them with a salute from the terrace when they plowed through the tall grass toward him. He was seated in a chair drawn up before an old wooden easel that had been set up on the flagstones. The terrace's awning, a tattered and stained striped canvas, had been unrolled onto its rusty metal frame, casting an uneven shade. Kenneth wore a bandage circling his head, his face nearly the same deathly white as the gauze wrapping. Under the ripped awning, its scalloped edge torn loose in places and fluttering, Kenneth looked to Alice like a shipwreck survivor, beaten and exhausted.

"My camarilla," he said, and turned partway in his chair, tossing out his hand to indicate Alice and Theo, addressing someone seated behind him in the shade. Alice hadn't noticed her at first. With her black skin and black dress, the woman seemed to disappear into the shadows. When she opened her mouth and laughed, her body seemed to organize itself around the sound. Her hair was divided into dozens of braided rows tipped with black beads that clicked as she shook her head, smiling. She had a strong neck and open face, eyes like a doe. Her big hands were folded in the wide bowl of her lap. Alice stared at her.

The children climbed up the steps and stood shyly on the terrace in the presence of this visitor.

"I am resurrected," Kenneth said. He put down the long, thin piece of charcoal he had been holding and set it on the easel. "I understand it was you two who called in the guard and rescued me." He touched his shirtfront and looked up at Alice. "I think I remember a bird landing on my chest."

She remembered the feeling of Kenneth's heart under her hand, the weak longing of its beating beneath her fingers, and blushed.

He turned away abruptly. "Miss Sidonnie Roberts," he said. "Who is about to take her leave of us after valiant service."

Alice noticed then the suitcase just inside the French doors, the raincoat draped over it.

"Good afternoon," the woman named Sidonnie said softly. She was a mesmerizing color, the rich deep black of the carved ebony chess pieces set up on the board in Archie's study. Alice thought of the queen, with her roughly carved crown. Beside this woman, Theo's tawny skin looked sandy. How could both of them be called black? Alice wondered.

"And what have you been doing all this fine morning?" Kenneth said.

Theo, who had been hanging back by the edge of the terrace behind Alice, spoke up. "Building a fort, down by the river," he said. "Only we need an animal skin for the doorway."

Sidonnie laughed again.

Kenneth raised his eyebrows. He put his hand to his chin and seemed to be considering the problem. "It's not native, of course," he said. "But would a zebra skin do?"

A zebra skin! Alice looked at Theo, marveling.

"It's heavy," Kenneth cautioned. "You'd have to drag it away as though you'd slain it on the plain."

"That's okay," Theo said. "I can do it."

"You have a zebra skin?" Alice thought of the tiger skin stretched out on the floor of Archie's study. She felt sure that Archie would not consider contributing it to the cause of their fort in the woods. She wanted to clarify matters. "It would be for *outside,*" she said.

"Naturally." Kenneth's eyes seemed to close a little, and his face sagged. With an effort he opened his eyes again. "It seems an entirely fitting purpose. It's in the attic, I think, or somewhere . . ." He waved his hand at the house behind him.

Just then, a car's horn sounded from the street at the front of the house. Sidonnie got to her feet.

"Your ride," Kenneth said.

Sidonnie came forward. She bent down over Kenneth, dwarfing him in his chair, and embraced him. His arms, thin as a child's, came up across her back. For a moment they did not move, Kenneth's face hidden against Sidonnie's shoulder, her eyes closed. Alice looked away.

When Sidonnie stood up, her eyes were wet. "You take care of this man," she said. She looked at Theo for a moment, her eyes resting on him.

Theo came to stand beside Alice. He looked up at Sidonnie in a straightforward way, his manner courtly. "We will," he said.

Kenneth reached over to take Sidonnie's hand briefly. "*Lux mundi,*" he said. "Great light of the world, or something like that. You've been wonderful. Thank you, my love."

"I'm sorry," she said, looking down at him. "You know I am." She turned back to the house, but Theo darted ahead of her. "I'll get your suitcase," he said. He dragged it over the doorsill and heaved it along the stones. "I can get it," he said, when she stepped forward to help him.

At that moment, they heard the sound of footsteps in the room, and Miss Fitzgerald's voice. "Kenneth, the taxi's here," she said, but she stopped when she stepped outside and saw Alice and Theo.

Sidonnie leaned down and put her hand on the suitcase's handle, next to Theo's.

Miss Fitzgerald's own hand disappeared busily into her sleeve and extracted a tissue. "Well, Sidonnie," she said, not looking at her. "Thank you for your trouble."

Sidonnie smiled down at Theo. "You stay here and see if he needs anything," she said quietly. "I'll be all right." She picked up the suitcase and moved carefully into the house past Miss Fitzgerald, who stepped aside to let her go and then, after glancing uncertainly at Kenneth, who sat slumped in his chair, turned to follow her.

Kenneth tilted back his head, his eyes closed.

For a moment the three of them were quiet. Alice glanced curiously at the drawing propped up on the easel. It was only lines of black charcoal, the suggestion of the lawn and the trees behind in a scribbled dark mass like a thunderhead.

"Let me have your arms," Kenneth said after a moment, not opening his eyes. They drew close to him and he held out his hands. Alice staggered as he grasped her forearm and pushed himself from the chair, but Theo put a hand on his back and Kenneth steadied himself on his feet.

"A wonderful woman, Sidonnie Roberts," he said, his eyes still closed. "Let's go inside."

"Who will cook for you now?" Alice asked as they walked slowly inside, Kenneth leaning on their arms. He had opened his eyes, but his expression was pained. She felt indignant on his behalf. The strained coolness of Miss Fitzgerald's goodbye to Sidonnie, whom Kenneth clearly loved, had appalled her. Was it everywhere, she wondered, this secret hatred inside people she thought she had known? She thought of Archie, holding Theo in his arms under the tree outside the hospital the night before. Archie didn't feel that way about black people, she thought.

They helped Kenneth to the settee where he settled back against the cushions. "Hope has been feeding herself all these years," he said. "And she's dying to feed me now."

Alice thought about the crowded rooms in the house. She imagined the kitchen, a welter of dishes and boxes and teetering pyramids of cans. In her own house, the kitchen with its friendly fireplace and long table, its polished wood floor and bowls of fruit, the candlesticks and vases of flowers and clock on the mantelpiece, the braided cushions on the chairs, the wallpaper of tiny blue windmills, was her favorite room. "Maybe Elizabeth could cook for you," she said. "She's a good cook. We could bring you supper every night."

Kenneth waved away her offer. "Don't worry," he said. "Really, Alice. Don't worry. What I eat is the least of my concerns." He took a deep breath, adjusted himself against the cushions again. "Now," he said, looking up at them from under his drooping eyelids. "I used to play in those woods when I was your age. Tell me everything about your fort."

Theo described it in detail, its provenance on the island, its stones, his plans for the construction of the roof. He sat down on the floor beside the settee. He wanted to build a landing pier out into the river, he said, and an outdoor fireplace. When they got a canoe, he told Kenneth, they could draw it up on the far side of the island onto the tiny half-moon beach. They would need a telescope, too. "Do you have a piece of paper?" he asked abruptly.

Kenneth pointed to a box on the floor. "In there," he said. "Help yourself." He lay back again, smiling faintly.

Theo bent over the paper, busily drawing. Inside the fort, he said, he imagined hammocks strung from the beams, a stone floor, shades made of woven branches for the windows that would roll down on a cord.

Kenneth asked questions, lying with his eyes closed and nodding from time to time.

"Let me see your drawing," he said finally, and Theo passed it up to him.

Kenneth sat up and looked at the paper, but he handed it back to Theo after a moment, and Alice thought that perhaps he had not been able to see it clearly.

"Magnificent," he said. "I'll find out what happened to the zebra. It will be a furbelow for your fort." He smiled. "*Furbelow:* an ornament, like a flounce or a ruffle on a dress. Spelled exactly as it sounds. Fur-below."

"Thank you for the mobiles," Alice said suddenly, remembering them and feeling ashamed that they had not said thank you before, that she could not think of the words to express their pleasure at the gift, their understanding of its great value.

He reached out and she came near, giving him her hand.

"I miss being outdoors, in the woods," he said. After a moment, with more conviction in his voice, he resumed. "But I'll be on my feet again, wouldn't you say? Only, this fall has been a bit of setback." He let go of Alice's hand and reached up gingerly to touch the bandage on his head.

Alice thought of what Archie had told her about Kenneth climbing mountains and looking down on the clouds, the shifting blue and white scaffolding of vapor beneath him, the valleys below. He could not climb a mountain now, she thought, and for a moment she felt inside herself the grief of that loss for him, a prisoner in this house. She was suddenly aware of the open doors behind her, the woods at the edge of the lawn, and beyond that the river twisting away invisibly toward the sea. It came to her with a shock that she hadn't been anywhere yet, that every road was open to her. Her life, she thought, had barely even begun.

"Where were we?" Kenneth said abruptly. "In the Lewis and Clark. They were presenting the Missouri Indians with medals for their chiefs, and whiskey and gunpowder."

"And the lost horses had come back," Theo said, stretching out on the floor as he had done the day before, his arms behind his head.

Alice sat down at the table and opened the book. The party had halted, waiting for the return of two men who had been sent off as scouts to look for Indians. Many Indian villages had been decimated by smallpox, Clark wrote. *I am told when this fatal malady was among them they Carried their frenzy to verry extraordinary length,*" Alice began reading, *"not only of burning their Village, but they put their wives & children to Death with a view of their all going together to some better Countrey. They Burry their Dead on the top of high hills and rais Mounds on the top of them."*

She was interrupted—snow had fallen on the explorers early in October, and the banks of the river were often lined with Indians come to view the curious party—when the door opened and Miss Fitzgerald came in with a tray. She did not seem to notice that Alice was reading aloud and set the tray down on the table with a clatter. She bore a tall glass of something foamy and yellow over to Kenneth on the settee. "Eggnog," she said. "Mother used to give us this. Remember?"

He took it from her clumsily—Alice wondered whether he had been asleep. "Rum," he said indistinctly, and took a careful sip. He cleared his throat. "Isn't that what's added to eggnog?"

"Oh, *Kenneth,*" she said, as if he'd been teasing her.

She wants to do it all for him, everything by herself, Alice thought, with a flash of understanding. She wants to be in charge. That's why she wasn't sorry to see Sidonnie leave.

"And here's a plate of cookies for the children," Miss Fitzgerald said. She didn't look at Alice or Theo. She took the plate off the tray and put it on the table, like setting a saucer of milk on the floor for cats. She stood at the table for a moment, gazing around the room, her eyes following the slowly revolving shapes of the mobile that Alice and Theo had hung.

They heard the sound of the lawn mower starting up outside. Alice turned to look out the French doors. Eli, wearing an old white tennis hat, came into sight, leaning over the mower and forcing it through the tall grass. The sun was lower in the sky now, and the light outside had softened. She noticed how the trees at the edge of the lawn stood together in a dense mass of dark green, just as Kenneth had rendered them in his charcoal drawing, a single solid shape against the sky.

"The industrious MacCauleys," Kenneth said. "The heroic

twins were here this morning, Alice, hacking away at the rock of Gibralter." He took a sip of the eggnog. "Do you think your father would simply adopt us? How could we earn our keep at the MacCauleys' house, Hope? Do you think we seem pitiful enough to be adopted?"

Alice was embarrassed that he should refer to the shameful state of the house in his sister's presence, but Miss Fitzgerald only stood quietly, her hands hanging limply at her sides, watching Eli outside as if she'd never seen a lawn mower before. Alice thought of all the times Miss Fitzgerald had come to the MacCauleys' house, her face bunched up under its headscarf, some matter of civic interest on her mind, a clipboard and a pen in her hand. How strange it was to discover that someone so apparently purposeful and in command should be simultaneously, privately, so helpless.

On their way home, Alice told Theo what Archie had said about Kenneth climbing mountains, about his having adventures and exploring the world.

"Now he's cooped up in that house with *her*," Theo said. He shuddered. "She is so weird. Why doesn't she ever say anything to us? She acts like we're not even there, like we're not even a person."

Alice noted that he had referred to them collectively as a single person. She was oddly pleased, even if it was just a syntactical error. "And he's *sick,* too," Alice said, rising to Theo's indignation. She heard the outrage in her voice. It seemed so unfair. Why did people have to get sick? A bell-shaped cloud of gnats hovered in the road before them. Alice waved her hands wildly in front of her face to disperse them. The late afternoon sun hung ahead of them, burning with a gold light under the trees' lowest branches, as if the road were a stage in a dusky theater, its upper reaches in darkness.

"I don't think he can see very much," Theo said. "But he can still walk around if he has his cane. He could get out if he had a guide dog." He spoke as if he were considering something. He took aim and kicked at a rock by the side of the road, sending it sailing into the weeds, and squinted after it.

They walked along in silence. When they came to the corner, Alice saw the mother of one of her friends from school, Mrs. Kiplinger, out in her side yard taking in laundry from the line. When she saw the children she stopped and waved. "Hello, Alice!"

"Hi," Alice said. She didn't want to stop. Mrs. Kiplinger was one of the mothers Alice thought felt sorry for her. She made a fuss over her, asking if she was hungry, as if no one ever thought of food in the motherless MacCauley house. She was always wearing some kind of tracksuit or athletic gear, her blond hair twisted into a knot at the back of her head. Sometimes Alice was invited to play with Sarah Kiplinger, who was in her class at school, but in general Alice preferred the games of boys to the dolls and tea parties most girls her age enjoyed. Still, girls weren't invited to play at boys' houses very often.

"We just took Sarah to summer camp this weekend," Mrs. Kiplinger said, bouncing over to the picket fence in her fancy sneakers, the basket of laundry under her arm. "I'm sure she'll send you a pretty postcard."

"That'll be nice." Alice nodded encouragingly, as if she'd been longing for a postcard from Sarah Kiplinger, away at summer camp.

"Who's your little friend?" Mrs. Kiplinger said brightly, looking Theo up and down.

"This is Theo," Alice said. "He's the O'Briens' grandson."

Mrs. Kiplinger's expression changed, and Alice saw an unguarded, almost greedy curiosity come over her face. Did everyone in Grange know that Theo's mother had married a black man? Alice wondered. And why did it seem to matter so much?

"Ohhh," Mrs. Kiplinger said, drawing out the vowel, her tone full of comprehension. She stared at Theo. "Oh, he *is*. Well, I know your grandmother, Theo. She's a lovely person."

Alice nodded again, more enthusiastic confirmation of Mrs. Kiplinger's many opinions: Picture postcards were nice. Helen O'Brien was nice. "Well, we better be going," she said. She could feel Theo beside her, a silent, glowering presence.

They trudged down the road toward home. Alice wanted to apologize for Mrs. Kiplinger, for her proprietary knowingness about Theo, for every adult's way of seeming to know more about you than you knew about yourself, but she wasn't sure what to say. Theo marched along next to her, looking at the ground. After a little while, he lifted his chin and sighed.

"I'm hungry," he said.

"Me, too," Alice said, realizing that he had identified exactly what she had been feeling. It was as if wind were gusting through emptiness inside her. She sighed, remembering that Wally and James would not be there when they got home. Maybe the twins wouldn't even be there for dinner, or Eli, or her father. This past school year, when she was alone for dinner, Archie being occupied with something at Frost, Elizabeth would make Alice scrambled eggs or baked beans on toast for supper. Elizabeth herself, if she was staying late because Archie wouldn't be home until after Alice's bedtime, ate different food she cooked for herself, strange-smelling concoctions mixed with rice, which she ate with her fingers. Once, Alice had asked if she could taste what Elizabeth was eating, and Elizabeth had put a little spoonful on a saucer for her.

"This is what Vietnamese babies eat," she had said to Alice. "Very good."

Alice had tried a little, but she hadn't liked the taste or the smell, and she had been unable to conceal her dislike, looking up apologetically at Elizabeth with watering eyes.

Elizabeth had laughed. "You're not a little Vietnamese baby, Alice," she had said. "Have to grow up with it."

Alice had smiled politely, not wanting to hurt Elizabeth's feelings, but she had felt strangely unfit, as if it were she who was the stranger in this country, not Elizabeth, who had continued to eat with a sure, knowing pleasure. After dinner that night, Elizabeth fixed them both bowls of orange sherbert and took Alice on her lap at the table, even though Alice was too big for lap sitting. "Never mind, never mind," she had said, holding her cheek to Alice's. "It doesn't matter that you are not Vietnamese baby."

They continued along the road, feet dragging. Lights were beginning to come on in the houses they passed. Here and there through the windows Alice could see the blue light of television sets being turned on.

"What do you eat for dinner at home?" she asked suddenly.

"Takeout," Theo said, shrugging. "Thai. Chinese. Indian. Mexican. Ethiopian."

Alice had never had Thai food or Indian food, let alone Ethiopian. "Doesn't your mom cook?" she said. She thought all mothers cooked.

"Yeah, she cooks." Theo didn't say anything else for a minute.

"We like takeout, though," he said finally. "In New York you can get anything you want to eat. I like dim sum."

Alice didn't know what dim sum was. She sensed that Theo's mother didn't really cook. Maybe it was because of her sickness, what Wally had called her being "blue" and depressed. She wanted to ask Theo about this, but she didn't know how to phrase the question.

"Your mom's dead, right?" Theo said.

Alice said, "She died when I was a baby. I don't remember her."

Theo nodded, as if something in his own experience compared to this, and he was familiar with the terrain. He did not say he was sorry the way adults did when they learned Alice's mother had died. Usually when children found out Alice didn't have a mother, they didn't say anything; they just stared at her as if she had described her mother's death for them in horrifying detail. Theo didn't seem impressed, though. He just walked along beside her.

Alice, feeling something behind her suddenly, glanced back and saw that their shadows trailed behind them, two ragged giants with flapping coattails and miniature heads, swaying along the street. She nudged Theo, who turned to look over his shoulder. He lifted his arms, and shadow arms flew out from the giant's side, two long sticks flapping into the darkness of the trees on the side of the road. It was a helpless gesture, as if the figure had suddenly taken fright and tried to lift off from the ground but had failed, its lead feet tied to the earth. Theo jumped, both feet off the ground, as if he were feeling what Alice felt, which was that she wanted to break free of this black, mournful figure attached to her ankles, to shake it away from her, leaving a paper man folded in accordion pleats on the road, lifeless as dust, like Peter

Pan's silken shadow lying over Wendy's knees while she searched for a needle and thread.

Alice had read in the newspaper about the tidal wave that had engulfed the beaches in Thailand this past winter. The animals had known something bad was coming, and goats and cows and dogs had tried to break free of their chains or their pastures and make for the hills, knocking down fences and wildly tearing stakes from the ground. Alice had imagined the animals streaming toward the mountains, running away from the still invisible tidal wave gathering out in the sea. One man, who finally understood what it meant when the animals started to run away, had gathered up his children and his wife and tried to hurry with them through the crowded streets, but the wave had overtaken them before he could get far enough away. He had survived, but his wife and his children had been torn from him in the wave that had crashed over their heads, and he had lost them in the swirling waters. Ever since then, Alice had tried to pay attention to Lorenzo's lazy meanderings around the yard, but she never sensed any urgency in his movements. Consulting her atlas, she had determined that there was no way a tidal wave could reach them in Vermont, but she had been sickened at the thought of the people trying to run, dragged down by their own weight, their own inadequate human instincts, their own fear . . . even by the people they loved.

She jumped, too, like Theo, and her shadow stayed right behind her, pitifully attached to her feet.

"Let's run," Theo said, flapping his arms, and he caught Alice's hand.

They ran the rest of the way home, the sun burning red in the sky ahead of them.

NINE

ALICE AND THEO were in the kitchen making ice cream sundaes on a Friday night two weeks later, when Archie came in the back door. Tad and Harry had left the week before to go back to Frost; Eli was out in the barn with his friend Sam, working on Sam's old black Saab, a car for which Theo had expressed fervent admiration, though he had been banned from the barn for talking too much while Eli and Sam tried to puzzle through a problem with the car's transmission. Elizabeth, who usually stayed until Archie arrived home from Frost, even if he was late, as he was this evening, had left early to go visit a niece who had just given birth to twins. She had been working all day in order to bring food to the new family, a succession of salty-smelling Vietnamese dishes and a pineapple studded with gumdrops on toothpicks. Alice, witnessing the hectic level of Elizabeth's preparations, had suffered a moment of worry that the arrival of the infant twins might mean that Elizabeth herself would leave the MacCauleys in order to help her niece instead. She had been relieved when Elizabeth, banging pots on the stove, had said that she was glad it wasn't going to be her, looking after those twin babies. "One time was enough for me," Elizabeth told Alice. "Your bad brothers, they wore me out. Lucky for you, you were a good baby."

Archie hung his jacket over the back of one of the chairs in the kitchen and sat down at the table, glancing at the stack of mail and the evening paper from Brattleboro folded in half by his place.

"Do you want a banana split, Arch?" Theo said, waving the ice cream scoop. "I can make you a humongous one."

It pleased Alice that Theo had developed an obvious affection for Archie. He spoke to him as if to a familiar his own age, using a jocular form of address that sounded to Alice as if it were an unconscious imitation of Archie's own faintly ironic manner of speaking to Theo. She thought that Archie's restraint on the night Theo had climbed into the tree at the hospital had elevated Archie in Theo's mind. Probably Theo had expected a punishment, and she knew herself that sometimes Archie's polite refusal to mention an obvious transgression, as if he were carefully allowing you to save face, had the effect of making you especially sorry for whatever you had done and especially grateful to him for his tact. Once Alice had cut off a length of the silky fringe from the drapes in the dining room to use as trimming for one of the fairy houses she built in shoe boxes. She knew that Elizabeth, who had discovered the hacked-up curtain, had reported this to Archie, but Archie had been only rather quiet and tender with Alice when he had come home that evening, as if aware of the enormity of her guilt, the possibility that one more ounce of disapprobation would have been overwhelming.

"Thank you, Theo, but I try to avoid ice cream until I've had my dinner," Archie said. "I assume Elizabeth fed you before she left?"

"I'll bring you a plate," Alice said. "It was meat loaf."

"You're lucky you didn't get some of that ooo-wong-tang or

whatever it was she made," Theo said gaily. "It smelled like a dead fish."

Theo's spirits had been restored after a funny dip earlier that evening. A dank summer rain had begun to fall around five p.m., forcing Alice and Theo inside. Theo had wandered around rest-lessly for a while and then finally settled on sliding down the fire-man's pole on the porch again and again, sometimes headfirst, muttering under his breath as if he were narrating a story to him-self. "You," he said, pointing to an invisible spot on the floor. "Take a brigade and protect us from the flank."

Alice, lying on her stomach on the upstairs porch with her chin on her folded arms, had watched Theo below her through the round hole in the floor. She concluded that in the game Theo was playing, he had the starring role as the beleaguered general. Hands laced behind his back, head down, he paced back and forth as if considering his strategic options. Alice had wanted to join in the game, but Theo was playing with such concentrated, even unhappy intensity that he took no notice of her when she sat up and dangled her legs through the hole, knocking her heels noisily against the fireman's pole. It was the first time he had excluded her from something, and after a while she had drifted away, bored and lonely.

When Theo grew tired of his game, he had come looking for her. She was stretched out in retreat on Wally's bed reading *Robert, the Quail,* which she'd already read once before. She ignored him when he first came into the room, but after a minute or two of him aimlessly clinking the pennies in the little bowl on Wally's bureau, she put down her book and turned around.

He was flushed, and the hair on his forehead was damp. "Alice," he said, as if he hadn't heard her. "My brain is going around and around." He looked troubled.

"What do you mean?" She sat up on the bed.

He shook his head, ran his hand back and forth over his hair. "It feels like I'm thinking too hard," he said. "Feels like I'm going to pop a cork. Blow a gasket."

"Maybe you shouldn't go upside-down on the fireman's pole," Alice said, but Theo shook his head. "That's not it," he said. "Being upside down is *good* for me."

A moment later, Elizabeth called them to come downstairs for supper before she left. Theo hadn't said much during the meal, but his spirits had seemed to revive as he put away a plate of meat loaf and three glasses of milk. "I've been thinking about Kenneth," he told her, as if the nature of the thoughts that had been circling him all afternoon, running at his heels like wolves, had finally become clear to him.

"Thinking what?" she had asked.

He had shaken his head. "Not sure. Just thinking," he said, but he looked less troubled somehow, less fatigued, as if the thoughts—whatever they were—gave him pleasure rather than hectoring him for solutions.

Archie got up now to fetch a bottle of red wine from the sideboard, uncorked it, and poured himself a glass, sitting back down at the table with a sigh and peering over his glasses at the plate Alice put before him, two thick slices of meat loaf, a heap of peppery succotash, mashed potatoes. In the fridge, Alice found a jar of the corn relish Archie liked and brought it to the table.

Archie ate while Alice and Theo built their sundaes and debated the merits of adding the leftover gumdrops. Finally they brought their bowls to the table. Theo scooted into the chair next to Archie and looked interestedly at the letters by his plate.

"They're moving your grandmother into another wing at the hospital, Theo," Archie said. He stood up to pour a second glass of wine and returned to his chair. "I spoke with your grandfather today."

"Does that mean she's getting better?" Alice said.

Archie hesitated. Finally, he said, "It can take a long time to recover from a stroke."

Theo licked his spoon. "Having a stroke is like getting hit by lightning," he said to Alice. "It fries your system."

Alice saw Archie stop, his wineglass halfway to his mouth, and regard Theo. "That's a very vivid way of putting it," he said after a long moment.

Helen's state had improved little since the night nearly three weeks before when she had fallen to the floor in her own kitchen, Theo standing helplessly in the room while O'Brien cradled Helen in his arms and shouted into the telephone. She could not speak, or chew her food, or stand up. She had a little use of her right hand, though she was, in fact, left-handed, like Alice herself, and she could write a few shaky phrases. The thought of Helen so incapacitated made Alice feel sick to her stomach. O'Brien would not let any of the MacCauleys see her, though one evening, Alice knew, Archie had simply forced his way into her room over O'Brien's protests that Helen would not want to be seen in such a state, to bring flowers to her bedside and kiss her cheek and hold her hand. O'Brien was hardly ever home since Helen's stroke, but Archie had dispatched Eli to keep the grass mowed, and Elizabeth had gone over one morning to clean out the refrigerator and do some laundry, and she had set Alice and Theo to vacuuming and dusting. Theo had run the vacuum cleaner at top speed through the house, racing behind it as though it were a runaway stallion, and when it was his turn with the feather duster, he had spent most of the time sneaking up on Alice and tickling her with it. Alice, who did not in general much like housework, had spent much of the morning laughing. Like most things, even cleaning was more fun with Theo around.

Theo did not seem dismayed by or even interested in his

grandmother's condition, and he expressed no desire to see O'Brien, which Alice felt, sadly, she understood. She did not completely understand, however, Theo's silence about his parents and his life with them in New York, unless it were just as Wally had said, that Theo's mother was depressed and his parents' marriage was falling apart and it was all too horrible for Theo to think about. Theo's mother had telephoned one evening, and when Archie had called Theo to the phone, Theo had not resisted being summoned. Yet, nor had he seemed especially happy. He and Alice had been playing Monopoly on the floor in the dining room after dinner, and when Archie came to door and said, "Theo? It's your mother on the phone for you," Alice had seen Theo look up, surprised. For a moment his face had opened with relief, but then just as quickly it had shut back down again, blank as a stone.

Curiosity overwhelming her, Alice had followed Theo and lurked at the end of the hall, listening.

Between silences, Theo had answered in a sluggish stream of monosyllables: "Yes. No. Yes. Uh-huh."

Alice had watched him scratch violently at his scalp. Then he had just stared at the floor, kicking gently at the leg of the telephone bench as he listened to his mother telling him something. "Okay," he said at last. "Uh-huh. Okay. 'Bye."

When he hung up, he put down the phone as if finally releasing something unpleasant from his grasp.

Together, he and Alice walked back to their game in the dining room.

"Do you want Boardwalk?" Alice said, reaching for something that would make him happy. He had won Park Place early on in the game and been outraged when Alice landed on Boardwalk a few turns later and promptly bought it. "I'll trade you Boardwalk for your railroads," she said.

He glanced at her suspiciously.

"The railroads and two hundred dollars," she said, not wanting her offer to sound too much like charity.

"Okay," he said, shrugging.

But somehow, she sensed, his heart wasn't really in it anymore.

It seemed to Alice that Theo had fallen into their lives as if out of the ether, with no cords binding him to anyplace else and no end in sight to his stay with them. His suitcase had remained in the guest room, but he slept every night in the spare twin bed in Alice's room, and Alice was aware, every time she entered her room, of the new smell of him there, lingering in the sheets. He had so completely filled Alice's attention that she had hardly noticed Tad and Harry's departure for Frost.

One night, Alice, who had come downstairs to say good night to Archie in his study, had asked her father how long Theo would stay with them.

"A little while longer," Archie said.

Alice had crossed the room and stroked the tiger skin with her bare foot. "Is it because his mother is sad?" she asked.

Archie had looked up at her over the tops of his glasses. "Has Theo spoken to you about his parents?"

The way he phrased it made it sound that, by confiding to Alice, Theo would have violated his parents' privacy, shown himself to be disloyal, or at least unreliable, in some way.

"No," Alice said. "Wally told me. But even if his mom is sad, don't his parents want him? Why are they leaving him here so long?"

Archie, who had been staring at his computer, turned back to the lighted screen as if the answer to Alice's question might appear there, like the enigmatic replies that floated up into Alice's Magic 8-Ball.

Alice was aware of being alone, without Theo beside her. She'd left him upstairs, hanging upside down off the bed and reading; he seemed to prefer this position for reading, saying it was easier somehow. Alice imagined the inside of Theo's head like a loose collection of nuts and bolts and wheels and cogs—like the contents of his toolbox, in fact—that somehow fell magically into place when he was upside down.

"Don't they miss him?" she repeated now.

"I'm sure they do," Archie said.

"Well, then why—"

"Sometimes, Alice—" Archie began, interrupting her. But then he stopped.

Alice felt the hair rise on her arms. Archie's silence, she understood, was the silence of someone who is too tired to answer an important question, someone whose experience in the world has finally overwhelmed his intentions to be a good parent, a parent who will answer his child's questions. It was also the silence of someone who believes that no answer he can provide will be understood. Alice was suddenly enraged.

"I'm not a baby," she shouted. She stamped her foot. "I'm not a baby, Archie. Tell me! What is wrong? Why doesn't anyone come to get him? Why don't they call here more often and talk to him? Doesn't anyone *love* him?"

Archie swung away from his computer screen toward her. "Alice," he began, and Alice saw with horror that she had scored some sort of winning point, achieved a terrible advantage. He did not know what to say. He had no answer for her.

She looked away from him, heat suffusing her neck and cheeks, prickling under her arms. The space inside her chest seemed to have become very small and tight, like a keyhole. On the floor, the head of the tiger faced her, his glass eyes fixed in an eerie stare. What a horrible thing to do, she thought suddenly, to have killed this beautiful, wild, mysterious creature and turned him into a rug to step on with your smelly feet. She closed her eyes for a moment. How could nobody love Theo, she thought, and the anguish of this possibility felt like a fist struck hard into her sternum, taking away her breath. Somebody, she thought, *had* to love him. She remembered James's exasperation with Theo the morning the mobiles had arrived from Kenneth, how he had snapped at Theo, when Theo was only trying to help. She remembered the twins teasing him about his toolbox. Even Eli had kicked him out of the garage, when all he wanted to do was watch them working on the car. Theo had only brought two T-shirts with him, she thought, and one pair of shorts, and only two pairs of underwear, but he'd packed, inexplicably, fifteen pairs of old man's black socks and a grown-up's belt long enough for a fat man. Alice knew what it was to be taken care of, and she knew that no one—at least right now and maybe not ever—was taking care of this boy.

She opened her eyes again. Archie was leaning back in his chair, watching her.

"I——" she began, and then she caught herself in horror. *I hate you,* she had been about to say. But she did not hate her father, she thought, and in her grief and remorse she pitched herself into his lap, sobbing. "I can't stand it," she wept, even while in her head she thought, with a curious cold detachment: *what* can't I stand?

Kenneth had taught them two words the other day, *stygian* and *halcyon,* which were almost like opposites of each other, she thought, one of them like the night and the other like the sun. What she felt now was the slow-moving, inexorable tug of something stygian, something as dark and perilous as the River Styx, the boatman Charon's grim face flickering in the mist. Recently the paper grocery bags at the store had been imprinted with the photographs and descriptions of missing children. Alice, reading the text on the bags as Elizabeth's groceries were packed up, had noticed that some of the children appeared to have been stolen by one of their own parents. Smiling little Anita from Sykesville, Maryland, missing her front teeth and wearing a dress with a wide lace collar, had disappeared in the company of her father, who was said to be armed and dangerous. This was part of that stygian darkness, too. As was the tidal wave in Thailand, and the tornado that came down in *The Wizard of Oz* and swept Dorothy up to Oz . . . and yet Alice had been disappointed at the end of that movie. Kansas was so dull, so plain, compared to the Technicolor landscape of Oz. Who would want to be *there*? And no one in Kansas believed anything Dorothy said.

Suddenly her head had begun to hurt.

She felt Archie's hands stroking her hair. Alice raised her face.

Archie gazed down at her. And then quietly, he said, *"Come away, come away, death, And in sad cypress let me be laid; Fly away, fly away, breath; I am slain by a fair cruel maid."* He smiled sadly. "You've no idea, Alice," he said, "how much I would—" He stopped. "I am sure Theo's parents love him," he finished. "It's just a difficult time for them, in their marriage, and his mother is going through a rough patch, emotionally, and . . ." He trailed off.

Alice got off his lap and stood up with cold dignity. She wiped her hand across her face. She was not comforted, but the sense that she did not know what she was saying, and that in the extremity of her feelings might say something unspeakable, had gone away; the danger had passed. What would happen to Theo? she thought.

"He's so smart," she said to Archie, as if pleading Theo's case. "He knows about so many things."

Archie nodded, as if he agreed. Then he leaned forward and took her hands for a moment, holding them in his own. "Try not to worry about things so much, Alice," he said. "I hate to see you worrying. You're just a child." Her gave her hands a last little shake and then let go.

Alice nodded, but it was only politeness, for she could not manage real relief in the face of this final offense. She was just beginning to discover, she thought, how very much there was to worry about.

That night, Alice and Theo had made a tent city in her bedroom by spreading sheets over the gap between the beds, and they slept side by side on pillows on the floor in the cool, dark cavern beneath the sheet. Theo's presence beside her, the smell of his bare skin and the warm exhalation of his breath, had filled Alice with sympathy and with contentment. It came to her that he smelled like the inside of the silky cloth pocket of her winter coat. She liked smelling coat pockets. Archie's were full of the scents of ink and Pep-O-Mint Life Savers, Wally's of tobacco, a smell she did not dislike, though she disapproved of the habit. The pockets of Eli's hunting jacket with the corduroy collar smelled of dirt and something chemical, like gasoline. That Theo's smell reminded her of something of her own gave her a secret thrill, as if he and she were aligned in an important way. Waking once during the night to find her head butted into his ribs and his leg flung over her own, she had taken in the smell of him. Sleepily, in a drowse of contentment and pleasure at his proximity, the soft darkness of the room, the sheet floating above them like the band of the Milky Way, she had turned her face to his warm skin, breathing him in and burrowing down beside him into the pillows. Sometimes, when they sat on the bank of the river by their fort and stared upstream, he tossed his arm around her shoulders as he talked, the way a pirate might embrace a mate, pointing out the ships on the horizon, the gold and silver weighted in their holds, the good fortune that would soon be theirs.

He never spoke about his parents. Alice was curious about them and suspicious about what she saw as their neglect of their boy, and she was certainly interested in Theo's life in New York City. But he offered her very few details, and she did not know how to ask him about his mother and her mysterious, sad condition, or his black father, or his parents' falling-apart marriage, the thing that had caused them to abandon Theo. Most of what Theo reported to know seemed to have come from television. When she asked him what his father did, he said once that he was a musician and another time that he was an agent, whatever that was, and another time that he owned a nightclub with a partner. She asked him what his mother did and he shrugged. "I don't know," he said, as if the question didn't interest him.

Archie had asked them to draw pictures that he would take to the hospital for Helen's room. Theo had not objected to this, and one evening they had worked across from each other at the planter's desk in the alcove of the living room, colored pencils in a coffee can and a box of watercolor paints and a glass of cloudy water between them. Theo executed a painting so extravagantly detailed and complete that Alice felt her careful watercolor of a still life of flowers in a vase was embarrassing. He had painted their fort from a vantage upriver on the opposite bank, though he had never stood there, of course, the river being too wide and deep at that point to cross.

"How did you know it would look like that?" Alice said, leaning over the desk on her elbows to marvel at the picture.

Theo, bent over so close to the paper, his nose almost touched it, just shrugged. "I don't know," he said. "I just did."

• • •

They had spent every morning over the past two weeks playing down by the river, and every afternoon at the Fitzgeralds', where Alice read aloud to Kenneth and Theo, Kenneth lying on the settee, and Theo stretched out in his accustomed position on the floor. They never went to the front door anymore, but always came up the steps to the terrace and the French doors opening onto Kenneth's room. One day they had crossed the flagstones but stopped at the open doors, horrified, at the sight of Kenneth, sitting bent over on the settee and retching into a bowl held on his lap by his sister, who had her arm around his shoulders. Miss Fitzgerald had straightened up and turned around as if she had sensed them there, and Alice and Theo had backed away hurriedly. Later that evening they had taken bicycles and gone back to the house, leaving the bicycles by the fence under a shower of blue hydrangea, and crept through the shadows across the lawn to the terrace. The room had been dark, but the doors were open, a fan inside the room blowing the curtain through the open doorway. *Get well soon, Kenneth!* they had printed in fancy letters on a piece of Archie's shirt cardboard, each of them doing alternating letters, and they had pushed this over the doorsill and then dashed back to the street.

Kenneth's left eye had been taped to his brow again, and his other eyelid drooped and sometimes fell closed. Alice could not get used to the sight of his face, the water seeping from his open eye and slipping down his cheek like tears. Where the eye had once seemed malevolent to her, though, it now appeared to be staring out at the world with an almost panicked entreaty, as if it were casting around helplessly for somewhere to alight and rest. Sometimes, while she was reading, she looked up to find it fixed on her in speechless longing. At these moments she felt the familiar flush creep up her neck and cheeks, but it was her own help-lessness she was aware of as much as Kenneth's, her and Theo's failure to arrest the speed of Kenneth's decline, to disarm the thing that was weakening him, the thing that had driven him back to Grange, to this house, to his boyhood memories, to his sister and the few rooms he now occupied.

Every day, though, the big room filled with objects unpacked from his boxes, more mobiles, now hung so thickly that the ceiling of the long room seemed to Alice to be constantly in motion with birds and insects, the leaping figures of men and women and deer and fish and lizards, curled streamers of colored cloud, suns and moons and stars. Thick rugs of richly colored and compli-cated patterns were unrolled over the wood floors, and books and record albums filled the shelves. One day a kaleidoscope appeared on the round table, a marvelous tube of polished black ebony, its lens filled with bits of colored glass that tumbled into a fan of intricate designs. On another day there was a strange brass instru-ment with a long black tube and a carved bowl like a pipe's. Ken-neth had procured this is Morocco, he told them. It was a hookah, for smoking opium, and he invited them to sniff the sour-smelling little bowl. From a box one afternoon he unpacked a menagerie of little animal figures carved from green soapstone. From another box came a pair of china peacocks, with painted tails and jewel-encrusted crowns on their heads.

Almost every day after their session of reading and conversa-tion, Kenneth made them a gift of something. They staggered home under the weight of these offerings: on Theo, Kenneth bestowed a cunning red leather martini kit containing a shaker made out of shiny rings that slid into each other like a telescope, a measuring cup like two little cones stacked point to point, a pair of martini glasses secured neatly under elastic straps, and a flask with a green glass hole in the flat circle of its belly. Kenneth also gave Theo a pair of binoculars in a tooled leather case made of alligator hide and a set of chisels in a rolled canvas pouch with clever pockets inside for the tools.

Upon Alice, Kenneth bestowed a black woolen poncho embroidered with flowers sewn in brilliant threads, a spirit lamp with an etched glass hurricane shade, a statue of the conjoined figures of Don Quixote and his squire Sancho Panza mounted on swaybacked horses, eight inches high and woven entirely of a silvery grass, and a necklace of faceted jet beads. The zebra skin had been waiting for them one afternoon, rolled up by the French doors and tied with twine, and they had dragged it to the fort, deciding to lay it inside rather than over the door, chiefly because it was so heavy that all of Theo's ingenious contrivances for keeping it up failed.

One day there was an old phonograph player on a round table painted like a drum in Kenneth's room, and he played records of operas for them, which Theo mimed, leaping around on the rugs, his hand to his chest, his mouth open, and his eyes squeezed shut. Another day Kenneth had the children string a line for him between two chair backs outside on the terrace, and he showed them how to construct a mobile of washers and paper clips that they bent with tiny pliers into geometric shapes. He'd gone shopping with his sister one morning and come back with a TV and a DVD player; movies came in the mail for him every few days. Together they watched *The Sound of Music* and *Singin' in the Rain* and *The Wrong Trousers,* with Wallace and Gromit, which Theo loved. Every day Kenneth wanted to know about the status of their camp in the woods. On some afternoons he was strong enough to walk outside to the terrace with them and down across the lawn that Eli had mown, out to the edge of the trees where he stopped, leaning on his stick and staring into the cool dimness of the woods as if he could see something there, flickering among the leaves. Sometimes Miss Fitzgerald came in while Alice was reading and hesitated in the doorway, as if waiting for them to see her there and stop. Though she could feel Miss Fitzgerald's eyes on the back of her neck as she bent over the book, Alice kept her voice steady, proceeding through the adventures of the explorers through the cottonwoods and over the plains and down through the lofty caverns of the Missouri. She read about their perilous sojourns in the small pirogues up the river in advance of the boat, the ice moving on the water and the travelers' vain attempts to thaw it and free their craft by dropping hot stones onto the floes, the distribution of rum to all the men on Christmas Day. Antelopes and elk and buffalo roamed across the plains. Alice imagined them advancing along the flat line of the horizon like the black silhouette figures at the puppet stage at school. Swans and wild geese flew overhead in formations of giant Vs. Bears reared up from the shallows of the river and charged the men, who escaped only to suffer other traumas—frostbite and fevers and snakebite. On either side of the river, the bluffs rose as high in some places as three hundred feet, and Lewis described the fantastic architecture of the cliff sides, the *"eligant ranges of lofty freestone buildings, having their parapets well-stocked with statuary . . . We see the remains or ruins of eligant buildings;"* he wrote, *"some collumns standing and almost entire with their pedestals and capitals; others retaining their pedestals but deprived by time or accident of their capitals, some lying prostrate an broken . . ."*

The accounts rarely failed to mention the game killed that day, and Alice sometimes felt she could smell blood souring the air as she read, or hear the calls of the wild geese, or the shouts of the men on the river. It was as if her life, her life in this room with Theo and Kenneth, sometimes melted away and was replaced by the world of the flat plains flowing for miles away from the banks of the Missouri, the wind of that other time and place in her hair and on her cheeks. As Lewis and Clark gave her their descriptions, Lewis's especially so full of poetry that she could feel his awe as every day brought him to a new vista, she understood that the language you used to describe something, so that someone else could see it, too, was important. She thought of Thomas Jefferson sitting alone in his house in Virginia, spreading over his knees the hides and skins Lewis and Clark sent back east, examining the tiny preserved leaves and plants with earth clinging to their roots, unfolding the pages of his explorers' letters and reading them by candlelight, his lips moving over the words. The image brought a lump to her throat.

The days seemed made up of equal parts pleasure and the anticipation of something Alice could not name, the two states sometimes so close together that they slid into one queasy sensation of perpetual alertness, like waiting for the curtain to rise on the stage at the theater. Helen continued to languish in her bed at the hospital. The O'Briens' house now had become unfriendly and cold without her. Only O'Brien was ever there, and usually just at night now, one light on in the kitchen, another in the garage. Alice knew Archie talked to O'Brien every day and two or three nights a week went to the hospital, sometimes to take O'Brien out to eat, but she did not know what had been decided about Theo. It was as if Archie and O'Brien were also waiting for something, some news or event that would make Theo's fate clear. But Theo himself seemed unperturbed. He did not say again, after that first night, that he missed his mother. He said instead that he was thinking all the time of how to help Kenneth, but that the right idea had not yet arrived. Both he and Alice wanted passionately to do something for Kenneth, something heroic on the order of Lewis and Clark's magnificent trek westward. But they could not think of what that thing might be.

And then finally, one day, Theo hit on it. Kenneth himself gave them the answer.

It was nearly the end of June now, and after a stretch of sultry days, with the sky a bleak white haze above them, wet heaps of solid clouds had built up in the west, tumbling down from the mountains and rolling in black waves across the valley. That day, Miss Fitzgerald had hovered around Kenneth's room all afternoon, coming in and out with mail, or flowers in a vase, or a tray with lunch, which he had refused to eat. Finally, after she had come in bearing an album of old photographs she wished him to look through, he had raised his voice. "I am sick of being in this room," he shouted at her. "You do not give me a moment's peace."

He had struggled to his feet from his place on the settee, grasped his cane, and staggered outside onto the windy terrace.

Theo and Alice, frozen in position, had met each other's eyes, Theo looking to Alice like a wary dog, prepared to run. But run where? Not through the creepy house where Miss Fitzgerald had retreated, dropping the photograph album on the floor and rushing from the room. And not out to the terrace, where Kenneth stood with his back to them, staring out over the grass toward the trees blowing in the coming gale, leaning on his cane, his shoulders heaving. They were trapped.

Finally, Theo had gotten to his feet and come quietly to the table to stand by Alice. He leaned against the arm of her chair. She pressed back against him with her shoulder, and he leaned closer, the two of them bolstering each other against the uncertainty, the unhappiness in the room.

"I just want to go for a walk!" Kenneth's bellow from the terrace outside startled them both so much that they jumped and then pressed tightly against each other, Alice in her chair, Theo beside her, shrinking away from Kenneth's rage.

"I want to go for a walk in the woods, *by myself*." Kenneth threw back his head and lifted his cane from the stones of the terrace as if to strike something, but it only whipped through the air. He staggered.

Alice felt Theo tremble beside her. Her hands were white-knuckled around the book.

Then Kenneth quieted, both hands on his cane now, leaning over it, his head down, defeated. "Forgive me," he said, loud enough for them to hear, but not in rage anymore, and Alice knew he was addressing them. "Do you know what this is like? Here's your word of the day. This is an ambuscade . . ." He did not finish his sentence, but he turned around and came back shakily into the room. "I'm tired," he said. He didn't look at them, making his way back to the settee and sitting heavily, his cane clattering onto the floor. "That's enough for today." He reached up and tore away the white X of tape that held open his eyelid. The eyelid fell, and Alice thought, for a moment, of what Kenneth would look like when he was dead. Somewhere in the house the telephone began to ring.

"Forgive me," Kenneth said again. He turned his face aside.

Alice looked at Theo.

He tugged on the sleeve of her shirt. *Let's go,* he mouthed.

Soundlessly, Alice replaced the book on the table and got to her feet. They tiptoed from the room out to the terrace, onto the grass, and home.

They did not speak of what had happened right away. They went to their fort, even though the wind was blowing hard by then, and the river looked whipped up and dangerous. Tiny leaves blew past the opening as they sat inside on the zebra skin, their chins on their knees, staring out at the wild air filled with scraps of green and yellow and white, bright against the bulging purple of the sky.

"A rope walk," Theo said at last.

Alice turned to look at him.

"He needs a rope walk," Theo said. "Like at your party. So he can go outside by himself. He needs something to hold on to, a line. He can put his hand on it and follow it."

Alice felt her heart begin to race. "We could clear a path," she said. "We could make a trail."

Theo jiggled up and down beside her in excitement. "Yes, yes!" He turned to look at her with shining eyes. "It could be huge, he could go as far as he wanted but all he would have to do when he got too tired is turn around and it would lead him home."

"Not like Hansel and Gretel," Alice said. "It would never disappear."

Theo gave a huge sigh and collapsed theatrically beside her, his shoulders sagging, his chin dropped to his chest. "That's it," he said. "I've been thinking it and thinking it, but I couldn't see it until just now." Then he jumped up. "Let's start right now," he said. "Let's go get some rope."

Alice scrambled to her feet. "There's rope in the barn," she said. "Tons of it, all kinds."

They stared at each other. And then, as if on cue, they both squealed with excitement and jumped up and down, grabbing for each other's hands, cavorting over the small promontory of their island under the rushing sky, a confetti of leaves whirling around them. When Theo pulled her to his chest and hugged her, Alice wanted to cry suddenly—more tears, she thought in surprise—but this time they were tears of exhilaration, as if her body was too small to contain this much feeling, and she hugged him back, her arms clasping him against her—he felt so bony and thin—with a gladness that was fierce and brave and somehow, suddenly, adult.

"Let's not tell," she said, drawing back from him, breathing hard. "Let's not tell anyone." And she liked the frisson of danger that swept over her as she said these words, the sense of a secret blooming between them like a rare and exotic flower.

"Okay," Theo said, his hands still on her shoulders.

"It'll be a surprise," Alice said.

"Yes," Theo said. "Let's surprise everybody."

TEN

THERE WAS PLENTY OF ROPE in the barn. From under the stairs up to the haymow they dragged out nests of heavy, hairy coils that seemed magnetically charged, straw and feathers and dirt and bits of twine woven into the braid. In the old horse stalls they found more: sleek lengths of tightly woven yellowing cord tied into figure eights and hung on nails, loops of slippery, synthetic cable under the straw, tangles of old clothesline, heaps of bristly twine. Alice was amazed at how much they collected. It took them a full morning to haul everything they found out onto the grass where they could inspect it. Theo did not seem surprised to have found so much—naturally, he said, as if he were an expert on such things, a barn would be a repository of old rope—but he and Alice were daunted by how much it weighed, especially the thick stuff. Also, a lot of it needed to be untangled, which meant finding a loose end and then one of them marching off with it across the grass while the other person stayed behind to wrestle with the writhing loops and coils.

After lunch that first day, they decided to take what they could carry to the Fitzgeralds' and begin from there, coming back for more when they ran out. Theo magnanimously offered to carry the heaviest rope, which he wore around his neck and hung over his shoulders like an ox's yoke. He walked with his neck stretched forward, his face turned toward the ground, one hand steadying the load on his shoulders, the other grasping his toolbox. He made Alice think of an old donkey, trudging along under his awkward burden.

At the Fitzgeralds' they went around the side of the house toward the terrace, as usual. They hadn't knocked at the front door since their first visit weeks before, and they had no wish to run into Miss Fitzgerald, in any case. They stopped at the gate now, looking across the back lawn toward the terrace to make sure Kenneth wasn't out in the sun, waiting for them, as he often was. They didn't want him to see the rope, having decided that they would wait to surprise him instead with the finished product. The terrace was empty, so they pushed open the gate and hurried across the grass to the edge of the woods where they pushed a few yards into the trees and then stood in the shade, breathing hard. Theo extricated himself from the coils over his shoulders, set down his toolbox, and stood up, resting a hand on Alice's shoulder as they stared into the thicket ahead of them.

"Do you have a machete?" he asked. "A machete would be good."

As they peered into the dusty, twinkling light that fell between the trees, the forest appeared impenetrable, a fortress of vines and thorns, the underbrush a wall fortified with fallen branches, here and there the felled trunk of a massive tree that had crashed to the earth, all of it banked high at the edge of the lawn by decades of grass clippings thrown from the mower, raked leaves, and detritus tossed from the garden into the woods.

The busy world and its ordinary sounds thrummed at their backs: through an open window in a house nearby, an unanswered telephone rang continuously; car doors slammed shut; a delivery truck reversed out of a driveway to a steady warning beeping. Ahead of them, the silence of the woods beckoning them into its shady, leafy quiet seemed formal to Alice, the hush of a great medieval hall. She always felt dwarfed in the woods among these big trees, aware of an alert listening that seemed to be taking place around her, a watchful attention that communicated the tolerance of something ancient for a younger, more heedless presence. Alice felt as if she were both the center of the universe, all the unseen eyes of the world trained upon her from deep within the leaves, and an insignificant interloper.

Over the weeks of her reading aloud to Kenneth and Theo from the accounts of Lewis and Clark's adventures, the strangeness of that new world and its inhabitants had been taking shape in her mind: the mysterious mound rising from the flat line of the prairie, thought by the Indians to be inhabited by demons eighteen inches tall and armed with spears; the peculiar tribe of the Flathead Indians, whose broad, compressed brows were obtained by clamping infants' heads between two boards; the ghastly ceremonial capes of the Chopunnish Indians, made of human scalps and ornamented with the dangling fingers and thumbs of warriors killed in battle. For Lewis and Clark, the world had produced an endless chain of danger and heroics, the assault of a giant black panther, the desperate predicament of men who clung above the white froth of one-hundred-foot falls, gashing handholds in the cliff walls with their knives in order to climb to safety. Everywhere they went the men were threatened, attacked, driven onward (or back) by mosquitoes or beasts, raging waters, snow and ice, disease, even irrational fear.

Now, as Alice stood by Theo's side and imagined cutting a trail among the trees for Kenneth, someplace he might set his uncertain feet, the woods seemed tame, domesticated by comparison with the wilderness encountered by Lewis and Clark. She stood quietly with Theo's hand on her shoulder, just as Clark must have stood beside his friend Lewis, she thought, the two comrades staring out at the shadows of the clouds racing over the plains, the herds of bison that moved over the brown earth in the far distance like swarms of bees or pools of spilled ink.

They were doing something good here, she hoped, something difficult and grown-up. And yet in the deep silence of the woods before them like a held breath, in the way her eye could find no final resting place, no end through the trees, in the solemn shafts of light that fell as though into a cavernous chamber, she felt awfully small somehow. Perhaps Lewis and Clark had felt that, too.

It was harder work than they had anticipated. To hold the ropes in place, they discovered they had to nail through them into the trunks of the trees; otherwise the ropes slipped and sagged toward the ground. And cutting a path was filthy, difficult business; they came away from their labors scratched and bleeding, their hands raw, welts rising on their arms and legs. But after a week, they looked back toward the Fitzgeralds' house and saw that they were well out of sight—maybe even earshot—of it, and that the path they had hacked through the brush was clear and smooth: a sleepwalker could have moved down it, gliding like a wraith. As they drew deeper into the woods, the going became a little easier. Here a deep sea of leafy cover spread over the ground, the neat thickness of the pile choking out the undergrowth, and the trees rose up around them like stanchions for a huge bridge. They did not talk much during their labors, beyond complaining cheerfully about the difficulty of the task, a way of confirming for each other and for themselves the virtue of the work, its heroic proportion. Theo backed away from the trail with vines gripped between his hands, staggering from side to side as though he was wrestling an alligator. Alice, on her knees, hacked away at roots. Sweat ran down her face.

Before too many days had gone by, Alice could hear the sound of the river from their position in the woods, though she could not yet see its silver spine through the trees. She could not exactly get her bearings. She had never walked down to the water from the Fitzgeralds' house, and though she thought their property was well above Indian Love Call, she could not be sure, and it made her a little uneasy that their path might be leading them in that direction. She noticed that the ground had become rockier, too. Now they spent as much time prying stones from the path with a shovel as they did trimming back branches to make the way clear, piling up cairnlike heaps beside the trail. Every so often they would close their eyes and take hold of the rope and start to follow the path, exactly as they expected Kenneth would. It was a strange feeling to walk with one's eyes closed, one's fingers slipping along the rope. Alice needed all her courage to keep her eyes shut, for her instinct was to open them at the least resistance underfoot or sound amid the trees. She did not understand why having one's eyes closed made the ground seem so unstable and why it felt like standing on the tilting deck of a ship, but each time she had to will herself to go forward after just a few steps. Theo pointed out that Kenneth could see *something*—it wasn't as if he was as blind as they were with their eyes closed—and so the experience wouldn't be so hard for him. Sometimes they just stood quietly and felt the wind on their faces and listened for what they could hear, the sibilant whisper of the leaves, the occasional cry of a bird. One day a pair of enormous pileated woodpeckers scared them to death, the giant birds starting up suddenly from a nearby tree and flapping through the branches overhead, their raw cries of alarm ringing through the woods.

The children returned to the house in the late afternoons filthy and silent with fatigue.

"What are you doing out there all day?" Elizabeth asked them suspiciously one night, as she set plates of chicken potpie before their streaked faces.

Glancing up from her plate, Alice was alarmed to see that Eli, who had joined them for dinner, was watching them curiously.

"You guys building a fort?" he asked Alice now.

"Mmmhmm." Alice did not raise her eyes to look at him. She shoveled chicken into her mouth. She did not want to lie about what they were doing, but she did want to keep it a secret, a surprise. They would all be amazed at what she and Theo had accomplished. She was amazed herself.

"So, where is it?" Eli reached for the butter dish. "Down by the river?"

"We can't tell you!" Theo said quickly.

Alice's head shot up; he had spoken too anxiously, too vehemently. That note of desperation in his voice—his fear that they would be discovered—had been a dead giveaway.

Eli held up his hands as if to ward off further attack.

"They're out hunting for buried treasure." Elizabeth came to the table and pulled out the chair next to Alice's. "They're digging a big, big hole to China, right?" She reached out and tousled Alice's hair.

Every night, after baths and dinner, Alice and Theo fell asleep as though someone had administered drugs directly to their veins. They left their filthy clothes in trails over the floor; they abandoned damp towels by the tub; they left filthy handprints on the sink. Sometimes after dinner they lay side by side on their stomachs on Alice's bed and tried to read a book together, but Alice was a much faster reader than Theo. It was annoying to have to ask, "Finished? Finished *now*?" over and over again every time she was ready to turn the page, though Theo never seemed to take offense at her impatience. He just said that he wanted to read the same thing she was reading, resorting to a sly and illogical flattery to get her to agree to this foolishness; she could *help* him if he didn't understand something, he said.

They could have read the same book but at different times and she could still have helped him, Alice wanted to point out but didn't. She couldn't figure out exactly why—or exactly when—Theo would want to be close to her, his hip bumped up against hers, his foot toying with her ankle. Sometimes he reached out absently and plucked one of her curls, watching as it sprang back into position. Sometimes he seemed off in his own world somewhere, and she had to repeat questions, startling him out of a reverie. But often he seemed to Alice almost like an extension of herself, and his physical presence beside her—even when he was jiggling with impatience, one leg going up and down as if he were operating a treadle, a habit she found annoying—had become as familiar to her as her own hand held before her face.

Sometimes she woke up in the middle of the night to find her cheek pressed to the book's smooth, cool page, Theo's breath puffing gently into the back of her neck. He still smelled rewardingly to her like her coat pocket, and like grass, and— she struggled to identify it from within the refined family of smells—something a little sour, like a pinecone.

He smelled like himself.

• • •

Days went by without them seeing Archie. Alice and Theo were sleeping later than he was in the mornings now, and he was often gone to Frost by the time they came downstairs, eager to hurry through their breakfast and get outside, back to the rope walk. Archie had been away for three days at a conference somewhere and then occupied with something at Frost in the evenings or going straight from work to the hospital to check in on Helen. One morning, however, he was still at the breakfast table when Alice and Theo came clattering downstairs. He set down the newspaper when they came into the kitchen.

"Are you my daughter?" Archie leaned across the table and held Alice's chin in his hand. When he touched her she suffered a sudden wave of longing for him, his magician's white hair, even his sad eyes. She had been missing him, she thought, without even knowing it.

"Hmm," he went on speculatively. "You look like Alice, but I haven't seen her in so long I can't be sure." He dropped her chin, kissed his thumb, and pressed it to the tip of her nose. "Hello," he said.

"It's Alice, all right," Theo said complacently. He reached for the box of Cheerios on the table and began pouring messily into his bowl. Cheerios bounced across the floor.

"Thank you for that confirmation, Theo," Archie said. He leaned back in his chair and held his coffee mug in his hands. "Elizabeth tells me you've been extremely busy excavating a tunnel to China."

"Ha!" Theo crowed triumphantly, as if this assertion of Elizabeth's proved that their secret was safe. And then he immediately glanced guiltily at Alice. Too late, he saw that no response would have been the wiser rejoinder.

Alice noticed her father watching Theo. After a minute

Archie spoke again. "You've been neglecting your friend Mr. Fitzgerald."

Now it was Alice's turn to look stricken. They had not been to see Kenneth in over a week now. She was not sure how many days they had been working on the rope walk. Nine, ten? Of course he would feel neglected; she saw that now, and she felt foolish. There were too many things to consider while attempting something heroic, she thought. How were you supposed to remember everything all at once? Kenneth didn't know that they'd been building the rope walk for him, and it hadn't even occurred to them that he might have been missing them . . . he had been so much in their thoughts every day that it did not seem possible that he could have felt forgotten.

Alice felt Archie's eyes resting carefully on her. The familiar telltale heat had risen into her cheeks.

"He called last night, wondering if perhaps you'd been borne away by fairies." Archie was watching Alice now.

"We didn't forget him," Alice mumbled into her plate. She didn't dare look at Theo.

There was silence at the table for a moment and then Archie said, "Well, perhaps you could go over there today and reassure him that you are still among the living."

Alice nodded. "Okay," she said. She still didn't look up.

"And . . . how is the piano? Have you been practicing?" Archie asked her then.

Alice knew she was turning scarlet now. She hadn't touched the piano since before her birthday.

"No," she said reluctantly. Yet suddenly, she wanted to play. Her fingers practically itched. She hadn't even thought about practicing these last few weeks. Theo had made her forget about everything. For a moment she felt a little flare of anger toward him, as if he had persuaded her to misbehave, and now she'd been caught. But a moment later her conscience corrected her. She had not been able to think of anything except Theo and their plans ever since he had arrived, but that had not been Theo's fault. She had been completely willing. Yet, how could she so easily have abandoned her old self? she wondered. What had happened to that early riser, the one who sat happily at the piano for an hour or more? (And whose skill was gratifyingly noted by Archie and Wally, praises she loved to hear?) What had happened to Helen, to the people and things she used to care about? She hadn't even written to Wally or James, and she always used to remember to send them pictures and letters. For a moment, desolation spread over her, like waking after a nightmare horribly uncertain about what was true and what was only a dream; had she lost something unrecoverable? And if so, what was it? She blinked down at her plate, her eyes prickling again. And *why,* oh *why* was she crying all the time?

Archie was silent for a moment, though she could feel him looking at her. "I'll be home for dinner tonight," he said finally, as though concluding something. "I may even come home early this afternoon."

"Okay." Alice flicked her gaze over to Theo. He had wolfed down his bowl of Cheerios and now sat across from her, tense as a greyhound, jiggling one foot, ready to go. There was a Cheerio stuck to the front of his T-shirt.

"Ready?" he said.

Alice slid out of her chair and came around the table to put her arms around Archie, duck her head under his chin.

"O, she would sing the savageness out of a bear," Archie said softly, and kissed her on the back of her neck.

• • •

After breakfast, Alice and Theo ran practically the entire way to the Fitzgeralds'. The cool morning air was invigorating; Alice felt comforted and reassured by the sunshine, the delicious-smelling fresh tar on the street across from Barrett and Rita's general store, the heady gasoline fumes that made the air around the pump shimmer in wavering bands of heat when someone stopped to fill up a car with gas. There was a plant sale taking place on the lawn of the library, where baskets of trailing geraniums and pink and white and purple striped petunias hung in the branches of the dogwood trees. At the art gallery across the street from the library, watercolor paintings had been set up on a folding screen on the sidewalk.

There were only a dozen or so commercial buildings along Grange's Main Street, and Alice had been inside all of them at least once: the general store and gas station, the town library, a tiny post office with a wall of ornate old brass post office boxes, the art gallery, a brick building with a lawyer's office on the second floor and a real estate business on the first, a medical and dental clinic in a white Victorian house with a porch on the second story, the town's office building and tiny police station, which shared an entrance, and the volunteer fire station. At the end of Main Street, across the village green from the narrow spire of the Episcopal church, stood a handsome restaurant and hotel popular with tourists called the Grange Inn. In a tradition begun by Alice's mother, Archie took Alice and the boys here for Christmas Eve dinner every year; the maple trees on the green were strung with twinkling lights, and Alice had baked Alaska for dessert and helped herself from bowls of oranges and ribbon candy and peppermint sticks. This ritual meal, with no light in the low-ceilinged dining room except from the candles and the fireplace with its mantel heaped with holly and pine boughs, filled Alice every year with a sense of well-being and pleasure so intense that it stole the power of speech from her. She sat beside Archie with shining eyes, watching the faces of her brothers, watching as the heavy white plates were lowered, steam rising, to the table, the golden bubbles sparkling and colliding in Archie's glass of champagne.

The only other notable public building in Grange was the old mill; a collection of town residents, Archie among them, had formed a nonprofit corporation and purchased the building many years before. It was used now as a community center for the town, with the summer theatricals staged there, dances held at Christmas and at the end of the summer, and a potluck dinner on the Fourth of July. The Red Cross set up a blood drive inside twice a year, and town meetings were held there, too.

Alice and Theo jogged down the street toward the Fitzgeralds'.

"You know what you don't have here?" Theo said out of the blue, puffing along beside her. "Dog poop. There's no dog poop anywhere on the sidewalks here."

"Is there a lot in New York?" Alice remembered seeing people in New York walking dogs on leashes. At Christmas, many of the dogs had been wearing jackets.

"Oh, my god," Theo said. "You wouldn't believe how much." He bounced along for a moment, apparently lost in reflection. "You're lucky, Alice," he said after a minute, and Alice, who understood suddenly that she had never really considered herself or her circumstances in relation to other people before, felt the morning darken slightly around her. She *was* lucky, she realized. She was lucky, and some other people were not, dog poop everywhere they put their feet. Yet somehow, this feeling of being lucky was not a good thing, the way you might have expected feeling lucky would be. On the contrary, it was a disquieting feeling, as though she'd been given a very large helping of cake when a hungry child next to her had been given none at all.

"Maybe you could move here," she said to Theo. "I mean, permanently."

There had been no discussion of Theo going home. It was still shocking to Alice that no one seemed to want him or even really miss him—not O'Brien; not, apparently, Theo's own mother or father. She knew, however, that having Theo with her forever was an eventuality too good to hope for; one was bound to be disappointed, the way she had been disappointed—so embarrassingly, miserably disappointed—on the Christmas when she had hoped she would be given a baby elephant to raise. Now, of course, she understood that asking for an elephant had been ridiculous, but how was one to know at the time whether one's longings were impossible to fulfill, when all you could feel was the strength of that wanting?

Theo lurched unevenly along next to her, one foot on the sidewalk, one in the gutter. "My dad would hate it here," he said.

Alice thought about this reply. She wanted to understand. "Because he's black?" she said. "Because there aren't any other black people here?"

"Alice. *I'm* black," Theo said obscurely. "Remember?"

Alice felt rebuffed somehow, but she didn't understand the logic of his comment.

"Maybe I'll move here when I'm grown up," Theo said then, sighing, and Alice had the sense again that there were things he was not telling her, that he did not know how to explain.

"Do you think you'll still be here then?" Theo asked. He stepped up out of the gutter and they stopped for a moment on the sidewalk to look at each other. Alice noticed a tiny green caterpillar, no bigger than a fingernail, swaying on an invisible thread in the air near Theo's ear. It hung there, curling and uncurling, twisting like a gymnast.

She paused. "I think so," she said, but as she spoke she realized uncomfortably that she might not be wholly in control of what happened in her future. "I hope so."

Theo regarded her for another moment, and then he shrugged and resumed his crooked walk along the sidewalk and gutter. "I'm probably going to get drafted anyway," he said. "That's what happens to guys. I'll probably get drafted and have to go to war and fight somewhere."

"Well, when you get back then," Alice said, breathless, hurrying to catch up with him. She did not want to think about war. "When you get back, you could come here."

"Okay," Theo said. "As long as I'm not dead."

They could hear voices as soon as they pushed open the gate to the Fitzgeralds' back lawn. At first Alice thought Kenneth had on the radio. Peals of theatrical laughter floated out the door, and she could hear piano playing, a Scott Joplin rag; she recognized the tune from Wally, who liked to run through it on the piano for fun. Alice and Theo, panting a little, climbed the steps to the terrace but stopped abruptly at the French doors.

There were two men sitting with Kenneth at the round table in the big room. Their backs were to the children, but they turned around at the sound of Alice and Theo's approach. Theo fell in quickly behind Alice. She felt his hand catch the back of her shirt and hold on.

"Well, well," Kenneth said. "I thought you had been eaten by bears."

Alice hesitated, uncertain. There was something a little mean about his tone. Was he mad at them? She stood uncomfortably in the door.

The two strangers in the room regarded Alice and Theo. One of them was Kenneth's age, an older man with a silver ponytail and deeply carved creases in his cheeks that reminded Alice of the face of an old Indian chief in her American history book at school; the other man was younger, with fuzzy blond hair, a wide mouth like a frog's, and an expression of hilarity and surprise. He was wearing a pink and white bow tie and, Alice noticed, no shoes.

"We've been building you a rope walk!" Theo spoke from behind Alice, his tone unmistakably defensive. He threw out the phrase with disdain and hurt and anger, the way you'd reprimand someone whose curiosity had spoiled a secret you'd been planning for a long time. She whirled around, shocked that Theo had spilled their secret so easily, and with so little provocation; he'd obviously heard something a little unfriendly in Kenneth's tone, too, but that was no excuse. Now they couldn't surprise Kenneth at all. She wrenched her shirt out of Theo's hand. He glared back at her, defiant.

Over at the table, the young man had opened his big mouth and begun to laugh. "A what?" he said. "What are they building?" He looked at Kenneth as if Kenneth could provide a translation.

Theo made a sound of fury, turned around, and ran off the terrace.

Alice stared after him, her face burning. Then she turned back to face Kenneth. She felt completely helpless. Why had Theo spoiled it?

"Alice—" Kenneth was struggling to his feet.

The older man stood up quickly and gave Kenneth his arm, his gesture solicitous and kind.

"I'm sorry," she said quickly. "I'm sorry we haven't come. He shouldn't have told you, though, because it was supposed to be a surprise."

"Come in." Kenneth was crossing the room toward her. "This is Alice," he was saying to his companion. "My *rara avis*."

"The Lewis and Clark. The ravishing hair." The man with the ponytail smiled and held out his hand. "Hello, Alice," he said. "I'm Gifford, an old friend of Kenneth's."

Alice shook his hand obediently, but her mind was whirling. Kenneth had told this man about her? He had said her hair was *ravishing*? She could feel the heat—embarrassment and also, she knew, pleasure—pulsing beneath her skin. No one had ever told her that her hair was ravishing.

Kenneth's eyelid was taped up again. His eye watered freely down his face, a trail of tears. "I hurt his feelings," Kenneth said to her. "I'm a monster. It's just that I hadn't seen you in so long, Alice, and you hadn't called . . ." He stopped. "I'm sorry. I'm so sorry."

The other man, Gifford, put his hand on Kenneth's shoulder. "Sit down, Ken," he said. He smiled at Alice. "We're having something ghastly that your friend Kenneth likes to drink— lemonade and beer mixed together—and the best barbeque potato chips in New York, but I can offer you an unpolluted lemonade. And chips. Please." He smiled at her again, his eyebrows lifted in inquiry, and his smile was charming, full of what Alice took to be an appeal that acknowledged both Kenneth's fragility and her own reputation as his good and caring friend; his smile seemed to say, *He needs you. Forgive him. He's suffering.*

The younger man hopped up and, grinning away, found another chair. He looked at her as if now he suddenly knew who she was, but she felt haughty toward him. After all, he had laughed at Theo.

Gifford poured her a glass of lemonade and passed the potato chips to her; she took one delicately from the bowl and held it in her fingers. Gifford and the young man—Henry de Something; it was a foreign name and Alice didn't hear it properly—were friends of Kenneth's from New York. Gifford was a choreographer, he told her; did she know what that was? She bridled a little at his assumption. Of course, she knew what a choreographer was. And Henry was a photographer, Gifford explained. Alice's eyes flickered skeptically over Henry—she thought she might like to be a photographer one day, but she didn't like the idea of this man and herself sharing similar enthusiasms. Gifford and Kenneth had been neighbors for nearly thirty years, Gifford told Alice. They had apartments in the same building, one right above the other, and years and years ago they'd had a beautiful wrought-iron circular staircase designed by Kenneth—of fish leaping from the waves—installed between their outside terraces, so that they could go between the two apartments without having to bother with the building's creaky old elevator inside or the fire stairs. Gifford and Henry had come to Grange to visit Kenneth, Gifford said, and also so that Henry could see about photographing Kenneth and some of his work for a magazine.

Gifford leaned back in his chair and gestured to the ceiling, the stirring shapes of the mobiles. "Aren't they wonderful?" he asked her. "Have you seen the great big one at the Guggenheim?"

All the while Kenneth sat silently, chin lowered to his chest, mouth turned down, brooding. He hadn't shaved in a few days and there was gray stubble on his chin and over his cheeks; Alice thought it made him look a little frightening. The only time she'd ever seen Archie unshaven was once when he was sick with the flu.

Alice had her back to the French doors, but when she heard

the bird call from outside—a completely unpersuasive imitation of the pileated woodpecker's hoarse cry—she knew it was Theo.

Henry began to laugh again; it was obvious no bird had made that noise. "Oh, my God," he said. "Is that your friend? That is so funny!"

But Kenneth looked up from his unhappy reverie, and Alice saw his gaze meet Gifford's. They both smiled, a sad, private smile, Alice thought, shared between them.

"Let him hear your loon," Kenneth said, and after a hesitation Gifford closed his eyes and cupped his hands to his mouth and tilted back his head.

There was a silence in which the fluting call of the loon reverberated, just as if a real loon had called across a lake in the darkness for its mate; the hair rose on Alice's arms, and the look exchanged between the two men was so powerful, so charged, that she felt a lump come in her throat, though she did not understand why.

And then Theo answered from outdoors with another insane woodpecker's call.

Kenneth began to laugh. Gifford leaned over and put his arms around him and Kenneth's hands came up and clutched at the back of Gifford's shirt.

Alice stood up and waited, her throat thick with an emotion she could not name. "I have to go now," she said finally in a quiet voice. "I hope you feel better, Kenneth."

Gifford looked around at her. He gave her another little smile and a nod, as if to say that he understood, that she should run along.

Alice waited on the terrace for a moment, searching the edge of the woods, and then she saw Theo, crouched just inside the shade by a fallen tree. She ran over the grass toward him.

Henry came out of the French doors onto the terrace, a camera in his hands. "Hey!" he called. "Children! What's a rope walk? Come on, tell me!"

Alice reached Theo and ducked down under a branch to join him. Together they watched Henry standing on the terrace in his bare feet and foolish bow tie, one hand shading his eyes.

"Yoo hoo!" he called. "I'll give you twenty bucks!" He started to laugh again.

"He's going to die, Theo," Alice said. She looked away from the stupid, annoying Henry into the dirt at her feet. "That other man is his friend, and he knows it, too. Kenneth's really dying."

"I know," Theo said.

For a moment Alice wondered how Theo knew this, but she did not doubt, as sometimes she did, that he was telling the truth. Somehow she knew that Theo had understood before her that Kenneth was dying. She stared down between her feet. It was amazing, she thought irrelevantly, distracted, how much stuff was on the ground in just one tiny little square: knobbed and smooth twigs, half-moon and palmate and tear-shaped leaves, even different kinds of dirt, gritty and flaked with mica or granular as sugar, black berries and green berries and tiny red berries like drops of blood, tendrils and vines and curls of silver or brown bark. There were hundreds of things, she saw, peering closer, things she couldn't even identify, just right here. She put up her hands to her eye and made her pretend camera, drawing a border around the tiny square of tapestry between her feet. It was hypnotic, like a hole drawing her down into it, Alice in Wonderland's magic rabbit hole. She dropped her hands and sat up, dizzy and sick at heart.

"I want to go home," she said.

"Me, too," Theo said.

· · ·

That night, Archie came home as promised by five p.m. Alice was already at the piano when he looked in at the door to the living room and smiled at her, a stack of books under his arm and his jacket held over his shoulder with one finger. She played the piano that evening for almost two hours, her concentration focused and sharp in a way that felt new to her, as if she was trying to block out everything around her, the whole teeming, crowded world, so as to make room for something else, something inside her head. Outside, the sun fell lower in the sky, lingering at the horizon and flooding the sky with pink light against which the trees stood out, black as ink. A few stars began to wink in the blue vault of the evening sky. Alice played Chopin's Prelude in B Minor and Bach's Prelude in C Major again and again.

At seven-thirty, when she finally stopped, Elizabeth called to her from the kitchen.

"You hungry? Go call your father, okay? Dinner is ready."

Alice wandered through the house in her bare feet, the soft light in the rooms setting everything aglow, the burnished wood of her mother's old secretary desk, the tarnished silver trophy bowls on the mantelpiece, the living room's rose-colored drapes that had worn thin over the years, the setting sun's golden light behind them now. She felt tired after playing the piano for so long, but peaceful, too. The painful scene at Kenneth's from earlier that afternoon, Kenneth and Gifford hugging each other, had dulled a little in her mind. Like exploring a recent wound, she probed gently at the idea of Kenneth and found she could just bear it. Was it possible that she and Theo were wrong, she thought, and Kenneth wasn't dying, after all? Maybe he was just very, very sick and everyone was worried he *would* die.

She found Theo and her father in Archie's study, where Archie was tilted back in his chair with a tumbler of Scotch in his hand, watching the television. Theo sat cross-legged on the floor beside him, his chin in his hands.

When Alice came to the door, Theo turned around. "They bombed the Tube in London," he said importantly. "I told you they were everywhere."

Alice stopped at the door.

"That's the London subway," Archie said, not turning away from the television screen. "People used to take shelter in the Tube stations during the Blitz."

Alice didn't know what the Blitz was, but it didn't sound like a good thing, or else why would people have needed to take shelter? She glanced out the window; an evening breeze had come up, and the leaves on the trees against the hillside moved a little, like a dark crowd in a stadium.

"And a hurricane wiped out a whole island," Theo said. "Hundreds of people died. There's another one getting ready out in the ocean, too. Also, there was a mud slide in California. Some dad went out to get ice cream and his kid's birthday cake, and when he came back his whole house was gone." His voice sounded oddly excited, and Alice saw Archie sit up in his chair and take notice of Theo as if for the first time.

"Dinner's ready?" Archie said to Alice. He drained his glass and set it on his desk. "Turn off the television, please, Theo."

With an expression of reluctance, Theo crawled forward and hit the button on the television set. "Don't you guys have a remote?" he said. "Remotes are great." But his face looked drawn and pale. Alice wondered how so many bad things could have happened in the world in just one day. It made her feel a little sick to imagine how many bad things lay ahead, if one day could contain so much tragedy.

• • •

"Let's not go in if these guys are still there," Theo said as they walked to the Fitzgeralds' the next morning.

They had decided to go straight to Kenneth and explain everything to him, if his friends had left. Theo had already spoiled the secret about the rope walk, they figured, and it might cheer up Kenneth to hear about it.

"It could be the thing that, you know . . ." Theo said.

"What?" Alice was carrying a bunch of black-eyed Susans that Eli had cut from the garden that morning. A bee swerved in front of her, and she waved the bouquet to shoo it away.

"You know . . ." Theo put his hands in his pockets. "Maybe it will make him want to live," he said. "Maybe it will save him."

Alice walked beside him, contemplating the enormity of this possibility. Could that really happen?

As if he were reading her mind, Theo said, somewhat stiffly, "Miracles do happen, you know."

Something about his tone made the remark sound a little too easy, Alice thought, even a little condescending. She frowned. She didn't believe in miracles, not really. Santa Claus had been a miracle, for instance, and he wasn't real.

Theo seemed to sense her skepticism. "My mom wants to go on a pilgrimage and have a miracle," he said, defensively. "In Spain. People have been going there for thousands of years. It's called the Road to Ipanema."

Alice frowned again. She knew a song called "The Girl from Ipanema" about a girl walking to the beach. Archie liked it. Regardless, this was more than Theo had ever divulged about his mother. "What do you do on a pilgrimage?" Alice asked.

"Get cured, dude! That's why people go."

He had begun to walk very fast. Alice hurried to keep up with him. "What's wrong with your mom?"

"Oh, she has depression."

He spoke breezily, but Alice knew him now, and she knew that he was telling her something important, that it had taken a great effort.

"That's like when you're sad," she said.

"Really, really sad. Like, kill-yourself sad."

He had slowed down a little. Alice leaned into him with her shoulder and bumped him gently. She didn't know what to say. He bumped her back a little.

"That won't happen," Alice said.

"I know," Theo said.

Then he sped up and started to run. "Race you," he called over his shoulder.

When they arrived at the house, Kenneth was alone, puttering around in the big room in a distracted way. He appeared surprised by their arrival, whirling around when Alice said his name from the French doors.

His friends had gone back to New York, he told them, but they were flying back again the next weekend to take the photographs. He was jittery and restless, and the prospect of his friends' return seemed to worry him or make him a little angry. He said, "I think they feel they need to . . . hurry it up." And then he added nonsensically, "I haven't been sleeping well," staring at them as if he were making some sort of appeal.

Miss Fitzgerald came in as they stood there. She was wearing what looked like an old pair of men's trousers, bunched up around her waist with a belt. She paused at the door, just long enough to convey to Alice and Theo her surprise and unhappiness at finding them there before she crossed the room to set a tray on the table. "Mr. Fitzgerald needs his medicine now," she said, as if this situation called for Alice and Theo's immediate departure.

"For God's sake." Kenneth came over to the table and sat down. "I'm just swallowing pills, Hope. Give me that." He reached out for the glass.

They hadn't seen Miss Fitzgerald in several days, and Alice thought she looked exhausted, almost worse than Kenneth. Alice turned away, embarrassed; it was awful, looking at Miss Fitzgerald and remembering how messy her house was and how nobody liked her. The twins had said they'd cleared out everything except the furniture from the first floor, but they hadn't been able to make much of a dent in the second floor before they'd gone back to Frost, and it had smelled horrible upstairs.

"You've had a lot of excitement, Ken," Miss Fitzgerald went on patiently and soothingly, as if she hadn't heard him, "a lot of visitors and—"

Kenneth burped suddenly, a loud, wet, fantastic burp. He gripped the arms of the chair, his face surprised, and Alice felt herself growing hot all over; it had sounded as if he might throw up.

Miss Fitzgerald's head swung around toward him; he looked up at her, his eyes desperate. Then he held up his hand. "I'm all right," he said. But he was breathing hard and sweat stood out on his forehead.

Suddenly, Theo approached the table. "Do you want to hear about the rope walk now, Kenneth?" he said.

Kenneth turned vaguely in Theo's direction; he was still breathing hard.

"It's so you can go out into the woods and walk by yourself. Alice and I have been working on it," Theo said, his voice quiet and steady. "It's just like those guard ropes in museums or the ropes along a ship's deck. We've got them going from tree to tree, and the path is completely clear, so all you have to do is walk along with the rope under your hand and walk for as long as you want and then you can turn around and come back. Nobody has to go with you. You can go by yourself." He took a few steps away, gliding over the floor as if he were skating, with one hand held out to his side. "We've got all the roots and rocks and everything out of the way, and we've nailed the ropes so they're the right height and everything." He skated back to Kenneth, sweeping over the imaginary ice. "See?"

Alice, who had been holding her breath while Theo spoke and now let it out in a gasp of relief, wondered whether Kenneth had just that moment gone completely blind, for his expression showed bewilderment.

"It's a rope walk. They had one at Alice's party," Theo said patiently. "That's where we got the idea."

Kenneth stared at him. "Extraordinary," he said at last. "Extraordinary, extraordinary children."

"It's not finished," Alice said hurriedly, coming to join Theo.

"We've got a *lot* of work to do," Theo said. "A *lot*."

"But it's going to be great," Alice said. Kenneth looked stunned; she wanted to reassure him.

"Tell me, Hope," Kenneth said then, turning away from them to speak directly to his sister. "Tell me what great act I performed in my life that has brought them to me, here and now, when I most need them."

But Miss Fitzgerald looked away from him and began busily putting the pill bottles and the water tumbler back on the tray. "Well, I don't know, Kenneth," she said, but her voice sounded angry. Alice, standing there watching her, thought with sudden, unhappy clarity that Kenneth had not been nice enough to his sister.

"Do you want some juice?" Miss Fitzgerald said. "You should have one of those Ensures. I got the chocolate ones. You haven't had anything—"

Kenneth didn't bother to answer her. He turned around to face Alice and Theo and held out his hands. "You're proof," he said. "I've been looking for it my whole life, but now I know. There *is* a God, and he made you and sent you to me." His hand as he took Alice's was cold and bony; she had to fight the urge to pull her fingers away. She was glad he was happy—and he was, clearly, happy and grateful—but she wished he had not ignored his sister like that.

"You are the cleverest children in the world," Kenneth said. "And the most good, the most kind and generous. Tell me everything. How exactly have you built this marvelous rope walk, and where does it go, and . . ."

It was very gratifying to describe it, really, all the places they'd found the rope, and how they'd had to carry it there, and how they'd had to hack off roots and branches, and how they'd decided where the path should go, and how they'd raked it smooth. At one point, though, Alice looked up from their conversation to realize that Miss Fitzgerald had left the room without any of them noticing. Alice felt unsettled by this, as though something strange had happened to time, the clock's pliant hands bending forward and back in a forbidden reversal to erase her presence there entirely. It was as if she had never come in the room that morning at all.

Over the next few weeks, Alice and Theo worked every morning on the rope walk and visited with Kenneth in the afternoons. Every day they gave him a progress report, telling him how far they'd come, what special sorts of difficulties they'd encountered and how they'd managed to overcome them. Apart from the weekend when his friends came back to visit and take pictures, and one two-day period when Kenneth had to go into the hospital, they did not miss a day, and his face lit up when he heard them come to the French doors in a way that made Alice's heart catch. She didn't think anyone had ever seemed so happy to see her as Kenneth was to see them. He loved hearing the news of the rope walk, how many feet they progressed each day. He gave Theo a beautiful silver tape measure with a pretty stone in the center that you pressed to release the measuring tape. Theo added it reverently to the collection in his toolbox.

One afternoon Kenneth produced the old photograph albums that his sister had tried to interest him in one day. There were funny black-and-white pictures of himself as a handsome baby wearing puffy white shorts and a blouse and little white shoes, and others of him as a young boy, with a sculpture of a giant flying creature he'd built out of chicken wire in the backyard of the Grange house, and still others of him as a young man, dashing in a naval uniform on the deck of a destroyer. He showed them pictures of his boyhood dog, a Jack Russell terrier named Winnie Churchill that could hold on to a rope with its teeth and be lifted clear off the ground. There were photographs of Hope Fitzgerald, too, as a heavy, round-cheeked baby in a christening gown and cap, or slender in white graduation robes, and then surprisingly buxom and pretty in a debutante dress with a bell-like skirt and a tight bodice. In nearly every photograph she had dark rings around her eyes, but Alice was astonished to see her smiling in some of the pictures, the even white teeth in her mouth, the way it changed the shape of her face into something pleasing. Alice realized she'd never seen Miss Fitzgerald smile, not a genuine smile, anyway.

Theo wanted to try building a bigger mobile, and one week

they worked outside on the terrace making hollow shapes out of chicken wire covered with papier-mâché and suspending them from arms made out of long curved pieces of wood Kenneth unearthed from the garage. He seemed to Alice much thinner than when they'd met at the beginning of the summer; she didn't like it when he wore his shirt unbuttoned too low on his chest, for she could not keep her eyes averted from the way his body seemed to fall in on itself, collapsed under his breast bone. And sometimes a smell came from him—she couldn't describe it; it was like air that wasn't real, she thought, struggling—that filled Alice with a distaste she tried to conceal for fear of hurting his feelings, moving her head aside when he leaned over the photograph albums beside her, pointing.

The days wore on through July, warmer and warmer, longer and longer, slow bees droning in the garden, the light of the sloping, golden afternoons so rich it seemed to melt over the towering trees at the edge of the lawn. Kenneth did some painting outside—he used a knife, not a brush, a technique Theo tried to copy and pronounced impossible—and it seemed to Alice, who stood marveling behind Kenneth at his easel, that somehow he caught exactly the quality of the long, falling rays that slanted over the garden. Sometimes the three of them lay on chaise longues out on the terrace and unrolled the awning for a little shade so Alice could read aloud to them outside. Kenneth's mood seemed milder, his voice softer, as if the heat and the sun and the light had reached under his skin to his bones, warming and comforting him, stunning him into quiet. Sometimes now when Miss Fitzgerald came to the door, a worried and worrying presence, he looked up in her direction and said, "It's time again, is it?" And she would nod. But he would get up without complaint. "Until tomorrow then, *amigos,*" he would say, taking his sister's arm and allowing her to lead him away into the back rooms where Alice and Theo had never been. Alice did not know what happened to Kenneth when his sister took him away like that, two old people bent over and hanging on to each other. She did not like to think about it, whatever it was—a sharp needle filled with medicine, a handful of pills, even a nap. The thought of Miss Fitzgerald forcing her brother to rest, lifting his feet to the bed—and Kenneth's new, almost docile willingness to cooperate, as if he had given up—made Alice feel sick. Better he should fight, she thought.

But soon the rope walk would be finished, and then he could step out into the trees by himself, into the perfect silence. Kenneth still taught them a word almost every day. Today's had been *sempiternal*.

"It means never-ending," he told them, "as in the prayer: world without end, Amen. As in: this summer." And he had closed his eyes and leaned his head back against the chaise longue. But Alice had stayed awake, cross-legged on the terrace with her chin in her hands, looking back and forth between Kenneth and Theo, who had curled up, his hands tucked between his knees, and fallen asleep with his mouth open.

Alice made her imaginary camera and took a picture, her tongue clicking soundlessly against the roof of her mouth.

ELEVEN

THE NEXT MORNING, for the first time in weeks, Alice woke up early. She knew it was early; the trees were thick black shapes against a faint light in the sky, and the house was as silent as if a spell had been cast over it. Not only was she up early, she thought, suddenly alert; she was up *first*. And it was Saturday; Elizabeth would not be coming, and Archie would be sleeping in.

Alice sat up in bed. Theo was sprawled sideways in the bed next to hers, his head half under the pillow, his feet hanging off the edge of the mattress. When Alice looked at Theo's palms and the pink soles of his feet, which at this moment were turned up vulnerably in her direction, she was always struck by how dark the rest of his skin seemed by comparison. Unless you looked at his hands and feet, she thought, Theo didn't look especially black at all.

The surface of the table between the two beds was cluttered with objects Theo had been collecting, including a quart Mason jar filled with ants and grasshoppers and beetles that was Theo's earthquake early-warning device. Cockroaches, which Theo said were the best insects for the job and easy to come by in New York, though apparently pretty scarce in Vermont, had been proven by scientists to go into a frenzy of activity before an earthquake, thereby serving as reliable predictors of disaster.

The day he had brought the jar into the bedroom, Alice had looked at the insects scrambling like people in a terrified mob stepping on each other in their haste to flee. "They look like they're in a frenzy now," she'd said.

Theo bent over next to her to look into the jar. "That's normal behavior," he said. "That is not a frenzy, Alice. A frenzy is . . ." He made a wild-looking face, tongue out, and shook his head violently as though trying to clear his ears.

Now, with Theo sleeping beside her and the house quiet, she leaned over from her bed to look into the jar. Only one beetle seemed to be alive still, scaling the glass and fruitlessly falling back onto the heap of its dead brothers and sisters. It always seemed to be Alice who noticed that all the early-warning system participants had died, sending Theo back outside to collect more. It would be better, he had told her, if they could keep a bird in their room; birds had "sub audio traducers" on their legs, he explained, that allowed them to tune in to frequencies beneath human hearing; these "traducers," he said, would alert them to an earthquake rumbling their way. Archie, however, had said no to a bird and Alice had felt secretly glad. Even though she didn't think she believed completely in the insects' power to anticipate an earthquake, the jar held her attention in a worrisome way. It was hard to fall asleep with the insects' desperate, fruitless assault on the glass walls of their prison taking place inches from your eyes, and she did not think she could ever look away from a bird in a cage whose only job was to warn you if disaster was coming. Plus, it seemed cruel.

Along with the Mason jar/earthquake early-warning system, Theo had also collected stones from the river, a dusty piece of honeycomb they'd discovered at the base of a tree while they were working on the rope walk, a lopsided bird's nest fallen from a rafter in the barn, and, one day, in the soft bed of needles under the pine trees, some grubby things made out of what looked like sticky, chewed-up dirt that Theo said were weevil nests.

"What's a weevil?" Squatting down on the pine needles, Alice inspected the objects Theo held in his hand. She had never heard of a weevil.

"You don't know what a *weevil* is?" Theo looked amazed. He had stood up, the nests held reverently in his cupped hands, and he and Alice headed inside. "A weevil is a parasite, Alice," he said, adopting his professorial tone. "It eats the bugs on animals, like raccoons and skunks and opossums, and then it makes these little nests out of its own poop. There's probably a hundred eggs in here."

They reached the bedroom, where Theo laid the nests carefully on the bedside table. He tapped one of them with his finger.

Alice looked at the nests. "Will they hatch?"

Theo looked at her blankly.

"The eggs," she said.

"Oh, no. Not now," he said airily.

"Why not?"

Theo looked exasperated. "Well, they can't be fertilized in *here,* can they?"

Theo spoke with his usual conviction, but something about it did not seem right to Alice. "I think maybe these are just clumps of dirt," she said. "I've never heard of a weevil. Maybe you mixed it up with *weasel.*"

"Alice," Theo said with infinite patience. "You do not watch television. There could be a new species discovered every day and you would not know about it because you are out of the loop, man. I saw this whole science show about weevils. They burrow

in the guts of dead animals. This"—he indicated the nest—
"could be part of a possum's bladder."

Alice made a disgusted face and turned away, but a moment
later Theo jumped on her from behind. She sank under him in
surprise, buckling onto the floor with Theo draped on top of her
like a rug.

"Alice is a weevil," he said breathily in her ear. "Alice is a
wascaly weevil."

"Stop it. Get off," she said, laughing.

"You are my weevil *pwisoner*," Theo said. "Now I'm going
to . . . *wick* you on your ear," and he stuck out his tongue.

Alice shrieked and rolled over, scrabbling under the bed for
safety.

Theo crawled in after her. "I see you, *wittle* weevil," he said in
a high voice, clutching at her ankle.

Alice shrieked again and crawled out the other side.

"I *wuv* you, *wittle* weevil," he called as she clattered downstairs, screaming and laughing. "Come back, *wittle* weevil. Come
back!"

He had chased her all over the lawn and into the barn that
afternoon. By the time he'd finally caught her, she was weak-
kneed from hysterical laughter, and he was panting. He tackled
her in the hay bales in the barn and they lay there, his arms
around her waist, his head resting for a moment on her stomach.
She felt the surprising weight of it; for its size, she thought, a
head was a very heavy thing.

"Your head is heavy," she said.

He rolled away and lay in the hay beside her. "That's because
my brain is so big." He turned and smiled at her.

"I knew you were going to say that," she said.

His face was close to hers, his tawny lion eyes behind curly
eyelashes traveling over her hair.

"Your hair is so weird," he said. He reached out a hand to touch one of her curls. "It's like mini-tornadoes."

Alice stayed still. Sometimes his hand brushed her cheek as he lifted a curl and watched it spring back into place, and she felt a strange fluttering in her chest at the accidental touch of his fingers against her skin, as though her heart had leaped upward on little wings, only to drop back to earth.

"Hey, Alice," he said. "When they come get me, let's hide, okay?"

"You mean, when you have to go home?"

"Yeah. Be thinking of good places to hide, okay?"

"Okay."

"Maybe we should store food there," he said.

"And a flashlight. And water."

"Now you're thinking." He tapped the side of her head and smiled at her. "Your brain is big, too, Alice," he said. And then he grinned. "Not as big as mine, but big."

The truth was that Theo's brain seemed to be in motion almost constantly, along with his body and his mouth. He reported one night at dinner that in fourth grade he had won the class chatterbox award.

Archie caught Eli's eye across the table and smiled. "Really!"

"I have a certificate," Theo said, as if Archie had asked for proof.

He loved to snap his fingers and to whistle and sing and he could make a convincing array of the percussive sound effects of rap music. He loved the names of rap artists, too, rattling them off for Alice as if speaking a foreign language: Busta Rhymes, Butta Babees, Wyclef Jean, Talib Kweli, Ludacris, Del tha Funkee Homosapien, 50 Cent. He especially loved to watch television, and he was appalled at Archie's restrictions, eventually wheedling Saturday-morning cartoons out of him, a novelty Alice enjoyed. Glancing at Theo as he sat on the floor beside her in front of the television set with his mouth hanging open, Alice thought that maybe he liked TV so much because it was the only time his brain was not in charge of things and he could rest. He was always planning something, or explaining something, or worrying about something. Alice discovered that he worried about bird flu, for instance, and he had persuaded her that she ought to be worried, too. He was in possession of terrifying statistics about the last pandemic; he said he had heard on a radio science show that the next one was just around the corner. For this reason, he informed Elizabeth one day, he had decided that he would no longer eat chicken, or duck, or any sort of fowl; it was too bad, he said, because Peking duck was one of his favorite Chinese dishes, but it really wasn't worth the risk.

"What are you talking about, bird flu?" Elizabeth had replied impatiently. "You don't eat chicken, you go hungry."

Theo was worried about many things: bird flu, tidal waves, terrorists, suicide car bombers, hurricanes, floods, forest fires, global warming, sexually transmitted diseases, cancer, kidnappers, earthquakes, mud slides, easy access to handguns, nuclear attack, asbestos contamination, and being struck by lightning or a meteorite. Alice, who felt as though after a long and shameful innocence, she had woken up finally to the horrible truth about the world, which was that it was falling apart, sometimes found herself wanting to fight the panic he incited in her; he could be pedantic, mordant, and terrifying. And yet, with Theo, Alice felt that she had entered the real world at last, a step as ennobling as it was frightening. The dangers she faced, the principles she would be asked to defend, the wisdom for which she reached would be real: real dangers, real principles, real wisdom. And though along with these would come real suffering, she thought she was ready. Theo believed he could do anything, and when she was with him, Alice thought she could do anything, too.

Unlike being awake in the middle of the night, usually a sign of emotional or physical distress, being the first one up in the morning had always filled Alice with elation, as if she stood before a secret door opening into a private world. She liked to move about the quiet house undetected, pretending that she was escaping from a jail cell or embarking on a mission to free a fellow captive, feats of daring that required masterful control and caution and stealth. She got out of bed now and peered round her doorway into the dim gray light of the hall.

Lorenzo slept in Archie's room unless he had been banished for snoring. He was overweight, barrel-chested, and short-legged, troubled by arthritis for which Archie patiently fed him pills that had to be wrapped individually in raw bacon, or else Lorenzo would spit them out. Archie had acquired him for James and Wally after their mother's death, but Lorenzo had never in his heart been anyone but Archie's dog, seeming to understand at the time that it had been Archie's need for comfort that had been the greatest, that it had been Archie who could imagine, better than his young sons, the ways in which the care of a puppy could serve as a distraction from pain. James, who could be unashamedly sappy, liked to get down on his knees to hug and kiss Lorenzo, speaking nonsense to him in a ridiculous baby voice, but all the children loved Lorenzo, and each of them throughout their childhoods had wept private tears into his warm shoulder; no one could seem so sympathetic about your sorrow as Lorenzo, nor possessed of such patience for your sad tale, whatever it was.

Theo, whose initial fear of dogs had worn off entirely, trailed around behind Lorenzo as if after a fascinating and rare species, especially once Tad and Harry had taken the three-legged Sweetums Lucille back with them to Frost, and Theo could no longer lavish concerned attention on him. He liked to pretend he was a dog, getting down beside Lorenzo on all fours with his bottom in the air to play, following him around the yard and lifting his leg behind Lorenzo; it was exhausting to be a dog, Theo reported to Alice, who sat on the porch with her chin in her hands, watching Theo pretend to pee on the hydrangeas. He also liked to lie next to Lorenzo on the floor in the living room and mimic Lorenzo's poses, especially the one in which Lorenzo balanced on his spine, front paws curled on his chest and hind legs spread wide like a shameless exhibitionist's, tongue lolling in loony fashion out of the corner of his mouth.

Eli, observing this behavior one day, had stopped to look down at Theo and poke him with the toe of his shoe. "You are one weird little dude, Theo," he had said, but Alice had been pleased at his affectionate tone. And Theo certainly seemed to amuse Archie, who listened to him with one eyebrow raised and a smile at the corner of his mouth, as if he were about to laugh.

Lorenzo lay now against Archie's closed bedroom door like a rug that had been rolled up and dumped there; Alice could imagine how Archie had had to push him out with his foot over the wood floors. When Lorenzo did not want to move, and he especially hated being evicted from Archie's bedroom, he acted as though he had been lobotomized, his eyes staring straight ahead into a middle distance, his limbs heavy as stone. He opened his eyes now as Alice appeared in her doorway, peeping around the doorframe. His head and tail rose reflexively, preparatory to an enthusiastic and noisy greeting of tail banging. One of the only commands Lorenzo ever obeyed was to flop instantly to the floor, eyes shut, if you pointed your hand like a gun at him. Tad and

Harry had taught him this trick, and it worked every time, proving the interesting scientific point—the twins said—that dogs could recognize and interpret the symbolic representation of a deadly weapon.

Alice was glad to see Lorenzo now. She felt strangely as though she had been away for a long time; she had missed him. When she knelt down and opened her arms, Lorenzo heaved himself up, stretched and yawned like a lion, and then came across the hall to her, bumping his shoulder into hers and nearly knocking her over, his tail wagging furiously. She put her arms around him and kissed his salty-smelling head.

With Lorenzo beside her, his collar in her fingers, Alice stepped into the soft pile of the Oriental runner that ran the length of the upstairs hall alongside the stairs. Its deep colors, pumpkin and garnet and glossy yellow, emerged in the fragile early light like something gradually being refreshed by water. Along the carpet's patterns of waterways and paths, roads and runways, cul-de-sacs and dead-ends, the younger Alice had built elaborate block villages, scooting model cars down the alleys or shepherding herds of plastic horses over the center ground of medallions in a game she'd called Capture the Ponies, in which Alice played a boy with a bewitching affinity for wild horses. The beautiful creatures ran from everyone who tried to capture them, except Alice, into whose outstretched palm they obediently laid their soft muzzles. This had been a very private game; given the circumstances of their mother's death it was understood that none of the children would ride horses, and Alice, though she had harbored a passionate love of horses for a while, had known never to ask for pony lessons.

She went quietly downstairs. In the back-porch mudroom she found a pair of her shorts crumpled up on the floor in one of the cubbies and a T-shirt of Eli's, which she pulled over her head, discarding her nightgown. From the pantry she got Lorenzo a dog biscuit and herself a Pop-Tart and then, holding the door open for Lorenzo, she went outside.

The grass was silver with dew, a cool landscape of dusky pearls. In the boxwood bushes next to the back steps, huge spiderwebs beaded with dew stretched like fantastic gilded nets over the leaves. Alice set out across the lawn in the morning's fragile light, her feet leaving dark prints behind her in the cold, wet grass. She crossed the gravel driveway and headed for the path to the river, but at the edge of the woods she stopped, shivering; wet grass clippings were plastered up to her knees, and goose bumps had raised themselves on her arms. She turned around. Her footprints across the lawn, coming to a stop at the driveway, were clearly visible. It looked as though something ghostly had followed her from the house and waited now invisibly at the edge of the grass, a shimmering substance in the early morning air. She had the uncanny feeling that when she turned around again, whatever it was would pick up and come along behind her, silent and dark and helplessly, intimately bound to her.

There was a set of twins in her class at school, and Alice had always felt envious of them, two red-haired boys with blotches of identical freckles across their identical faces. At one point, Alice had felt strongly that she herself must have had a twin—perhaps one who'd died or been given away. She had asked Archie about it.

He had seemed startled by the question, even a little upset. "Good God, Alice. No, of course not," he'd said. "Who gave you that idea? Tad?"

She had not known how to explain to him that she had found the idea tantalizing, that it was a wonderful thing to imagine two of yourself, so that you would never be alone.

• • •

The morning opened up like a kaleidoscope around her, bird, feather, leaf, flower, branch, treetop emerging as the sun rose. The sky itself was like a moving river overhead, clouds with bruised-looking undersides pouring in. Alice thought she could smell rain coming, maybe even hail again; there was that burnt, sulfurous edge to the air that she remembered from the afternoon of her birthday party. By the water, the poplars flashed the pale undersides of their leaves, a flurry of white against green. Alice climbed down to the river where she began hopping along on the rocks at the edge, Lorenzo crashing along beside her through the underbrush on shore, nose to the ground. Now and then, out of old habit, Alice stopped to squat down and examine the rock pools for minnows, stirring the water with a stick and watching the sand in the shallows swirl up into the clear depths like smoke. At one point, a heron rising from the banks across the shore and flapping off downriver startled her. Theo had probably never seen a heron, she thought, and she realized at that moment that she had not been alone without him, except from time to time in the house when they puttered in separate rooms, since her birthday weeks before. It was sort of boring, being by herself now. And then, realizing that, she had to reckon again with the fact that one day, no matter what she wanted, Theo was probably going to have to leave. A sullen, unhappy weight settled in her chest. No one cared what she wanted, she thought. Archie didn't care. She fished moodily in the shallows with her stick.

Lorenzo heard the noise before she did, lifting his nose from his investigations in the weeds to go utterly still, head turned toward the woods. The leaves of the trees rustled wildly in the cool wind that had come up, a shuffling overhead like conversation in a crowded room, and the trunks of the slender saplings by the water's edge bent toward the ground.

Glancing up and noticing Lorenzo's alert posture, Alice turned to follow his gaze into the moving trees.

Lorenzo began to bark. Alice stood up.

Baying wildly, hackles raised, Lorenzo had taken a warning position, feet planted wide.

Alice started to call him; he was scaring her, barking like that.

She thought then of her own dark footprints in the wet grass, the baleful, invisible presence she had sensed behind her earlier as she had left the house. A shiver ran over her. Her childhood seemed to have taken place long ago, in an unreal and summery haze of gold and silver. Today, the invisible companion she had once imagined for herself was no longer the benign imaginary twin of her childhood, the friend who kept her company when all the others had gone away, the playmate who was completely known to her because she was unable to imagine anything other than her own simple self. Now this intimate stranger had become something tenebrous and unpredictable and divided, with injuries to nurse and a brooding sensitivity, a being both familiar to her as herself and at the same time completely mysterious. For the first time in her life, Alice longed to escape from herself, to shed her own skin. This new person who was dragging her into the future was not at all whom she had imagined becoming, the heroic figure who balanced on the bowsprit and faced the waves, color in her cheeks and wind in her hair. This new self was restless, unhappy, frightened, a crybaby. Alice hated her.

She started over the rocks toward Lorenzo, who was still barking wildly. She slipped and almost lost her footing entirely. Then, just as she recovered her balance, a flock of birds lifted abruptly from the trees at the river's edge in sudden alarm, and

Alice, ducking instinctively as though the flock might veer into her, stumbled again and this time went down with a hard jolt into the water, skinning her elbow on the rocks, her backside painfully hitting the jagged edge of a boulder, one leg sinking into the river up to her thigh. She scrambled, arms flailing, to avoid falling in altogether. The water was breathtakingly cold, so cold she could feel it like an ache in her ears. All around her, the river's sound was huge.

"Alice! Hi, Alice! Are you okay?"

She looked up to see Theo, fighting his way through the brush, coming in her direction.

Recognizing him, Lorenzo bounded joyfully, tail wagging, through the trees toward Theo.

Alice struggled out of the water and sat down on the rock, reaching for her aching foot. She'd knocked her ankle hard going down into the pool. It was the cold that was making it hurt so much, she thought, but something else lay behind the heat that was suddenly present behind her eyelids, the tears that threatened.

"Alice! I've got a picnic!" Theo called.

He came to the water's edge, scrambled over the rocks toward her. He was hauling a grocery bag and his toolbox.

"Did you break your leg?" His face was wet with perspiration and streaked with filth, his T-shirt smeared with dirt and grass stains.

She stared up at him. Had he been *crying*?

"I woke up and you were gone," he said then in a different tone, standing over her, and in his voice she heard accusation and understood that he had felt deserted.

"I just went outside," she said. She'd been worrying about him leaving, she thought, and now *he* was mad at *her*?

He set down the bag and his toolbox, balancing them with studied carefulness on a rock. Then, businesslike, his face composed, he turned around. "Let me see your foot," he said. He sat down next to her on the rock and lifted her leg gently, experimentally, as if he were testing its weight. "I've got some first aid, you know," he said. "I mean, I couldn't *operate* on you or anything, but I know how to tell if a bone is broken." He peered down at her ankle, touched it gently with his finger. "Does this hurt? No? Good. How about this?" He manipulated her ankle in the other direction. "No?"

He patted her ankle, set her foot back down on the rock without looking at her. "I think maybe it's just a slight sprain," he said. "You can lean on me, if you want to."

Alice reached down and probed her foot. "It's okay," she said.

Theo looked away in dignified silence. The wind ruffled up his hair, pressed his T-shirt to his back.

"It might be just a little weak," Alice said after a minute; this concession to his vanity as a medical expert was easy enough to give. She didn't like seeing him hurt, anyway. "What did you bring for the picnic?" She was starving, she realized.

He turned back to her, gratitude washing over his features. "Apples," he said, fishing around inside the bag. "Bread. Jelly. I forgot a knife, but we can use my screwdriver."

"I'm hungry," she said.

"Well, you're lucky I came along," he said. He gave an indulgent sigh. "Without me, Alice, you'd be in a homeless shelter, you know that? Up a creek with no paddle."

He handed her an apple and she took it and rubbed it against her T-shirt. Then, just for a moment or two, she leaned her head against his shoulder. Theo stayed still, his hand inside the grocery bag. The water rushed past them, silver braids between the rocks. Alice felt very tiny, sitting there on the rock, her temple pressed against Theo's bony shoulder. She felt the force of the water behind them, watched it rushing away before them.

"You know what?" Theo said. "This is the happiest I've ever been."

Alice sighed and then sat up and took a bite of her apple. "Me, too," she said.

The rain held off, but the air was electric, the sky a thunderous, cinematic landscape of purple cloud towers and theatrical shafts of light. They decided to hurry and go work on the rope walk until the rain began, as it surely would at some point. The wind had grown stronger over the morning, irregular gusts giving way to a steady beating. Alice felt excited, reckless, a little giddy; dramatic weather always did that to her.

When they reached the point in the woods near the Fitzgeralds' where they had stopped work, Theo began immediately hacking away at the underbrush, but after a desultory sweeping of the path, Alice gave up and walked ahead into the trees, wanting to see what lay ahead, where they were going. After a few minutes fighting through the brush, she stopped and listened. The wind moved the leaves high in the trees above her head with a heavy rushing sound, as though an army massed overhead, but she could hear something else now, too.

She could hear the falls of Indian Love Call, she realized; now she was absolutely certain that that was where they had ended up.

She hadn't realized they had come quite so close; she would have said they were farther upriver than that. She glanced over her shoulder. Behind her, she could hear Theo whacking away energetically at the weeds. Alice pressed on into the trees, bending branches to slip through them. Then, abruptly, as she skidded down into a rocky, root-strewn gully and clambered up its far side, she saw the white emptiness of sky straight ahead. A moment later, she was standing at the edge of the high bank, looking down over the falls and the foaming basin of Indian Love Call. The water rushed past, disappeared over the edge where a hazy blur hung in the air. The air in front of her face was full of cold spray, her ears full of the falls' thunder. Alice reached out and grabbed a sapling close at hand.

She wanted to back away, to retreat before Theo came to find her and saw the falls for himself. Archie had said this was a dangerous place, and now she knew, as she had not known before, that she ought to obey his injunctions about the falls, that she ought to have nothing to do with them; she could hear the dead Indian bride's terrible wailing for her lover, the sound of the falls themselves like the rush of your own blood in your ears.

But it was too late. Theo was behind her and then next to her, and when she put out her arm to hold him back from the edge, his eyes were round with awe.

In the next instant, thunder crashed overhead, a brittle fork of lightning lit up the sky, and the rain began.

Instinctively they pulled back from the falls into the shelter of the trees.

"C'mon," Theo shouted, and they ran back through the woods toward the Fitzgeralds', Lorenzo galloping along, panting beside them. In less than a hundred yards, they'd reached the rope walk, and even in the chaos of the storm Alice registered with a thrill of pride how successful they'd been. The path was completely clear; as she ran, she reached out every now and then and grabbed at the rope, its reassuring presence beside her.

They broke through the trees at the edge of the Fitzgeralds' lawn and raced across the grass and up the steps to the terrace, but the lights were out in Kenneth's room. Alice pressed up reluctantly against the glass; remembering the time they'd found Kenneth on the floor, she felt afraid to look inside. But when lightning cracked overhead, offering in the glass of the French doors an instant's weird reflection of her and Theo's streaming faces, the phosphorescent half-moon of lawn behind them, and the dark edge of the woods behind that, she turned the handle and they pressed inside. Lorenzo, terrified of the storm, scrabbled on the floor in his haste to get inside and nearly tripped her.

They stood just inside the doors, water from their drenched clothes, their streaming hair and faces, pooling at their feet. There was a pillow on the daybed, its white pillowcase standing out in the dark like a slab of ice or stone.

Lorenzo trembled against Alice's calves. "Kenneth?" she called. She put a hand down to comfort the dog. "Good boy," she said. "It's okay."

"Where's Kenneth?" Theo said, behind her.

"I don't know." Alice called again in the echoing darkness. "Kenneth?"

There was no reply. After a minute Theo said, "Do you think *she's* here?"

"I don't know," Alice said, feeling irritated. It was unnerving, no one answering her. "How should *I* know?"

There was another pause, and then Theo spoke again, his voice an appalled whisper. "Maybe she *killed* him!"

At Alice's feet, Lorenzo shook himself, spraying water. Alice winced.

"I think she's a witch," Theo said.

"She's his *sister*," Alice said. "She wouldn't *kill* him. *God.*"

"Haven't you ever heard of sistercide?" Theo said. "I saw this episode of *Unsolved Murders* once. That's when sisters kill their—"

"Stop it," Alice said. "She didn't kill him."

It was raining so hard outside that the water bounced off the stones of the terrace and noisily struck the French doors as if little stones were being flung against the glass. They couldn't walk home in this, Alice thought. They'd have to call Archie. But where was the phone? There was usually a cordless one in here somewhere. She began to tiptoe across the room.

"Hey! Where are you going?" Theo said anxiously.

"I'm looking for the phone," she said in a loud whisper. "We need to call Archie."

But there was no sign of the phone. Alice looked back over her shoulder through the French doors, but it was dark as night out there, and the rain beat hard against the glass, streaming down the panes.

In the hall outside Kenneth's room, she called out again. "Kenneth? Miss Fitzgerald?"

Theo had followed her and now his hands gripped the back of her shirt. Lorenzo, whimpering, shivered against her legs. There had to be a telephone somewhere, she thought. She called out again into the hallway, louder this time, but no one came.

"There's no one home," she said. "C'mon. We need to find the phone and get out of here."

Theo was the one who dragged Archie into the house and made him see what they had found. When Archie's car pulled up in front of the Fitzgeralds', Alice and Theo were standing just inside the front door, watching for him, but Theo ran down to the car through the rain and yanked open the front passenger door. "You've got to see this, Archie," he said, leaning inside. "You've got to come inside. You've got to *do* something."

Alice thought that because she had seen it before, she wasn't as horrified as Theo by what they'd seen. The house looked better, in some ways, than it had when she'd come inside the first day, because the boys had been able to carry out so much stuff, at least from the first floor. Still, what was left behind was pretty awful. Against the old wallpaper, like the outlines of furniture that hadn't been moved in decades, stood the dingy silhouettes of the heaps of trash that had leaned up against the walls. Alice could see how already Miss Fitzgerald had started to pile things back up again.

Theo had been speechless when they'd looked into the kitchen, which was walled in by boxes and stacks of newspapers and cans and egg cartons and God only knew what else. No wonder Sidonnie had left, Alice had thought. It didn't even look safe.

It had taken them forever to locate a telephone. Finally, Theo still clutching the back of her wet shirt, Alice had steeled herself to head upstairs, despite the awful smell, and she had found an old rotary phone on a nightstand in what was obviously Miss Fitzgerald's bedroom. The bed itself was neatly made, an incongruity that made Alice's throat tighten inexplicably with emotion. Mostly what seemed to be stored in this room were clothes, heaps and heaps of clothes.

Archie, running with Theo from the car to the Fitzgeralds' front door and ducking against the ferocity of the rain, had stopped beside Alice just inside the hall. Once, she had wanted Archie to come inside and see it, but now she found that she was glad she wouldn't have to conduct this awful tour. Theo's horrified enthusiasm was enough for both of them. At first, though he had allowed Theo to drag him into the house, Archie had protested against proceeding any farther; it was dark in the front hall, and Alice forgave him for what she recognized, even as he hung back fishing for a handkerchief in his back pocket with which to wipe off his glasses, as cowardice. He didn't want to see it, she thought. In a way, she couldn't blame him for that.

But Theo would not take no for an answer, and he hauled Archie by the arm through the rooms.

Alice sat down at the bottom of the stairs, her chin in her hands, and listened to Theo exhorting Archie to see first one awful room, and then another. Through the open front door, while Lorenzo crowded against her knees, she watched the rain falling into the street. Where had the Fitzgeralds gone? Kenneth hardly ever went anywhere. She hoped they wouldn't come back now; her scalp prickled with fear at the thought of it. She wished Archie and Theo would hurry.

In the front hall again, Theo started up the stairs, buoyed by a strange excitement. "You're not going to believe it up here," he said, turning sideways to push past boxes on his way to the stair landing, but Archie said, "That's enough, Theo."

He stood at the bottom of the stairs looking up at Theo, his hand on the newel post, his face colorless in the gray light of the hall. "Come on down now," he said. "That's enough."

He ushered them out the front door, pulling it closed carefully behind him. Alice and Theo ran for the car, Lorenzo leaping into the backseat, but Archie stayed for a minute on the front step as if hesitating. Alice watched him from the car, a short, dark figure bent inside his old raincoat. Somehow that first day when she was still riding the wave of her horror at the condition of the Fitzgeralds' house and had imagined bringing Archie inside, she had thought that having Archie see it would be like transferring something heavy from her own arms to his, like relieving herself of a burden. And yet now that it had happened, she felt not better but worse, as if by dragging Archie into it, she had somehow made the whole thing more awful . . . more troubling, more bewildering, more real.

All three of them were quiet on the short drive back home. Even Theo's brittle excitement seemed to have subsided, and in the backseat he leaned away from Alice, staring out the car window. Alice, too, rested her forehead against her cold window and watched the spray thrown up by the tires. Behind them, the Fitzgeralds' house, and all it contained of sadness and trouble, disappeared behind curtains of rain.

When they got home, Archie put the car in the garage and sent them inside to take hot showers. When Alice came downstairs in dry clothes, he was in the kitchen scrambling eggs in a bowl. He'd made a small fire in the fireplace, and Lorenzo lay in front of it, steaming. A bottle of red wine had been uncorked on the counter, a glass poured. It was still raining, though the intensity of the storm had weakened a bit. Archie had stripped off his wet shirt and pulled on an old sweatshirt from Frost belonging to one of the boys. His white hair was still damp, disarranged on top of his head.

Alice sat down at the table and hooked her feet over the rungs of her chair. "What are you going to do?" she said.

"About what?" Archie concentrated on the eggs.

Alice sat up. "About the house."

Archie didn't answer her at first. "Bacon or sausages?" he asked, opening the refrigerator.

"Theo likes bacon," Alice said automatically. "Archie? What are you going to do about the Fitzgeralds?"

"I'm going to think about it," Archie said at last. He turned away from her to put four pieces of bread into the toaster.

Alice waited.

"I'm not sure," he said then, and, putting down the knife with which he'd sliced the bread, he turned around and looked across the kitchen at her. "It's not a crime, Alice," he said. He rubbed a hand through his hair and then reached for his wineglass. He leaned back against the stove, the glass in his hand, regarding her.

"Well, can't you just *help* them?" Alice said.

"How could I help them?" Archie said. "By telling them I prowled through their home this afternoon while they were out?

I already knew from Kenneth and the boys that things were a mess. Kenneth's not hiding anything."

He took a drink from his glass and watched Alice.

Alice met his gaze for a moment and then looked away. She could hear Theo banging around upstairs in James and Wally's room, where he sometimes went to hang upside down on the ship's rigging.

"I thought you could fix it," she said, staring at the floor.

She heard him set down his wineglass.

"I know," he said. "I know you did."

She wanted to understand this, she thought, the awkwardness, the impediments, the delicacies; she *did* understand. But still, despite all that . . . Archie should be able to do *something*, she thought. Why did he have to make it so complicated?

After a minute, she stood up. "I'm going to find Theo," she said.

"Alice—" Archie began in a warning tone, but she didn't stop. She didn't even look at him as she left the room.

That evening after dinner, Theo sat down at the desk in the living room and began to draw. He worked feverishly, crumpling up sheets and tossing them to the floor, pushing others aside, chewing on his pencil. Alice pulled up a chair beside him and sat on her knees, resting her cheek on her folded arms on the table, watching his hands move across the paper. Across the room, the windows were closed against the rain, and Alice could see their reflections wavering in the old glass.

It would be beautiful, Theo said, and she began to see, in the pattern of his drawings, what he meant, the rope bridge Theo imagined would span the river above the falls. It wouldn't have to be very long—the river wasn't more than thirty or forty feet wide at that point, and that was nothing compared with how far they'd come already, he said. He leaned over the paper in the lamplight and drew various designs, some more elaborate than others, geometric shapes that looked to Alice like cat's cradle, the string game she played at school, where the patterns you made on your fingers—the Crane Flying Away, Apache Door, Pillars of the Sun—could be passed from person to person. He showed her what the rigging of the George Washington Bridge across the Hudson River looked like, sketching across the page with a fast hand, and the Brooklyn Bridge over the East River; you could make up endless variations on those themes, he said, showing her. It was all just a matter of engineering. The bridges he drew looked like lace; they looked like spiderwebs.

For their friend Kenneth, Theo said, this would be the crowning moment of his journey on the rope walk. He could stand by himself above the falls and hear that sound, feel the water on his face. Even if he couldn't see very well anymore, even if he was weak and couldn't walk very far, their rope walk would bring him out into the world, the wild world. And not like a baby with a babysitter, but by himself, just like Lewis and Clark. He would be an adventurer again, just like when he was younger and climbing up mountains.

Could they really do this? Alice wondered. Did Theo really know how to build a rope bridge? How would they get it across the river? Where would they get the rope to make it? How did he know it would hold someone's weight, Kenneth's weight?

"You'll see," he said. "You'll see. Kenneth can even help us. He can design anything."

Archie came through the room at one point, a book in his hand. He stopped at the desk and leaned over to look, resting a hand on Alice's head. She pulled away from his hand and sat up.

Archie glanced at her, but then he looked away, and he didn't try to touch her again.

"Building bridges?" he asked Theo.

"Mmm-hmm." Theo ran the tip of his tongue over his lips. His upper lip had become red and chapped. Alice had noticed that prolonged hard thinking did this to him; it was as if his mouth had to work to siphon off some of the overflow energy from his brain.

"Very nice," Archie said. He leaned closer, pulled his glasses down off the top of his head and settled them over his nose. "Your grandfather ever show you the designs for the bridges he built?"

Theo stopped drawing and looked up Archie.

"You could ask him," Archie said. "You've clearly inherited the talent." He looked at his watch then. "It's been a long day," he said, straightening up. "Time for bed."

"Ten minutes," Theo said, turning back to his drawing.

"Now," Archie said.

"Five," Theo said.

"*Now.*" Archie tapped his watch.

"Okay," Theo said. He tossed his pencil to the table. "Come on," he said to Alice.

"Good night, Theo. Good night, Alice," Archie said, when they had reached the doorway.

"Good night," Theo said. Alice said nothing.

"Alice?"

She knew she ought to say something. She knew she would regret it if she didn't. "See you," she said finally, flinging it over her shoulder in a casual way. It lacked all the intimacy of a true good night, of a kiss or an embrace, and she knew that. But it was the best she could do. Hearing it, she thought she'd struck just the right note of casual indifference.

TWELVE

IN AUGUST, the weather turned hot and still, and Theo and Alice began a list of insects. In the attic they uncovered earwigs, a plague of ladybugs, and a wasp's nest that whirred alarmingly when they put their ears to it. Black crickets and grasshoppers and the otherworldly praying mantis hid in the grass, elephant stag beetles and grubs labored under the pine trees, cornucopias of white larvae grew in the damp and chilly brick basement. They discovered shiny green beetles in the vegetable garden, fat gray ticks on the dog, katydids that issued their lisping chirps in the azaleas. Bees crawled out of their nests and gathered in Eli's flower borders near the house. A colony of anthills behind the barn disgorged hundreds of red ants, and flies collided against the window screens. Here and there, swarms of gnats created mysterious places where the air seemed to shiver and vibrate like a kind of weak warp in the fabric of the sky. For days, Alice and Theo went around with a magnifying glass and Archie's field guide, trying to identify what they found. Alice was not squeamish about bugs, but she had never focused on them so intently as she did in Theo's company. The experience made her feel big and ungainly, like a giant swollen balloon figure bobbing along in the sky at the Macy's Day Parade, which Archie had allowed her to watch on television at Thanksgiving. The ethereal damselflies, the lacewings and orb weavers, the ruffled caterpillars with their fiery fringes of red hair, the water striders skimming the river on their filaments of legs, all these delicate creatures made a living, moving tapestry of the earth, wondrous and strange.

One weekday afternoon, Theo was stung between the eyes by a yellow jacket. His forehead swelled so dramatically that his eyes were almost squeezed shut. Elizabeth drove him in to the doctor's office in Brattleboro.

"What will they do to me?" Theo worried in the car, holding a towel full of chipped ice to his head.

"You might have to get a shot." Alice sat beside Theo in the backseat with a bowl of ice and a dish towel in her lap. The degree to which the swelling altered his appearance was shocking. He looked like a freak. "Eli has to get them for bee stings," she said, trying to give Theo the comfort of company in his misery. "He can even give them to himself."

She was not prepared for the tragic dimensions of Theo's horror at this prospect.

"Oh, God," Theo moaned, clutching the armrest. "Oh God, oh God . . ." He leaned his head back against the seat and closed his eyes, which were already squeezed nearly shut from the swelling in his face. "I have to try and clear my mind," he said. "Otherwise I'm just going to . . . freak out."

"No freaking out!" Elizabeth said, alarmed, from the front seat, glancing at Alice in the rearview mirror. "Tell him no freaking out."

At the doctor's office, Theo screamed as if he were being murdered. Alice, sitting in the waiting room and listening to him, staring without seeing at an ancient copy of *Highlights,* was both mortified on his behalf and sorry for him. Other patients exchanged worried looks. Alice's heart beat as though she'd been running for miles, and when Theo finally came out, led into the waiting room by a nurse and Elizabeth, who gripped his arm as though he were a dangerous prisoner of war, he looked defeated and humiliated, and his face was even more swollen than before.

For a day he looked very strange, with a bulging Neanderthal brow and beady eyes. Once he got over the trauma, however, he could not keep away from his own image in the mirror. "Man! I look like something out of *Star Trek*!" he said to Alice, enraptured.

It was cooler down by the water, and there were fewer bees, so Alice and Theo spent a lot of time splashing in the river and fishing, experimenting with bait: marshmallows, cherry tomatoes from Eli's garden, bits of fungus foraged from the woods. After heavy lobbying from Theo, Archie was persuaded to allow them to build a cook fire on the stones at the little beach, and Alice showed Theo how to construct a careful tent of kindling, adding bigger pieces once they had a good blaze going. On most days they grilled hot dogs there for lunch. Theo said they were the best hot dogs he had ever eaten and that he would never tire of them. Alice thought she had never enjoyed a hot dog more, either.

The late summer evenings lasted a long time, gold and silver hours with the sun setting at one end of the sky and the moon rising at the other, a phenomenon that thrilled Theo, who liked to pull Alice down onto the grass to lie with him and watch the stars come out. He was transfixed by this alignment of the planets, the fact of their own position as a tiny speck on the celestial curve.

"You know what? Scientists have proven that the human mind cannot really even *think* about distances like those up there," he told Alice, head tilted back, eyes traveling across the sky. "We just can't imagine it."

For a boy who relished the barrage of factual information available on television, Theo was, Alice discovered, surprisingly superstitious. He believed, for instance, that a simultaneous sunset and moonrise was auspicious. On these occasions, he informed Alice, the ancient Mayans staged bloody ceremonies to propitiate the gods; he'd seen a *National Geographic* special about this. He also developed a secret handshake that he and Alice should exchange for good luck, a complicated choreography including a midair finger wagging that Theo said was actually a gang symbol Alice should take care never to duplicate on the streets of New York. Once they got it down, Theo wanted to perform this handshake dance every ten minutes. It was fun, jumping up and down, dropping to a squat and kicking like a Cossack, leaping up to slap hands in the air, wriggling around in a contorted dance, shaking fingers and bumping hips, ending with a double palm slap, one up high, one down low.

"Yo Alice," Theo would say, and hold up his hand invitingly. That was the signal to go into the routine.

Theo didn't like to be alone at all if he could help it. He even peed with the door to the bathroom ajar, facing the toilet but craning his head around to yell things to Alice through the open door. "Alice," he said one day, slinging an arm around her shoulder. "You know what? You are a good listener."

Was she? No one had ever told her that before. It was a whole new way to think about herself. Not quiet. Not shy. Just a good listener.

Listening and looking. A whole life could be spent that way, she sensed, and there would be no end to the discoveries possible. It must be how Lewis and Clark had felt, she thought. The world never ran out of ways to surprise you.

• • •

Kenneth's absence from home on the day Alice and Theo had found the Fitzgeralds' house empty was only the start of what turned into a prolonged stay the hospital; Kenneth had pneumonia, Archie had told them at dinner the night after their sorry exploration of the Fitzgeralds' house.

Theo, sitting in what was by now his accustomed place at Archie's right, said he'd had pneumonia, once. "Oh man, it was horrible," he said, worse even than chicken pox, and he'd had chicken pox so badly that he'd even gotten sores inside his nose and ears and on his lips. "And you don't want to know where else," he said. "The doctor said he'd never seen a worse case," he announced cheerfully, twirling spaghetti onto his fork.

"I'm sure he never had," Archie said blandly, but Alice saw him exchange a smile with Eli across the table. It bothered her that sometimes Archie didn't seem to take Theo seriously. And it was patronizing and humiliating to smile over somebody's head like that, like you knew something that other person didn't know. She would never do that when she grew up, she promised herself.

Alice knew that it was stupid to be jealous of someone who'd had so many sicknesses and injuries, so much apparent misfortune, but she couldn't help how she felt. Everything seemed to have happened to Theo. He'd broken his arm and his leg (on separate occasions), his nose and a finger (playing baseball), and once he had developed a cyst on his lower eyelid that caused it to start gushing blood during a holiday concert performance at his school. And yet, she did feel a little jealous. Theo's life seemed to have been full of drama, near-death experiences, and narrow escapes. She wasn't sure she believed him about everything he claimed to have suffered. But just when she thought he'd gone too far, he would provide a convincing detail, such as exactly how they'd had to cauterize the cyst on his eye, the smell of burning in the room when a hair accidentally got in the way.

"Yeah, my whole eyeball filled up with blood. It was like I was looking out at the world and the whole thing was, like, drenched in blood," Theo said. "It was cool."

Yes, Alice thought, squinting and trying to imagine it. That would be cool.

It took them only one day's work during Kenneth's stay in the hospital to bring the final section of the rope walk up to the river's edge overlooking the falls. On the crumbling bank they lashed their last length of rope, an old clothesline that Elizabeth had discarded because of rust stains that ruined the sheets, to a tree whose gnarled roots lay exposed, curled like long fingers over the steep bank. From here, they agreed, turning from the shade of the trees to gaze out warily over the tumult of foam and cool spray, the rope bridge could be launched across the span of the water toward the far bank. It was certainly the most dramatic spot on the river, and despite her vague misgivings about the place, Alice agreed that it was a fitting final destination for the rope walk.

"He should go *somewhere*, anyway," Theo said, "not just round and round in circles. That's boring." This, he said, throwing out his arm to indicate the rushing current, the flat horizon edge of the top of the falls, the mist that hung in the air beyond, *this* was a destination. "He can just stand here and listen to it, feel the spray on his face," Theo said, closing his eyes and striking a pose that reminded Alice of the painting of Washington crossing the Delaware, a framed poster of which was in her classroom at school.

Yet the problem of the bridge defeated even Theo. What they needed was an elephant, he fretted, a giant, sure-footed creature that could trudge across the river carrying one end of a bridge to the far shore. Probably it couldn't even be accomplished without an elephant, he complained, and as Alice was no help in providing information on how they might procure the services of an elephant, they would just have to wait for Kenneth to recover before proceeding any further. Surely Kenneth would be able to help them overcome the temporary defeat of the engineering dilemma before them. Theo had drawn a beautiful bridge: two parallel spans, cables of heavy braid, with a section patterned like crossed bootlaces in between. "I know it'll work," he said. "I just don't know how."

They had labored all summer on the rope walk, and when they looked back at it from the river now, they could see it winding away through the trees, an innocently meandering path illuminated here and there where the sunlight fell through gaps in the leaves. To Alice it looked magical, like something made by elves or fairies.

The season was at its fullest, the leaves on the trees large and silky, brushing softly against one another, the flowers bowed under their own weight, the heavy air itself like a colossal heart or set of lungs, beating and breathing around them. Archie let Alice and Theo sleep outside sometimes, and she and Theo lay in sleeping bags on the front lawn under the stars, staring up at the night sky.

"Can you feel it?" Theo whispered.

"What?"

"The earth, turning under us."

Alice closed her eyes and concentrated. "Yes!" She opened her eyes in surprise.

"Me, too." Theo was silent for a moment. "Whoa," he said. "It's kinda scary."

On a Friday morning toward the end of the third week of Kenneth's stay in the hospital, Archie announced at breakfast that he would drive Alice and Theo in to the hospital to see him that evening.

"I have meetings all day today but I'll try to get home by six tonight," he said to them at breakfast, finishing his coffee and pushing back from the table. "Make sure you're ready to go." He looked over his eyeglasses at Theo. "That means shoes," he said pointedly.

Alice, who knew that one of Theo's sneakers, which were his only pair of shoes, had been missing for four days, reminded herself to look in the boys' rooms to see if there might be an old pair of shoes that would fit Theo; he had very big feet, wide and flat as flippers.

Theo had appeared unconcerned when his shoe had gone missing, and he did not seem worried now, despite Archie's warning. He ate his pancakes that morning with the zeal and steady concentration that characterized his behavior at all meals. At breakfast one day he had eaten a dozen pieces of cinnamon toast and fifteen sausages; even Eli, who had the biggest appetite of the MacCauley boys, though he was the smallest, had been impressed. Theo ate with a contented, trusting cheerfulness that somehow made Alice feel sorry for him; it was so easy to make Theo happy, she thought, and yet his happiness also seemed so much in peril, assailed on all sides by the many things he found to worry about, not to mention the parents who seemed to have forgotten about him altogether.

One day, when they'd been out all afternoon on the river fishing and working on their fort, Alice had discovered a crumbly granola bar in the pocket of her sweatshirt.

"Here," she'd said, offering it to Theo, who had recently announced that he was starving; he was often starving. "Look what I found in my pocket."

Theo's expression had been rapturous. Then he had hesitated. "You don't want it?" he said.

Alice had shaken her head.

The granola bar had disappeared like a fly into the mouth of a lizard; one flick of the tongue and it was gone.

"That was good." Theo had looked sad. "You have the best granola bars here, Alice."

"They're just regular granola bars," Alice had said. And then she felt mean, as though she were draining the moment of pleasure for him.

But Theo had shaken his head. "We can't get your brand in New York," he'd said. "I don't know why not. I mean, you can get fruit from Bora Bora in New York, and they sell special magical medicinal roots from the Chinese rain forest on the sidewalk, so why not these granola bars?"

In all their weeks together, Alice had not directly asked Theo about whether he wanted to go home to New York. Partly she was worried about unleashing a torrent of homesickness he might have been keeping bottled up inside; partly she did not want to think about when he would have to leave, a future that seemed so bleak to her, she could not exactly believe that it would come true. Yet it still seemed strange, strange and troubling, that Theo rarely mentioned his parents, that since that first night, when he'd said he missed his mother, he had never confessed to homesickness of any kind. But Alice could not forget the fact that just as O'Brien and Helen had dropped out of their lives, and Theo's parents seemed to have ceased to exist, Theo did *have* parents. He had parents, and he lived in an apartment, and he went to school. He had a whole life in New York that she tried to imagine from the stream of information about television shows and ethnic takeout restaurants he described. And one day soon, for now it was August, and there were only a few weeks left before school would begin again, he was going to have to go home. Sometimes, she caught herself indulging in a fantasy in which she and Theo ran away together, piloting a boat downriver like Huck and Jim, or living up in the woods in a cleverly designed shelter Theo would build. In these fantasies, she surprised herself by taking on domestic duties that felt thrillingly exotic to her—he would hunt, she would cook. But the idea sometimes also made her feel a little embarrassed around Theo. She did not really think of herself as a girl, per se.

Finally, though, perhaps because now she sensed that Theo's affection for Grange and the MacCauleys—and even Alice herself—was sufficiently genuine and compelling, she summoned the courage. "Do you *want* to go home to New York?" she said.

Theo licked the inside of the granola bar wrapper. "Ha! And get blown up by a suicide bomber? Get gassed on the subway? Drink poisoned water? Open an anthrax letter? No thanks, man! It's dangerous in the city." But then he fell silent. He busied himself baiting their fishing hooks. When he finished, he handed Alice her rod, onto whose hook he had impaled a worm, a task from which Alice shrank. "I don't know," he said. "Not like it is," he added obscurely.

"What do you mean?" Alice said.

"I want to go home when my mom isn't sick anymore," he

said. "When my dad is happy, and she's happy, and they're not going to get a divorce." After a minute, he said, "They've forgotten about me, anyway."

Alice looked over at him from her perch on the rock beside him. The way he said it, his tone of voice, made her feel hot with anger on his behalf.

"They haven't forgotten you," she said. She felt a little disloyal to Theo, insisting on this, because his parents certainly seemed to have forgotten him, and Alice had thought the same thing of them, that they must be heartless, terrible people to leave their boy with strangers all summer, to make only the occasional phone call. But defending them in this instance seemed better than agreeing with him.

Theo gazed into the water for a minute or two. Then he made the sound of a phone ringing and held up his hand to his ear theatrically, his pinkie lifted. "Hello? Mom? Dad? Hey, wow, you guys don't have to call every *day,* you know! Yeah, I'm great. Thanks for asking. I'm having a great time. Okay, be seeing you."

He pretended as if he were snapping a cell phone shut and stowing it in his pocket. Then he jumped. "Ooops. Got it on vibrate." He pretended to extract the phone again and answer it. "Yeah, Mom! Hey! Thanks for calling, man. Yeah, I really miss you, too. Okay, 'Bye."

Alice didn't know what to say in the face of this heartbreaking sarcasm. How did you explain parents who didn't seem to worry about their child, who were content to have him gone all summer long? There wasn't anything she could tell Theo, she realized. Instead she leaned toward him until her shoulder touched his, and then she bumped him gently. When he didn't respond, she nudged him again, a little harder, and finally he nudged back. "Stop," he said.

"Stop," she said, imitating him.

"*Stop* it!" he whined in complaint.

"*Stop* it!" she whined back.

"A-lice!" he said warningly.

"A-lice!"

"You are so *stu*pid," he said.

"You are so *stu*pid," she said back, automatically.

He smiled then, but he said nothing, shaking his head, lips pressed together maddeningly.

In his hospital bed, Kenneth, Alice thought, looked as fragile as a leaf that had fluttered toward the ground and come to rest on the white sheets. He was frail and pale, his skin shiny, stretched tight. He wore a patch over one eye, and the other eyelid drooped sadly. There was an IV in his arm; where the needle entered his flesh was a disturbing wad of cotton padding and tape.

When Alice and Theo came to the door of the room, Kenneth was sitting up in bed, wearing a gray NYU sweatshirt. He held an enormous book close to his face under the bright light of what looked like a sun lamp; Alice recognized it from her friend Sarah Kiplinger's house, where in the winter Sarah's mother lay like a corpse under a sunlamp in her bedroom, with cotton balls over her eyes.

Alice knocked lightly on the open door.

Kenneth looked up over the page. For a moment his expression was apprehensive, with the disoriented uncertainty of someone who steps into the shadows after being in the bright sun. Alice remembered her birthday party, when she had felt that he was watching her as if through a periscope. That he was seeing her, but not directly with his eyes.

"Alice," he said then, as if it had been years. "Thelonius."

The happiness in his voice made Alice feel guilty. He sounded as though he thought they had forgotten him. She stepped forward to offer the heady-smelling bouquet of late summer lilies. "We brought you flowers from Eli," she said. Theo shuffled behind her in an old pair of Wally's moccasins, still hanging on to her shirt annoyingly. She reached behind her to disengage his hand, but he wouldn't let go.

Kenneth rested the book he'd been holding facedown on the sheet beside him and took the flowers from her, inclining his face into the trumpets like a man bending to drink deeply from a pool of water. Alice almost reminded him that he would get sticky pollen all over his face that way, but then she stopped. Maybe he wanted it, she thought. Maybe he wanted to roll around in pollen until he was covered with it. The hospital smelled awful, a nauseating odor of bleach and ammonia insufficiently masking other smells underneath, smells whose origins she did not want to think about too closely. She'd been breathing shallowly through her mouth ever since they'd stepped inside, and now she felt a little light-headed. The sunlamp by Kenneth's bed emitted a faint, disconcerting buzzing sound.

Theo tugged on her shirt. She glanced at him.

With a gesture, Theo indicated Kenneth, whose shoulders shook silently as he bent over the flowers. He had turned his face away from them.

What should we do? Theo's look said.

Alice turned back to Kenneth helplessly. "I'm sorry we didn't come before," she said. "Archie only said today that we could come, now that you're better."

That their arrival, or maybe just the sight of the beautiful flowers, had so unsettled him, made Alice feel desperate. She looked away across the shallow, inconsequential ranges of Kenneth's thin legs under the sheet, over the old radiator, and out the window. The evening sky had turned a deep, glowing indigo; how fragile the planet was, awash in the sky, the spangled galaxies and whirlpools of solar systems all around them. How small she was, how small everyone was, even taken all together. Yet the blue of the evening sky was also the kind of color that made you want to spread your arms and soar into flight. She gazed out the window, remembering from her flying dreams the delicious sensation of tilting on currents of air. The world was full of these sorts of invitations, she realized, vertiginous doorways into itself that were revealed magically in midair like stones rolling away from before the mouths of caves. You wanted to eat the world, and swim in it. It was that beautiful.

Kenneth coughed and lifted his wet face. Alice looked down at him again, her attention returning to the room. On the sheet beside him was a box of slides, some of them spilled onto the blanket. A rust-colored blotch stained the sheet. In an open box of chocolate-covered cherries, most of which were gone, a few had been smashed open, the cordial seeping out onto the ruffled white paper cups. Alice looked everywhere but at Kenneth's face. She did not want to look directly at his face.

Kenneth leaned over and took a Kleenex from the table beside the bed, blew his nose.

Then Theo stepped out bravely from behind her. "Guess what?" he said. "We finished the rope walk!" He extracted a wad of papers from his pocket, his drawings for the rope bridge. "But we've got a little problem," he said.

Kenneth was still holding the bouquet. Alice stepped forward to take the flowers from him.

Kenneth blew his nose again, looked up, and smiled shakily at Alice, an apology. "I don't know what's the matter with me," he said. "I'm a mess." Then he drew a breath. "At the nurse's station, in the hall," he said. "They'll give you a vase. Let's put these beauties in water, shall we?" He turned to Theo. "I would love a problem," he said. "I would love any problem of yours. Come and show me."

Alice thought that she could not have sat down on the bed beside Kenneth at that moment, but Theo plunked himself down unconcernedly and began unfolding his drawings and spreading them out on the sheets. "Well, we've hit the falls," he said. "You know, Indian Love Call? And we want to build you a rope bridge that goes over the river. See? Here."

"It goes . . . *where*?" Kenneth had taken one of Theo's drawings and brought it close to his face, reaching up to tilt the sunlamp in order to see better. His nose almost grazed the paper, as if he were inhaling it or tasting it. His posture, his hungry, almost ardent exploration of the drawing, reminded Alice, as she stood there with the flowers in her arms, of her own yearning into thin air from the edge of her windowsill, the way she inclined toward that bright, busy emptiness, seeing there the crack in the rock, the secret fissure in the wall, the door hidden by ivy that would open, if only you could find your way through, into a secret garden, the dusty backstage and marvelous winding catwalks of the world, the echoing pavilion in which the clanking, whirring, brilliant machinery of the universe was stored.

"It goes right up to the edge, at the top of the falls?" Kenneth said.

"The very, very edge," Theo said.

In the hall, Alice stopped at the door and looked in both directions. She could hear the muffled sounds of music and voices from television sets behind the closed doors. At the end of the hall in one direction stood an empty gurney pushed up against the wall. She thought she and Theo had passed the nurses' station when they had come up on the elevator, and so she turned in that direction.

When she rounded the corner, she nearly collided with Miss Fitzgerald. For a moment Miss Fitzgerald was so close that Alice could smell her, the stale odor of the airless rooms of the Fitzgeralds' house. Alice gasped and drew back instinctively.

Miss Fitzgerald recoiled, too, as if Alice, though clearly in retreat, had threatened to strike her. Then, casting a quick look around, as if to make sure no one would overhear her, she said, "Don't you ever go creeping about in my house again, Alice MacCauley," she said. "Bad little girl."

Alice, wide-eyed, took another step backward. How did Miss Fitzgerald even know they'd been there? That had been weeks ago, anyway. Heat flooded her face and neck. In her ears, the throb of her own heartbeat was deafening. Standing before Miss Fitzgerald, Alice felt as if she was burning up, that a fire inside her was squeezing the breath out of her. Yet as she looked up fearfully at Miss Fitzgerald in the midst of that conflagration of shame and anger and fear, she thought something clearly and slowly; she thought how unfair it was that Kenneth had been so handsome, was still handsome, even though he was sick, when Miss Fitzgerald herself, with her terra-cotta face like the pinch pots they made at school in art, was so ugly. But as soon as Alice thought this—or, she didn't even think it; she *felt* it, including her sense that this unequal distribution of physical wealth between the Fitzgerald siblings was a cruelty—it was as if Miss Fitzgerald read her mind and was forced, by necessity, to defend herself against the devastation of Alice's sympathy.

Miss Fitzgerald's expression was suddenly wild with injury and disbelief. "There is nothing *wrong* with us," she said. Trembling, she looked at the flowers in Alice's arms and then back to Alice herself. "I am *fine*," she said, but it came out on a moan that made the hair rise on Alice's arms. "We're *fine*! Your father does not need to *help* us."

Alice, terrified, stared up at Miss Fitzgerald. It must have been awful, she thought, looking up into Miss Fitzgerald's face, and it was as if she were telling herself a story, then, reminding herself of familiar details: Miss Fitzgerald being alone all those years when she hadn't wanted to be, never getting married or having children, turning out to be such an ugly woman after having been a promising-looking girl, never playing the piano well enough to really teach anyone anything.

And then her brother coming at last to live with her but being so terribly sick.

There was a rightness to these conclusions, Alice knew; she struggled to hang on to the truth of them, because part of her did not want to feel sorry for Miss Fitzgerald. She did not want to know anything about Miss Fitzgerald's terrible life; she hadn't asked for any of this. Yet though she could easily hate Miss Fitzgerald for being mean and creepy and annoying, that hate would provide only a bleak ending, Alice sensed, bleak and incomplete.

At that moment, the doors of the elevator opened. Archie, who had dropped off Alice and Theo and gone to park the car, stepped into the hallway. The sight of him in his rumpled jacket, with his glasses perched crookedly on the top of his head and a book under his arm, struck Alice with a powerful wave of relief.

She did something she hadn't done in a long time. She ran toward him and jumped into his arms, hooking her legs around his waist and burying her face in his neck.

Alice could feel his surprise, but he put his arms around her. "Everything all right?" he said. "Hope? Everything all right here?"

Archie, with Alice beside him hanging on tightly to his arm, made his way to the nurses' station, where he borrowed a vase for the now-crumpled lilies. Miss Fitzgerald, apparently humiliated at Archie's arrival, had excused herself at the elevators; she'd forgotten the newspapers for Kenneth in the car, she said, hurrying away.

"She found out we were in the house," Alice told her father. "She's really mad."

"Yes," Archie said. "I know. I called her. And the word is angry," he added automatically. "She's angry, not mad . . ." He trailed off.

"You *called* her?" Alice was amazed. She had thought Archie wouldn't do anything.

"Just to see if I could help." He tilted the vase under the spigot of the water fountain at the end of the hall and began filling it. Then he said, "You understand why she's upset, Alice?"

"I think so."

"I'm afraid my phone call was one of those kindnesses that looks like cruelty," Archie said. "Or perhaps it was only a cruelty. I don't know. She must have known that the boys would come back after that first trip over there and tell me what they'd seen. Maybe she thought I was punishing her when I called, rubbing it in." He straightened up, and Alice handed him the lilies. "She's been living like that for years, obviously. It's not very nice, I grant you, but maybe it's really none of our business."

He was speaking to her candidly, Alice thought, just as if she were a grown-up like him. She felt a rush of affection and gratitude for Archie, as well as guilt that once she had thought him feeble and incapable of action. "What did you *say* to her?" she asked.

"Not very much. I just told her I'd been in the house, and that I was sorry for the circumstances, and was there anything I could do. For her or for Kenneth. She thanked me for the boys' help."

Alice reached out and touched the flowers in the vase. "Isn't it so sad, Archie, that her name is *Hope*?" she said.

Alice saw immediately that Archie was upset by Kenneth's appearance. The uncomfortable surprise that crossed his face when they stepped into Kenneth's room was enough to revive the lurching, sick sensation in her stomach. Theo sat at the end of the bed with the hospital tray pulled up before him, drawing away.

"How are you?" Archie said to Kenneth. He approached the bed and gave Kenneth his hand. "Or are you very tired of hearing that question?"

"Never. Of course not." Kenneth said.

"Can we bring you anything?" Archie pulled a chair closer to the bed. He sat down, still holding Kenneth's hand. "I saw Hope at the elevator," he said. "She was just going back down. Left the newspaper for you in the car, she said."

"They're sending me home tomorrow or the next day. I don't seem to be ready to die just yet, and they need the bed," Kenneth said. He smiled.

Archie smiled back automatically, but Alice saw that it was a pained smile. He made an indefinite noise of protest or apology. Then, abruptly, as if he was finding speech difficult, he bowed his head.

Kenneth watched Archie. "I've known your father since he was a little, little boy, Alice," he said, not looking away from Archie's bowed head. Silence filled the room. "Archie?" Kenneth said at last, and his tone was inquiring, like a child's. Alice felt the hair rise on her arms. "Archie? What's the line? *I am so out of love with life . . .*"

At the end of the bed, Theo lifted his head, suddenly alert. He met Alice's gaze, and Alice knew that he had been listening, too.

"Come, come," Kenneth said awkwardly after a minute, letting go of Archie's hand and pushing himself up in the bed to sit straighter. "I haven't stumped you!"

"Measure for Measure," Archie said quietly.

"Terrible words. Godforsaken." Kenneth looked vaguely around the room as if trying to remember where he was. "Well, I made my bed, didn't I?" he said at last, as if there had been another conversation going on, one Alice had missed. "That's what they'll say, Archie. I know that. And, strictly speaking . . ." He gave a short laugh. "I'm just full of aphorisms."

Alice did not understand the conversation between her father and Kenneth, but she felt that she had been excluded from it suddenly. She wanted to go home. She moved over to Theo, who leaned back from his paper so that she could see what he'd been drawing. He'd sketched a huge catapult on the bank of a river.

"With every problem comes opportunity," Kenneth said. "That is the lesson young Theo is learning, Alice." Then he stopped. "I'm getting more unoriginal by the moment."

Archie looked at the children. "I need to take them home, Ken. I didn't realize it had gotten so late." He got to his feet. "I'm sorry. Alice? Theo?"

"Coming." Theo gathered up his drawings and slid off the bed.

Alice did not want to look at Kenneth. All her comfort with him, the ease he had inspired in her, the way he had enchanted them—the whole summer and the surprise of their long, happy afternoons together, she and Theo and Kenneth—was gone. Had it only been a trick? This was a sad thought, a wearying thought. How were you really to know anything, or anybody, she wondered? She felt as though a light had been extinguished, and she was in the room with a stranger to whom something very, very bad was happening.

"Word of the day, kiddos," Kenneth said then from his place against the pillows, surprising her. "It's a pretty one. *Bagatelle.*" His voice suddenly had become very kind and familiar, as if he knew exactly what Alice was feeling and wanted to comfort her, reassure her. He reached out and turned off the sunlamp, and the room sank immediately into a gentle, elegant dusk, its surfaces— polished sheets, enamel sink, IV pole with its bag of bright liquid—shone like silver. In his bed, Kenneth looked like an old portrait of himself, all cracked surfaces and planes and angles and chiaroscuro shadows, one black and blazing eye addressing the world out of the grime of centuries. Alice blinked.

"What's it mean?" Theo said.

"Nothing," said Kenneth. "A petty trifle. Nothing to worry your heads about."

"*What* is?" Theo looked confused.

Kenneth waved, his hand swinging in the dark. "Whatever weighs on you, whatever you're worried about, the woe of the world. I take it away. *Poof.* It's nothing but a *bagatelle.*"

Theo smiled. "Thanks!"

"You're welcome," Kenneth said, but he was looking at Alice. "Thank *you.*"

One by one, a few days before the traditional end-of-summer dance at the hall in Grange, the MacCauley boys came home. They brought with them: the three-legged dog Sweetums Lucille; a loud motorcycle Tad and Harry had traded for their car and whose appearance sent Archie into a disbelieving rage; several six-packs of beer; a buxom, raven-haired girl whom James introduced as "Katya, the love of my life," who had a serious manner and a violin; four tennis racquets, one of which had its strings broken as though it had been used to volley bricks; a plastic sandwich baggie of pot that Theo found in the bathroom medicine cabinet and identified correctly for Alice; a bong, also identified by Theo; heaps and heaps and heaps of dirty laundry.

All of a sudden, the house got very noisy, very messy. Wally played the cello on the porch, the twins blared music from the stereo in their bedroom, Katya wandered around outside in bare feet and gauzy peasant dresses playing the violin. Lorenzo, in a kind of psychic dog pain, stood baying on the lawn, and Sweetums Lucille answered from her tether at the side of the barn. Elizabeth shouted at the boys, the telephone rang, tempers flared. The boys' bathroom smelled ferocious. Archie was hardly speaking to Tad and Harry, because of the business with the motorcycle. The septic tank backed up, and the lawn had to be excavated.

Alice and Theo tried to stay out of the way, but it seemed that there was nowhere to go, nowhere to hide.

"You still here?" Tad said to Theo.

The dance was held in the old high-ceilinged hall in Grange on the last Saturday night in August. Alice and Theo hung around watching the band, a group of expressionless older men playing swing. They also watched the couples moving around the dance floor. Some of the older people danced so comically, especially the older men, and with such foolish expressions on their faces, that Alice and Theo enjoyed making fun of them for a while. They sat on the dusty open staircase that led up to the loft and looked down over the heads of the couples moving below them. Tall standing fans had been set up by the open front doors to direct the cooling night air into the room, but heat still rose from the dance floor to Alice and Theo, perched on the steps. Leaning over the stair rail, Alice surreptitiously made her imaginary camera and took a picture, a kaleidoscopic image of the dancers twirling beneath her.

Alice followed James and Katya with her eyes. James wore a tuxedo jacket and khaki shorts and a white tuxedo shirt open at the neck. He was easily the most handsome man in the room, Alice saw. He looked like an old-fashioned movie star, with his shiny black hair slicked back, his high cheekbones and straight nose. Katya was barefoot in a strapless silver sheath of a dress. She was drawing looks from everyone in the room.

"Don't have a heart attack, Archie," Wally had said when Archie had come into the kitchen earlier that evening a few minutes after James and Katya had left to walk over to the hall. "But Katya's wearing a surgical glove to the dance. I just wanted to warn you."

On the dance floor, James pressed Katya to him with one hand on her lower back, looking down into her upturned face. Katya's slim, pale hand rested delicately on the back of James's neck, her hair flung over her shoulders.

"Whoa," Theo mumbled, round-eyed. "Look at *Katya*."

On the steps, Alice crossed her arms over her knees and rested her chin on her forearms. On the step below her, Theo kept jabbing her leg with his elbow and saying, "Look at that old guy," or, "Look at that lady with the turban."

But Alice could not take her eyes away from James and Katya.

"I'm bored," she said after a while. "Let's go."

From the step below her, Theo looked up in surprise. "Okay," he said.

Alice stalked off past him down the stairs. After a minute, Theo scrambled after her.

He caught up with her on the dark street that led back to the MacCauleys'. Here and there a few lights were on in the houses they passed, but most people were at the dance, and only their porch lights had been left on. The porches looked like a series of small empty stages floating in the darkness up and down the street.

"What's the matter?" Theo said.

"Nothing." Alice took deep breaths of the mild night air, which smelled sweet and yeasty. Her flip-flops made little slapping sounds against the sidewalk.

"*Some*thing," he said. "Are you *mad*?"

"No!" But she knew she sounded mad. She felt mad, though she could not have said precisely why. It had something to do with James and Katya, and herself and Theo. She was embarrassed, too, about how she had felt, watching James, watching Katya tilt back her head and expose her long, lovely neck to James, who bent forward, Katya draped in his arms, and brushed her throat with his lips.

The air felt good now against Alice's hot cheeks.

"Hey, Alice," Theo said awkwardly after a moment. "You want to go home and make popcorn?"

Alice stopped and turned to look at him. They stood under a tree, its branches inclined over the sidewalk, enfolding them in a fragrant darkness. She couldn't see Theo's face clearly, but she could still hear the music spilling out of the open doors of the hall into the street behind them.

She sighed. "Okay."

She turned away from him and started to walk again. There were things inside her that she did not know how to say, things that both excited her and embarrassed her, that filled her with vague longing and also with fury. Theo caught up and fell quietly into step beside her. Then he brushed her shoulder with his own, bumping her gently. She shrugged him off, but he came back again, leaning into her, insistent. And then she felt his hand find hers in the dark, and he held on.

His hand was warm and dry and small.

Alice's heart flew up into her throat, fluttering wildly inside her. Her pulse sounded in her ears like a deep bell, ringing and ringing into the dark street around them. A deep, sweet happiness spread over her, making her shiver.

He didn't look at her, but he swung her hand a little when she stole a glance at him, as if to say, *Yeah, that's my hand, holding yours.*

Alice woke up sometime in the middle of the night. She and Theo had slept outside, side by side in sleeping bags on the lawn in the front yard. It should have been dark—she knew it was night, because out beyond the strange light that seemed to surround her, it was utterly dark and still and quiet—but she could see Theo's face beside her as clearly as though it were daylight. She rolled over in her sleeping bag to crane her neck and look back at the house. Nearly every window was lit with a hectic light. Alice blinked, puzzled. And then she heard voices.

"Don't fucking wake them up! God, Archie. Don't wake them *up!*" It was Wally's voice. "Archie?" He was pleading.

Alice sat up in her sleeping bag. *Wake up who?*

Archie said something undistinguishable. Then she heard the sound of the screen door to the porch opening. Archie and Wally stepped outside. "I need to ask them about it," Archie said. "Tonight. Now. I need to be able to go and speak to Hope. If it's true, then I'm at fault, too."

Alice lay frozen in her sleeping bag. She saw Wally sit down on the porch steps and put his head in his hands. Tad came out onto the porch, and then Eli, but they didn't go any farther, lurking by the front door. From inside, she thought she could hear Harry's voice, and then Katya's. Was someone crying?

Beside her, there was a sudden alarmed whirring and clicking in the grass, the angry sound of an insect disturbed, one of the beetles that buzzed furiously when flipped onto its hard, shiny green back. She drew away sharply from the sound as if whatever it was might sting her or bite her.

Archie came across the grass toward her. Suddenly she felt trapped inside the sleeping bag, as if she wanted to get up and run but couldn't.

He stopped before her and stared down at her for a minute, his expression unreadable. "You're awake," he said.

Alice, bewildered by his tone, which was cold and sad and distant, looked into his face and then past him to the house. On the porch, under the yellow light, Wally sat motionless on the steps, his head resting in his hands. Tad leaned up against the wall of the house, his arms folded, staring down at his feet. Next to him, Eli turned in the light from the door and looked inside, his hands in his pockets, as if watching something in the hall.

Archie was still in his tuxedo, but he had unbuttoned his collar and his bow tie hung limply around his neck. His white hair was flattened on his head, as if he had been lying down.

"What *time* is it?" Alice said. She struggled to sit up.

Archie put his hand to his wrist as if to check his watch, but he did not pull back his sleeve.

"It's about quarter to five," he said, and Alice noticed then that there was a light in the sky on the eastern horizon, a sliver of bright red interrupted here and there by the dark tops of the trees.

Alice looked back at Archie's grave face and then up at the

boys on the porch. "Why's everyone up?" she said. "Is the dance over?"

"Please come inside, Alice," Archie said. "And would you wake up Theo, too, please?" He turned away from her and walked back to the house, slowly mounting the porch steps and disappearing inside. Her brothers stayed on the porch, exactly as they had been.

Alice scrambled to extricate herself from her sleeping bag, scraping her knee painfully on the zipper. She reached out and shook Theo roughly. The grass was cold and wet. She heard the whirring noise again, a little farther off, and she drew away fearfully.

Theo moaned and scrunched down into his sleeping bag, one hand emerging to try to draw it over his head.

"Wake up," Alice said. "Theo, wake up. Wake up!" A terrible urgency and fear was building inside her.

She jostled Theo again. Her legs were soaking wet and cold from kneeling in the grass. She began to shiver.

Theo rolled over and squinted up at her painfully as if she were shining a flashlight into his face.

"Something's happened," she said. "Get up."

"What?" He sat up, bleary-eyed and blinking. "Why are all the lights on? What time is it?"

"Just get up," she said. Her teeth started to chatter.

Theo stared at her for a second and then wriggled out of his sleeping bag. He stood on the grass in his bare feet, in his striped T-shirt and his wrinkled shorts.

He looked helpless, she thought, stupid and helpless, with his hair standing up crazily and his face creased and bewildered. Once he had begun holding her hand as they had walked back from the dance, he had seemed not to want to let go of it for the rest of the night, and they had fallen asleep on their backs, hands clasped, staring silently up at the clouds crossing the face of the moon, the black depths full of stars appearing and disappearing. She had drifted off, aware of the pulse in his hand, the steam of their breath rising above them into the cool night air.

She'd been wrong, she thought now. When she'd met Kenneth, and when Theo had taken her hand, she had thought that the life that lay ahead of her had been fully revealed to her, all the complicated, grown-up things that she could not have identified before because she did not know what they were. But those had been only a prelude, she understood now, only the parade's first weak players in their tattered uniforms and tarnished instruments, the dirty urchins and toothless, unfit volunteers who staggered out from the side streets to join the throng, beating old pie tins or the lids of metal garbage cans, anything to make a noise. They had been only the shabby, raucous harbingers of the real thing, the future that came on relentlessly rolling down the street on massive, creaking wheels, ropes straining and whining, a dark and shapeless mass that organized itself blackly against the horizon.

"Foolish," Archie said, closing his eyes, his face sagging, leaning back in his desk chair as if defeated. "All of it."

They had found Kenneth on the rocks below the falls, he told Alice and Theo. They had followed the rope walk, just as Miss Fitzgerald—hysterical, pointing, accusing—had said they should, and once they reached the end, well, it was obvious, Archie said, where they should look next.

"How could you be so stupid?" he asked them, and Alice had gone cold with fright.

In his study, with the dawn light creeping into the room, Archie had raised his gaze at last to Alice and Theo, taking them in as though he was surprised; they were too small and insignificant in their rumpled T-shirts and bare feet and sleep-creased faces to have accomplished anything, much less anything of such magnitude. "Didn't you realize that he could fall from there?" he'd said. *"Alice?"*

The tiger skin on the floor had seemed to raise its heavy head, teeth bared.

"He didn't fall," Alice said, bewildered but certain. "He jumped."

She knew it. She didn't want to know it, she thought, looking back at Archie. But she felt it inside herself, the truth of it.

Archie stared back at her. "There wasn't any note, Alice," he said. "He didn't leave a note."

She shook her head. "It doesn't matter," she said at first.

Then she said, surprising herself, "Yes, he did. I know he did."

Archie stood up abruptly then, as though he didn't want to look at them anymore. "I need to go speak to Hope," he said. "I consider myself at fault, for not supervising you properly this summer."

He looked at them for one more minute. "This will be with us for a very long time," he said. "Forever. Do you *understand* that?"

There was a black man standing in the driveway beside a white car. His hair was close-cropped, revealing the shape of his blue-black head. From her windowsill, Alice pretended to take a picture of its perfect oval. She had heard the tires coming down the lane, the slam of a car door. And then there were voices downstairs, and the sound of the screen door below her windowsill opening and then banging shut. Tad came down the porch steps into the brilliant light of the day carrying Theo's battered suitcase, the duct tape on the corner of it glinting in the sun. A moment later, the screen door squeaked again and Harry appeared on the steps, hoisting Theo's toolbox in his arms.

Alice frowned and raised her camera to focus on an empty square of sky above her, an uninterrupted royal blue, like the field of the flag.

Below her windowsill, the door banged again and suddenly Theo ran thudding down the porch steps and across the lawn, hurtling into the man who stood by the white car. The man staggered as Theo hit him, and then, in a gesture whose emotion Alice could read even from the distance of her windowsill, bent over like a puppet released at the waist and put his arms around him. Archie came slowly down the steps, offered his hand to the man who let go of Theo for a moment to shake hands. Then the man reached behind him as if to extract a wallet from his back pocket. Archie held up his hands and took a step away, shaking his head. He was saying something, but Alice couldn't make out what it was. Theo's face remained pressed to the man's stomach.

Harry reached out and roughed up Theo's hair, but Theo didn't turn around.

Alice's heart leaped in gratitude toward Harry for that gesture.

The man bent over and picked up Theo's suitcase. Archie picked up the toolbox. Awkwardly, because Theo was still pressed against him, the man shuffled with Theo so that he could put the suitcase in the trunk. Then he turned and took the toolbox from Archie. They shook hands one more time, and then Theo, like water sliding down the man's shirtfront, slipped into the backseat of the car without ever speaking to Archie or showing his face and sank down below the level of the window. For a long moment the figures on the driveway remained standing there, frozen in position, as if none of them knew what to do next.

Theo must be lying on the seat, or curled up on the floor mat, Alice thought, straining from her windowsill to see.

Once she had hidden in Archie's car during a game of hide-and-seek, and she remembered the feeling of making herself small enough to fit on the gritty floor mat, curled up tight with her nose full of the smell of dirt and gravel and engine oil.

Neither she nor Theo had cried. After Archie had dismissed them from his study two nights ago, they had crawled underneath the porch in the dirt while the sun rose, and they had looked out at the lawn and the sky through the bars of the lattice. Later in the morning, Wally had come outside to find them, and he had made them come inside. Silent with shame, they had stood in the kitchen, hands and faces filthy, while he made them peanut butter sandwiches. Alice had asked if they could take the sandwiches upstairs and Wally had said yes. Sometime in the afternoon, Archie had come upstairs to Alice's room and asked Theo to go with him. Theo had not come back. Wally had brought Alice a mug of tomato soup and some crackers in the evening. She had fallen asleep on the floor under her bed, and when she had woken up the next morning, all of Theo's belongings were gone. She had wanted to go look for him, she had wanted to find him, but she had been afraid to come out of her room. When Wally had come upstairs to try to get her to come down for breakfast, he had said that Theo was still asleep, that Archie had not wanted him in Alice's room anymore.

"It wasn't your fault, Alice," Wally had said. "Come here. Come on. You're breaking my heart."

But she had shied away from him, shinnying under the bed again, banging her head on the box spring, tears springing to her eyes.

And now she couldn't even see Theo.

She knew he was in the car; she could imagine how he was lying with his face pressed against the vinyl into the crack of the seat, smelling all the things that had fallen back there, pennies and matchbooks and pieces of paper and old pencils and French fries.

Finally the man got into the car and backed up and then turned the car around and headed up the lane.

Alice leaned from her windowsill.

Just before the car pulled out of sight, she saw Theo's face emerge against the rear window, staring back at the house. Was he looking at her window? She remembered her flying dreams, when she had launched out into the air, swooping up toward the moon, the hills falling away beneath her, the tops of the trees a soft, dark mass below.

She leaned from her windowsill toward Theo's disappearing face, and she knew that the air would not hold her, that it was only air, thin and insubstantial, that if she fell she would tumble over and over until she hit the ground.

THIRTEEN

THE FIRST SNOW of that winter began toward the end of a bitterly cold day in early November. Alice had gone to school that morning with a headache. When she got off the school bus at the top of the driveway at five that afternoon, she was shivering with a fever. The bus pulled away, leaving her standing alone in the unnatural silence of the snowfall. Heavy, cottony snowflakes sank gently through the violet air. The snow fell so thickly that Alice could not see fifteen feet ahead of her, and in the last light of the day, the lane dropped off into nothingness, a hallucinatory white blur filled with a flickering interior light and a smoky, hissing cold. Head bowed, the snow forming epaulets on her shoulders, Alice set off toward the house.

When she came through the back door into the kitchen a few minutes later, Elizabeth turned around from the stove.

"Why you all red in the face?" she said in surprise.

"I don't feel very well," Alice said dully. She sat down on one of the kitchen chairs without taking off her coat and let her backpack slide to the floor. In the warmth of the room, the snow melted immediately to form a puddle under her soaked shoes. A cold trickle ran down the back of her neck, and then another over her forehead and into her eye.

Elizabeth crossed the kitchen and plastered a hand to Alice's forehead.

Alice leaned back her head and closed her eyes. Elizabeth's hand was wet and heavy; at that moment Alice felt as if her neck wouldn't support the weight of her own head much less Elizabeth's hand, but Elizabeth's touch was comforting, anyway. Helen had often taken Alice in her arms and laid her cheek alongside Alice's, but Helen was still in the nursing home, speechless and ill; when Archie had taken Alice to visit her, she had been changed almost beyond Alice's recognition of her. It seemed that there were not many people to touch or comfort Alice anymore. Her teacher, Mrs. White, absently rubbed Alice's back a little sometimes as she came around the room to look over the students' shoulders at their work, and occasionally Elizabeth gave Alice one of her hard little squeezes in a way that made Alice think Elizabeth was sorry for her. In the mornings, Archie kissed Alice goodbye with a careful formality, and sometimes with what she recognized as longing, but she did not want to sit in his lap any longer, and, as if sensing that she would rebuff him, he had not invited her.

Archie had made Alice write to Miss Fitzgerald, a stiff letter of contrition and apology full of formal phrases that had been painfully difficult to compose. Archie had sent her back to rewrite the letter three times, but in the end Alice had not meant any of it, at least not the part in which she had been forced to acknowledge culpability, stupidity, guilt.

Sorrow, she had felt. The sorrow was deep and black, like water that rose inside her sometimes and took her breath away.

She had been furious at Archie for making her write that letter.

"You don't believe me," she had said to Archie.

"It had a terrible end, Alice," Archie said. "Regardless of what you and Theo intended. He got to the end of it and fell."

"Not regardless!" Alice had shouted. "Not *regardless*!"

"Don't shout," he had shouted back at her.

"I want to talk to Theo," she said, struggling to control her voice. "Give me his phone number."

"Goddamn it, Alice." Archie had put his hands on his head and rubbed his scalp furiously as though something was eating away at him. "Enough. No. You two did enough damage. No."

"I don't love you anymore," Alice said to his back as he left the room.

"Go upstairs. Get into bed," Elizabeth said now. "I'll come up in a minute, bring you some Advil." She left her hand on Alice's forehead for a moment, though, looking down at her. "Poor thing," she said. "You sick."

Upstairs, the hall was cold and dark. Last year, when the boys had gone back to school, Alice, wanting to enliven the house's abandoned spaces, had assigned each of their rooms a particular purpose: she had read books stretched out on her stomach on Wally's bed under his ship wall lamp with the shade shaped like a sail; she had done her homework in Eli's room at his desk beneath the dormer window; she had carried her paints and colored pencils and the box of paper scraps and scissors and glue into the twins' room so she could work on art projects on the floor in there.

This year, however, the boys' rooms had remained dark and undisturbed. Sometimes Alice quietly opened the doors and stared inside, but the rooms had the same remote museum quality as her mother's dressing room. They were like shrines, sad and old and even a little frightening, as if when Alice turned the doorknob something inside hurried to hide, flattening itself up against the wall and camouflaging itself against the pattern of the old wallpaper.

In her bedroom now, Alice didn't turn on the light. She bent to take off her wet socks. The effort it took to tug them over her heels was absurdly exhausting, and she sat down on the striped chair by her window and gazed out at the snow. Maybe it would snow so much she couldn't go to school tomorrow, she thought. Or maybe she'd be too sick to go. Being out of school and in her dark bedroom, with the quiet, snow-filled night creating between her and the rest of the world a gulf of white silence, she felt a little better, just shivery and small and dull.

It was a relief to be away from school. For the first few days this past fall she had been an object of intense and wary scrutiny on the part of her classmates; the news of Kenneth's death and Alice's role in it had spread quickly throughout Grange. Once the children's interest in her passed, though, Alice had failed to do anything to help restore herself to public acceptance. She was quiet, as she had always been quiet. She didn't know what people thought, whether they blamed her and Theo, or Kenneth himself, or nobody at all.

Her class was studying geography in social studies, and Alice liked maps, as she liked math. She appreciated the certainty of those subjects, their unequivocal boundaries. She especially liked coloring in the maps. At home she'd been working on a map of the world on an old sheet spread out on the floor of the dining room. She'd started one and then had to turn the sheet over and start again once she had figured out how to make a grid with a ruler and a piece of string so that the continents and oceans were more or less to scale. It was absorbing to draw in the rivers and mountain ranges, the seas and chains of little islands, the lakes and deserts. It was the kind of project Theo would have liked, she thought, and sometimes lying on her stomach on the floor and coloring, she tried to pretend he was lying there beside her. When she had the idea of drawing a tiny sea serpent in the Pacific Ocean, she knew that Theo would have liked that detail. Inspired, she had lifted down the atlas from the bookshelf in the living room and looked up information about the countries— climate, principal exports, crops—that would give her more ideas for drawings. She'd drawn apple trees, salmon leaping upriver, bundles of grain, blue and silver snowflakes falling on the Swiss Alps, the French Pyrenees, the Carpathians, the Andes. She did not think her illustrations approached Theo's skill, but she found the hours of lying on her stomach on the dining room floor diverting. She couldn't seem to think about anything when she was coloring, and that was a comfort.

It distressed her that she didn't seem able to concentrate on books. The familiar stories had lost their charm for her; they seemed silly. And sometimes she didn't bother to do her home-work, either. When Mrs. White asked her about it, she just said she was sorry.

"It's all right, Alice," Mrs. White said kindly. "But I know you *can* do the work. I'd just like to understand why you're *not* doing it."

Who cares? Alice had thought, looking at the floor. What does it matter, anyway? The future for which she had been preparing herself, in which she would do her homework and get good grades and become a brave and successful person, had become like a quaint idea from a story. People were not what she had imag-ined them to be—not her father, not O'Brien, not her brothers, who seemed to have abandoned her to the remote wilderness of Archie's care. The world she had loved so passionately from her bedroom windowsill just six months before, the spring morning that had unfolded brilliantly at her feet, now seemed distant and insubstantial. It seemed, in fact, like a place she had gone to once with a terrible and casual indifference, without any recognition of its value, and from which she was now painfully and mysteriously excluded. It was as if she could no longer find the gate or the key and did not know how to get back there. Or, worse, it was as if that place, that region of her past that was her childhood, its magic conveyed by the rich careless offerings of the world's beauty, had disappeared entirely from the map, the roads leading to it rubbed away, a gray blur where it had been once, as if a mountaintop were enveloped in cloud.

Meanwhile, she could not make herself do many of the things that had once felt like requisites of the life she had led before, indeed, that had been among its pleasures. The only dependable happiness was to be outdoors; she found the river's rushing colloquy comforting. She did not think that the river had tried to drown Kenneth, any more than she believed that the rope walk had killed him. He had used the rope walk, as he had used the falls and the river.

Archie was persuaded that if Kenneth had intended to kill himself, he would have left a letter; that none had been found was evidence that whatever had happened at the edge of the falls, it had not been premeditated. Archie acknowledged that, perhaps, finding himself poised there, Kenneth had simply . . . taken the opportunity. But if that opportunity had not presented itself? Archie had let the question hang. And in the silence that grew between them as Alice had stood before her father, Alice felt the ground pull away from beneath her.

"I blame myself," Archie said, not looking at her. But she knew he blamed her.

Alice did not ask herself to imagine what had happened, Kenneth moving shakily hand over hand through the dark, still woods that evening when everyone else in Grange, including his sister, was at the dance, sweating under the lights; Alice and Theo had seen her there, working alongside some of the other women serving punch and cake. Kenneth's death was too much to think about, too much to consider, the details too shocking; she was sensible about protecting herself in this way and would not make herself picture it. But she could not believe that he had simply fallen to his death; he had known exactly where he was going, she thought. What she could not understand was how he could have ended his life without giving Alice and Theo—especially Alice and Theo—some kind of explanation. Without saying goodbye.

As they crouched in the dirt under the porch the morning after Kenneth's death, Theo had said, "He had AIDS. He knew he was dying. Everybody who gets AIDS dies eventually. Maybe everyone in the whole world will get AIDS. I just don't think he wanted to be alive like that anymore, and with *her*."

Alice hadn't said anything.

"He was sick," Theo said. "He was in pain." After a minute, he added, "Maybe it was kind of a brave thing to do. He just . . . you know. *Whoosh.* Flew."

"Maybe," Alice had said. She had felt grateful to Theo for this version of events, for the way it calmed the sick sensation in her stomach, the hideous rise of guilt.

Theo had been quiet for a time, and they had crouched there

together, staring out through the bars of the lattice. "It was meant to be *nice,*" he had said finally, and Alice had been glad to hear the anger in his voice, because she felt angry, too.

Alice stared out her bedroom window now into the swirling blur of the snow falling through the evening air. Her head throbbed and her neck and back ached. Once she had wanted to take on a hundred enemies at once, sword flashing, cape flying. Now she felt both surrounded and curiously alone; she did not know which way to turn.

For days after Theo had been sent home, Alice had wandered around outside or lay on her bed. From time to time Wally had come in and pulled up a chair, sitting quietly near her and smoking cigarettes as if in open, angry defiance of Archie.

"Kenneth must have been suffering, Alice," Wally said the day after Theo had been taken away "I don't think he meant to hurt you. I don't think he was even thinking about you. Maybe he just had a flair for the dramatic. Or maybe he couldn't think of any other way."

"I want Theo," Alice had said. She rolled over away from Wally. The wallpaper was coming loose at its seam; she reached out and picked at it.

"Listen," Wally said. "You tried to do something wonderful, right? You just have to remember that."

Alice sat up on her bed and turned to face him. "Why did Archie make Theo leave?"

"Archie just wants the whole thing to go away," Wally said. "This is exactly the kind of thing Archie hates. People talking about him."

"He hates me," Alice said.

Wally had shaken his head. "No, he doesn't. He's just . . . he feels like it's his fault. Like he should have known what you guys were doing."

"We didn't want anyone to know. It was supposed to be a surprise."

"Yeah, well . . ." Wally put out his cigarette in the coffee cup he'd brought upstairs. "How long did it take you guys to build that, anyway?"

"All summer."

"I don't think I could have done that at your age. It's impressive, really." Wally leaned forward, looking at her bedside table. "Why do you have all those dead bugs in that jar?"

Alice looked at the jar. The last valiant earthquake detectors had fallen on their backs to the bottom of the glass amid the dead leaves and broken twigs. It was awful, she thought, as sad and terrible as a battlefield. She flopped back down on her bed and closed her eyes.

"It's Theo's earthquake-warning device," she said. "Why isn't Archie mad at *Kenneth*?"

"Well, he is. But Kenneth's . . . you know."

"Dead," said Alice, eyes still closed. "You can say it."

Being separated from Theo was the worst thing that had ever happened to her. She knew that her mother's death had been more important in terms of terrible things to happen to a person, but because she had not felt that loss, she could not compare it to this. She had tried calling directory assistance in Manhattan and in Brooklyn and the Bronx, but she didn't know where exactly Theo lived, nor his father's first name—there was no listing in his mother's name—and there were dozens of Swanns in the directories. Every day she saw something or thought something that she knew Theo would have liked. At night in bed she crept her fingers together over her breastbone and clasped her hands there over her heart, but it was not the same, holding your own hand.

When Elizabeth came upstairs with a glass of water and an Advil, Alice got into bed.

Elizabeth tugged the sheets and blankets into place around her while Alice swallowed the pill. Then, sighing, she sat down on the chair where Alice had been sitting by the window. "That's some snow!" Elizabeth said.

Her head with its neat cap of hair was silhouetted against the silvery light of the snowstorm outside the window. Her voice sounded to Alice very far away. "Maybe I should stay here tonight," she said. "Roads might get bad."

"Don't leave," Alice said groggily from bed. "Elizabeth?"

"What? Wow. Look at that snow, Alice!"

"Don't leave, okay?"

"Okay. Shhh. Go to sleep."

Alice woke up the next morning feeling light-headed but otherwise well. She stood at the window for a moment, looking out at the landscape. Against the snow that lay over the ground, the firs were a deep, velvet green, iced in silver. Recovering from illness often gave her a fragile sense of euphoria, especially if she woke, as she did this morning, to clear weather, the skies an achingly brilliant blue. As she went downstairs, her head felt pleasantly separated from her body, as if her legs and torso were a ship that moved beneath her, cumbersome and heavy, sensitive to currents that her mind, skimming along in the thin air above, could not detect.

"Lucky day for you," Elizabeth said cheerfully, when Alice found her in the dining room surrounded by an armada of the silver and her polishing rags and a blaze of winter sunlight. "Big water pipe broken at school. You get free vacation. No homework, even. Right?"

"Really?" Alice sat down on a chair in the sunshine. When she reached out to touch the tarnished garland of roses on the coffee pot, Elizabeth made a noise of caution.

"Sorry." Alice withdrew her hand.

"You feel better?" Elizabeth said.

"Much," Alice stretched. She stood up and wandered into the kitchen to make herself a piece of toast, which she ate standing at the back door, looking out into the brightness of the morning and over the pure, unbroken whiteness, the slow crystalline dripping of water from an icicle hanging from the gutter of the garage. There were interesting patterns of purple shadows over the snow, the blurred mauve silhouette of a squirrel running along a power line, the immense shadow of the house itself. The world had been simplified, laid out in blocks of color: white, green, blue, gray.

From the dining room, Elizabeth called, "You want scrambled eggs?"

Alice turned away from the window and went back to the dining room. "No, thank you," she said. She squatted down in front of her map on the floor. She had been working lately on North America, drawing in the rivers in the west, the Missouri and the Snake and the Columbia. She had drawn in the outlines of Montana and Wyoming and Idaho, sketched the tumult of the Rocky Mountains, where Lewis and Clark and their party had been shocked to discover not the fabled Northwest Passage and a gentle slope down to the Pacific, but only the endless rugged heaves of Clark's "Shineing Mountains" stretching far

away into the distance, the snow-covered ranges of the Bitterroots that would nearly destroy the Corps of Discovery and its
brave leaders.

Alice lay down on her stomach at the edge of her map and
traced her finger along the Missouri to the Great Falls, where the
company had portaged the canoes. The journal entries from
those weeks, and the ones over the next two months, when the
explorers crossed the Continental Divide, had been the most har-
rowing in Lewis and Clark's accounts of their voyage west. Theo
had stopped falling asleep in the afternoons when she read, as
caught up as she was in the story. From time to time, Lewis and
Clark had been forced to part company and consider alternate
routes, leaving each other handwritten notes pegged to trees,
articles of faith in the midst of such a vast wilderness the dimensions of which Alice found astonishing. How had the two friends
found the courage to believe they would see each other again?
How had they possibly expected to find each other's valiant messages fluttering against the brown bark of one tree in a million?
Every time she read about days when Lewis and Clark had to
separate, or send a man off to look for a packhorse gone astray, or
then more men to look for *that* man when he failed to return,
Alice's anxiety had risen. She had been alone in the woods
enough times herself, halted suddenly by a prickling at the nape
of her neck, an alarm that rippled through her like the wind in
the trees, to imagine the explorers beyond the grip of danger or
even their own fear. She wanted them all to stay together, but
time and time again they bravely had bid each other farewell and
set off, sometimes one man utterly alone. Had they never suc-
cumbed to fear, Alice wondered? They had written in their journals. They had gathered specimens of roots and moss and plants.
They had met Indians and bartered for horses and information
and dogs and beaver skins. They had taken their bearings, made

their careful drawings and their maps. Somehow, miraculously, they had survived.

The sheet was warm now in a patch of sunlight falling through the window where the curtains were drawn back. Alice could smell the acid fumes of the silver polish, hear behind her at the table Elizabeth's vigorous efforts with the cloth. Alice rested her chin on her folded arms and let her gaze wander over her map. Here the men of the Corps of Discovery, stranded by hail and snow in the steep passes of the Bitterroots, had slaughtered their horses to eat and to stay alive, here they had killed a coyote, here in desperation they had melted down and eaten some of their tallow candles.

And yet, it probably wasn't exactly right *here,* she thought. She rested her chin in her hands, looking at the lines she had drawn. Then she consulted the atlas spread open on the floor beside her. She couldn't tell exactly, looking at the modern atlas, where Lewis and Clark's trail had gone. In the edition from which she'd been reading to Kenneth and Theo, there had been a map on the flyleaf of the book much like the map in her copy of *The Hobbit,* with its drawing of the Misty Mountains and Mirkwood and the Desolation of Smaug. In James and Wally's room there was an edition of *The Wind in the Willows* with its absorbing map of the Wild Wood and Surrounding Country. The map on the flyleaf of the Lewis and Clark journals had shown the explorers' trek westward with little black symbols like a chain of arrowheads or tiny footprints crisscrossing the plains, and though she knew that the voyage had been a real one across a real continent, the landscape in the black-and-white drawing had seemed as mythical and exciting as an imaginary place. The little track had veered north toward Canada and then descended in a crooked dip through the mountains, a scooped path like the bowl of the Big Dipper, before stretching out on the runaway lap down the Columbia toward the Pacific Ocean. She looked at her own map and then back at the atlas. She would like to draw Lewis and Clark's route on her map, she thought.

She looked up, startled, as the bough of a fir tree just outside the window released its burden of snow, the drift sliding heavily down the slippery needles and crashing into the shrubs beneath the window. Dry snow rose like a smoke signal into the still, cold air outside. In the silence of the house she could hear the faint, raspy ticking of the clock in the hall, the vigorous rubbing sound Elizabeth made with her cloth. And then another load of snow slipped free, following the first. A second puff of dry snow exploded and hung suspended, sparkling in mid-air. Alice blinked. A third branch dipped, strained; snow slid hissing toward the ground. A fourth went. A fifth. Each time, Alice blinked as though a gun had been fired beside her ear, a signal going off to bring her to her feet, like Lewis and Clark's men bolting from sleep as a buffalo bull charged into their camp.

She sat up abruptly. What had happened to the edition of Lewis and Clark's journals she had taken to Kenneth's? What had happened to *all* the books she and Theo had brought with them on that first day they'd gone to visit Kenneth? Were they still there on the table in Kenneth's room?

On one of the last days she had read aloud to Kenneth and Theo, when she came to Clark's triumphant journal entry at the explorers' first view of the ocean, Alice had had difficulty controlling the emotion in her voice. *"Great joy in camp we are in view of the Ocian,"* he had written, *"this great Pacific Octean which we been so long anxious to See. and the roreing or noise made by the waves brakeing on the rockey Shores (as I suppose) may be heard disti[n]ctly."*

"Whew," Theo had said from the floor. "I thought they'd *never* get there."

That evening, Archie came in the back door while Alice was eating her supper. Elizabeth had made her tomato soup and a grilled cheese sandwich and had pulled up the rickety little bamboo side table to one of the armchairs before the fireplace in the kitchen. The house was cold, and Alice was wearing her pajamas and a pair of heavy socks and one of Wally's hats with the fake fur earflaps.

"Feeling better?" Archie said, putting a hand on Alice's head briefly as he stood by the fire and unwound his scarf. He sat down in the chair across from her. "It's snowing hard again," he said to Elizabeth. "You should go on home before it gets worse."

Elizabeth leaned down and gave Alice a hug on her way out the back door. "Dinner's in the oven," she said to Archie, pulling on her mittens. "You *eat* it, okay? Don't forget. I don't want to come back tomorrow and find it in there again, hard like a old rock."

"No. Of course not." Archie stood up, his scarf in his hand. "Thank you." He looked embarrassed, Alice thought, glancing up at him. Maybe he often forgot about his supper.

He came back a few moments later with a glass of wine and the mail. Alice swiveled in her chair, her back to the fire so she could watch the snow through the window. The snowflakes seemed to be engaged in a battle, colliding and whirling like people running wildly in all directions.

In the chair on the other side of the fireplace, Archie unfolded the newspaper and held it up before his face.

Alice looked at the gray front page of the newspaper. There was a picture of a crowd of people, their expressions violent.

Archie reached out from behind the paper and picked up his wineglass.

Alice watched the newspaper for a minute, but Archie stayed hidden behind it. She picked up her soup cup and looked into it. She stuck her tongue down into the cup and licked. Everybody in the whole world seemed to be angry, she thought.

"Don't forget about your dinner," she said at last.

"What?" Archie didn't lower the paper.

"In the oven," Alice said.

"Oh. No, I won't." He lowered the paper at last. He folded it on his lap and tilted back his head, closing his eyes. He looked old and tired, Alice thought. Once Archie had played Prospero in one of the plays in Grange, and she'd been frightened of him in his cape and stage makeup, with long black lines painted on his face and his hair wild.

She looked down into her cup again and with her tongue reached for the last of the soup at the bottom. It was very quiet in the room, just the fire hissing and crackling gently at their feet, but Alice's thoughts were whirling. She looked over at Archie, trying to reach him with her mind. Could she communicate with him that way, tell him what she was thinking without actually saying the words? She tried, concentrating fiercely, but her efforts did not seem to be successful. He didn't even open his eyes. She tried saying it very distinctly inside her head—*I'm going to go look for the Lewis and Clark*—but Archie just sat there, his eyes closed. It gave Alice a sad sense of freedom. There were all sorts of things she could hide from her father. There were continents that separated them now.

It was neither as cold as she had expected it to be at midnight, nor as dark. The moon was nearly full, and even though snow was falling lightly, she could see the moon behind the clouds, a blurred lamp high in the sky. The snow-covered fields around the house gave off an unearthly light.

The explorers had worn only moccasins on their feet, Alice thought, as she had pulled on her snow boots and her coat, tied a scarf around her neck, pulled down the flaps of Wally's hat over her ears.

An enormous lightheartedness came over her the minute she stepped outside and quietly pulled the back door closed behind her, dispelling the fear she had felt lying in bed a few minutes before when, wide-eyed, she had clapped her hand over her clock, the alarm set to go off at midnight. Had she actually fallen asleep? She couldn't be sure.

The snow was beautiful, a benevolent fall of light through darkness. She tipped up her face and held out her arms.

When she crossed the lawn and started up the lane, she became aware of movement in the woods beside her—a silent herd of white-tailed deer, twenty, maybe thirty creatures in all, moving alongside her a few feet into the trees, their heads down, searching for something to eat. A few paused, lifted their heads, and turned to look in her direction and then moved on parallel with her as she walked uphill. When she looked back for them after a few minutes, they were gone, but she felt comforted, knowing they were nearby, coughing into the trees, their white tails flickering.

No one would be able to see her tracks in the snow. She would walk along the road—it was too deep in the woods to make good progress there now, anyway—but if anyone came by she could just duck into the trees or behind a parked car. Still, no one would be out at this hour, and not on a night like this, she thought, even though it was so beautiful, the snow twinkling around her, the breathing silence. Why *didn't* people come outside in a snowstorm and walk around? Falling through the street-lights, coming on endlessly from somewhere high in the sky, the snow was so lovely it almost made her want to cry. She wished Theo were with her.

At the houses along the street, paths along the front walks had been shoveled, and cars had backed out of garages and left tracks in the driveways, but already these were filling up with new snow. There were electric candles in the windows, wreaths on a few front doors, Christmas lights wound around porch railings or through the branches of trees in the front yards. In the falling snow, the scene was tranquil and lovely; Grange looked like a perfect storybook town, Alice thought, in which nothing bad could ever happen. No terrorists or suicide bombers or psychopaths or serial killers, no tidal waves or hurricanes or floods or avian flu. And yet once, she remembered, startled, all this land had been covered with an inland ocean through which great dinosaurs had stepped and whales had swum.

There were no Christmas lights on at the Fitzgeralds'. The car was parked in the garage, but the garage doors had been left open, probably so Miss Fitzgerald wouldn't have to shovel away the snow to open them, Alice thought. It would be hard, if you were an old lady, to shovel all that snow. Alice stared up at the house. Miss Fitzgerald's bedroom was at the front of the house facing the street, as far away as possible from Kenneth's rooms. The windows were dark. Alice thought of the crowded rooms inside the house, the narrow passages between stacks of boxes like trails made by small animals, and she shuddered. Snow slipped down the back of her neck. She lifted her hood, shook the snow from it, and pulled it over her head.

Rather than leave her footprints down the front walk and across the lawn, even if they would soon be filled with snow, she broke through the hedge behind the garage and pushed through the low branches of the cedars there toward the semicircle of lawn at the back of the house, where Kenneth's big room gave out onto the terrace. At the edge of the trees, near where the rope walk had begun, she stopped. Every window in the house was dark. Alice thought of Miss Fitzgerald, asleep in her bed in the dark. She had not seen her since Kenneth's death except once from the car when Archie had stopped to get gas. Miss Fitzgerald had been walking along the sidewalk with a bag over her arm. She had not seemed to notice Archie's car nor Alice sitting alone, frozen in the front seat.

Alice's heart began to beat fast. She was warm inside her coat, but her fingers and toes were cold. Suddenly she felt afraid to be standing there watching the house with the woods at her back. There was no way to get to the house now except straight across the lawn, up the steps to the terrace, and to the French doors.

She scanned the house one more time, but there was not a single light on anywhere, as far as she could tell. Again she thought of Miss Fitzgerald, lying alone in her bed. It must be lonely without Kenneth, Alice thought. She knew she would be very lonely, if it were her.

She slipped on the steps going up to the terrace because she couldn't tell under the drifts where they began, and her mittens slipped, too, when she grasped the handle of the French doors and it did not turn. Were the doors locked? Her pulse pounded painfully in her ears and against her throat. She glanced behind her, as if someone from the house next door might be watching her from a curtained window.

She had not even considered the possibility that the doors would be locked; the doors at her own house were never locked.

She shook the doors lightly, despairingly. A thin layer of snow fell off the mullions. And then she pulled off her mittens with her teeth and put her bare hands on the handle. She could feel her head sweating under Wally's hat.

When she opened the doors to the boys' rooms at home, sometimes banging the door against the wall suddenly so as to surprise the thing that lived in there and came out to dance alone in the gloom of the long winter afternoons, she was never truly afraid. She was sure about the magic that lived in those empty rooms—it was perhaps the only magic in which she still believed, the magic of the thing you could not see—but she never mistook it for something larger than herself. The thing left behind all alone in those rooms and abandoned by her brothers, who long ago had left their own childhoods behind, was a small thing, even a mean thing, but it was a lonely thing, too, like Peter Pan's ragged, lifeless shadow, and she was not afraid of it. Indeed, she was sorry for it and longed somehow to comfort it, to sew it to her foot as Peter Pan had sewn his shadow to his heel and then, boy and shadow reunited, risen crowing into the air. One day, she thought, she would surprise the thing that lived in those empty rooms, that wandered back and forth like a wraith from her mother's dressing room and into the boys' rooms, bleating and moaning, and it would sweep out the door and flit away into the trees to take up residence inside an owl's nest or a mouse's hole. In a way, it would be like setting it free.

Now, though, her hand on the French doors, she was afraid. She pressed her fingers along the cold length of the handle and then, with a sharp heave, pushed down hard. The door swung suddenly open. It had not been locked, after all.

The white light from the French doors, full of the soft shadows of the moving snowflakes falling like the shadows of rain down a windowpane, lay over the floor. Nothing had been moved; nothing had changed. Kenneth's mobiles hung from the ceiling, stirring in the air she had disturbed by opening the door. The fur throw lay across the settee as if Kenneth had just tossed it aside. One of the leather chairs had been pulled up to the easel, the paper unfurling from its roll onto the carpet. His books were on the shelves, his telescope pointed toward her where she stood just inside the open French doors, the snow falling silently in the darkness behind her. On the round table where she had sat to read were the stacks of books and papers, the shiny ebony head of the African woman with her knots of hair, the carafe of water, half full. Alice ran her eyes over the room lovingly; that it had not changed seemed to her like a miracle or a dream.

And then she looked up. In the round silver mirror across the room over the fireplace, she saw a face and screamed.

She had screamed before she realized who it was, that she was looking at her own reflection.

She clapped her hands over her mouth, but it was too late. The sound had already escaped her. She stood still for one moment, horrified, and then she whirled around and ran out of the room across the terrace through the snow, slipping and falling down the steps and across the drifts that lay over the lawn. In a moment she was in the trees, and then there was nothing but silence and darkness and the snow falling gently around her.

When she lay in her own bed again, she could not close her eyes. She had crept in through the kitchen door, shoved her wet coat and hat into one of the cubbies on the porch, and slipped up the stairs and into her bed, but her body still seemed to be moving through the snow-filled night, the deer running silently beside her, hidden in the trees. As she had neared her own driveway, a car's headlights had blazed up once out of the darkness behind her, and Alice had felt herself pick up speed as though wolves were at her back. She had not known she could run that fast. In her ears now, as she pulled the covers up to her chin with cold fingers, she could still hear her feet thudding, like the sound of the surf crashing inside the dry, pristine vessel of the conch shell.

Surely her scream had woken Miss Fitzgerald.

If Miss Fitzgerald had come downstairs to investigate, running a flashlight's shaky beam over Kenneth's rooms, she would find the French doors open.

If Alice was lucky, she thought, Miss Fitzgerald would not notice Alice's tracks in the snow; she might assume the wind had blown the doors open. But she would shut them now, for sure, and probably lock them.

Alice was sure the book had been on the table, where she thought she had left it, but it might have been picked up and moved, stuck into a shelf somewhere, or fallen behind one of the paintings stacked against the wall, or kicked under a chair by Kenneth's shoes, filled now with dust.

There had been so many places Alice might have looked, she thought, and now she had wasted her chance. It was over. She would never get back inside.

FOURTEEN

ALICE WAS LYING on the couch, rereading *To Kill a Mockingbird,* when Archie came to the door of the living room. It was the last Sunday in March, a chilled, rainy afternoon with the feel of ice at its edges, the metallic cold smell of the thaw in the air. Alice had been outside earlier in the day and found snowdrops blooming under the dogwood trees.

"I've got to go up to the college," Archie announced from the doorway. "Someone's called in sick, and they need a dean at the admissions fair."

Alice did not look up from her book. She had heard the telephone ring, heard Archie answer it, noted the weary tone of resignation in his voice when, after some moments of his listening silence, he finally replied to whoever had called. She heard his annoyance now. He liked to spend Sundays reading and dozing in his study, and she was sure he did not want to interrupt his day with a trip to Frost. Nor did Alice want to go with him. It was nearly an hour's drive there and then another hour back, and it was boring to have to sit coloring or reading in her father's office. These events always took much longer than he said they would, anyway. "Okay," she said carefully, not looking up from her book, avoiding his eyes.

"Alice?" Archie put his hand on the door frame, preparatory to returning to his study to collect his papers, shut down his computer, and turn out the lights. The gesture meant that now the clock was ticking; he assumed she would get up from the couch, find her shoes, get ready to go with him.

"Um, I don't really feel like going to Frost," she said. She kept her tone carefully even; it was important that she should not sound as if she were whining. Her eyes stayed deliberately on the book before her. "I'll be fine here."

Archie hesitated.

Alice studiously followed the words on the page, not daring to risk it and look up to assess how seriously he was considering her proposal. Would he actually go without her? He didn't usually leave her alone unless he was just doing a quick errand in Grange. But she was almost eleven. She could stay home by herself; she knew plenty of kids who stayed home by themselves. And it would be so boring at Frost, especially in the rain. Finally, though, she couldn't resist; she looked up, her expression as bland and noncommittal as she could make it, a wide-eyed face that she hoped denied all contrivance.

Archie frowned. "I'll call Elizabeth," he said.

Elizabeth, reached on her recently acquired cell phone, was organizing a fiftieth birthday party for a friend at her church. She could not come in to stay with Alice. Why didn't Archie just drop off Alice at the church? Elizabeth proposed. Alice could come to the party. It would be fun!

Alice, who had come into the hallway and was following Archie's side of the conversation with growing comprehension and alarm, rolled her eyes. This would be even worse than having to go to Frost. *Please,* she mouthed to Archie. *No.*

Then Archie tried calling Tad and Harry, to see if Alice could spend the afternoon with them at Frost; the boys could take her to the gym to shoot baskets or for a swim in the indoor pool. But Archie couldn't reach either of the twins; neither one seemed to have a phone with him. More likely, Archie said, growing visibly further annoyed by the moment, they had run out of minutes.

Alice waited in the hall beside him while he held the phone to his ear, trying the twins a last time.

Finally, he looked at her. "You won't go outside, though," he stipulated. He hung up the phone. "All right? I'll be home by six."

"No problem," she said without thinking and then watched his mouth tighten. Archie hated that expression. He also hated the phrase "My bad," which the twins used regularly. "I'll be fine," she said hastily, to distract him. "I'll just read. I won't go anywhere."

Twenty minutes later, Alice watched from the kitchen window as Archie drove away up the driveway, the taillights of his car at first clearly visible through the rain, then flashing unsteadily and finally disappearing altogether, as if the car had plunged off the steep shoulder of the lane or been swallowed up by the gusts of the storm, restless inflated shapes like the gray sails of an enormous boat that swept over the treetops and across the fields.

Despite having told Archie that she would be fine by herself, she found that once he had actually gone, she was uneasy about the hours stretching ahead. The afternoon seemed gloomy and full of foreboding. She was surprised, really, that he had left her. He hadn't even argued with her, she thought.

She got up and wandered through the dining room and the living room, turning on lights against the watery, gray darkness, but this was almost worse, in a way; with every light on, and the rooms ablaze with a hard, demanding glare, the emptiness of the house intensified, ringing with silence.

Back in the kitchen she climbed onto a wobbly-legged chair to turn on the radio on the mantelpiece over the fireplace. She found an oldies station and stood on the chair, holding on to the mantelpiece and listening to a Buddy Holly song she recognized, watching herself sing along in the mirror: *Peggy Sue, Peggy Sue*.

After a while, she went upstairs, planning vaguely to root around in the boys' closets for something interesting to look at among the jumbled shoes, and the slick ties that had slipped from their hooks and fallen to the floor, and the stacks of worn paperbacks with their covers creased and folded back unevenly.

In Eli's closet, in a cardboard file box under a snake's nest of tangled wire hangers, she found sixteen dollars and some spare change, a copy of *The Prophet,* and a lot of Eli's old school papers; they all seemed to be marked with a red A inside a circle, or "100%" or "Excellent!" written across the top.

In the closet in James and Wally's room she found two cardboard cartons of sheet music and a gym bag that, when she unzipped it, caused her to reel back: it was full of rank-smelling, dirty clothes. Scattered on the floor of the closet were various papers and envelopes. She took up a handful and flipped through it: bank statements, mailings from Princeton, letters, including one to James from a girl named Jenny, penned in a round, childish hand, the tail of the Y on Jenny formed into a tiny heart. Alice skimmed the contents. *Hey Cutie! I miss you! So, what are you doing this summer?* The letter was full of references to people Alice did not know, and she put it aside, bored. Inside an old hiking boot that rattled when she lifted it to move it aside, she found a harmonica, delicate scales of rust like a fossil across its shiny surface. She raised it to her lips and blew. The sound was eerie—it made the hair on her arms rise—and she dropped it on the floor of the closet where it fell soundlessly onto a pile of clothes.

She was on her hands and knees, her brothers' shirts and sport jackets brushing her head and shoulders, when she heard a distinct noise from downstairs, a dull thud like a door banging open against a wall.

A jolt of pure fear went into her stomach. In the closet, she flattened onto the floor and froze. After a minute, her heart pounding, she moved—just her head, a fraction of an inch—so that she could see behind her into the bedroom. In the silence she registered the urgent ticking and creaks of the house, as though a conversation were taking place around her between the walls and the window frames, the ceiling and the floorboards, a dissatisfied, murmuring conference.

Maybe Archie had come home, having forgotten something. This was a comforting thought; the possibility that it was Archie downstairs, and not something else, sent relief washing over her. Still, if he found her looking through the boys' things, he would be mad. She waited another minute, and then she inched backward out of the closet and crawled over to the window on her hands and knees to look out for his car. But the driveway, when she peered over the window ledge, was empty, only the rain disturbing the surface of the water in the puddles. No car, at least, had approached the house.

Alice sat alert and fearful on the floor beneath the windowsill. What was she frightened of? Murderers? Terrorists? Madmen?

Suicide bombers? Yes, yes! All those things, all the horrors Theo had invoked, the faces of strangers intent on harming her, the figures who moved now out of the dark recesses in her imagination, places she had not even known were there, had not wanted to explore, was afraid to own. A dark mass pressed itself invisibly against the comforting world she could compass now with her eyes, the solid, reassuring planes of its surfaces—beds, bureau, bookshelf—even the leaking roof of clouds fleeing overhead, all of it braced like an insubstantial firmament against the oppressive darkness beyond. When she had recognized Theo's fear, she had not been scornful. She had known, deep in her heart, that he was right: the world was terrifying.

An image of Miss Fitzgerald emerged in Alice's mind like a figure coming clear out of the gloom, a woman at the end of a dark hallway, all alone and intent as a ghost, with all the power of a ghost to accost and accuse.

The week before, when Archie had come upstairs one evening to say good night to Alice, he had sat down at the end of her bed and quietly told her that Miss Fitzgerald was planning to leave Grange. There was Kenneth's estate to be settled; it was complicated, all his papers and the art, of course, Archie had said. Apparently Kenneth had bequeathed his books and several valuable drawings to the library in Grange. As soon as all that had been taken care of, Miss Fitzgerald was going away.

"What about the house?" Alice had looked at Archie in the darkness, thinking of the mess, the boxes and stacks and the bad smell and the darkness, the little paths threading through the confusion like the tracks of small animals in the woods. "Where's she going?"

"Someone's bought the house," Archie said. "A friend of Kenneth's from New York."

Who would ever buy that house, Alice thought, once they'd seen it inside? "Did *she* tell you this?" Alice wished she could see her father's face clearly.

Archie had hesitated. "I have it from a reliable source," he said finally. "It was . . . apparently arranged. Kenneth arranged it. She's going to Florida, a cousin there."

Archie had stood up then and looked down at her. Then he put out his hand and stroked her hair back from her forehead. "It's all right, Alice," he said, surprising her, as if he understood, after all, though they had never spoken of it, that for these many months Alice had been terrified she would run into Miss Fitzgerald, that the news that she was leaving now would be a relief to her.

"Don't think about it anymore now," he said. "I just wanted to tell you."

At his touch, Alice had closed her eyes. *I forgive you,* her heart had cried inside her, and though she had not said the words aloud, she had felt for the first time since Kenneth's death the possibility that one day she *could* pardon her father—for his lack of faith in her, for his failure to comfort her, for his denying Theo to her. It would happen with time, perhaps, just as their aloofness from each other had begun to ease slightly over the passing months. The sensation of joyful release that had swept over her for a moment, the reckless sense that she could go back to how things had been before, had been wonderful, as if her body had become buoyant, filled with air.

Yet now, crouched by the windowsill, listening to the menacing quiet downstairs, she could not banish the figure of Miss Fitzgerald from her imagination. There she was, her lank hair running with rain, her face pressed to the glass, looking for Alice.

Alice made a wild run for the doorway, out onto the upstairs landing, and clattered downstairs. She would not be trapped up there in a bedroom where she had no chance of escape. Theo would not let himself be cornered like that. Theo would run for it. Downstairs in the front hall she hesitated for a moment, shrinking back—every doorway seemed to contain an ominous threat—and then she fled through the living room and into the old brick passage that led to Archie's study, slamming the door closed behind her.

There was a little window in the passage with a deep sill and interior shutters, a window Alice had always been drawn to for its cunning proportions, like a window in Mrs. Tiggy Winkle's house. She had been gripped by that story when she was younger, as much for its mysteriousness as its superficial charm, the hedge-hog turned washerwoman who carried on a normal-sounding domestic conversation with the little girl of the tale, and then, just as the little girl turned back from their walk together to bid her a polite goodbye, turned into a hedgehog again, running brown and prickly into the gorse. Had little Lucy only imagined it all or was the transformation of hedgehog to washerwoman something that just happened occasionally? Why had Lucy been allowed to see this essentially private transformation? Had she, in fact, somehow *caused* it? The line between illogic and reality, or between magic and insanity, had been strangely blurred in that story, just as the farm animals' laundry drying in Mrs. Tiggy Winkle's kitchen—the ducks' long yellow stockings, the lambs' wooly coats—had been familiar and reassuring, reasonable expla-nations in and of themselves for Mrs. Tiggy Winkle's existence.

Alice stopped at the window, breathing hard, and put her hands on the sill. Rain slid down the windowpane, but no rav-aged face met hers in the glass.

Lorenzo wandered lazily into the hallway from Archie's study and sat down beside Alice's feet, idly lifting a leg to scratch once behind his ear. He gave a mighty yawn.

Alice touched her fingertip to the cold glass of the window and watched the raindrops jerking down the pane. Outside, the leaves on the trees hung down darkly, clumped like braces of dead birds.

Here was only the ordinary rain, she thought, her ordinary finger. Here was the ordinariness of her two shoes, the frayed cuff of her sweater against her wrist, the dust thick on the windowsill. Here was the dead fly on its back, curled up like a tiny, weightless sarcophagus. Here were two spiral peppermints, one cracked into pieces inside its wrapper like an ancient mosaic. Here was a dirty mug, on its side a faded and chipped painting of the state of Texas, and in its depths a dry, cracked film of something sad and brown, old tea or coffee, like the surface of the desert.

Alice thought of Theo and wondered if it was raining in New York, if he was looking out the window just as she was. In New York, though, one did not have to stand around and stare out at the rain, she thought. There were too many interesting things to do and see. Theo would not be bored. He was never bored. And he was not thinking of her. Perhaps he had stopped thinking of her long ago, wanting to put the whole summer with its sad ending out of his head. He had never called her.

She leaned her forehead against the window's cold glass and closed her eyes. At her side, Lorenzo lay down, sighing.

Alice opened her eyes and looked down at the windowsill; it was piled with stray belongings that had found their way there over time. There was a stack of books, three with long German titles; a tennis ball the color of a spoiled lime; a black felt-tipped pen missing its cap, frayed like an exploded, spent firecracker. A tarnished silver dish holding a collection of intricately shaped foreign coins balanced on top of the stack of books. Several torn envelopes of what looked like junk mail, the paper yellowed, stuck out from between them.

Below all these was a mysterious black case with a zippered top. Alice felt interest flicker inside her, a flame struggling in the damp, but it did not blow into something strong enough to move her.

The rain moved down the windowpane. Behind Alice in the silence of the afternoon lay the bright lights of the empty living room, like a stage that had been cleared after a performance. Ahead of her was the open door to Archie's darkened study.

Somewhere in what now felt like her distant past there had been a beautiful May morning when she had turned ten years old, and for the first time happiness and sadness, beauty and cruelty had begun to join together inside her, entwining themselves inextricably like the tendrils of a vine up the trunk of a tree. There had been a dead moth on the windowsill, she remembered, a lovely moth in a powdered wig. She had worn on her arm the silver bracelet her father had given her. The light of the day had balanced for a few minutes just at the horizon's edge.

When Archie came home just after six o'clock, Alice was in the living room, the contents of the mysterious black case from the windowsill spread over the floor beside her, the camera and its different lenses lined up on the rug. She was reading the instruction book. She had spent the afternoon looking through the camera, figuring out how to attach the lenses, adjusting the focus. She had looked at the rain. She had looked through the crack under the door to the bathroom. She had looked at the spines of books and their chipped golden letters. She had looked at the blossoms of the pink geranium fallen to the radiator in the kitchen, an ant on the cutting board like a pilgrim crossing the Sahara, the cracked surface of the old globe in Archie's study, with its ornate, italicized labels.

She heard the back door open and close and then Archie's voice.

"In here," she called back.

Archie came into the living room and sat down on the couch behind her, unwinding a scarf from around his neck. "Where'd you find that?" he said. He sounded surprised.

Alice looked around at him. "It was on the windowsill in the hall by your study," she said. "Underneath some junk."

Archie leaned over and picked up one of the lenses, hefting it thoughtfully in his hand.

"Why?" Alice said. He might try to take it away from her. "No one wanted it," she said quickly.

For a moment, Archie was quiet. Then he said, "It was your mother's, Alice. She loved to take pictures. I should have remembered about it long ago."

Alice felt her cheeks redden and heat bloom over her neck. Her *mother's* camera. This had been her mother's. A deep comfort, tugging at her ankles like a tide as if to bring her down into its arms, sang in her ears.

On the June evening three months later when the lights went out in the Grange library, the power failed first with a precipitous diving descent in the register of sound. The lights shuddered once and then went out. A resonant hush spread around Alice in the darkness of the reading room.

On Wednesdays, in the summer months, the building was open until nine p.m., and Archie allowed Alice to stay until it closed on those nights and walk home by herself. Few people came in for the evening hours. Except for the librarian, Alice was usually the only person there after seven p.m. In the short aisle between the stacks at the back of the room, Alice reached out and took hold of the bar of the rolling book cart that had been next to her when the lights went out. She couldn't even see her own hands; she tested them against the cart's handle. The darkness had a way of taking away the sensation of things, as well as the sight of them. Her feet felt as if they had fallen away beneath her. She waited. Like a swimmer going deep underwater beyond the light of the sun, she felt the palpable weight of nothingness like water around her. Then suddenly, in the silence, she could hear again the rain outside. The room, though still invisible, settled back around her in the darkness.

Alice stood there quietly, alert. She was not frightened, though she could feel the possibility of fear waiting for her. It was strange how electricity masked the actual sound of things, she thought, this deep silence that must be there all the time, lying beneath the hum of the lights. How quiet it was, an immense, blanketing quiet like a snowfall. She closed her eyes for a moment, but that was too much. She opened them again, straining to see. Relaxing her grip on the book cart for a moment, she gave it a little shove, keeping her fingertips on the bar. She knew where she was, after all, even if she couldn't see anything. She began to shuffle forward, but though she would have said that she could have felt her way blindfolded across the familiar room, it was as if the proportions of the space had been dramatically and unpleasantly altered. She stopped. Dark continents poured out beneath her, tilting away toward an invisible horizon, a precipice of further blackness. She was aware less of what she might run into than the feeling that she might run into nothing at all. The lights had gone out, and with them the whole world had emptied, all of it sliding away fast.

Then she remembered the watch that James had given her for her eleventh birthday a few weeks before. Her hand emerged from somewhere to find her wrist, to feel for the face of the watch. In its green glow she saw that it was just before nine o'clock. She pressed it again. The watch, her wrist, her arm, rose up out of the darkness for a moment and then, when her fingers released the knob, vanished.

She lifted one hand from the cart's handle and touched the camera hanging at her neck. Since discovering it on the windowsill outside Archie's study a few months before, she had kept it with her almost all the time, taking so many pictures at first that Archie finally balked at the cost of developing the film and told her she would have to learn to use more discretion. At Alice's insistence, he had finally opened up some boxes in the attic and retrieved her mother's old albums, the photographs she had taken, as a young girl, of the streets and buildings in Oxford, the flowers in her father's garden, the horses she had ridden. The weight of the camera reassured Alice now, and blindly she felt for the lens cap, took it off, and aimed the camera into the darkness.

The click of the shutter was like a gunshot going off in the room. Her pulse leaped forward in the echoing silence that followed. Why hadn't the librarian, Mrs. Emerson, come to find her and see if she was all right? Maybe she was in a back room or had gone to use the Xerox machine? Maybe she, too, like Alice, was paralyzed somewhere in the darkness of the library? Alice called out, but there was no answer.

She was aware of Kenneth's mobiles moving gently and invisibly high above her head in the reading room; a memory of him in his torn straw hat on the terrace, sketching the line of trees at the edge of the lawn, came to her. Somewhere in that tree line had been the dark opening where the rope walk had begun.

Alice took hold of the cart's handle again—there it was, surprising her with its solid familiarity—and pushed the cart a few steps forward. It tried to sway away from her on its wobbly wheels, and she tightened her grip on the handles. She was not afraid of the dark, she thought. She had never been afraid of the dark.

It had been Theo who had been afraid.

Archie had carried Theo into her bedroom that first night, and now it was as if she could feel Theo's fingers gripping the back of her shirt the way he did when he was nervous or unsure, feel his breath on the back of her neck.

When she heard Mrs. Emerson call her name, she started with relief.

"Here I am," she called back, and she saw the little beam of Mrs. Emerson's flashlight come bouncing toward her across the room.

"Alice? Are you all right? Of course I couldn't find the flashlight," Mrs. Emerson said in exasperation, reaching Alice and directing the light into her face. Alice cringed. Mrs. Emerson was only the Wednesday-night librarian, working part-time just to give her something to do, she had told Alice, who felt a little sorry for her—often Mrs. Emerson seemed to need someone to talk to; she liked to show Alice her needlepoint efforts, complain of the difficulty of the patterns. Mrs. Emerson had drawn-in, reddish eyebrows that reminded Alice of a clown's.

"I was in the lobby coming back from the ladies'," Mrs. Emerson said in an accusing tone, as if the power failure had been specifically arranged to inconvenience her in the bathroom. "And then the lights went out!"

She turned around and began walking back across the room. Alice abandoned the cart and followed the bouncing point of light that was Mrs. Emerson.

"I'll have to try and find the keys," Mrs. Emerson was saying, and then suddenly there was a roar, and the lights came back on. They dimmed once, filling the room with a damp brown light, and then they flared again.

Alice blinked.

Mrs. Emerson bustled across the room to the librarian's desk. "I'm going to put this flashlight right here in this top drawer," she said. "You'll remind me what I've done with it, Alice, in case the lights ever go out again while we're here."

She stepped behind the desk and then stopped. A worn cardboard box had been set crookedly on the surface of the desk, balancing halfway atop the keyboard of the computer. Mrs. Emerson leaned over the box and lifted the flap. "Well, who brought this in?" she said. She lifted out a couple of books from inside the box, glanced at them, and then set them back inside. "Well, it can wait," she said impatiently. "I'm going to go find those keys. I think they're in the Xerox room, and then we can lock up and go home." She left the room, clicking away on busy heels.

Alice moved toward the desk and the carton of books. Her nose had detected something, something familiar, but for a moment she could not place it. Then, with distaste, she realized what it was.

It was the Fitzgeralds' house.

James would have said she was lying, but she knew she was right. She could smell it.

She put her hands on the box and opened the flaps. Inside was a stack of books, perhaps twenty volumes jumbled together. Alice began lifting them out of the box and stacking them on the desk, but she knew even before she reached the bottom of the carton and her fingers found the familiar shape of Lewis and Clark's journals, the furred binding of its cover, that it would be in there. And inside the book, as she had known it would be, was Kenneth's letter.

The envelope, with her name printed on it in Kenneth's big handwriting, was not sealed, but it was impossible to tell if it had been sealed once and then opened carefully without tearing the paper—opened carefully, read, considered, and then in a moment of incalculable suffering and cruelty put away again— or whether it had been overlooked entirely, never been opened, never been seen at all. She would never know, Alice realized, and for a moment she was angry at being denied this final knowledge. It was quite possible, she realized, that she would never see Miss Fitzgerald again now, that their last meeting had already taken place. Heat rose into her cheeks. She had aimed her camera into the darkness when the lights had been out, sensing something in the room. Had Miss Fitzgerald been standing there when Alice took the picture?

Alice opened the envelope and took out the letter.

Dear Alice, Kenneth had written. *I know you will forgive me, for the hand that made you fair hath made you good, as well. That's a weak paraphrase of Shakespeare, I think, but you know that already, being your father's daughter. Thank you for everything you and Theo have done for me in these my last weeks and, most especially, for my beautiful rope walk, which will take me away from the certain awful end I fear so much and lead me instead to the places I remember from my boyhood, the woods, the river, the clouds in the sky, the underwater filled with bubbles. If I'd ever had children, you are the ones I would have chosen—hardworking, brilliant, generous. If I am brave enough for the one necessary moment ahead, I want you to know that I hope by it to spare everyone, including myself, a lot of trouble. Word of the day:* redivivus. *Your great friend and admirer, Kenneth Fitzgerald.*

Alice folded the letter. She crossed the room, the letter in her hand, to the big, heavy dictionary on its stand under the window. She loved the enormous book. The pages were delicate, nearly transparent, with tiny inked illustrations of plants or famous people's faces or strange animals or machines or mountains.

She turned the pages of the book until she found the word.

Redivivus, she read. *Revived, reborn, or brought back to life.*

She put the book and the letter into her backpack and went outside. The rain had stopped, and in the deep black clearings between clouds overhead there were stars far away, so many it looked as if there had been an explosion up there, showers of sparks now falling toward the earth. She walked down the steps of the library and turned toward home. Beneath the streetlights, the sidewalk under the trees was wet and gleaming; soft leafy shadows moved weightlessly over the ground. She could hear the wind moving in the trees; water pattered down, scattered droplets striking the leaves and startling her with their other-worldly coldness when they touched her head and the back of her neck. There was a wild smell in the air, as if things had been stirred up, and she realized she could identify its component parts—the old, mineral smell of half-buried stones on the mountains, the pinch of fertilizer from bags torn open and spilling onto the floor in garden sheds, the warm breath of overturned soil, pungent as molasses. And now in her love of the world, there was less fear and more longing. The shock of knowing exactly how things could be lost had started to wear off—the past year had done that—so that now, coming hand over hand through starlight and moonlight and lamplight, she thought not of the future, of what would happen next, nor of the past, but only, for a moment, of the shining present.

In Helen's room at the nursing home, an orchid had been placed on the windowsill in an Oriental pot. Its single spray of tiny yellow blossoms, like sleeping bees, drooped in the heat from the radiator that rose up in blurry waves to the open window, where the evening breeze stirred the curtain.

Alice sat on a hard chair beside the bed and looked at Helen's sleeping face. Until Helen went into the hospital, Alice had never seen her in a nightgown. Helen had been a careful dresser, old-fashioned brooches on her sweaters or the lapels of her jackets, pressed trousers, a cream-colored coat soft as a fawn, with a bright, cherry-colored collar, a scarf printed with a pattern of water lilies around her neck. Because of the polio, she'd worn ungainly black shoes that laced up with heavy cords, but her shoes had been the only things about Helen that were not delicate or small or neat.

Along with the camera, which she took everywhere, Alice now carried Kenneth's letter, too, and she reached up and touched the pocket of her shirt, reassuring herself that it was there. She had not shown the letter to Archie. She and her father were just beginning to recover some of their ease with each other, as if the shadow of last summer's events was finally with-drawing, and she understood that Archie would always see Ken-neth, his life and his death, as the place where Archie's protection of Alice had been breached, that no matter what she had to tell Archie about Kenneth, he would not be happy to hear it. In Archie's mind, Theo, too, was part of Archie's failure, Alice understood. And, as always, it was Theo she most wanted to talk to now.

Yet though her desire was great, her trepidation was great, as well. Perhaps Theo didn't ever want to speak to her again—he could have found out her telephone number easily enough. But talking on the telephone was probably not something that would even occur to Theo, she thought, and maybe he had been forbid-den to call her, anyway. He had returned to his old friends in New York, his takeout restaurants and Peking duck, and had forgotten all about her. It was painful to think about him not remembering her, not longing to see her, the way she longed to see him. Still, since finding Kenneth's letter a few nights before, she had wanted to come and see Helen; seeing Helen connected Alice to Theo.

Sometimes Alice sat at the table in the kitchen to do her homework in the evenings while Elizabeth fixed dinner and listened to the evening news, its litany of grim tidings: the report of a dozen miners trapped thousands of feet below the ground, a suicide bomber who blew up himself and twenty guests at a wedding party in Faluja, the collapse of the roof of a skating rink in Germany, killing dozens of children. She felt the ache of fear in her stomach at the news, the endless tide of disaster and calumny, the bewildering reports of injury and wrongdoing. If Theo were listening, he, too, would be afraid, she thought, and she longed both for comfort and to comfort. Elizabeth, with the sturdy, implacable body of a survivor of the world's harm, had become even more infinitely precious to Alice and tolerated without complaint Alice's fierce, sudden hugs when she came home from school.

O'Brien had met Alice and Archie in the lobby of the nursing home when they'd arrived that evening, and Archie had taken O'Brien down the street to a restaurant where they could get something to eat, while Alice had made her way down the hall to Helen's room. Alice had not forgiven O'Brien for his treatment of Theo last summer, his inexplicable coldness, but when she had looked up into his face in the lobby this evening she had felt sorry for him, despite her anger. He had aged over the past year almost as much as Helen herself, whose once quick, knowing expressions had been smudged and blurred by the effects of the stroke.

Helen had been sleeping since Alice had pushed open the door with her fingertips and looked into the room a few minutes before. Many of Alice's drawings had been taped to the wall by Helen's bed, as well as Theo's drawing of the fort he and Alice had built on the river. Alice looked at the drawings for a while, and then she turned her attention to Helen, the arrangement of shadows and forms that created Helen's face in the blue light of the evening. She reached down and took off the lens cap of the camera and raised it to her eye, bringing Helen's face nearer, pushing it away, bringing it near again, looking at the way the light from the window fell across the bottom half of Helen's face, her shoulder, the ribbon of her bed jacket.

Then, with a start, she realized that Helen had opened her eyes and was looking at Alice.

Alice lowered the camera. She was afraid that she had offended Helen by looking at her that way, as though Helen were an insect under a microscope. She had never been alone in the room with Helen before; usually Archie was there, too, and O'Brien. She was afraid of not really knowing Helen anymore—behind her altered expression, was Helen the same person she had been before? When Archie and Alice came to visit, Helen listened to Archie's slow reporting of events in Grange and at Frost, bits of news about the boys, with what seemed like comprehension on her face. Archie said she understood what was said to her, but she did not speak much, because she couldn't control the words she said; sometimes she reached for a word but another one came out instead, Archie explained, and this was a strain, embarrassing and disconcerting, as well as hard work.

Helen had come into full wakefulness now, and her face, as she seemed to recognize Alice, was restless, almost excited. Alice, reading urgency in Helen's expression, leaned toward the bed, meaning to try to help Helen with the pillows behind her, as she had seen Archie and O'Brien do.

As Alice brought her arm forward, Helen reached up and clumsily caught Alice's wrist. Alice looked down in alarm at Helen's hand closed on her arm.

"Helen?" she said. "Are you okay? Do you need something?"

Helen let go of Alice and began to fumble inside the sleeve of her bed jacket. The piece of paper she withdrew was tiny, crumpled up, and she extended it in Alice's direction, her eyes on Alice's face.

Alice took the paper and unfolded it. On it was printed a telephone number and two words in Theo's wobbly handwriting. *Call me.*

It was Theo's voice, answering the phone.

"Hello?" he said.

Alice heard a siren wailing in the background. It seemed to approach through the telephone and then recede, a pulse of alarm that crested to panic and then fell away in a correction, a diminution of alarm, the all clear of silence. But Alice knew that Theo was still there, his breath in the phone reaching her across the distance between them.

"Hello?" he said again, and now he sounded suspicious. Suspicious, and worried.

"It's me," she said. "Alice."

A moment of silence followed. Then Theo said, in a whisper, "Wait a minute."

A loud crackling followed, as though someone were crumpling up a paper bag right next to the mouthpiece. Alice pulled the phone slightly away from her ear.

"Alice?" When he came back on he was whispering still, but his tone was eager. "Alice, I'm under my bed. Can you hear me?"

"Yes." She turned, dazed, and looked out the open front door into the evening. If she ducked a little, she could see the night sky, the first stars appearing there.

More crackling. "Can you *still* hear me?" he said.

She felt a flutter of impatience and annoyance. "What are you *doing*?" she said. Wasn't he surprised to hear from her?

His voice was muffled. "I'm just pulling a blanket down over the edge of the bed, so no one can see me," he said. "Wait a minute."

She waited. Then she heard a breathy sound, as if he were blowing wetly into the phone.

"Alice, I've missed you so much," he said, suddenly near. His voice in her ear was so close he might have been standing beside her.

A thrill flew over her skin, like the evening breeze stealing toward her through the open door. Alice felt her breath catch in her chest, a little sob. Why did being around Theo sometimes make her want to cry? Why did she want to cry when she felt so happy?

"Alice?" he said. *"Alice?"*

"Yes," she said. "I'm here." She realized she was whispering, too, although there was no need for it. Archie was at Frost, Elizabeth was cleaning up the dishes and listening to the radio in the kitchen.

"You got my message?" he said. "What took so long? God!" His tone was accusing, as though Alice had bungled an important maneuver. "My mom took it at *Christmas* when she went up there to see them. She understood, Alice. She, like, got it. She said I couldn't call you, though, because Archie would be mad. So that was all I could do, send you a secret message."

Alice was speechless. All this time, she had imagined Theo had forgotten about her. "Is she better?" she asked finally. "Your mom?"

"What? Oh, yeah. Kinda. But my parents are getting divorced. Wait a minute . . ."

There was another crashing and crinkling sound. "Hold on," Theo whispered.

Alice listened. She began to walk toward the screen door, the blue light of the evening captured there, the telephone cord stretching out behind her.

He came back on the phone. "Okay," he said. "I'm recording this now."

"You're *what*?"

"Yeah. With my tape recorder."

"Why are you recording it?" She had so much she wanted to tell him, she thought. But he interrupted her thoughts again.

"Why? *Why am I recording it?* So I can listen to it again," he said.

"So you can listen to *you*?" she said, confused.

"No, Alice," he said, and his tone was tender suddenly, forgiving, as though she was a loveable dunce. "So I can listen to *you*, Alice, when we get off the phone. So I can hear *your* voice again. I'm recording *you*. I'm recording us." He hurried on before she could say anything else. "What's happened there, Alice? Are you okay?"

She took a breath, and then she told him about Kenneth's letter, about finding it in the Lewis and Clark, about the lights going out in the library that night.

"Wow," he said, a few times. "Oh my God. That's amazing."

"Do you want to hear his letter?" Alice said.

"*Yeah* I do."

She took it out of her pocket and unfolded it. When she had finished reading it to him, he said, "Man. Nothing like this has ever happened to me before, Alice."

"Me, neither," she said.

They were quiet, and she thought of how their voices ran down the telephone lines toward each other. Another siren intruded then, its wail so loud she felt the ambulance must be about to burst through the walls into Theo's apartment. It was a terrible sound, announcing the approach of catastrophe, the nearness of death. Yet it was valiant, too. Someone was fighting for his life. Someone else was trying to help him.

"That's so *loud*," she said, and she heard the protest in her voice, the indignation. "It sounds like it's coming right at you, under your bed, like it's going to run you over. Like it's going to come through the phone and run *me* over."

"I know," Theo said. "But it's okay, Alice. Don't worry. You get used to it."

She listened to the sound of the siren fading away, the whine shrinking to a tiny black dot and then, pop, vanishing into a hole. And then all she could hear on the other end of the phone was Theo, all those many miles away down the long, echoing corridor of their connection, breathing into her ear.

The passages of Lewis and Clark's journals quoted here are taken from *The Journals of Lewis and Clark* edited by Bernard DeVoto, Houghton Mifflin Company, 1953. This edition is based on the *Original Journals of the Lewis and Clark Expedition* edited by Reuben Gold Thwaites in 1904–5. The version of the story I imagined Alice reading aloud to Kenneth Fitzgerald and Theo would likely contain more narrative and fewer of the actual journal entries themselves, whose archaic and erratic spellings, while perfectly consistent with an account being composed in the wilderness with neither typewriter nor editor, can make for rather difficult reading.